W9-CDZ-908

*Her fate and desire
will hinge upon a man . . .
and a mattress.*

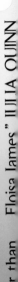

"Nothing gets me to a bookstore faster than   Eloisa James" JULIA QUINN

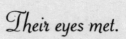

Their eyes met.

His face could have been granite, for all the emotion she saw on it.

But his eyes...his eyes were different. They locked with hers and she could have sworn that she read something there.

Longing. Perhaps.

Olivia almost shook her head as she hurried back down the corridor after her sister. Of course it wasn't longing. No one could possibly feel that, not for her.

She was a plump, long-in-the-tooth woman without much more to recommend her than her betrothal to a duke's heir, and she needed to keep that in mind.

Longing! She almost snorted.

What could a duke possibly long for? The world lay in front of him, his for the asking.

Just as it would for her, once she became a duchess.

By Eloisa James

ATTENTION: ORGANIZATIONS AND CORPORATIONS
Most Avon Books paperbacks are available at special quantity discounts for bulk purchases for sales promotions, premiums, or fund raising. For information, please call or write:

Special Markets Department, HarperCollins Publishers, 10 East 53rd Street, New York, New York 10022-5299. Telephone: (212) 207-7528.   Fax: (212) 207-7222.

Eloisa James

The Duke Is Mine

AVON

An Imprint of HarperCollinsPublishers

This is a work of fiction. Names, characters, places, and incidents are products of the author's imagination or are used fictitiously and are not to be construed as real. Any resemblance to actual events, locales, organizations, or persons, living or dead, is entirely coincidental.

AVON BOOKS
An Imprint of HarperCollinsPublishers
10 East 53rd Street
New York, New York 10022-5299

Copyright © 2012 by Eloisa James
Excerpt from *The Ugly Duchess* copyright © 2012 by Eloisa James
ISBN 978-0-06-202128-1
www.avonromance.com

All rights reserved. No part of this book may be used or reproduced in any manner whatsoever without written permission, except in the case of brief quotations embodied in critical articles and reviews. For information address Avon Books, An Imprint of HarperCollins Publishers.

First Avon Books mass market printing: January 2012

Avon Trademark Reg. U.S. Pat. Off. and in Other Countries, Marca Registrada, Hecho en U.S.A.
HarperCollins® is a registered trademark of HarperCollins Publishers.

Printed in the U.S.A.

10 9 8 7 6 5 4 3 2 1

If you purchased this book without a cover, you should be aware that this book is stolen property. It was reported as "unsold and destroyed" to the publisher, and neither the author nor the publisher has received any payment for this "stripped book."

This book is dedicated to my dear friend, the wonderful novelist Linda Francis Lee. In a moment of despair, when I realized that I had to throw away 175 pages of my version of The Princess and the Pea *and begin again, Linda coaxed me through the grief and replotted my entire novel over two glasses of wine. You're my Lucky Duck, Linda!*

Acknowledgments

My books are like small children; they take a whole village to get them to a literate state. I want to offer my heartfelt thanks to my village: my editor, Carrie Feron; my agent, Kim Witherspoon; my website designers, Wax Creative; and my personal team: Kim Castillo, Franzeca Drouin, and Anne Connell. Others kindly provided specialized knowledge: more thanks go to Thomas Henkel, Ph.D., professor emeritus of physics, Wagner College; Annie Zeidman-Karpinski, science librarian, University of Oregon; and Sylvie Clemot of Rueil Malmaison, France. I am so grateful to each of you!

Prologue

Once upon a time, not so very long ago . . .
(or, to be exact, March 1812)

. . . there was a girl who was destined to be a princess. Though to be absolutely precise, there was no prince in the offing. But she was betrothed to a duke's heir, and from the point of view of minor gentry, a coronet was as good as a crown.

This story begins with that girl, and continues through a stormy night, and a series of tests, and if there's no pea in the tale, all I can say is that if you read on, you *will* encounter a surprise in that bed: a key, a flea—or perhaps a marquess, for that matter.

In fairy tales, the ability to perceive an obtrusion as tiny as a pea under the mattress is enough to prove that a strange girl who arrives on a stormy night is indeed a princess. In the real world, of course, it's a bit more complicated. In order to prepare for the rank of duchess, Miss Olivia Mayfield Lytton had learned something from virtually every branch of human knowledge. She was prepared to dine with a king, or a fool, or Socrates himself, conversing on subjects as far-flung as Italian comic opera and the new spinning machines.

But, just as a single dried pea was all that was needed to determine the authenticity of the princess, one crucial fact determined Olivia's eligibility for the rank of duchess: she was betrothed to the heir to the Canterwick dukedom.

Less important were the facts that when this tale begins Olivia was twenty-three and still unmarried, that her father had no title, and that she had never been given a compliment such as *a diamond of the first water*. Quite the opposite, in fact.

None of that mattered.

One

In Which We Are Introduced to a Future Duchess

41 Clarges Street, Mayfair
London
The residence of Mr. Lytton, Esq.

Most betrothals spring from one of two fierce
emotions: greed or love. But Olivia Lytton's was
fueled neither by an exchange of assets between like-
minded aristocrats, nor by a potent mixture of desire,
propinquity, and Cupid's arrows.

In fact, the bride-to-be was liable, in moments of
despair, to attribute her engagement to a curse. "Perhaps our parents forgot to ask a powerful fairy to my
christening," she told her sister Georgiana on their way
home from a ball given by the Earl of Micklethwait, at
which Olivia had spent generous swaths of time with

her betrothed. "The curse, it hardly needs to be said, is Rupert's hand in marriage. I would rather sleep for a hundred years."

"Sleeping has its attractions," her sister agreed, descending from their parents' carriage before the house. Georgiana did not pair the positive comment with its opposite: sleep had attractions . . . but Rupert had few.

Olivia actually had to swallow hard, and sit in the dark carriage by herself a moment, before she was able to pull herself together and follow her sister. She had always known that she would be Duchess of Canterwick someday, so it made no sense to feel so keenly miserable. But there it was. An evening spent with her future husband made her feel half cracked.

It didn't help that most of London, her mother included, considered her the luckiest of young women. Her mother would be horrified—though unsurprised—by Olivia's lame jest linking the dukedom with a curse. To her parents, it was manifestly clear that their daughter's ascension of the social ranks was a piece of singular good fortune. In short, a blessing.

"Thank God," Mr. Lytton had said, oh, five thousand times since Olivia was born. "If I hadn't gone to Eton . . ."

It was a story that Olivia and her twin sister Georgiana had loved when they were little. They would perch on their papa's knees and listen to the thrilling tale of how he—plain, unremarkable (albeit connected to an earl on one side, as well as a bishop *and* a marquess on the other) Mr. Lytton—had gone to Eton and become best friends with the Duke of Canterwick, who had inherited his grand title at the tender age of five. At some point, the boys had sworn a blood oath that Mr. Lytton's eldest daughter would become a duchess by marrying the Duke of Canterwick's eldest son.

Mr. Lytton showed giddy enthusiasm in doing his part to ensure this eventuality, producing not one but two daughters within a year of marriage. The Duke of Canterwick, for his part, produced only one son, and that after a few years of marriage, but obviously one son was sufficient for the task at hand. Most importantly, His Grace kept his word, and regularly reassured Mr. Lytton about the destined betrothal.

Consequently, the proud parents of the duchess-to-be did everything in their power to prepare their first-born daughter (the elder by a good seven minutes) for the title that was to be bestowed upon her, sparing no expense in shaping the future Duchess of Canterwick. Olivia was tutored from the moment she left the cradle. By ten years of age, she was expert in the finer points of etiquette, the management of country estates (including double-entry accounting), playing the harpsichord and the spinet, greeting people in various languages, including Latin (useful for visiting bishops, if no one else), and even in French cooking, though her knowledge of the last was intellectual rather than practical. Duchesses never actually touched food, except to eat it.

She also had a thorough knowledge of her mother's favorite tome, *The Mirror of Compliments: A Complete Academy for the Attaining unto the Art of Being a Lady*, which was written by no less a personage than Her Grace, the Dowager Duchess of Sconce, and given to the girls on their twelfth birthday.

In fact, Olivia's mother had read *The Mirror of Compliments* so many times that it had taken over her conversation, rather like ivy smothering a tree. "'*Gentility*,'" she had said the morning before the Micklethwait ball over marmalade and toast, "'*is bestowed on us by our ancestors, but soon blanched, when not revived by virtue*.'" Olivia had nodded. She herself was a firm believer in the benefits of blanching gentility, but long experience had taught her that expressing such an opinion would merely give her mother a headache.

"*A young lady,*" Mrs. Lytton had announced on the way to the Micklethwait ball, "*loathes nothing so much as entering parley with an immodest suitor.*" Olivia knew better than to inquire about how one "parleyed" with an immodest suitor. The *ton* understood that she was betrothed to the Duke of Canterwick's heir, and therefore suitors, immodest or otherwise, rarely bothered to approach.

Generally speaking, she tabled that sort of advice for the future, when she hoped to indulge in any number of immodest parleys.

"Did you see Lord Webbe dancing with Mrs. Shottery?" Olivia asked her sister as they walked into her bedchamber. "It's quite affecting to watch them stare into each other's eyes. I must say, the *ton* seems to take their wedding vows about as seriously as do the French, and everyone says that inclusion of marital fidelity into French wedding vows turned them a splendid work of fiction."

"*Olivia*!" Georgiana groaned. "You mustn't! And you wouldn't—would you?"

"Are you asking whether I will ever be unfaithful to my fiancé once he's my husband—if that day ever arrives?"

Georgiana nodded.

"I suppose not," Olivia said, though secretly she sometimes wondered if she might just snap one day and break every social rule by running off to Rome with a footman. "The only part of the evening I really enjoyed was when Lord Pomtinius told me a limerick about an adulterous abbot."

"Don't you *dare* repeat it!" her sister ordered. Georgiana had never shown the faintest wish to rebel against the rules of propriety. She loved and lived by them.

"There once was an adulterous abbot," Olivia teased, "as randy—"

Georgiana slapped her hands over her ears. "I can't believe he told you such a thing! Father would be furious if he knew."

"Lord Pomtinius was in his cups," Olivia said. "Besides, he's ninety-six and he doesn't care about decorum any longer. Just a laugh, now and then."

"It doesn't even make sense. An adulterous abbot? How can an abbot be adulterous? They don't even marry."

"Let me know if you want to hear the whole verse," Olivia said. "It ends with talk of nuns, so I believe the word was being used loosely."

That limerick—and Olivia's appreciation of it—pointed directly to the problem with Miss Lytton's duchess-ification, or, as the girls labeled it, "duchification." There was something very *déclassé* about Olivia, no matter how proper her bearing, her voice, and her manners might be. She certainly could play the duchess, but the real Olivia was, dismayingly, never far from the surface.

"You are missing that indefinable air of consequence that your sister conveys without effort," her father often opined, with an air of despondent resignation. "In short, Daughter, your sense of humor tends toward the vulgar."

"'*Your demeanor should ever augment your honor*,'" her mother would chime in, quoting the Duchess of Sconce.

And Olivia would shrug.

"If only," Mrs. Lytton had said despairingly to her husband time and again, "if only *Georgiana* had been born first." For Olivia was not the only participant in the Lytton training program. Olivia and Georgiana had marched in lockstep through lessons on the comportment of a duchess, because their parents, aware of the misfortunes that might threaten their eldest daughter—a fever, a runaway carriage, a fall from a tower—had prudently duchified their second-born as well.

Sadly, it was manifest to everyone that Georgiana *had* achieved the quality of a duchess, while Olivia . . . Olivia was Olivia. She certainly could behave with exquisite grace—but among her intimates, she was sarcastic, far too witty to be ladylike, and not in the least gracious. "She looks at me in *such* a way if I merely mention *The Mirror of Compliments*," Mrs. Lytton would complain. "I'm only trying to help, I'm sure."

"That girl will be a duchess someday," Mr. Lytton would say heavily. "She'll be grateful to us then."

"But if *only* . . . ," Mrs. Lytton would say, wistfully. "Dearest Georgiana is just . . . well, she would be a perfect duchess, wouldn't she?"

In fact, Olivia's sister had mastered early the delicate art of combining a pleasing air of consequence with an irreproachably modest demeanor. Over the years Georgiana had built up a formidable array of duchess-like traits: ways of walking, talking, and carrying herself.

"'*Dignity, virtue, affability, and bearing*,'" Mrs. Lytton recited over and over, turning it into a nursery rhyme.

Georgiana would glance at the glass, checking her dignified bearing and affable expression.

Olivia would sing back to her mother: "Debility, vanity, absurdity, and . . . *brainlessness*!"

By eighteen years of age, Georgiana looked, sounded, and even smelled (thanks to French perfume, smuggled from Paris at great expense) like a duchess. Mostly, Olivia didn't bother.

The Lyttons were happy, in a measured sort of way. By any sensible standard they had produced a real duchess, even if that particular daughter was not betrothed to a duke's heir. As their girls were growing up, they told themselves that Georgiana would make a lovely wife to any man of rank. Alas, in time they stopped saying anything about their second daughter's hypothetical husband.

The sad truth is that a duchified girl is not what most young men desire. While Georgiana's virtues were celebrated far and wide throughout the *ton*—especially amongst the dowager set—her hand was rarely sought for a dance, let alone for marriage.

Mr. and Mrs. Lytton interpreted the problem differently. To their mind, their beloved second daughter was likely to dwindle into the shadow of a duchess, without becoming even a wife, because she had no dowry.

The Lyttons had spent all their disposable income on tutors. That had left their younger daughter with little more than a pittance to launch her on the marriage market.

"We have sacrificed everything for Olivia," Mrs. Lytton often said. "I can't understand why she is not more grateful. She's the luckiest girl in England."

Olivia did not view herself as lucky at all.

"The *only* reason I can countenance marrying Rupert," she said to Georgiana, "is that I will be able to dower you." She stripped off her gloves, biting the tips to pull them from her fingers. "To be honest, the mere thought of the wedding makes me feel slightly mad. I could bear the rank—though it isn't my cup of tea, to say the least—if he weren't such a little, beardy-weirdy bottle-headed chub."

"You're using slang," Georgiana said. "And—"

"Absolutely not," Olivia said, throwing her gloves onto her bed. "I made it up myself, and you know as well as I do that the *Mirror for Bumpkins* says that slang is—and I quote—'*grossness of speech used by the lowest degenerates in our nation.*' Much though I would like to attain the qualifications of a degenerate, I have no hope of achieving that particular title in this life."

"You shouldn't," Georgiana said, arranging herself on the settee before Olivia's fireplace. Olivia had been given the grandest bedchamber in the house, larger than either their mother's or father's chambers, so the twins generally hid from their parents in Olivia's room.

But the reprimand didn't have its usual fire. Olivia frowned at her sister. "Was it a particularly rotten night, Georgie? I kept getting swept away by my dim-witted fiancé, and after supper I lost track of you."

"I would have been easy to find," Georgiana replied. "I sat among the dowagers most of the night."

"Oh, sweetheart," Olivia said, sitting down next to her sister and giving her a fierce hug. "Just wait until I'm a duchess. I'll dower you so magnificently that every gentleman in the country will be on bended knee at the very thought of you. 'Golden Georgiana,' they'll call you."

Georgiana didn't even smile, so Olivia forged ahead. "I like sitting with the dowagers. They have all the stories one would really like to hear, like that one about Lord Mettersnatch paying seven guineas to be flogged."

Her sister's brows drew together.

"I know, I know!" Olivia exclaimed, before Georgiana could speak. "Vulgar, vulgar, vulgar. All the same, I loved the part about the nursemaid costume. Truly, you should be glad you weren't me. Canterwick stalked up and down the ballroom all night, dragging Rupert and me behind him. Everyone groveled, tittered behind my back, and went off to inform the rest of the room how uncommonly unlucky the FF is to be marrying me."

Between themselves, Olivia and Georgiana generally referred to Rupert Forrest G. Blakemore—Marquess of Montsurrey, future Duke of Canterwick—as "the FF," which stood for foolish fiancé. On occasion he was also "the HH" (half-wit husband), "the BB" (brainless betrothed) and—because the girls were fluent in both Italian and French—"the MM" (mindless *marito* or mindless *mari*, depending on the language of the moment).

"The only thing lacking to make this evening absolutely and irredeemably hellish," Olivia continued, "was a wardrobe malfunction. If someone had stepped on my hem and ripped it, baring my arse to the world, I might have been more humiliated. I certainly would have been less bored."

Georgiana didn't reply; she just tipped her head back and stared at the ceiling. She looked miserable. "We should look on the bright side," Olivia said, striving for a rousing tone. "The FF danced with both of us. Thank goodness he's finally old enough to attend a ball."

"He counted the steps aloud," Georgiana stated. "And he said my dress made me look like a puffy cloud."

"Surely it could not have surprised you to discover that Rupert lacks a gift for elegant conversation. If anyone looked like a puffy cloud, it was I; *you* looked like a vestal virgin. Far more dignified than a cloud."

"Dignity is not desirable," her sister said, turning her head. Her eyes were full of tears.

"Oh, Georgie!" Olivia gathered her into another hug. "Please don't cry. I'll be a duchess in no time, and then I'll dower you and order such beautiful clothing that you'll be the wonder of London."

"This is my *fifth* season, Olivia. You can't possibly understand how dreadful it feels, given that you've never really been on the market. No gentleman paid me any attention tonight, any more than they have in the last five years."

"It was the dress and the dowry. We all looked like ghosts, but not transparent. You, of course, were a willowy ghost, and I was a particularly solid one."

Olivia and Georgiana had worn matching gowns of frail white silk, caught up under their bosoms with long ribbons trimmed with seed pearls and tasseled at the ends. The same streamers appeared on the sides and the backs of the gowns, rippling in the faintest breeze. On the page, in Madame Wellbrook's pattern book, the design had looked exquisite.

There was a lesson there . . . a dismal one.

Just because fluttering ribbons look good on a stick-thin lady portrayed in a pattern book does not mean that they will be, when festooned around one's hips.

"I caught sight of you dancing," Olivia continued. "You looked like a bouncy maypole with all those ribbons trembling around you. Your ringlets were bouncing as well."

"It doesn't matter," Georgiana said flatly. She brushed away a tear. "It's the duchification, Olivia. No man wants to marry a prude who acts as if she's a ninety-five-year-old dowager. And"—she gave a little sob—"I simply can't seem to behave any differently.

I don't believe that anyone titters behind your back, unless from jealousy. But I'm like nursery gruel. I—I can *see* their eyes glaze over when they have to dance with me."

Privately, Olivia agreed that the duchification program had much to answer for. But she wrapped her arm tighter around her sister and said, "Georgiana, you have a wonderful figure, you're sweet as honey, and the fact that you know how to set a table for one hundred has nothing to do with it. Marriage is a contract, and contracts are about *money*. A woman has to have a dowry, or no man will even consider marrying her."

Georgiana sniffed, which served to demonstrate how upset she was, as she normally would never countenance such an unrefined gesture.

"Your waist makes me positively sick with envy," Olivia added. "I look like a butter churn, whereas you're so slim that I could balance you on the head of a pin, like an angel."

Most young ladies on the marriage market—Georgiana included—were indeed ethereally slim. They floated from room to room, diaphanous silk sweeping around their slender bodies.

Olivia was not one of them. It was the sad truth, the canker at the heart of the ducal flower, another source of stress for Mrs. Lytton. As she saw it, Olivia's over-indulgence in vulgar wit and buttered toast stemmed from the same character defects. Olivia did not disagree.

"You do *not* resemble a butter churn," her sister stated, and wiped away a few more tears.

"I heard something interesting tonight," Olivia cried. "Apparently the Duke of Sconce is going to take a wife. I suppose he needs an heir. Just imagine, Georgie. You could be daughter-in-law to the most stiff-rumped starch-bucket of them all. Do you suppose the duchess reads her *Maggoty Mirror* aloud at the dining table? She would adore you. In fact, you're probably the only woman in the kingdom whom she *would* love."

"Dowagers always love me," Georgiana said with another sniff. "That doesn't mean the duke will give me a second glance. Besides, I thought that Sconce was married."

"If the duchess approved of bigamy, she would have put it in the *Mirror*; therefore, its absence suggests that he is need of a second wife. My only other, rather less exciting, news is that Mother was told of a lettuce diet tonight and has decided that I must try it immediately."

"Lettuce?"

"One eats only lettuce between the hours of eight and eight."

"That's absurd. If you want to reduce, you should stop buying meat pies when Mama thinks you're buying ribbons. Though, to be honest, Olivia, I think you should eat whatever you want. I want quite desperately to marry, and even so, the idea of marrying Rupert makes me want to eat a meat pie."

"Four pies," Olivia corrected. "At least."

"What's more, it wouldn't matter how slim you became by eating lettuce," Georgiana continued. "The FF has no choice but to marry you. If you grew rabbit ears, he would still have to marry you. Whereas no one can countenance the idea of marrying me, no matter what my waist looks like. I need money to—to bribe them." Her voice wavered again.

"They're all port-brained buffoons," Olivia said, with another squeeze. "They haven't noticed you, but they will, once Rupert dowers you."

"I'll likely be forty-eight by the time the two of you walk the aisle."

"On that front, Rupert is coming over with his father to sign betrothal papers tomorrow evening. And apparently he is leaving directly thereafter for the wars in France."

"For goodness' sake," Georgiana said, her eyes widening. "You really *are* going to become a duchess. The FF is about to become the BB!"

"Foolish fiancés are often killed on the battlefield," Olivia pointed out. "I think the term is 'cannon fodder.'"

Her sister gave a sudden laugh. "You could at least try to sound sad at the prospect."

"I would be sad," Olivia protested. "I think."

"You'd have reason. Not only would you lose the prospect of being 'Your Grace'd' for the rest of your life, but our parents would hold hands as they jumped off Battersea Bridge to their watery deaths."

"I can't even imagine what Mama and Papa would do if the goose that promised golden eggs was turned into *pâté de foie gras* by the French," Olivia said, a bit sadly.

"What happens if the FF dies before marrying you?" Georgiana asked. "Legal or not, a betrothal is not a wedding."

"I gather these papers make the whole situation a good deal more solid. I'm certain most of the *ton* believes that he'll cry off before we get to the altar, given my general lack of beauty, not to mention the fact that I don't eat enough lettuce."

"Don't be ridiculous. You *are* beautiful," Georgiana said. "You have the prettiest eyes I've ever seen. I can't think why I got plain brown eyes and you have those green ones." She peered at her. "Pale green. The color of celery, really."

"If my hips were like celery, then we'd have something to celebrate."

"You're luscious," her sister insisted. "Like a sweet, juicy peach."

"I don't mind being a peach," Olivia said. "Too bad celery is in fashion."

Two

In Which We Are Introduced to a Duke

Littlebourne Manor
Kent
Seat of the Duke of Sconce

At the precise moment that Olivia and Georgiana were engaged in an agricultural wrangle over the relative merits of peaches and celery, the hero in this particular fairy story was certainly not behaving like the princes in most such tales. He wasn't on bended knee, nor on a white horse, and he was nowhere near a beanstalk. Instead, he was sitting in his library, working on a knotty mathematical problem: specifically, Lagrange's four-square theorem. To clarify my point, if this particular duke ever encountered a beanstalk of unusual size, it would doubtless have spurred a leap in early botanical knowledge regarding unusual plant growth—but certainly not a leap up said stalk.

It should be obvious from the above that the Duke of Sconce was the sort of man repulsed by the very idea of fairy tales. He neither read nor thought about them (let alone *believed* in them); the notion of playing a role in one would have been preposterous, and he would have rejected outright the notion that he resembled in any fashion the golden-haired, velvet-clad princes generally found in such tales.

Tarquin Brook-Chatfield, Duke of Sconce—known as Quin to his intimates, who numbered exactly two— was more like the villain in those stories than the hero, and he knew it.

He couldn't have said at what age he'd discovered how profoundly he did not resemble a fairy tale prince. He might have been five, or seven, or even ten—but at some point he'd realized that coal-black hair with a shock of white over the forehead was neither customary nor celebrated. Perhaps it was the first time that his cousin Peregrine had called him a decrepit old man (a remark that had led to a regrettable scuffle).

Yet it wasn't only his hair that set him apart from other lads. Even at ten years of age, he'd had stern eyes, fiercely cut cheekbones, and a nose that screamed *aristocrat*. By thirty-two, there were no more laughter lines around his eyes than had been visible twenty years earlier, and for good reason.

He almost never laughed.

But Quin did have one major point of resemblance with the hero of *The Princess and the Pea*, whether he would have acknowledged it or no: his mother was in charge of choosing his wife, and he didn't give a hang what criteria she applied to the task. If she thought a pea under a mattress—or under five mattresses—was

the way to ascertain the suitability of his future duchess, Quin would agree, just as long as he didn't have to
bother about the question himself.

In this crucial fashion, he was as regal—as *real*—
as the nameless prince in the fairy tale, as dukified as
Georgiana was duchified. He rarely saw a doorway
without advancing through it as if he owned it. Since he
owned a good many doorways, he would have pointed
out that this was a reasonable assumption. He looked
down his nose because he was taller than most. It was
there to look down, and arrogance was his birthright.
He couldn't conceive of any other way of behaving.

To be fair, Quin did acknowledge some personal fail-
ings. For example, he seldom knew what the people
around him were feeling. He had a formidable intelligence and rarely found other people's thought patterns
very surprising. But their emotions? He greatly disliked
the way people seemed to conceal their emotions, only
to release them in a gassy burst of noise and a tearful
exposition.

This antipathy to displays of feeling had led him
to surround himself with people like his mother and
himself: to wit, those who responded to a problem by
formulating a plan, often involving experimentation
designed to prove a stated hypothesis. What's more, his
selected few did not cry if their hypotheses were proven
incorrect.

He rather thought that people shouldn't have so
many emotions, given that feelings were rarely logical, and therefore were of no use whatsoever. He had
embarrassed himself once by falling into a slough of
emotion—and it hadn't ended well.

In fact, it had ended miserably.

The very thought sent a pulse of black pain through
the region that he generally supposed to house his heart,

but he ignored it, as was his habit. If he paid attention to how many times a month, a week—a *day*—he felt that little stab . . . There was no point in thinking about it.

If there was one thing he had learned from his mother, it was that regrettable emotions are best forgotten. And if one cannot forget (he couldn't), then that personal failing should be concealed.

As if thinking of his mother brought her to his side, the door to his library opened and his butler, Cleese, intoned, "Her Grace."

"My plans are in order, Tarquin," his mother declared, entering on the heels of Cleese's announcement. She was followed closely by her personal assistant, Steig, and by her personal maid, Smithers. Her Grace, the dowager duchess, preferred to have a little flock of retainers in tow wherever she went, rather as if she were a bishop trailed by anxious acolytes. She was not a tall woman, but she projected such a formidable presence that she achieved the impression of height, albeit with some help from a towering wig. In fact, her wig bore a distinct resemblance to a bishop's miter. They both advertised the wearer's confidence in his or her rightful place in the universe: to wit, on top.

Quin was already on his feet; now he moved from behind his desk to kiss the hand his mother held out. "Indeed?" he asked politely, while trying to remember what she was talking about.

Fortunately, the duchess did not view responsiveness as an obligatory aspect of conversation. Given a choice, she would prefer to soliloquize, but she had learned to give addresses that could almost be classified as interactive.

"I have selected two young ladies," she pronounced now. "Both from excellent families, it hardly needs saying. One is from the aristocracy; the other is from the gentry, but recommended by the Duke of Canterwick. I think we both agree that to consider only the aristocracy is to show anxiety about the matter, and the Sconces need have no such emotion."

She paused, and Tarquin nodded obediently. He had learned as a child that anxiety—like love—was an emotion disdained among the aristocracy.

"Both mothers are aware of my treatise," his mother continued, "and I have reasonable faith that their daughters will surmount the series of tests I shall put to them, drawn, of course, from *The Mirror of Compliments*. I have put a great deal of thought into their visit, Tarquin, and it will be a success."

By now Quin knew exactly what his mother was talking about: his next wife. He approved of both Her Grace's planning and her expectation of success. His mother organized every aspect of her life—and, often, his as well. The one time he had engaged in spontaneity—a word and an impulse he now regarded with the deepest suspicion—the result had been disastrous.

Thus the need for a *next* wife. A second wife.

"You shall be married by autumn," his mother stated.

"I have the utmost confidence that this endeavor, like all those you undertake, will be a success," he replied, which was no more than the truth.

His mother didn't flicker an eyelash. Neither of them had time for flattery or frivolous compliments. As his mother had written in her book, *The Mirror of Compliments*—which rather surprisingly had become a best-selling volume—"A true lady prefers gentle reproof to extravagant compliment."

It hardly need be said that Her Grace would have

been extremely surprised if offered a reproof, gentle or otherwise.

"Once I have found you a wife who is worthy of her position, I shall be happy," she said now, then added, "What are you working on?"

Quin looked back at his desk. "I am writing a paper on Lagrange's solution to Bachet's conjecture regarding the sum of four squares."

"Didn't you tell me that Legendre had already improved on Lagrange's theorem?"

"His proof was incomplete."

"Ah." There was a momentary pause, and then the dowager said, "I shall issue an immediate invitation to the chosen young ladies to join us here. After due observation, I shall make a choice. A *reasoned* choice. There will be no succumbing to light fancy, Tarquin. I think we both agree that your first marriage made patently clear the inadvisability of such behavior."

Quin inclined his head—but he didn't entirely agree. His marriage had been inadvisable, surely. Terrible, in some lights (the fact that Evangeline had taken a lover within a few months spoke for itself). Still . . .

"Not in every respect," he said now, unable to stop himself.

"You are contradicting yourself," his mother observed.

"My marriage was not a mistake in every respect." He and his mother lived together quite comfortably, but he was well aware that the household's serenity was dependent on the fact that he generally took the path of least resistance. When necessary, however, he could be as firm as the dowager.

"Well," his mother replied, eyeing him. "We must each be the judge of that."

"*I* am the judge of my marriage," Quin stated.

"The question is irrelevant," she replied, waving her fan as if to brush away an insect. "I shall do my best to steer you in such a way that you shall not fall into the same quagmire. I feel quite exhausted at the mere memory of the tempests, the pique, the constant weeping. One would think that young woman had been raised on the stage."

"Evangeline—"

"A most improper name for a lady," his mother interrupted.

According to *The Mirror of Compliments*, interruption was a cardinal sin. Quin waited a moment, just long enough that the silence in the room stretched to a point. Then he said, "Evangeline was deeply emotional. She suffered from an excess of sentiment and recurring problems with her nerves."

His mother shot him a beady look. "I trust you are not about to instruct me to speak no ill of the dead, Tarquin."

"Not a bad precept," he said, taking his life in his own hands.

"Humph."

Still, he had made his point. He had no particular objection to allowing his mother to organize the matter of a second wife. He fully realized that he needed an heir. But his first marriage . . .

He chose not to entertain other people's opinions on the subject. "To return to the matter at hand, while I am certain that the parameters you have formulated are excellent, I have one stipulation as regards the young women you have selected."

"Indeed. Steig, pay attention."

Quin glanced at his mother's assistant, whose quill was at the ready. "The giggles should have worn off."

His mother nodded. "I shall take that point under advisement." She turned her head. "Steig, make a note. At the express request of His Grace, I shall devise another test, to determine whether the subject is overly given to giggling and other native signs of innocent enjoyment."

"In-no-cent en-joy-ment," Steig muttered, writing frantically.

Quin had a sudden vision of a haughty duchess with a huge ruff, like the faces of his Elizabethan ancestors up in the portrait gallery. "I don't mind enjoyment," he clarified. "Just not giggling."

"I shall dispense with either candidate if she seems likely to indulge in overwrought expressions of pleasure," his mother said.

Quin could readily picture himself bound by marriage to yet another woman who felt no pleasure in his company. But that wasn't what his mother meant, he knew.

Besides, she had already left.

Three

**In Which the Merits of Virginity and Debauchery
Are Evaluated, and Debauchery Wins**

Olivia and Georgiana had scarcely finished their discussion regarding the desirability of peaches over celery when their mother entered the room.

Most women in their forties allow themselves to take on a soft roundness. But, as if in reproach to her unsatisfactory elder daughter, Mrs. Lytton ate like a bird and ruthlessly confined what curves she had in a whalebone corset. Consequently, she looked like a stork with anxious, beady eyes and a particularly feathery head.

Georgiana instantly rose to her feet and curtsied. "Good evening, Mother. How lovely that you pay us a visit."

"I hate it when you do that," Olivia put in, pushing herself to a standing position with a little groan. "Lord, my feet hurt. Rupert trampled them at least five or six times."

"Do what, my dear?" Mrs. Lytton asked, just catching Olivia's remark as she shut the door behind her.

"Georgie goes all gooey and sweet just for you," Olivia said, not for the first time.

Her mother's frown was a miraculous concoction: she managed to express distaste without even twitching her forehead. "As your sister is well aware, *'A lady's whole pilgrimage is nothing less than to show the world what is most requisite for a great personage.'*"

"Show *unto* the world," Olivia said, making a feeble gesture toward mutiny. "If you must quote *The Mirror of Senseless Stupidity*, Mama, you might as well get it right."

Mrs. Lytton and Georgiana both ignored this unhelpful comment. "You looked exquisite in your plum-colored sarcenet tonight," Georgiana said, pulling a chair closer to the fireplace and ushering her mother into it, "particularly when you were dancing with Papa. His coat complemented your gown to a turn."

"Have you heard? *He* is calling on us tomorrow!" Mrs. Lytton breathed the pronoun as though Rupert were a deity who deigned to enter their mortal dwelling.

"I heard," Olivia said, watching her sister tuck a small cushion behind their mother's back.

"You'll be a duchess by this time tomorrow." The tremble in Mrs. Lytton's voice spoke for itself.

"No, I won't. I'll be formally betrothed to a marquess, which isn't the same thing as actually being a duchess. I'm sure you remember that I've been unofficially betrothed for some twenty-three years."

"The distinction between our informal agreement with the duke and the ceremony tomorrow is just what I wish to speak to you about," their mother said. "Georgiana, perhaps you should leave us, as you are unmarried."

Olivia found that surprising; Mrs. Lytton was fluttering her eyelashes in such a way that suggested she was in the grip of deep anxiety, and Georgiana had a talent for soothing aphorisms.

In fact, just as Georgiana reached the door, their mother waved her hand: "I've changed my mind. My dear, you may stay. I have no doubt but that the marquess will dower you shortly after the marriage, so this information may be relevant to you as well.

"A formal betrothal is a complicated relationship, legally speaking. Of course, our legal system is in flux and so on." Mrs. Lytton looked as if she hadn't the faintest idea what she was talking about. "Apparently it is always in flux. Parts of the old law, parts of the new . . . your father understands all this better than I.

"Under current interpretation of the law, your betrothal will be binding, unless the marquess suffers a fatal accident—when, of course, it would be invalidated by his death." She snapped open her fan and waved it before her face, as if such a tragedy was too terrible even to contemplate.

"Which is all too likely," Olivia said, responding to the fan as much as to her mother's words. "Inasmuch as Rupert has the brainpower of a gnat and he's apparently going into battle."

"'*Civility is never out of fashion*,'" Mrs. Lytton said, dropping the fan below her chin and dipping into *The Mirror of Compliments*. "You should never speak of the peerage in such a manner. It is true that in the tragic event of the marquess's demise, the betrothal will come to nothing. But there is one interesting provision that falls under the provenance of an older law, as I understand it."

"Provision?" Olivia asked, creasing her brow—unluckily just as her mother glanced at her.

"'*Cloud not your brow with disdainful scorn*,'"

Mrs. Lytton said automatically. Apparently duchesses remained wrinkle-free for life, doubtless because they never frowned.

"If you were to . . ." Mrs. Lytton waved her fan in the air. "To . . . to . . ." She gave Olivia a meaningful glance. "*Then* the betrothal would be more than legally binding; it would turn into a marriage under some sort of law. I can't remember what your father called it. 'Common,' perhaps. Though how a *common* law could have any application to nobility, I cannot say."

"Are you saying that if I tup the FF, I become a marchioness even if he dies?" Olivia said, wiggling her sore toes. "That sounds extremely unlikely."

The fan fluttered madly. "I'm sure I don't know what you intend to say, Olivia. You must learn to speak the English language."

"I expect that the law is designed to protect young women," Georgiana interrupted, before her mother could elaborate on the subject of Olivia's egregious linguistic lapses. "If I understand you correctly, Mother, you are saying that should the marquess lose his composure and commit an act unbecoming his rank as a peer, he would be forced to marry his betrothed bride, that is, Olivia."

"Actually, I'm not entirely sure whether he would be obligated to marry Olivia, or whether the betrothal would simply turn into a marriage. But most importantly, should this occurrence result in—in an *event*, the child will be declared legitimate. *And* if the betrothed were not deceased, then he would not be allowed to alter his mind. Not that the marquess would think of such a thing."

"To sum it up," Olivia said flatly, "bedwork is followed by bondage."

Their mother snapped her fan shut and came to her feet. "Olivia Mayfield Lytton, your incessant vulgarity is unacceptable. The more unacceptable, because you are a duchess-to-be. Remember, all eyes will be upon you!" She stopped to take a breath.

"Might we return to a more important subject?" Olivia asked, rising reluctantly to her feet once more. "It seems that you are instructing me to seduce Rupert, although you unaccountably neglected to give me a tutor in that particular art."

"I cannot *bear* your rank vulgarity!" Mrs. Lytton barked. Then, remembering that she was the mother of a duchess-to-be, she cleared her throat and took a deep breath. "There is no need for any . . . *exertion*. A man—even a gentleman—merely has to be given the impression that a woman is ready for intimacy and he will . . . that is, he will take advantage of the situation."

And with that, Mrs. Lytton swept out the door without so much as a nod to either of her daughters.

Olivia sat down once again. Her mother had never been very interested in shows of maternal warmth, but it was painfully clear that quite soon Olivia would have no mother at all—merely an irritated, and irritating, lady-in-waiting. The thought made her throat tighten.

"I don't want to make you uneasy," Georgiana said, seating herself as well, "but I would guess that Mama and Papa are going to lock you in the root cellar with the FF."

"They could move the matrimonial bed down to the study. Just to make sure that Rupert understands his duty."

"Oh, he will understand," Georgiana said. "Men come to it naturally, as I understand."

"But I never had any particular sense that the FF was of that sort, did you?"

"No." Georgiana thought for a moment. "At least, not yet. He's like a puppy."

"I don't think he'll mature by tomorrow evening." "Puppy" wasn't a bad description of Rupert, given that he had turned eighteen only the week before. Olivia would always fault her papa for leaping into matrimony before the duke, and then proceeding to procreate at the same headlong rate.

It was tiresome to be a woman of twenty-three, betrothed to a lad of barely eighteen. Especially a boy who was such a callow eighteen.

All through a light supper before the ball Rupert had babbled on about how the glory of his family name depended upon his performance on the battlefield— even though everyone at the table knew that he would never be allowed near a battlefield. He might have been "going to war," but he was the scion of a duke. What's more, he was an heir for whom there was no spare, and as such had to be kept from harm's way. He'd probably be sent to another country. In fact, she was rather surprised that his father was allowing Rupert to travel outside England at all.

"You'll have to take the lead," Georgiana suggested. "Begin as you mean to go on."

Olivia slumped a little lower on the settee. She had known, of course, that she would have to bed Rupert at some point. But she had vaguely imagined the event taking place in the dark, where she and Rupert could more easily ignore the fact that he was a good head shorter than she was and more than a stone slimmer. That didn't seem likely if they were locked into the library.

"That's one good thing about your figure," Georgiana went on. "Men like curvaceous women."

"I can't say I've noticed. Except perhaps when it comes to Melchett, the new footman with the lovely shoulders."

"You shouldn't be ogling a footman," Georgiana said primly.

"He ogles me, not the other way around. I am merely observant. Why do you suppose we aren't simply getting married *now*?" Olivia asked, tucking her feet beneath her. "I know that we had to wait until Rupert turned eighteen, though frankly, I thought we might as well do it when he was out of diapers. Or at least out of the nursery. It's not as if he's ever going to achieve maturity as most people think of the word. Why a betrothal, and not a wedding?"

"I expect the FF doesn't wish to marry."

"Why not? I'm not saying that I'm a matrimonial prize. But he can't possibly hope to escape his father's wishes. I don't think he'd even want to. He doesn't have a touch of rebellion in him."

"No man wants to marry a woman his father picked out for him. Actually, no woman either—think about Juliet."

"Juliet Fallesbury? Whom did her father choose? All I remember is that she ran away with a gardener she nicknamed Longfellow."

"*Romeo and Juliet*, ninny!"

"Shakespeare never wrote anything relevant to my life," Olivia stated, "at least until they discover a long-lost tragedy called *Much Ado about Olivia and the Fool*. Rupert is no Romeo. He's never shown the least inclination to dissolve our betrothal."

"In that case, I expect he feels too young to be married. He wants to sow some wild oats."

They were both silent for a moment, trying to picture Rupert's wild oats. "Hard to imagine, isn't it?" Olivia said, after a bit. "I simply cannot envision the FF shaking the sheets."

"You shouldn't be able to envision *anyone* shaking the sheets," Georgiana said weakly.

"Save your tedious virtue for when there's someone in the room who might care," Olivia advised her, not unkindly. "Do you suppose that Rupert has any idea of the mechanics involved?"

"Maybe he's hoping that by the time he comes back from France, he will be an inch or two taller."

"Oh, believe me," Olivia said with a shudder, "I have recurring nightmares about the two of us walking down the aisle in St. Paul's. Mother will force me into a wedding dress adorned with bunches of tulle so I'll be twice as tall and twice as wide as my groom. Rupert will have that absurd little dog of his trotting at his side, which will only call attention to the fact that the dog has a better waistline than I do."

"I shall take Mother in hand when it comes to your gown," Georgiana promised. "But your wedding dress is irrelevant to this discussion as pertains to tomorrow's seduction."

"'*Pertains to*?' I really think you should be careful, Georgie. Your language is tainted by that pestilent *Mirror* even when we're alone."

"You'll have to think of tomorrow as a trial, like Hercules cleaning out the Augean stables."

"I'd rather muck out the stables than seduce a man who's a head shorter and as light as thistledown."

"Offer him a glass of spirits," Georgiana suggested. "Do you remember how terrified Nurse Luddle was of men who drank spirits? She said they turned into raging satyrs."

"Rupert, the Raging Satyr," Olivia said thoughtfully. "I can just see him skipping through the forest on his frisky little hooves."

"Hooves might give him a distinguished air. Especially if he had a goatee. Satyrs always have goatees."

"Rupert would have trouble with that. I told him tonight that I thought his attempt to grow a mustache was interesting, but I was lying. Don't satyrs have little horns as well?"

"Yes, and tails."

"A tail might—just might—give Rupert a devilish air, like one of those rakes who are rumored to have slept with half the *ton*. Maybe I'll try to imagine him with those embellishments tomorrow evening."

"You'll start giggling," Georgiana warned. "You're not supposed to laugh at your husband during intimate moments. It might put him off."

"For one thing, he's not my husband. For another, one either laughs at Rupert or bursts into tears. While we were dancing tonight I asked him what his father thought about his plan to win glory, and he stopped in the middle of the ballroom and announced, '*The duck can dip an eagle's wings but to no avail!*' And then he threw out his arm and struck Lady Tunstall so hard that her wig fell off."

"I saw that," Georgiana said. "From the side of the room it looked as if she was making a rather unnecessary fuss. It just drew more attention."

"Rupert handed back her wig with the charming comment that she didn't look in the least like someone who was bald, and he never would have guessed it."

Georgiana nodded. "An exciting moment for her, no doubt. I don't understand the bit about the duck, though."

"No one could. Life with Rupert is going to be a series of exciting moments requiring interpretation."

"The duck must be the duke," Georgiana said, still puzzling over it. "Perhaps dipping the eagle's wings should be clipping? What do you think? That implies Rupert thinks of himself as an eagle. Personally I consider him more akin to a duck."

"Because he quacks? He would certainly be alone in visualizing himself as an eagle." Olivia got to her feet and rang the bell. "I think it would behoove me—there's a twopenny word for you, Georgie—it would behoove me to keep in mind that I'm being invited to have intimacies with a duck in my father's library tomorrow night. And if that doesn't sum up my relationship with our parents, I don't know what could."

Georgiana gave a snort.

Olivia waggled a finger at her. "Verrrrry vulgar noise you just made, my lady. Very vulgar."

Four

That Which Is Engraved on the Heart of a Man (or Woman)

The following evening, Olivia was positioned on the sofa in the Yellow Drawing Room some two hours before the Duke of Canterwick and his son Rupert were due to arrive. Mrs. Lytton kept rushing through, squeaking this or that order to the servants. Mr. Lytton was more given to agitated pacing than to rushing. He fiddled with his cravat until it had utterly wilted, and he had to go off to change.

The truth was that her parents had prepared the whole of their married life for this moment, and even so they didn't really believe their good fortune. She could see the incredulity in their eyes.

Would the duke truly go through with this marriage, based on a schoolboy promise years ago? Inside, they were not convinced.

"'*Dignity, virtue, affability, and bearing*,'" her mother whispered to her, for the third time that evening.

Her father was more direct. "For goodness' sake, keep your mouth shut."

Olivia nodded. Again.

"Aren't you the least bit nervous?" her mother hissed, sitting down beside her.

"No," Olivia stated.

"That's—that's unnatural! One would almost think you didn't want to be a duchess." The very notion was clearly inconceivable to Mrs. Lytton.

"Insofar as I am about to formally betroth myself to a man whose brain would make a grain of sand loom large, I must wish to be a duchess," Olivia pointed out.

"The marquess's brain is irrelevant," Mrs. Lytton said, frowning, and then instantly soothing her brow with her fingertips, in case a wrinkle had sprung up. "You will someday be a *duchess*. I never thought about brains when I married your father. The very consideration is unladylike."

"I feel quite certain that Father evinced a normal intelligence," Olivia said. She was sitting very still so that her ludicrously unnatural ringlets wouldn't tangle.

"Mr. Lytton paid me a call. We danced. I never considered the question of his wits. You think too much, Olivia!"

"Which may not be a drawback, given that any woman who marries Rupert will have to do the thinking for two."

"My heart is palpitating," Mrs. Lytton said, with a little gasp. "Even my toes are qualmish. What if the duke changes his mind? You . . . you are not all that you could be. If only you could stop trying to be *witty*, Olivia. I assure you that your jests are not funny."

"I don't try, Mama," Olivia said, starting to feel a little angry, even though she'd promised herself that she wouldn't wrangle. "I simply don't always agree with you. I see things differently."

"You indulge in coarse wit, no matter how you wish to phrase it."

"Then Rupert and I will make quite a pair," Olivia said, just stopping herself from snapping. "Dim-witted and coarse-witted."

"That's just the sort of thing I'm talking about!" her mother accused. "It's unnatural to jest at a moment like this, when a marquess is about to plight his troth to you."

Olivia *was* calm. She knew perfectly well that Rupert's father would arrive, at the appointed hour, and bearing whatever papers were necessary to effect the betrothal. The bridegroom's presence hardly seemed relevant.

The Duke of Canterwick was a hardheaded man who had no interest in finding his son a compatible spouse; instead, he was looking for a nursemaid. A fertile nursemaid. He didn't need money, and the dowry her parents had scraped together—which was more than respectable for a girl of her rank—was of no importance.

It was her hips and her brains that had prompted the duke to go through with his promise, as he'd told her coolly on the day she'd turned fifteen. Her parents had thrown a garden party for their daughters, and to everyone's enormous surprise, His Grace had joined them. Rupert had not accompanied him because he'd been only eleven years old at the time, and barely out of short pants.

"My son is a buffle-headed idiot," the duke had said to Olivia, staring at her so hard that his eyes bulged a bit.

Since her opinion accorded with the duke's, Olivia had deemed it best to say nothing.

"And you know it," he had said, with distinct satisfaction. "You're the one, my girl. You've got the brains, and you've got the hips."

She must have twitched, because he'd said, "Hips mean children. My wife was rail-thin, and look what happened to me. There are two things I want in my daughter-in-law, and one is hips and the other is brains. I don't mind telling you that if you didn't have those two assets, I'd toss over my promise to your father and look about until I found the right woman. But you're the one."

Olivia had nodded, and since then she had never doubted that she would marry Rupert someday. His Grace, the Duke of Canterwick, was not a man who permitted mere technicalities—such as Rupert's or her feelings—to stand in the way of a decision.

As the years passed and the duke didn't bring his son to the altar, even as her parents grew more and more nervous, Olivia still didn't worry. Rupert was a buffle-headed fool and he wasn't going to change.

Her hips weren't going to change, either.

When a carriage bearing the ducal crest was finally observed to have turned into Clarges Street, her father took up a position at Olivia's right shoulder, while her mother sat beside her, her profile to the door, and twitched her skirts into place.

The duke entered the room without allowing their butler to announce him. In fact, the Duke of Canterwick was not the sort of man who would ever allow another man—other than royalty—to precede him. He looked like what he was, a man given to labeling ninety-nine percent of the world's population *insolent upstarts.*

A particularly observant person—such as Olivia—might have noticed that in reality the duke's nose entered the room first. He had a magnificent proboscis in the front, a doorknocker of a nose. But he made it work. Olivia rather thought that it was the way he held his head high and his chin forward.

He looked as if his presence was the only thing that made other people visible, though even she had to admit that this particular notion was more than unusually far-fetched on her part. "'*A lady does not stoop to fanciful notions,*'" her mother would have said, quoting, naturally, *The Maggoty Mirror.*

Alas, fanciful notions were all that seemed to run through Olivia's head, even as she curtsied with consummate grace and gave the duke a smile nicely calibrated between awe and respect.

Rupert, on the other hand, got a smile pitched between familiarity and respect (the latter entirely feigned).

"There you are!" Rupert said, with his usual enthusiasm.

Olivia curtsied again, and held out her hand. Since he reached only to her shoulder, Rupert didn't have to bend far to kiss her glove. It was unfortunate that he had inherited his father's nose but not the duke's dominating personality; his nose just seemed to force one to pay more attention to his mouth. Which invariably hung open, his lower teeth visible in a glistening pout.

She was never happier to wear gloves than when receiving Rupert's salutations. He invariably left a wet spot on the back of her hand.

"There you are," he repeated, straightening with a huge smile on his face. "There you are, there you are!" Rupert was given to statements that meant nothing at all.

In fact, as Olivia agreed with his statement—indeed,

here she was!—she puzzled over the differences between Rupert and his father.

The Duke of Canterwick was very intelligent. What's more, he was ruthless. It was Olivia's considered opinion that most people allowed feelings to get in the way of logic. Canterwick didn't.

Given that level of clear thinking, it was rather odd that his son was not only patently disadvantaged when it came to thought, but also given to excesses of emotion. Rupert made people think uneasily that he was about to burst into song—or worse, into tears. You definitely thought twice about mentioning a recent funeral—even for an elderly great-aunt—if Rupert was assigned to sit beside you at a meal.

"And here's Lucy!" he said, even more enthusiastically. Lucy was a very small, rather battered-looking dog whom Rupert had found abandoned in an alley a year or so before.

Lucy looked up at Olivia with an adoring expression, her thin, rather rat-like tail whipping from side to side like a metronome set to *molto allegro*.

"No meat pies today," Olivia whispered, leaning down to pull up one of Lucy's long ears.

Lucy had the best manners of them all. She licked Olivia's hand even given that disappointment, and then trotted after Rupert.

He was bowing and scraping before her parents, which gave Olivia an excellent view of his potato-shaped nose and pendulous lower lip. It occurred to her, not for the first time, that she was set to marry the sort of man whom people wished were invisible. Or if not invisible, at least silent. She swallowed hard.

"Now," His Grace announced, "I would never be clear in my conscience if I wasn't absolutely certain that

Miss Lytton wished this union with my son as dearly as we do. A promise between schoolboys should not force a young person into holy matrimony."

"Told him that myself," Rupert said, with palpable satisfaction. "No one could force me into marriage. My own decision. Clippings don't answer."

"No one is trying to clip your wings," his father snapped.

Mr. and Mrs. Lytton looked at their prospective son-in-law with identical expressions of alarm and confusion.

"My son means to say that he is deeply enthusiastic about marrying Miss Lytton once he has returned from his military service," the duke clarified.

Mrs. Lytton's eyelashes fluttered madly.

"First I'm going to do our name proud," Rupert put in. "Glory, and all that."

The duke cleared his throat, glowering at his son. "The question of the moment is not your intent to prove your military prowess, Son, but whether Miss Lytton cares to wait for you until you have returned. The poor lady has been betrothed to you for some time."

Rupert's face twisted into an almost comical expression of anxiety. "Must win glory for the sake of the family name," he said to Olivia. "What I mean to say is, I'm the last of the line. The rest all killed in the Culleron Door."

"Culloden Moor," his father said. "The Jacobite rising. Fools, every one of them."

"I completely understand," Olivia said to Rupert, resisting the impulse to draw her hand away from his.

He hung on with a tight grip. "I'll marry you as soon as I come back. Trailing glory, you understand."

"Of course," Olivia managed. "Glory."

"There is no need to worry in the slightest about my daughter," Mrs. Lytton told Rupert. "She will wait for you without a second's thought. For months, nay, for *years*."

Olivia thought this was a bit much, but obviously she was not in charge of the timetable. If her parents had their way, she would indeed wait another five years for Rupert to wander back to England, wreathed in glory—or, more likely, ignominy. The idea of Rupert in a war was distinctly frightening: men of his type should not be handed a penknife, let alone anything as lethal as a sword.

"Now, now, my dear lady," the duke said to Mrs. Lytton. "One can hardly trust a mother to plumb the depths of her daughter's heart."

Mrs. Lytton opened her mouth to dispute this statement; without question, she considered herself to have plumbed the depths of Olivia's heart and found there nothing but an engraved plaque that read *Future Duchess of Canterwick*:

But the duke raised a hand, politely but firmly. Then he turned to Olivia. She dropped another perfectly calibrated curtsy.

"I shall speak to Miss Lytton in your library," His Grace announced. "Meanwhile, Rupert"—he all but snapped his fingers—"do inform Mr. Lytton about the situation in France. My dear sir, the marquess has been studying the situation with some fervor, and I'm sure he can enlighten you as to the grave dangers posed by the debacle on the other side of the Channel."

They left the room on a stream of Rupert's babble. Olivia allowed herself to be seated when they reached the library; the duke stayed in his favorite posture, feet spread, hands behind his back, as if he were standing on the prow of a ship.

He'd have made a good ship's captain, now Olivia thought on it. That nose would have come in handy when it came to smelling the storm winds, or sniffing out rotten goods in the hold.

"Just in case you're worried, my dear, Rupert will be going nowhere near the French shore," His Grace announced.

Olivia nodded. "I am very happy to hear it."

"He'll be landing in Portugal."

"Portugal?" Olivia echoed, thinking that she had been right: Rupert was indeed being kept a whole country away from the battle.

"The French are fighting in Spain at no great distance," the duke said. "But Rupert is landing in Portugal, and there he will stay. He wishes to be at Wellington's side, but I simply cannot allow that."

Olivia inclined her head again.

The duke shifted from foot to foot, the first time that Olivia had ever seen him show the faintest hint of uncertainty. Then: "He's a biddable lad, as you'll discover. Generally does what he's told, without much fuss. He learned to . . . He can even dance now. Not the quadrille, of course, but most of the rest. But when he does get an idea in his head, he simply won't let go of it. And here's the problem: he's convinced himself that he will not marry until he achieves military glory."

Olivia didn't twitch an eyebrow. But the duke read something more subtle in her face.

"Astonishing, isn't it? I blame his tutors for spending altogether too much time beating the history of our family into his head. The first duke led five hundred men into battle—and the best way to describe that engagement would be a glorious and epic defeat. But of course we put a different gloss on it amongst ourselves. Or at least those fools of tutors did. Rupert wants to lead a troop of men and come home covered in glory."

Olivia was suddenly aware of a feeling of pity for the duke, something he would undoubtedly resent.

"Perhaps he might lead a small skirmish?" she suggested.

"Precisely my thought," the duke said, sighing. "It's taken a bit of maneuvering, but he'll be heading up a company of one hundred men."

"And what will he do with them?"

"Lead them into battle," the duke said. "In Portugal, a nice distance from any soldiers who might be inclined to fight back."

"Ah."

"Of course, anytime I let him out of my sight, I worry."

Olivia would worry too, if she had the faintest affection for Rupert. He was just the type to commit suicide. Oh, he wouldn't have it in mind as such. But he would wander into the Whitefriars with a jeweled snuffbox in his hand and a diamond set in his cravat. Suicide.

The duke thumped his walking stick on the flagstones before the fireplace, rather as if he were trying to even out the stone. "The truth of it is that I'm concerned about the possibility that Rupert won't go through with the marriage if I force him to the altar."

Olivia nodded again.

The duke looked at her fleetingly and then gave the flagstone at his foot another good prod. "I could deliver him to a church, obviously, but I would be unsurprised if he said no at the crucial moment, even if I filled St. Paul's with witnesses. He'd cheerfully explain exactly why he didn't want to say his vows, and he would certainly be happy to tell everyone that he planned to marry you after he achieved—" His voice broke off.

"Military glory," Olivia finished his sentence for him. She was feeling very sorry indeed for the duke. No one deserved to be humiliated like this.

"Precisely." Another thump sounded, along with the distinct sound of splintering wood.

"I have no doubt but that the marquess will return from Portugal satisfied with his prowess," Olivia said. It was true, too. As long as someone was at Rupert's shoulder who could describe marching down a country road as valiant subjugation of an (invisible) enemy, Rupert would come home happy.

"I'm sure you're right." The duke leaned his splintered walking stick against the fireplace and sat down opposite Olivia. "What I have to ask you is something that no gentleman should ever address with a young lady."

"Something to do with common law?" Olivia inquired.

His brow creased. "Common law? What does that have to do with anything?"

"The old law and the new law? My parents said something about older and newer rules pertaining to betrothals . . ."

"English law is English law, and to the best of my ability, common law has no bearing on a betrothal." The duke gave her a clear, penetrating look. "Women shouldn't be meddling with matters of the law. Though you must develop some familiarity, because God knows you won't be able to let Rupert make decisions on his own. But I'll teach you all that. As soon as you're married, you'll come to the estate and I'll start training you."

Olivia considered it a great triumph that her smile didn't slip, even though her heart was racing and a panicked voice in her head screamed: *Training? More training?*

His Grace didn't notice her silence. "I'm going to have to teach you how to be a duke, since Rupert isn't up to the task. But you're smart enough for it. I saw that when you were fifteen."

Olivia swallowed and nodded. "I understand." Her voice sounded rather faint, but the duke wasn't listening anyway.

"You may not know this, but our title is derived from an ancient Scottish dukedom," he said. He still didn't meet her eyes. He reached over and picked up his cracked walking stick and held it in his lap, examining it as if he thought it might be worth repairing.

"I am aware of that fact," Olivia said. The duke obviously had no idea of the extent of her knowledge of the Canterwick holdings and history. She could have told him the name of his second cousin thrice removed's firstborn child. And the name of that cousin's seventh-born child, the one notorious for having been born in the common room at the Stag's Head Inn after his mother had drunk too much ale.

"Due to our ancestral roots in Scotland, a case can be made that Scottish inheritance rules apply."

"Ah."

The duke pressed down deliberately on his knee, and the walking stick broke in two. He did not raise his eyes. "If you were to conceive a child now, before my son goes to Portugal, that child would be legitimate under Scottish law. I want to be quite clear about this, however: you would not become a marchioness until my son returned and wed you. There are those who might say unkind things about you, as they would of any woman carrying a child without the benefit of matrimony, although, of course, you would be put immediately under my protection."

"Yes," Olivia murmured.

"I would give Rupert no chance to refuse his duty. In fact, if a happy event were to occur, I would immediately send proxy marriage papers after him, to be signed in Portugal. As long as there was no mishap as regards the papers—and I see no reason why there should be—you would be a marchioness before the child was born."

He paused. "In the event that something were to happen to Rupert before the proxy papers could be signed, you would have the satisfaction of being the mother of a future duke."

Olivia had a terrible impulse to quote a choice line from *The Mirror of Compliments*: "*Nothing is more precious than a virgin's honor!*" But she remained silent, not even venturing to point out that the baby might be a girl, a possibility that didn't appear to have occurred to the duke.

"Whether or not a child ensues, I will gift you with a jointure and a small estate of your own," Canterwick continued.

"I understand," Olivia managed. If she understood him correctly, the duke had just offered her an estate in exchange for losing her virginity out of wedlock. It was an astonishing thought.

"I have tasked Lady Cecily Bumtrinket to accompany you to the country. You cannot stay at Canterwick Manor, of course, until either the proxy papers are signed or my son returns to marry you. It wouldn't be proper."

"Lady Cecily Bumtrinket?" Olivia repeated. "Could

I not simply remain at home until either of these events occur?"

"It wouldn't be appropriate for you to remain here any longer." The duke glanced about the room with just the faintest hint of indifferent disdain. "You and your sister will stay at the Duke of Sconce's estate until we are able to resolve all the little legalities. The dowager duchess planned to invite a young lady to the country in order to assess her befittedness for the position of duchess. I convinced her that your sister was also a suitable candidate. Her invitation is a tribute to your parents, as I shall inform your mother shortly."

Olivia murmured, "Georgiana will be gratified by the confidence shown in her."

"And so she should," the duke stated. "I have taken the liberty of informing Madame Claricilla on Bond Street that she is to outfit both you and your sister as befits your new station, within a fortnight. You must learn, my dear, that we dukes tend to keep to ourselves. We may crossbreed, rather like dogs and horses, but we prefer to keep each other's company."

Olivia's mind was reeling. Apparently she was part of a crossbreeding experiment. And she was to stay with the Dowager Duchess of Sconce? The very duchess who had written that dreadful tome, *The Mirror of Compliments*?

The duke rose, and at last he did look at her. His eyebrows were rather bushy and intimidating, combined with his great beak of a nose, but nevertheless she could see both kindness and despair in his eyes. "Don't worry," she said impulsively, coming to her feet. "Rupert and I will do our best."

"It's not his fault, you know," the duke said. "He wasn't breathing at birth, and the doctors believe that had an effect on his brain. It isn't . . . your children won't take after the poor boy."

Olivia took a step forward and picked up the duke's hand. For the first time in their many meetings, she felt a genuine fondness toward him. Of all the people and things attached to the dukedom of Canterwick, her father-in-law would be one of the very few of whom she was not wary. "We will do our best," she repeated. "And Rupert will be safe in Portugal. It's very kind of you to allow him to follow his dream. I'm sure he will be happy to have traveled outside England."

The corner of the duke's mouth quirked up. "His mother would have wanted it. I know that. She would have told me that I had to allow him to grow to a man, no matter how much I'd prefer to keep him tied to my apron strings."

Olivia blinked. She knew very little about the duchess; her parents had always said she was ill and lived in seclusion.

"Elizabeth almost died during his birth," the duke said heavily. "She lived, but she was never the same again. She can't eat by herself; she doesn't recognize me. She lives in the country."

"Your wife *and* son were impaired by the same event?" Olivia blurted out, before she could catch herself.

"Aye," the duke said. "That's the devil of it. But Rupert has a good heart. He's a kindly, cheerful soul, and if I don't think about what might have been, the two of us rub along fairly well together. And my dear, I've talked to you about your brains and your hips, but the most important thing is that you've always been kind to him. It's not easy. He tends to jabber, but you have never made fun of him."

Olivia tightened her grip on his hand. "I promise to be kind to him," she said, and in that moment, it was as if she said her vows.

The duke gave his odd smile again. "I'll send him to you."

And he was gone.

Five

Events That Warrant No Introduction

$\mathcal{R}$upert customarily entered any room with a hearty stream of greetings; having been coached as to the proper salutations, he took a clear delight in observing the appropriate rules. But now he walked into the library without a word, his eyes lighting on Olivia's face and sliding away.

Olivia let fly a silent, if heartfelt, string of oaths directed at their parents. She had forgotten—again—to consider what Rupert might be thinking of all this. From the look on his face, she and Georgiana had been right in their surmise that Rupert had not been tutored in the particular situation he now faced.

No more than she had, actually.

But then, people had been getting through the business for years. Luckily, her father kept a brandy decanter in the library, and she handed Rupert a brimming glass and poured one for herself as well, and the devil with the fact that her mother considered spirits to be unladylike. Still without a word, they sat down on the sofa before the fire.

"Left Lucy in the sitting room," he said suddenly. "Didn't seem right."

Olivia nodded. "She will be more comfortable there."

"No, she's not comfortable," he stated. "My father doesn't like her. Says that she's fit for hunting rats and nothing else. She doesn't wish to kill rats. She wouldn't even know how. And your parents don't care for her, either."

"My parents never allowed us to have a pet of any sort," Olivia said.

"You like dogs, though," Rupert stated.

"Yes."

"Said I'd do it because of that."

Olivia blinked. "What?"

"Marriage."

Apparently she had underestimated Rupert's strength of will; she hadn't realized that he was allowed any part in the choice of his duchess. Nor had she the faintest idea that the meat pies she'd saved for Lucy comprised her audition for the role.

She would have eaten them herself.

"It's not that I don't like you," Rupert said earnestly. "I do. But you like Lucy too, don't you?"

"She's a dear dog." They were on common ground now. She and Rupert had spent many an evening in the last year talking of Lucy.

But Rupert seemed to have exhausted the subject of Lucy, and with his silence the air turned edgy and nervous again.

"We needn't do it, you know," she said, after a bit.

"I must," he said, taking a big gulp of brandy and shuddering. "Told my father I would. Be like a man. Do—*be* a man." He looked confused.

Olivia took a sip and thought about how much she'd like to throw her parents and the duke off Battersea Bridge. "Shall we not, and tell them we did?" she offered.

He turned to look at her for the first time, eyes round. "Lie?"

"More like a fib."

He shook his head. "I don't lie. Not a gentleman's thing to do, lying. Better to man up." He took another shuddering gulp.

In his own way, Rupert was admirable, Olivia thought, realizing for the first time that he would have made a rather exceptional duke, if he'd had possession of all his faculties. He had his father's strength of will, with an extra layer of honor that his father was conspicuously lacking.

"I understand," she said.

"No time like the present," Rupert offered.

"Shall I turn down the lamps?"

"How would I see what I was doing?"

Good question. "Of course," Olivia said hastily.

He stood up, putting his now empty glass on a side table. "I know how to fall in. I fall in; you fall backwards." He seemed to be reassuring himself as much as her. "Easy business. They all say."

"Wonderful," Olivia said. After a second's hesitation, she stood up and then moved behind the sofa to remove her drawers. Then she came back around to the fire, wondering if she should take off her slippers.

A quick look at Rupert showed that he was not planning to do so. His breeches were pushed down around his ankles. She took another, larger sip of brandy.

"Perhaps you'd better finish your glass," Rupert suggested.

She gulped the remains of her brandy and then looked again at her fiancé. He was rather red in the face and his eyes were slightly glassy. Apparently, he had refilled his glass while her back was turned.

"What ho," he said, rather faintly, and drank it off as well.

Olivia took a deep breath and put her glass down. Then she lay back on the sofa, pulled her skirts up to her waist, and steeled herself.

"Right," Rupert said. "Do you suppose I should put one knee here, next to your hip? There's a pillow in the way."

They wrestled with placement of their limbs for a moment or two until he was more or less in position.

"Do you want some more brandy first?" Rupert asked. "Painful for a woman. My father says."

"No, thank you," Olivia said. Unfortunately, what brandy she'd already taken had gone straight to her head, and she had a burning wish to giggle. She could just imagine what her mother would say to that.

"If you feel like crying, I brought three extra handkerchiefs." Rupert displayed no particular urge to get on with the business.

"Thank you," Olivia said again, choking down more giggles. "I never cry."

"Really? I cry all the time," Rupert said, blinking at her.

"I remember how you wept at the garden party when that dead sparrow fell out of a tree."

Rupert's face crumpled at the memory.

"It was just a bird," she added quickly.

"Quick, bright . . . wild."

"The sparrow?"

He seemed to have entirely forgotten what they were supposed to have been doing, even though he was on his knees, holding his tool in one hand. His eyes weren't glassy anymore, but focused. "I wrote a poem," he told her.

Olivia wasn't entirely certain, but she was fairly sure that his tool wouldn't be effective in its current state. "What sort of poem?" she asked, putting her head back on the cushion. Life with Rupert would have its own rhythm. There was no point in rushing it.

"Quick, bright," he said again, "a bird falls down to us, darkness piles up in the trees."

Olivia raised her head. "Is that the whole poem?"

He nodded, eyes on hers.

"It's lovely, Rupert," she said, and meant it. For the first time in her life, almost, she truly meant what she was saying to her fiancé. "'Darkness piles up.' I love that."

"In the trees," he said, nodding vigorously. "I cried for the bird. Why don't you ever cry?"

She had never cried, even once, after meeting Rupert for the first time. She was ten years old; he was five. It was the morning when her dreams of the fairy-tale prince she was to marry crashed to the ground.

Even though he was only aged five (and she only ten), she knew something was gravely wrong with his brain.

But her mother had scoffed when she said as much. "The marquess may not be as quick as you," Mrs. Lytton had said, "but that is like expecting a duke to learn flower arranging. *You* are too clever for your own good."

"But—" Olivia had said, desperation rising in her chest.

"You are the luckiest girl in the world," her mother had stated. The utter conviction on her face had made the words die in Olivia's mouth.

Even all these years later, after it became clear that Rupert was lucky to have mastered speech, let alone literacy, her mother had never altered her opinion an iota.

"Perhaps you should begin," Olivia suggested to Rupert. She waved her hand toward the general area of endeavor.

"Right," Rupert said gamely. "On with it." As Olivia watched, he swayed back and forth slightly. "Bit too much brandy," he muttered, but applied himself to the appropriate place.

It bent in half.

Rupert blinked down. "It's not working. This part is supposed to be easy."

Olivia propped herself up on her elbows. It looked as if he were holding a piece of old celery. Bendy and—though one wouldn't want to say so aloud—flaccid.

"Try again?" she suggested.

"I suppose this is the right place?"

"Yes," she said firmly.

Rupert tried again, muttering to himself. Olivia let him get on with it, only slowly realizing that he was whispering, "*In, in, in.*" Giggles built up in her chest again, so she bit her lip hard.

After a while she said, "I've heard that this sort of thing never works on the first try."

Rupert didn't look up at her. He held his private parts in a fierce grip that looked desperately uncomfortable. "This is easy," he repeated.

"I think it needs to be stiff in order to work," Olivia ventured.

He blinked at her. "Do you know a great deal about

the matter?" He didn't seem in the least censorious, just curious.

"It's just a wild stab in the dark," Olivia replied. She was fighting giggles again because the phrase *lame duck* kept running through her mind.

"I thought the most important thing was size," Rupert said.

"I believe I have heard the same," Olivia admitted cautiously.

Rupert gave himself a shake. "This is big. I know that."

"Lovely!"

"But it doesn't work." He dropped it and looked at her, his eyes miserable. "Another thing that doesn't work."

Olivia wiggled backward and managed to sit up. "Do you know how you never lie, Rupert?"

He nodded.

"We'll just lie on the sofa together." She patted the cushion beside her. "Then, we tell them that."

"You mean . . . not tell?"

"It wouldn't be a falsehood."

"No."

"We'll just say that we lay together on the sofa."

"Lay together," he repeated. "I'd rather . . . I . . . Don't tell Father? Others? Please?"

Olivia took his hand—the other hand. "I'll never tell, Rupert. Never."

His smile was quick and bright.

Considerably later the same night, Olivia scowled at her sister. "Our parents requested that Rupert and I conjoin without the benefit of matrimony, and we complied, just as if we were a pair of breeding hounds."

"There's no need to put it in such a depressing fashion. Although," Georgiana added, with one of her rare smiles, "after this evening Rupert's prospects as a breeding hound are somewhat in question."

"If you smiled at men like that, Georgie, you'd have more proposals than you could manage."

"I *do* smile," Georgiana protested.

"But your smile often looks as if you were thinking about the fact that they are lower than the rank of duke," Olivia pointed out. "You could try smiling at them as if they *were* dukes."

Her sister nodded. "I take your point. At any rate, one shouldn't compare one's future husband to a breeding hound."

"*His Grace* characterized it as such. After which he informed me that he would reward me for this evening's work with a jointure and an estate. A small estate, I believe he said. I had no idea of how rich a strumpet could become from a mere hour or two of debauchery."

"Olivia!" But her sister's protest had no force.

"You're to benefit from my strumpethood, my dear. He's told Madame Claricilla to outfit both of us *according to my new station*."

Georgiana's eyebrows flew up.

"The fruits of sin. I am thinking of Cyprians in a whole new light, I promise you. You and I are both getting an entire wardrobe, and I shall refuse to have a single white gown or trailing ribbon."

"You are not a strumpet," Georgiana protested. "You were obeying Mother and Father's wishes."

"To that point, may I say that I deeply resent the fact that Mother spent years insisting that a lady's life should revolve around the protection of her chastity, only to toss out that precept the moment she thought I could have a child by Rupert?"

Georgiana chewed on her lip for a moment. Then she said, "You're right, of course. Our parents are showing an excess of enthusiasm for this marriage, and have done so all along."

"Given that poor Rupert is harebrained as they come, yes." Olivia rolled over on her back again. She felt exhausted, and deeply sad; the effects of the brandy had decidedly worn off. She had realized at the age of ten that her married life would be conspicuously different from that of other women. But she hadn't realized just how appalling the reality might be.

The very idea of having breakfast with Rupert, let alone years and years of breakfasts, made her feel despairing.

"Even if the marquess had a distinguished brain, our parents shouldn't have been party to a distasteful encounter such as you just described," Georgiana stated.

"His brain is distinguished, all right," Olivia muttered. "There are very few like it. Though his poetry is truly lovely, in a fragmented sort of way."

"I hesitate to ask," Georgiana said, "but why was Mother so vexed, after the duke and the FF left? Her voice carried even to my chamber, so I hesitated to come down for some time. Yet it sounds as though everything went according to her best hopes; the betrothal papers are signed, and as far as she knows, you may be carrying a future duke. Not to mention her fervent reaction to the possibility of my becoming a duchess."

"Oh," Olivia said. "That was Lucy." Even thinking about it made her start smiling.

"Lucy?"

"Rupert's dog, Lucy. Surely you remember her."

"Who could not? It's not that she's the only dog in the *ton*—Lord Filibert's poodle has gained some notoriety, given its green bows—but Lucy is the only one with flea-bitten ears."

"Unkind," Olivia said, laughing. "I think the bite to her tail proved more detrimental to her beauty."

"Beauty may be in the eye of the beholder, but one would have to be blind to praise Lucy."

"She has very sweet eyes," Olivia protested. "And it's rather adorable the way her ears turn inside out when she runs."

"That is not a characteristic I ever considered essential to an attractive dog."

"Mother doesn't admire it either. In fact, she was truly vexed by the idea that I might be seen with the dog by anyone of consequence."

Georgiana raised an eyebrow. "Lucy isn't going to Portugal? I thought Rupert was never separated from her."

"He believes the trip might be dangerous, so he asked me to care for her in his absence."

"Most people do say that about battlefields. So where is Lucy? She certainly wasn't in the drawing room by the time I joined you. Is she in the stables?"

"In the kitchens, being bathed," Olivia said. "Rupert demanded that she remain with me at all times. Of course, Mother was entirely sweet to his face, but she flew into a temper the moment the door closed. She considers Lucy to be an utterly inappropriate companion for a future duchess. Which makes her the perfect companion for me, you have to admit."

"Lucy does not have an aristocratic air. It's the rat tail, I think."

"Or that long waist. She looks like a sausage with legs. But she will smell like an aristocrat. Mother sent her down to the kitchens to be bathed in buttermilk."

Georgiana rolled her eyes. "Lucy may be enjoying the buttermilk, but the idea is preposterous."

"Mother also suggested that bows or some sort of embellishment might make her more suitable as a lady's companion." In the whole, long, rather horrible day, the only bright spot was the expression on their mother's face when Rupert, a tear rolling down his cheek, put Lucy's leash into Olivia's hand.

"Lucy with bows on her ears—or that tail—does not appeal," Georgiana stated firmly.

"Do you know what's bothering Mother the most? I think she's afraid that everyone will call Lucy a mongrel and then think the same of me. Bows for Lucy and ribbons for me, if you see what I mean."

"You can squash any such pretentiousness. Mother may despair of you, Olivia, but you and I both know that if you feel like playing a stiff-rumped duchess, you can do it with more flair than almost anyone."

"It's not always possible to disguise the truth," Olivia said. "Look at poor Rupert and his celery stick, for example."

"I think your experience in the library was unusual. All the conversations I've had with married women gave me the strong conviction that men needed nothing more than a woman and a modicum of privacy."

"Rupert obviously needed more than a captive woman and a sofa. But I'm not sure his experience says much about the rest of mankind."

"What did you say after you left the room?"

"Nothing. I promised Rupert that I would never tell—you don't count. His father should have known better than to think a duck could rise to the occasion, so to speak."

"Did Rupert obey you?"

"In every detail," Olivia said, with a flash of triumph. "He was a bit unsteady on his legs—I think he should probably stick to cider in the future—but he managed to bow without falling over, and then to leave without revealing the fact that neither of his two most important organs are functioning."

Georgiana sighed. "You really mustn't."

"I'm sorry. It just came out of my mouth."

"Jests like those should never come out of a lady's mouth."

"If you're casting aspersions on my claims to propriety, you're not saying anything that Mother hasn't concluded long ago," Olivia said. "Enough about my character deficits. In all the excited talk of your aptitude for the position of Duchess of Sconce, did Mother mention Lady Cecily Bumtrinket?"

"What an extraordinary name. No."

"Well, as Mother told you, the Duchess of Sconce, author of the *Mirror for Mooncalves*, apparently agreed with Canterwick's suggestion that you are a suitable match for her son. And Lady Cecily, who I gather is the dowager's sister, has been recruited to introduce us to His Grace. The only dark lining to this silver prospect is that we have to actually meet the grand arbiter of propriety herself, the duchess of decorum, the—"

"Stop!"

"I'm sorry," Olivia said, wrinkling her nose. "I start to babble when I'm miserable. I know it's a fault, but I can't bear to cry, Georgie. I'd much rather laugh."

"I would cry," Georgiana said, scooting over and tugging gently at a lock of Olivia's hair. "The very idea of Rupert's taking down his breeches makes me feel tearful."

"It was worse than I had imagined. But at the same

time, Rupert is such a good soul, poor cluck. He really—there's something very sweet about him."

"I think it's wonderful that you are able to respect his merits!" Georgiana said, with rather more enthusiasm than called for.

Olivia shot her a sardonic look.

"At any rate," Georgiana added hastily, "I suspect that such intimacies are always embarrassing. Most of the dowagers refer to the experience in the most disdainful terms."

"But think of Juliet Fallesbury and her Longfellow," Olivia pointed out. "Obviously, she didn't run away with a gardener because of his horticultural skills. At any rate, since Rupert is off to the wars at the crack of dawn, you, Lucy, and I will be taken to the country to meet the Duke of Sconce and his mother."

"A lovely prospect," Georgiana said, her eyes darkening. "I can't wait to see the duke's eyes roll back in his head from the utter tedium of sitting next to me."

Olivia gave her a tap on the nose. "Just smile at him, Georgie. Forget all those rules and look at the duke as if he might be likable. Who knows, maybe he is? Just smile at him as if you were a pig and he the trough, promise?"

Georgiana smiled.

Six

Her Grace's Matrimonial Experiment Commences

May 1812

$\mathcal{B}$ack in his study following the evening repast, Quin was dimly aware that his mother's house party had commenced. There had been a great deal of commotion in the entryway shortly after the meal, which suggested that at least one prospective wife and her chaperone had arrived.

He had a reasonable amount of curiosity about the young women his mother considered suitable candidates for matrimony. But just at that moment a cascade of giggles bounced its way up the stairs and into his study.

The giggler would surely fail his mother's tests regarding enjoyment, innocent or otherwise, so it would be a waste of time to greet her. He pulled off his coat and cravat, threw them over a chair, and sat back at his desk.

He had discarded polynomial equations for the moment, and returned to the problem of light. He'd been puzzling over light since he was a boy, ever since he'd met a blind man and realized that to him the world was dark. He had asked his tutor whether that meant that light existed only because we have eyes; the man had guffawed. He hadn't understood the larger question.

For a moment Quin gazed through the window of his study at the growing darkness outside. His study faced west, and its windows held the oldest glass in the house, the kind that was bottle thick and blurred, slightly bluish in hue. Quin liked that because he was convinced that, somehow, glass held the answer to the mystery of light.

He'd been taught at Oxford that light was made up of particles streaming in one direction. But light came through his old glass in ribbons, and the ribbons didn't act like a flowing river. It was more as if they were waves coming into the shore, bending slightly, adapting to imperfections in the glass . . .

Light came in a wave, not a flood of particles. He was convinced of it.

The problem was how to prove it. He sat down at his desk again, pulling over more foolscap. Light splits into separate color ribbons in rainbows. But rainbows are impractical and hard to pin down. He needed to . . .

By the time he raised his head again, the house was quiet and the window at his shoulder had turned black. For a moment he stared at it, then shook his head. Light was enough to worry about at the moment. The absence of light was another question. Besides, there was rain beating at the windows, a spring storm. Water . . . water was made of particles . . .

He stood up, legs stiff, and then froze in the middle of a stretch. What in the devil was causing that noise?

He heard it again, a distant thudding that sounded like the knocker on the front door. It was far too late for anyone in the household to respond. Cleese would be snug in his bed, and the last footman long since retired to the servants' quarters on the fourth floor.

Quin snatched up the oil lamp on his desk and ran lightly down the great marble stairs that led to the entry. He put the lamp down, drew back the bolt, and swung open the heavy door. Light fell out—in ribbons—from behind his shoulder into the dark, but there was no one to be seen, merely a moving blur of white in the middle distance.

"Is someone out there?" he shouted, keeping well back from the water sluicing off the pediment above the door.

The blur he'd glimpsed in the rain turned and ran back toward him. "Oh, thank goodness you're still awake," a woman gasped. "I thought no one heard me."

She moved into the circle of light falling over his shoulder, still talking, though he stopped listening. She was obviously a lady—but not just any lady. She didn't look as if she belonged in this world, let alone the world of Littlebourne Manor. The very sight of her was a blow to a man's senses, as if one of Homer's sirens had somehow traversed both eons and continents, and arrived at his doorstep to bewitch him.

Dark hair fell sleekly down her shoulders, making her skin look translucent, as if it had its own source of light. He couldn't see the color of her eyes, but her eyelashes were long and wet.

Then he suddenly realized that rain was pouring down her shoulders and she wasn't even wearing a pelisse. She was certainly as wet as a siren, or did he mean a mermaid?

He reached out and picked her up, swinging her into the entry, out of the rain. She gasped and started to speak, but he put her down and spoke over her voice: "What on earth are you doing out there?"

"The carriage turned over, and I couldn't find the coachman, and he didn't respond when I called," she said, shivering.

Quin found it hard to concentrate on what she was saying. Her hair was like skeins of wet silk, lying dark and sleek over her shoulders. Her dress was drenched, and it clung to her skin, showing every curve of her body . . . and what a body!

Belatedly he realized that her narrowed eyes indicated that she did not care for his survey.

"I can assure you that your master would not wish you to stand about parleying with me," she said sharply.

He blinked. She thought he was a servant? Of course, he wasn't wearing his coat or cravat, but even so, no one in his life had ever taken him for anyone but a duke (or, in the days before his father died, a duke-to-be). It was oddly freeing.

"*Parleying*?" he asked, rather idiotically. This drenched woman looked wickedly intelligent, far more so than the bran-faced debutantes he'd met back when he was last in London for the season.

"I am not—" She broke off the sentence. "I shall repeat my request. Would you please fetch the *butler*?" She sounded as though she was talking through clenched teeth.

Quin had the feeling he was having a hallucinatory

experience. He'd heard of this sort of thing, when men lost their minds and suddenly kissed the vicar's wife.

He always thought imprudence of that nature indicated a profound lack of intelligence, but as he wasn't inclined to question his own aptitude, he'd have to change his mind. In fact, it was a good thing the mermaid wasn't the vicar's wife, because he would likely kiss her and never mind her sanctified husband.

"You look very chilled," he said, observing that her teeth were chattering. No wonder she sounded as if her jaw was clenched. What she needed was a warm fire. He bent down and scooped her into his arms without a second thought.

She was soaked, and water instantly drenched his breeches . . . which just made him realize all the more sharply that his body agreed with his mind. If the mere sight of her had aroused him, now that she was in his arms the situation was made worse. She was gorgeous, a soft, fragrant, wet—

"Put me down!"

As if in punctuation, a sharp bark sounded around his ankle. He looked down and saw a very wet, very small dog with an extraordinarily long nose. The dog barked again, in a clear command.

"Does that animal belong to you?" Quin asked.

"Yes," his visitor said. "Lucy is my dog. Will you please put me down!"

"Come," Quin said to the dog, and "In a moment," to the lady, who was beginning to struggle. He moved toward the drawing room only to realize that the fire in that room would be banked for the night. But there was a coal stove in Cleese's silver room that was easily stoked.

"Where are you going?" she said indignantly as he

changed direction. "The coachman is out there in the rain and—"

"Cleese will arrive in a moment," he told her. Her lips were fascinating: full and plump, and a deeper rose color than any woman's lips he'd seen before. "He'll take care of your coachman."

"Who is Cleese?" she demanded. "And—wait! Are you taking me into the servants' quarters?"

"Don't tell me that you're one of those ladies who has never been through a baize door," he said, turning so that he could back the two of them through the door, and then keeping it open for the dog. "Your dog looks rather like a rat thrown up on the banks of the Thames," he added. The silver room was just to the left, so he kicked the door open.

"Lucy does not look like a rat! And what does that have to do with anything? I am Miss Olivia Lytton and I *demand* . . ."

Olivia. He liked it. He looked at her eyelashes and her plump lips. Her eyes were a beautiful color, a kind of pale sea green—or was it the color of new leaves in the spring?

"Put me down, you rudesby!" she was saying fiercely, and not for the first time.

He didn't want to do that. In fact, he felt very strongly about the question, which was unlike him. Generally, he didn't care strongly about anything other than polynomial equations. Or light. But Miss Lytton was rounded . . . beautifully rounded in all the right places. She felt right in his arms. He particularly liked the soft curve of her bottom. Not to mention the fact that she smelled wonderful, like rain and, faintly, of some sort of flower.

"I shall inform your master!" She had a definitely threatening tone. Rather like a queen.

He placed her gently on Cleese's sofa, then threw a shovelful of coal into the stove and gave it a stir. Yellow flames surged up just as he swung the stove door shut, and they threw out enough light so that he got a good look at her face. She was furious, eyes narrowed, arms wound around her chest as if he were a ravisher.

He would be happy to oblige.

Her dog had hopped onto the sofa as well, and was perched next to Miss Lytton. The beast was only slightly larger than a Bible, but she had the fierce eyes of an attack dog.

In fact, Lucy and Miss Lytton had a certain resemblance, though not in the nose.

A person would always know what Miss Lytton was thinking, he realized, lighting the Argand lamp on Cleese's sideboard. At the moment, her eyes were full of rage.

"If you don't fetch your master this very moment, I shall have you let go. Dismissed, and without a reference!"

Her dog barked a sharp underline to that threat.

He felt a strange sensation bubbling up in his chest. It took a second before he realized it was laughter. "You're going to have me dismissed?"

She leaped to her feet. "Stop looking at me like that! If you had a brain that was bigger than a mouse's willy, you'd realize that I have been telling you something important!"

At that he surprised himself with a laugh. His mother was not going to appreciate Miss Lytton's colorful use of the English language. "I cannot lose my position. I was born to it."

"Even a family retainer should not be tolerated if he oversteps the bounds of propriety."

That sounded faintly familiar, probably because it was the sort of thing his mother said. It created an odd contrast to *mouse's willy*. He'd never met a lady who'd admitted to knowing terms of that sort.

Following his gut instinct, Quin took a step toward her, just enough so that he caught her enticing scent again. He expected her to scream at him, but she didn't.

"I am not a footman," he stated.

Their eyes met. The world of logic and reason—the world that Quin inhabited on a regular basis—peeled away. "And you are very beautiful," he added.

She blinked. And then, just as if she were the vicar's wife and he was a man who'd suddenly lost his mind, he bent his head and brushed his lips over hers.

They were soft and berry colored, like a raspberry tart. It was a gentle kiss, at least until he pulled her against his chest. His body turned to flame and the kiss changed, turned dark and deep. He gave a silent groan and put a hand to her cheek, tilting her head so that he could kiss her again . . .

Her cheek was very cold to the touch. He straightened, reluctantly. "I had better fetch you a blanket."

That snapped the invisible thread that had kept them staring at each other. Just like that, all the outrage flooded back into her eyes. Quin felt a deep sense of rightness. He *could* read her, just like a book.

"I suppose you are the duke," she said stiffly. "I realize now that you sound like one, though I might add that you are not behaving like one."

"I am not the one who was throwing around references to willies, whether belonging to small rodents or other mammals. The last time I heard that word I was five years old."

He was fascinated to see that although a trace of pink

was stealing into her cheeks, she tilted her little nose firmly in the air. "Lady Cecily is out there in the rain, as is my sister. Why aren't you sending people to rescue them, not to mention that poor coachman? It's cold and wet."

She had the bearing and tone of a duchess, he thought, and then: Lady Cecily?

"Lady Cecily *Bumtrinket*? My aunt? Lady Cecily is out in the rain?" As she started an explanation that had to do with her carriage and the missing coachman, Quin finally snapped out of his trance. He yanked the cords connected to Cleese's rooms, the kitchens, and the fourth floor. For good measure, he pulled open the door and bellowed, "Cleese!"

Then he turned back to Miss Lytton. She was shivering, her arms still wrapped around that magnificent chest of hers. He felt for his coat and realized that he wasn't wearing it, nor even a waistcoat. No wonder she'd decided he was a footman. A gentleman is never seen in disarray.

Livery hung on the wall, and he grabbed a coat.

Her eyes were dark and suspicious, but she took the garment. She wasn't fast enough, so he threw the coat around her shoulders himself and pulled it tight, even though he didn't like seeing her luscious bosom disappear under a swaddling of black cloth.

"What happened?" he demanded.

"I've been trying to tell you. We hit a pillar at the end of the drive," she said. "I think Lady Cecily is fine, but she's injured her ankle and her ear hurts where she struck the edge of the window. My sister and I were unhurt, luckily, but I couldn't find the coachman anywhere. The horses seem to be sound, though it was so dark I couldn't be completely certain."

Quin was quite aware that what he most wanted to do was scoop up his watery visitor and then sit down, with her on his lap. At the very least, he didn't want to leave her.

The very thought was a shock. He had felt like this once before.

The first time he met Evangeline, he had felt intoxicated. He had seen her dancing, as delicate and joyful as if she were floating on the wind, and he had succumbed on the spot. Even now, after the years of disappointment and grief, he could remember the sense of wonder he'd felt.

But he could also feel his scalp prickling. He was at risk of succumbing again. As if he were a mad hare in the springtime . . . just what his mother warned that he shouldn't do.

What's more, given Miss Lytton's creative vocabulary—not to mention the fact that she allowed a man she believed to be a footman to kiss her—she was as unlikely a candidate for the role of Duchess of Sconce as Evangeline had been.

If there was one thing he knew in his bones, it was that he never, ever, wanted to fall under the spell of a woman again. Nor did he wish to humiliate himself by marrying a second wife who had no respect for her marital vows. He took a deep breath and willed the world to reassemble itself.

He was the Duke of Sconce. This young lady had been summoned to his house as a prospective duchess, and she was clearly, definitively, ineligible. That was the end of that.

True, his impulsive kiss suggested to him that he should make a greater effort to find a mistress. It wasn't like him to accost strange women who appeared on his doorstep, no matter how revealing their attire might be.

He pulled himself upright. "Miss Lytton, I trust you will forgive me if I leave you for the moment."

"Certainly," she murmured. She was looking at him with a rather amused curiosity.

He bowed.

"Your Grace," she said, still clutching the coat to her neck. It had to be his imagination that there was a faintly mocking tone underlying her salutation.

He headed out the door without another word.

Seven

Ineligible! And More So Every Moment

Olivia took a deep breath as the duke disappeared into the corridor. She felt as if her mind was darting in fifteen different directions, all at the same time. Who could have thought that the mere absence of a coat would emphasize a man's shoulders so much? At first she'd thought the duke's eyes were black, but then she'd realized they were gray-green, fringed with surprisingly long lashes.

And he'd *kissed* her. She actually touched her lips, thinking of it now. Her first kiss. She sat down and Lucy leaped onto her lap. A bundle of wet fur could not make her gown any wetter than it already was, and Rupert's little dog was shivering terribly, so she bundled her inside the coat and pulled it closed.

She had imagined that Rupert would kiss her when they consummated their betrothal. While she hadn't been looking forward to his salutation, her imagination had been proved wrong: he hadn't made the slightest attempt. Apparently his father had not included kissing in his instructions for marital congress.

But this duke had kissed her as if it were his right. As if *he* were her fiancé. And . . . he'd said she was beautiful. Olivia pulled the coat a little tighter and thought about that. She'd been complimented before, of course. She was to be a duchess someday, and on occasion men had flattered her in a halfhearted sort of way.

Still, the Duke of Sconce had had no idea of her future rank when he'd told her she was beautiful. The thought was like a bright little coal in her heart, a happy spark.

Her mind skipped to a different subject. She'd never seen hair like his. Black as midnight, except for one white streak in the front, and falling loose around his shoulders. Of course, he'd presumably been called from his bed. Undoubtedly he wore his hair tied back during the day.

Lucy made a little snorting sound, so Olivia glanced down, only to see a gleam of pink leg showing through her skirts. Perhaps that was why the duke had stared so intently. She couldn't bear wearing corsets while riding long distances in a carriage—but generally, there was no one to see her but her sister.

Just as she peeked into the coat to see whether, in fact, her breasts were as visible as her knees, a middle-aged man trotted through the door, pulling his livery over his right shoulder. "What is it?" he panted, seeing her. "Lord, and aren't you half-drowned, then? Has the bridge to the village gone under water again?"

"The village?" she echoed.

The moment he heard her voice, his entire demeanor changed. He straightened, and something indefinable shifted every feature in his face. He transformed from a rather annoyed, sleepy man into the butler of a great house.

"Please accept my humble apologies," he said, bowing. "I am Cleese, the butler. On seeing you in my silver room, I assumed . . . has there been some accident?"

A footman poked his head in at the door, with another at his heels, their livery pulled on in a haphazard fashion. "Our carriage drove into the gatepost," she explained. "Lady Cecily Bumtrinket's ankle is injured. She is not badly wounded, but the coachman must have been thrown clear. I couldn't find him at all. I called out, but when no one answered, my sister and I decided that I should come to the house, while she stayed with Lady Cecily."

She suddenly felt exhausted. "I am Miss Olivia Lytton," she continued, "and while I would not wish to disturb Her Grace, we are expected."

"Your rooms await you," the butler said reassuringly. "If you would accompany me, Miss Lytton, I'll have you upstairs, dry and comfortable, in a moment. I gather your maid is not travelling with you?"

"There were two carriages with our maids and trunks, but apparently they weren't following closely."

"Likely the other carriages missed the turn in the dark. It's quite common when a driver hasn't visited the manor before." More footmen appeared at the door, and the butler sent them flying in different directions. Then he turned back to her again. "Mrs. Snapps, the housekeeper, will dispatch a maid to your bedchamber, Miss Lytton. And I will send up a hot bath and drinks, perhaps a light repast, if you wish."

"But what about Lady Cecily and my sister?" Olivia asked. "I can't simply retire without knowing they are safely indoors. Not to mention the coachman, who might be lying dead in the ditch. And the horses."

"I will send—"

But whatever suggestion the butler was about to make was interrupted by a flurry of noise in the entry. Olivia jumped to her feet. Lucy skittered to the floor, the coat slid from Olivia's shoulders, and she saw Cleese's eyes slide below her neck and then jerk away, as if mortified.

One downward glance revealed that her garments were doing absolutely nothing to conceal her breasts. They were perfectly outlined, nipples and all, by her wet clothing. Her cheeks hot, she managed to resecure the coat and then walked past Cleese back down the servants' hallway.

Lady Cecily was standing in the middle of the entry, propped up on one side by the duke, who was now thoroughly drenched, and on the other by Georgiana. Her sister was a distinctly bedraggled version of her normally duchified self.

Olivia couldn't help noticing that the duke had rather remarkable cheekbones, emphasized by his sleek hair. And that a soaking wet shirt was as revealing on him as it was on her. Fine linen clung to muscular shoulders— she tore her eyes away. What on *earth* was she doing, ogling the man her sister was likely to marry?

Just then the door closed behind Cleese, at her back, and the wet arrivals looked up.

"My dear Olivia, you are the heroine of the hour!" Lady Cecily called instantly. "Rushing through this tempest; why, you could have drowned—though, of course, drowning is apparently quite a pleasant death, as those things go. That is, as deaths go. Much better than being hanged, by all accounts." She tapped the duke's arm. "Miss Lytton, this is my nephew."

Lady Cecily's hair looked as if a flock of swallows had turned it into a community nest, but other than that and her sprained ankle, she seemed little the worse for the accident.

Olivia curtsied. "It is an honor to meet you again, Your Grace."

"Indeed," the duke said, turning to his aunt. "Miss Lytton and I have already met, in a manner of speaking. My sartorial disarray led her to the logical conclusion that I was a member of the staff."

Olivia must have been out of her mind when she came to that conclusion. Even without a coat or cravat, the duke had a kind of ironclad self-possession that declared "aristocrat."

In fact, he looked astonishingly ducal. She couldn't see the slightest trace of the man who had laughed when she blurted out that hopelessly unladylike comparison between his brain and a mouse's privates. Instead he looked like a pasteboard portrait of a duke, staring down his nose at her in a superior fashion.

So be it. He must have suffered a temporary lapse into madness, only to revert to his title. "I apologize for my misapprehension, Your Grace," she said, sinking into a deep curtsy.

"I'm surprised that you didn't recognize him immediately," Lady Cecily put in cheerfully. "I always think that there's a sort of squint about the eyes that identifies a Sconce. Even those born on the wrong side of the blanket have just a touch of it."

The duke's eyes may not squint, but they were as startling gray-green as Olivia remembered. And cold, with just a trace of condemnation. As if she had tempted *him* to kiss her. Which she certainly had not. "As a matter of fact," she said, "I do believe I see exactly what you mean, Lady Cecily."

Georgiana gave a little gasp, which she covered with a cough. "What my sister means, Your Grace, is that you have the unmistakable look of a Sconce."

"That's exactly what I said." Olivia smiled at the duke's stiff features. "From now on I'll recognize that squint anywhere."

"I am happy to welcome you to my house, Miss Lytton," he said, dismissing the question of the squint as beneath him. Olivia had the feeling that he often ignored trivialities of that sort. "I trust that you, Lady Cecily, and your sister plan to make a long visit. My mother, the dowager duchess, will be most happy to greet you tomorrow morning, as will my cousin, Lord Justin Fiebvre, who is paying us a visit before he returns to Oxford University."

He had a very deep voice, deeper than her father's. It made him sound . . . it was very manly, Olivia thought, before she jerked her mind away from the subject.

Georgiana deserted Lady Cecily and trotted over to Olivia's side, giving her a little pinch. "What on earth are you doing, making fun of the duke?" she whispered. "He hasn't a squint!"

"Our driver was found in the ditch quite uninjured," Lady Cecily said, "and my dear, he reeked of gin. Reeked! A knavish type he must be, soaked in drink. If it had been up to him, we could have died right in the carriage and been eaten by vultures."

"Eaten while still in the carriage?" the duke remarked. "That would be quite unusual."

"It's a wonder we didn't drive straight into a river! Or into a mail coach. We should have examined his fingernails before we entered the carriage. Were you aware that a man who has a slightly longer fingernail on the little finger is invariably an inebriate?"

"The duke was remarkably surprising," Olivia whispered back. "He just—I'll tell you later."

"You didn't say something unladylike *already*," Georgiana groaned.

"No! Well, I did, but I'll tell you later. But are you feeling quite all right, Georgie? I think Lady Cecily landed on top of you."

"Five more minutes in that carriage alone with Lady C, and I'd have been a candidate for Bedlam," Georgiana breathed, so quietly that she could scarcely be heard.

Olivia squeezed her hand. Olivia and Georgiana had survived the past five days in the carriage by reverting to the games they'd played as children: betting on the number of times that Lady Cecily mentioned her "dearest friend"—Lady Jersey, one of the patronesses of Almack's—just as they used to bet on their mother's references to *The Mirror of Compliments*.

"I was not aware of any parallel between a man's character and his fingernails," the duke said now, to Lady Cecily. Olivia could have told him that his aunt was a treasure trove of odd theories, mostly to do with the digestion. Olivia didn't believe a single one.

"Oh, it's very true," Lady Cecily assured the duke. "I expect it's the very first thing Bow Street Runners look for when they apprehend a criminal."

"I always heard the telltale sign was a squint, myself," Olivia remarked. For some reason the duke's implacable expression made her long to tweak his nose, although she didn't quite dare look to see how he took her comment. So she added hastily, "Have the carriages with our maids and trunks made an appearance?"

"I had a new gown in one of my trunks," Lady Cecily said instantly. "And although you haven't suckled the milk of the court, my dear, and thence come to be a proper courtier, anyone could understand the need to recover my fringed gloves. I wore those gloves when I met the Spanish ambassador and he paid me a great compliment, though I couldn't tell you what it was, as he didn't speak English."

Cleese broke in the moment Lady Cecily paused for breath. "There is, as yet, no sign of the service carriages, Miss Lytton. I have taken the liberty of assigning a lady's maid to each of you, who will be happy to aid you until your own servants arrive."

"But I must have my maid," Lady Cecily said, nimbly taking up the new subject. "No one but Harriet can make my face. You know what they say, dear." She peered at Georgiana and Olivia through dripping strands of hair. "*A woman's past her prime at twenty, decayed at four-and-twenty, old, and insufferable at thirty.* My dears, you're not yet four-and-twenty, are you?"

"We have one year before we are entirely decayed," Olivia stated.

"I am glad to hear it," the duke put in, rather unexpectedly. "My squint may well indicate a marked state of decay."

Olivia raised an eyebrow. There was just the faintest gleam in his eye . . . his comment *almost* suggested a sense of humor. What a peculiar man he was.

"Decay!" Lady Cecily hooted. "As if we would accept such a description of *you*! Men do not decay."

Olivia felt nettled all over again. "Lady Cecily," she asked, "why on earth should men not decay, if ladies do?"

"Oh, men *do* decay," Lady Cecily said, not one to be stumped by any question that might possibly be construed as within her area of expertise. "That is, they rot, which is all the same thing, isn't it? Mr. Bumtrin-ket always used to say that a man who can't go diddly-diddly-up when required is rotten to the core."

Olivia choked, but otherwise Lady Cecily's comment was met with silence. She stole a look at the duke and found that very subtle gleam in his eye again. He looked as sober as an alderman, but possibly, just possibly, he was laughing inside.

Then she took another look and changed her mind. No one with a face that righteous could have a sense of humor. What's more, he had presumably been raised according to the precepts found in the *Mirror for Poker-Faced Peacocks*. The ability to laugh would have been trained right out of him.

"At any rate," Lady Cecily said, picking up the conversation again, "my nephew is famous all over the kingdom for the clever things he does with numbers. More than an accountant could do, I expect. *Better* than accounting. Such clever things."

"It is an honor to meet such a renowned mathematician," Georgiana said.

Olivia glanced to the side and saw with an odd little flip of her stomach that her sister was smiling at the duke. Of course, it would never occur to *this* man that Georgiana's smile signaled condescension—because it wouldn't. He was a duke. They were perfectly suited for each other. It was positively disgusting to think that she had kissed—no matter how unwillingly—her future brother-in-law.

The duke was as susceptible to Georgiana's smile as she had always known men would be. His eyes softened perceptibly and he said, "Lady Cecily exaggerates, Miss Georgiana." It was rather astounding the way he could murmur something self-effacing and yet look so proud.

"You mustn't be modest," Olivia said, unable to resist. "Accounting is *such* a useful skill. And it's quite brave of you to have realized your desire to be an accountant, given your elevated position, Your Grace."

Beside her, Georgiana gave a tiny, and likely involuntary, moan. The duke's eyes shifted from her sister's face.

"Most dukes haven't the wits for simple fractions," she finished, giving him a smile that didn't include a hint of her sister's worshipfulness.

"If I may, I suggest that we repair to the chambers that Cleese has kindly prepared for us," Georgiana said, sticking an elbow into Olivia's ribs.

"Yes, indeed," Olivia said, feeling a little ashamed of herself. She had done it again; the moment she became aggravated by flagrant displays of propriety, she abandoned all the ladylike traits her mother had instilled in her. "If you would be so kind, Cleese," she said, turning to the butler.

"I shan't retire until I have a warmed milk and brandy," Lady Cecily announced. "I've drunk it every night since my thirteenth birthday, and I assure each of you that it has made all the difference with my digestion. There are any number of diseases that I might have caught and haven't, because I cleanse my stomach every night."

"Withers, bring a hot milk and brandy to Lady Cecily's chamber as soon as possible," Cleese said, proceeding to the foot of the steps. "If you would please follow me, my ladies, I will escort you to your chambers."

"You'll have to haul me up, Nephew," Lady Cecily said. "Just wait until the young ladies reach the top of the steps, if you please."

Olivia couldn't resist turning about when she and

Georgiana neared the top of the flight of marble stairs. Her shoulders were prickling, as if . . . Sure enough, he was watching them.

The jokes she and Georgiana had made about satyrs leaped into her mind. There was something fierce and powerful about the duke's face that would suit a satyr. He had sharp cheekbones, but it was his eyes . . . they burned with the kind of utterly contained power that one could imagine of a satyr.

She loathed a goatee, but she had to admit that the fashion would suit his faintly exotic look. His hair had begun to dry, and the shock of white fell over his brow.

"Olivia," Georgiana said sharply.

Olivia blinked and turned away.

Georgiana, of course, did nothing so ill-bred as to ogle the duke from the top of the stairs. Instead she dropped a curtsy, giving both the duke and her ladyship a measured, affable smile. Then she sent one sharp-eyed glance toward Olivia that said *follow me*, turned, and walked down the hallway after Cleese.

For the first time in her life, Olivia felt a deep longing to possess her sister's figure rather than her own. Georgiana looked so slim and elegant, even in a drenched costume.

Whereas she herself undoubtedly looked like a loaf of bread, wrapped in a heavy coat, wet skirts clinging to her legs. Which weren't nearly as nicely shaped as her sister's.

"I'll just lean on your arm, Nephew," Lady Cecily was saying. "I certainly don't wish to be carried up the stairs like a bundle of linens."

Olivia started down the hallway, planning to escape before the duke reached the top of the stairs and had a good look at her wet gown from the rear.

"I hope you don't mind my saying this," Lady Cecily told the duke, "but your hair looks a little disordered. My husband used to wear a little net cap at night that kept his hair neatly in place. Your valet will find you one, Nephew; I shall give him the proper direction."

Olivia giggled at the thought of the duke in a hair net. She glanced over her shoulder and . . .

Their eyes met.

His face could have been granite, for all the emotion she saw on it.

But his eyes . . . his eyes were different. They locked with hers and she could have sworn that she read something there.

Longing. Perhaps.

Olivia almost shook her head as she hurried back down the corridor after her sister. Of course it wasn't longing. No one could possibly feel that, not for her.

She was a plump, long-in-the-tooth woman without much more to recommend her than her betrothal to a duke's heir.

Longing!

What did she possess that a duke could possibly long for? The world lay in front of him, his for the asking.

Just as it would for her, once she became a duchess.

Eight

Defining the Qualities of a Fairy-Tale Prince

O livia woke the next morning to the sound of her bedchamber door opening. She had no idea what time it was. The dowager duchess favored old-fashioned bedding, which meant that Olivia might as well have been sleeping in a cave. The very air around her looked blue, reflecting the watered silk that hung around her bed.

"Norah?" she asked drowsily. Late the night before, after they'd all retired, her maid had appeared, none the worse for wear. It turned out that the service carriages had missed the sign for Littlebourne Manor altogether and had gone several leagues out of their way before the coachman had at last conceded to stop and ask for directions.

"No, it's me," came a cheerful voice. Bright sunshine spilled onto the coverlet as the bed curtains were whipped aside to reveal Georgiana.

Olivia gave a little groan. "What time is it?"

"After eleven. You slept through breakfast, but you must accompany me to luncheon. The duke will be there."

Olivia yawned and pushed herself up against the carved headboard. "Lord knows I wouldn't want to miss the chance of being patronized again." Though, in truth, ducal condescension wasn't foremost in her mind when she thought of His Grace. She was not an early riser, but she would make an exception tomorrow and go down to breakfast if she thought . . .

Of course, the duke wouldn't kiss her again, and she most certainly would never allow it. He was likely temporarily maddened by lust—there she was, practically naked. Still, one had to think that he liked what he saw.

That thought made Olivia feel a glow of happiness. She always felt fat, but he hadn't seemed to notice. He didn't look at her as if she could stand to lose three stone—or even just one.

"Oh, Olivia!" Georgiana said, pulling back the curtains all the way to the foot of the bed and then sitting with a little bounce at her sister's feet. "Isn't this the most wonderful party?"

"Don't sit on Lucy!" Olivia cried.

Georgiana poked at the little ball she now saw under the covers. "You allow that dog to sleep *in* your bed? I've heard of canines sleeping *on* the bed, and that struck me as quite unhealthy. I'm sure this is even more insalubrious."

Olivia shrugged. "Rupert told me that's where she likes to sleep, and sure enough, she burrowed down there directly last night. She's something of a toe warmer, if I need one."

"Did you even hear what I said? Isn't he wonderful?" Georgiana demanded. She had been sitting in her customary prim fashion, hands clasped in her lap and ankles neatly crossed, but now she pulled up her knees and sat sideways on the bed. Her face broke into a beaming smile. "He's . . . he's everything I dreamed of."

"He is?" Olivia felt as if her mind were wading through treacle.

"Tall, and so handsome," Georgiana said. "And intelligent, Olivia! A proper mathematician—which is not at all the same thing as an accountant." A faint frown creased her brow. "You really must try to be more polite. What if he takes a dislike to you and we're asked to leave? I'll never meet anyone like him again."

"I won't," Olivia said automatically. "I mean, I will. I'll fawn on him as much as he could wish." Of course Georgiana loved Sconce. He was a perfect match for her: he had rank, bearing, *and* intelligence. And Georgiana was so exquisite, far more beautiful than Olivia.

"I just never thought," Georgiana said dreamily. "I never truly believed there was anyone for me. And all the time, here he was. He's so distinguished, and brilliant, and"—she giggled suddenly—"he looked wonderful drenched in rain yesterday."

Olivia nodded. That was true enough.

Georgiana's mouth curled in a naughty smile that Olivia had never, ever, seen on her sister's face. "This is *terrible* of me, Olivia, but did you look closely at him when he came out of the rain?"

"No," Olivia said, mendaciously.

"He—his breeches were wet and—oh Olivia, I think I have an idea why Juliet Fallesbury called her footman *Longfellow*!"

"Who are you, and what have you done with my

sister?" Olivia said, laughing. "Did you hit your head last night, Georgie? Are you feeling yourself?"

"I'm absolutely fine and actually, I feel happier than I have in years. The only thing that's worrying me is you."

"Me?" Olivia frowned at her. "I wasn't so impolite to Sconce. I merely teased him. I honestly don't think he gave it a second thought." Thank goodness her sister had no knowledge of that kiss.

"No, no, you and Rupert! I actually couldn't sleep last night. I kept thinking about how wonderful the duke is, and the way he smiled at me—he didn't look bored once, Olivia, not once—and then I remembered that you had to marry Rupert, and it broke my heart."

"Ah well," Olivia said, summoning up a jaunty tone. "You know I could never rub along with someone like the duke. I would die from pure *ennui* if he launched into a display of mathematical brilliance."

"He's a genius," Georgiana said with conviction. "Anyone could see that. He's a genius, and at the same time, he's not peculiar or crazed in the head."

"Amazing, given that his mother wrote the *Almighty Mirror*."

"You must stop making fun of the dowager's book. What if you accidentally mock the title in her presence?"

"I expect that she would survive the shock."

"Please," Georgiana pleaded, "*please*, Olivia. This is my chance. Mother said that she was quite certain the dowager intends to select her son's bride. She heard it from one of Lady Cecily's bosom friends. You mustn't insult Her Grace in any way, or she might overlook me for that honor."

"She couldn't," Olivia said with conviction.

"I want . . . I truly want to marry Sconce." Georgiana said it on a near whisper. "I know that's a terribly unladylike thing to say, but it's true. When he appeared out of the darkness to rescue us last night, it felt like the moment in a book when the hero appears. And then he spoke. His voice is so deep—steady and true—that I realized that he really was the prince in a fairy tale. Do you know what I mean?"

Yes, Olivia thought. Yes, I know exactly what you mean.

But there was absolutely no point to thinking such a thing, let alone voicing it.

"Princes have never appealed to me," she said instead. "Though I will admit that that type of man does seem oddly given to permitting his mother to choose his wife. If he doesn't select her on the basis of something as idiotic as her footwear. If the duke were really a hero, he would have saddled a white horse rather than running out in the rain looking like a butcher's boy. All those little details are very important when it comes to literature."

Georgiana groaned. "Stop jesting for a moment, Olivia! I always thought there was no prince for me. I just couldn't imagine him."

"What about the white horse?" Olivia inquired.

Her sister swatted her. "Be serious. What I'm saying is that I want to marry the duke. The way I've never wanted anything before."

"Then you shall have him," Olivia said, swinging her legs out of bed. The whole conversation was making her feel rather odd. Of course she had no claim on the duke. That kiss meant nothing. Nothing! He was always meant to be Georgiana's husband.

She walked over to the dressing table and pushed

back her heavy mop of hair. "All that rain last night made my dress turn transparent, and I looked as if I were completely naked. You should have seen the mortified look the butler gave me. When my coat slipped, he got a direct eyeful. I thought he was going to faint."

"Then he was foolish," Georgiana said loyally. "I'm sure you look as lovely naked as you do dressed."

"Better," Olivia said consideringly. "Although I'm hoping that the new gowns will make a difference in that respect. I didn't order a single gown that caught up under my breasts and billowed out at my waist. The style works only for women whose hips don't match their breasts, whereas it makes me resemble a milk cow."

"Gentlemen like a bovine air," Georgiana pointed out.

"You *did* hit your head," Olivia said, laughing. "That was a joke, Georgie! A proper joke."

Her sister rolled her eyes. "Hardly. What will you wear to luncheon? It's so warm that we're eating on the terrace."

"Interesting. I wouldn't have thought that the dowager ever countenanced irregular eating habits. You see, Georgie, I am already learning to appreciate her."

"You must, if she's to be my mother-in-law." Georgiana hopped off the bed. "Do you think it's possible? The maid told me last night that Lady Althea Renwitt is in residence. What if the duke has already fixed his interest? Althea is an aristocrat. I don't suppose you remember her?"

"Not in the slightest. Is she one of the new flock on the market this year?"

"Yes. She's got the most beautiful eyes," Georgiana said, sinking into a chair. "And pretty hair, the color of buttercups. But she's a little . . . well, silly. I'm not sure that I can picture the duke with her."

"Silly, is she? Then she won't care for His Soberness."

"I have no doubt but that Althea would be happy to be a duchess even if Sconce were as crazy as a bedbug—which he's not."

"Room for only one bedbug-brained duke in this kingdom," Olivia said cheerfully, "and I've already got the monopoly on him. How do you suppose Rupert is doing in Portugal, by the way? He must have gone ashore by now."

Georgiana waved her hand dismissively. "I expect he's missing Lucy, but fine otherwise."

"Which reminds me that I'd better ring for Norah. It's surprisingly difficult to take care of a dog. It seems as if she's always having to go out, or eat, or be given her bath."

"Olivia!" Georgiana said impatiently. "This is *not* the moment to talk about you or your dog. Do you think the dowager has already made up her mind to choose Althea? Her name sounds appropriate for a duchess."

"I think it sounds like some odd sort of digestive. *Drink Althea for your bowels!* Lady Cecily would love it. Do you suppose, Georgie, that her ladyship is perfectly unconscious of how odd it is for a woman with the surname *Bumtrinket* to be constantly talking about her digestion?"

"Only you would notice such a thing. It certainly never occurred to me."

"The duke noticed as well. I saw a gleam in his eye that might have been a guffaw in a man who knew how to laugh."

"My point is that the dowager duchess will certainly look for birth along with elegance. I do hope that she hasn't already decided for Althea. Or even worse, perhaps Althea has already caught the duke's fancy," Georgiana fretted. "She's very sweet."

"I don't think so," Olivia said, bundling up her hair and then reaching over to pull the bell.

"You don't think the duchess has chosen a daughter-in-law, or you don't think the duke has settled on Althea?"

"I don't think the duke has any idea whom to marry. He doesn't have the right look about him," Olivia said flatly. And—she added silently—presumably he wouldn't be kissing strange women, no matter how revealing their clothing.

"What kind of look would he have if he had made such a decision?"

"Less dashing. At the moment he has a kind of highwayman appeal that suggests that he wants every woman in his vicinity to lust after him."

Georgiana frowned.

Olivia spoke before her sister could disagree. "His hair, Georgie? Loose around the shoulders? And where was his coat last night? He couldn't be more obvious if he were one of those men who drift around the Pump Room at Bath looking for plump-in-the-pocket widows."

"How can you even say such a thing?" Georgiana cried. "The duke would consider such behavior far below him."

"All right, he's only midway to a highwayman," Olivia allowed. "He has the hair and the glamour, without the steed or the pistol. Although if he shouted *Stand and deliver*, I expect half the debutantes at the Micklethwait ball would have happily tipped up their heels."

"Tipped up what?"

"Fallen on their backs," Olivia elaborated, poking her sister. "I love you, Georgie, but you are a bit of a goose when it comes to jokes."

"I know," Georgiana said, wrinkling her nose. "I never understand them. At least I never understand yours."

"I expect that says more about my poor sense of humor than your comprehension," Olivia allowed. "I think I'll wear the violet gown to luncheon."

"Do you think it's perhaps a bit daring for the time of day? I thought of that gown as more an evening dress."

"Actually, I had all my dresses cut to the same low measure. I decided that since my curves aren't going to disappear due to gorging on lettuce, I might as well flaunt them. If men like the bovine appeal, as you said, they're certainly going to get it from me."

"I have no curves to flaunt," Georgiana said, turning so that she could see herself in the glass. "Do you think that the duke is the sort who likes a more generous figure?"

Olivia was strongly of the opinion that the duke was, indeed, of that sort, given the way his eyes had darkened at the sight of her wet gown. But there was no point in saying so. "I doubt it," she said diplomatically. "He was quite stiff, didn't you think? I expect he would disapprove if you showed the slightest bit of cleavage. Conduct unbecoming to a future duchess."

Georgiana brightened. "I'll wear the pink pleated gown, then. I love the way the sleeves peak into little triangles."

There was a scratch at the door, and Norah entered.

"Good morning," Olivia said, smiling at her maid. "I'm hoping you could hand Lucy to a footman so she can visit a grass patch. But first you must tell us everything you can about Lady Althea Renwitt." She ignored Georgiana's scowl—*The Mirror of Compliments* was very censorious with regard to inappropriate informality with one's staff—and added, "We're all a-flutter to know whether she poses any true competition to Georgie in the ducal sweepstakes."

There was nothing Norah liked better than relating conversations from below-stairs, which, generally speaking, tended to be far more lively than the conversations above-stairs. Her eyes sparkled as she closed the door. "Lady Althea and her mother only arrived yesterday evening, shortly before you, and the duke did not come down to greet them. So the first he'll be meeting her is at luncheon. Miss Georgiana, I have to add that Florence is waiting for you in your chamber. She's *that* anxious to start the dressing because Lady Althea's maid is terribly proud of herself. Her name is Agnès, in the French way, because that's where she's from. She went on and on about *politesse* last night, and no one had the faintest idea what she was talking about. Florence is determined to knock her into the shade with Miss Georgiana's appearance at the luncheon." She stopped to take a breath.

"How nice to be a betrothed woman with no worries about my appearance," Olivia said, standing up and stretching. "I did tell you that a curling iron is never coming near my head again, didn't I, Norah?"

Norah bent over to tie a ribbon to Lucy's collar. "As long as Mrs. Lytton doesn't think that I had anything to do with that decision, miss, I'm just as happy not to be wielding those hot sticks. I've burned myself many a time."

"I suppose I'll be off," Georgiana said. But she paused and shot Olivia a look.

Olivia obediently turned back to her maid. "Before you go, Norah, did you hear any gossip below-stairs about Althea? What's she like?"

"Cleese isn't one to allow prattle, as he calls it. *But* Lady Althea's maid did say a bit about her mistress." Norah paused. "Though of course I shouldn't repeat tittle-tattle, given that Agnès seems a dreadfully critical woman."

"Norah!" Olivia said. "Don't be a noodle!"

Norah relented. "Agnès allowed as how her mistress was more giddy than a hen in the rain."

"How on earth does rain affect chickens?" Georgiana asked, looking perplexed.

"They drown, Miss Georgiana," Norah explained. "They turn their beaks up to see the sky, and then they drink too much water, and then they fall over. A whole flock of them can go that way, just like dominos going down in a row."

"I think you can safely interpret that to mean that Althea *Henwitty* isn't going to beat you in the category of raw intelligence," Olivia said, with some satisfaction.

Norah gave a little snort of appreciation.

"I must not keep Florence waiting," Georgiana said with a stiff little smile. "Thank you, Norah, for . . . for . . ."

"For snitching on the enemy," Olivia put in.

Georgiana whisked out the door before having to agree to something so antithetical to her sense of propriety.

Norah looked after her. "Miss Georgiana is just perfect for the duke; that's what everyone is saying below-stairs. He's as smart as a whip, they say, but terribly lofty. Not as much as his mother, who takes the prize, but a gentleman who never forgets who he is, if you see what I mean."

Sometimes he forgets, Olivia thought to herself. That was no duke who grabbed her in the silver room last night.

"His mother, the dowager, is even worse," Norah continued. "They all warned me that if I see her in the corridor, I should drop a curtsy, then put my back to the wall and look at the floor. If she deigns to speak to me, I should drop another curtsy before I dare to look up."

Olivia snorted, but thought it best not to comment. "Just look how excited Lucy is to see you."

Norah reached down and pulled Lucy's long ears. "She is ugly, but there's something very taking about her all the same."

"Do you think she's trying to tell you something with all that hand licking?" Olivia asked.

"She can smell bacon on my hands. I helped clear the breakfast dishes."

"Still, you'd better take her out before she piddles on the carpet."

"Her Grace doesn't like animals at all," Norah said, moving reluctantly toward the door. "The dowager, I mean. Apparently the shape of paws makes her almost faint. Isn't that odd? If she even sees an animal running along on its paws, she goes all queer-like."

"Very odd," Olivia agreed.

"And did you hear about the duke's first wife?" Norah said, lingering by the door.

"I knew of her existence, of course, but you'll have to tell me any details later. The last thing I want is to have to explain to the housekeeper why my bedchamber has an unfortunate smell."

"She was no better than a trollop," Norah stated.

"No!" It didn't suit Olivia's image of the duke to think of him married to a hussy.

"Terrible! A very glad eye, if you see what I mean, miss. Very glad indeed. Always out with the carriage, hither and yon, and taking no more than a groom with her."

"That's dreadful," Olivia said, thinking of the duke's closed face. No wonder he had such a bleak look about him.

"Dreadful is the word," Norah said with emphasis. "And—"

But at that moment Lucy lost patience and piddled on the floor.

And that was the end of that particular conversation.

Nine

Introducing Lord Justin Fiebvre

*A*s Quin allowed his valet to dress him that morning, he was happily aware that whatever madness had possessed him the previous night had been washed away by a few hours of good sleep.

Actually, more than a few hours of sleep, given that it was very nearly time for luncheon.

He felt like himself again, a man who valued reason and the intellect above all else. Obviously, he'd have to keep his distance from the nubile Miss Lytton. There was something about her that brought out his least reasonable side. He would go so far as to describe himself in the grip of a somewhat compulsive lust.

He'd even dreamed about her during the night, and it was the kind of dream he hadn't had in years. Not since the early days of his marriage.

In his dream, he had entered a room to find Olivia,

her back to him, reading a book. He had walked over to her, his entire body one fiery throb of anticipation, and without saying a word, he had bent over her, running his fingers down the side of her face, her neck . . .

As his caress swept down, he realized that she was wearing nothing more than a light wrapper. And then she turned her face up to him, smiling, and reached her arms up to pull him closer. Her dressing gown fell open and—

It was embarrassing to have dreams of that sort. Yet there was something about Miss Lytton's smile, her hips, even the way she kept insulting him that drove his pulse to a faster rhythm.

But if a man didn't learn from his mistakes, then he was less intelligent than any member of the animal kingdom. Even animals quickly learned to avoid a forest fire.

He turned as his valet twitched the bottom of his coat, then he regarded himself in the glass. His mother firmly believed that a duke should both look and carry himself like a member of the aristocracy at all times; it was very lucky that she had not been there to see it when he'd blundered downstairs without his coat.

His coat had been made by a Parisian tailor who had fled to London. It was dark plum and severely cut, but it had unmistakable Continental flair, with mother-of-pearl buttons and an occasional glimpse of the green silk that lined his collar and cuffs. Quin never spent much time thinking about his appearance, but he was quite certain that he did not look like an accountant.

His man, Waller, handed him a starched linen cravat. Raising his chin, Quin began swiftly folding it into the Mathematical. "Miss Lytton arrived with a small cur at her heels."

"Yes, Your Grace," Waller said, bobbing his head. "The dog remains with her at all times, except when being given a daily bath. It's been quite the subject of conversation below-stairs, as the animal cannot be said to present an aristocratic appearance."

"It looks like a rat," Quin said. "Mind you, a friendly rat."

"Very sweet, by all accounts," Waller agreed.

"Has my mother been informed?" Quin carefully inserted a pearl-and-diamond pin in the folds of his cravat.

"Not to the best of my knowledge," Waller replied, offering Quin a pair of gloves and a pressed handkerchief, and adding, "Mr. Cleese feels that it is not his place."

"Coward," Quin remarked.

He caught Waller's smile as he left the room.

His mother would be extremely displeased. She could not abide animals of any sort. Animals, in her view, were dumb brutes controlled by only the basest of instincts, incapable of the civilized behavior on which her sense of order depended. She never rode, and he had been allowed no pets as a child. In fact, it could transpire that Miss Lytton's visit would be a brief one once the dowager learned of the dog.

After all, Miss Lytton was clearly ineligible, even if the mongrel were not taken into account. She was far too given to pleasure—the kiss briefly slipped through his mind—and she had giggled the night before. What's more, she'd giggled at *him*, at the idea of him wearing a nightcap.

But her sister seemed to be quite different.

Quin thought about Miss Georgiana as he descended the stairs. She had uttered an anguished gasp when her sister compared him to an accountant. She appeared to have a delightful sense of command and self-control, to be the sort of woman you could count on never to embarrass you, in public or private.

One had only to think of Evangeline to recognize how deeply important the trait of being dependably self-restrained was to a successful marriage.

Cleese met him at the bottom of the stairs and directed him through the library; luncheon was to be taken on the terrace overlooking the gardens. Quin walked toward the open doors onto the terrace, irritably aware that his heart had speeded up. Of course he wasn't excited by the idea of seeing the trollopy Miss Lytton.

Rather, he told himself, he merely felt a natural level of anxiety given that he was about to spend time with two young ladies, one of whom would quite likely become his wife. A man with his unhappy marital history had every right to feel unsettled at that prospect.

Of course, the first person he saw was Olivia Lytton. He actually stopped for a moment at the sight, frozen just inside the door leading to the terrace. She wore a very soft, violet-colored gown that seemed to be made of silk and lace. Bands of silk wound around her body, crisscrossing low over her breasts in a way that tempted him to unwrap her like a present. She had the curves of a Rubens painting, one of the lush goddesses of the hunt.

She leaned forward, laughing, and Quin's breath caught in his throat. Her hair was pinned up, but tendrils fell around her face. She was . . .

He glanced down. His severely cut coat was not designed to disguise reactions of this sort. A compulsion, he told himself, walking a bit uncomfortably back into the library. Lust, he told himself. His body agreed with that last word, though lust hardly seemed a strong enough word for the fierce desire coursing through him.

There was a sound at his feet, and he looked down. Miss Lytton's little pup was standing there, its odd face cocked to the side and its skinny tail wagging furiously. Quin knelt and scratched the dog under its floppy ears. "You are a coquette," he stated. "Lucy, isn't it?"

The dog's tail whipped back and forth in evident agreement, and she licked Quin's hand enthusiastically.

He took a deep breath and stood. He had himself in control again. He pulled on his gloves. "Come on, then," he said to Lucy. "Let's join the rest on the terrace."

But when he reached the door, the dog melted off to the side, disappearing behind the curtains. The party was clustered at one end of the terrace, looking quite flowery and picturesque. With a faint pulse of alarm, he realized that he was the only man.

His mother turned to greet him. "There you are, Tarquin," she said. "I wish to introduce you."

Quin walked forward and joined the circle. The dowager began at her left. "Miss Georgiana Lytton, my son, the Duke of Sconce." Miss Georgiana bore only a faint resemblance to the sodden woman he had helped from the toppled carriage. Her hair was warm brown with streaks of bronze, and pinned in loops and curls about her head. Her eyes were lively and intelligent, but above all, she carried herself with a kind of natural grace and dignity that was a pleasure to see.

He bowed. Georgiana dipped her head and dropped a pretty curtsy. His mother watched with noticeable warmth in her eyes.

It's done, Quin thought as he kissed Georgiana's

glove. She was perfect. She even looked like a duchess-to-be. She was wearing something pink with lots of tiny pleats. It wasn't at all like her sister's gown—it didn't make him rage with lust—but one had to assume it was *à la mode*, with short sleeves that belled around her shoulders with a kind of elegance gifted only by a French *modiste*.

She looked as if she were ready to have her portrait painted and stuck up on the wall with all the other duchesses who'd lived in his house.

"Miss Lytton, may I present the duke," his mother said, her voice altering just a shade. "Miss Lytton is Miss Georgiana's twin sister." Olivia was clearly not a favorite in the marital sweepstakes, which didn't surprise him in the least.

Olivia curtsied, rather less deeply than her sister had done, and then Quin swept into a bow. Her hair was far darker than her sister's.

"Miss Lytton," his mother continued, "is betrothed to the Marquess of Montsurrey. While the marquess has not been in company overly much, I'm sure you've met his father, the Duke of Canterwick, in the House of Lords."

Quin froze in mid-bow at the word "betrothed," then his lips touched Olivia's glove. He felt her fingers trembled in his hand; perhaps it was his hand that trembled around her fingers. He straightened.

"Indeed," he said. "Best wishes on your betrothal, Miss Lytton. I'm afraid that I have not had the pleasure of meeting the marquess."

She smiled at him. She had dimples. No, only one dimple, in her right cheek.

"Rupert is heading a company against the French," she said. "He is quite patriotic."

"He must be so," Quin said, pulling himself together and giving a silent nod to the absent marquess. He himself had thought of serving in the war against France but had deemed it impossible. Given that his father was dead and he had no brothers, he was responsible for an enormous estate that stretched across three English counties, not to mention the land in Scotland. He simply could not leave. "I have the greatest respect for those men who are defending our country against the incursions of Napoleon."

"May I present Lady Althea Renwitt and her mother, Lady Sibblethorp," the dowager said, ignoring the question of Napoleon. She didn't approve of the war; the French had been most objectionable when they slew their nobility, but she couldn't see why England should risk English lives on that account. Quin had given up trying to explain it to her. "Lady Althea, Lady Renwitt, my son, the Duke of Sconce."

Lady Althea was quite small, and had two dimples to Olivia's one. She smiled in such a way that both dimples and a great expanse of teeth were in evidence, and said, "It is a pleasure to meet you, Your Grace." Then she giggled.

"My sister, Lady Cecily, will be unable to join us, as she injured her ankle in last night's debacle," his mother said. "I don't doubt but that Cleese will wish to begin luncheon now. We are hopelessly uneven, of course. And there is no sign of Lord Justin." She turned to Lady Sibblethorp. "My brother's son. His mother was French, and I expect he inherited the propensity to be late from that side of the family. Sometimes he does not join us until the second remove."

Quin thought that the more likely explanation was that Justin took longer to dress than a woman. But still, he felt a little better remembering that his cousin would be at luncheon as well. While Justin couldn't precisely be said to have achieved manhood at age sixteen, half a man was better than none.

At that very moment he heard the click of heels. They all turned, to find Lord Justin Fiebvre making his characteristic flamboyant entry. He paused for a moment in the doorway, threw back the lock of hair that constantly—and, one had to believe, deliberately—obscured his eyes, and cried, "Such beauty! I feel as though I am entering the garden of the Hesperides."

Lucy was tucked under his arm, her long snout nuzzling the shot silk of a quite extraordinary pearl-colored silk coat, embroidered with silver arabesques and pale blue beads.

The dowager straightened her shoulders, a sign of irritation. She allowed Justin to vex her, which was foolish, to Quin's mind. Justin was not entirely English nor entirely adult, but under all the frills he was a decent fellow.

"Lord Justin," she stated. "May I inquire as to why you are carrying that—that animal under your arm?"

"I found this little sweetheart in the library," he replied, grinning. "I couldn't leave a lonely girl all on her own."

From the way she was eyeing him, the dowager considered the coat inappropriate for a country luncheon—though it was difficult to distinguish her sartorial disapproval from her patent dislike of dogs.

But Justin had a charming habit of ignoring his aunt's displeasure. He had a sunny disposition and preferred, as he often said, "to see happiness."

"Now who is the mistress of this charmer?" he asked,

looking from person to person as he stroked Lucy's head.

"She is mine," Olivia said, moving forward. "I left her in the library because she seemed to be so afraid to come into the sunlight. I'm afraid that Lucy is not a deeply courageous dog."

"We don't all need to be brave," Justin said. "I, for one, count myself among the cowardly yet respectable majority. Your Lucy is utterly charming."

"*If* you would be so kind as to join us, Lord Justin," the dowager cut in, "I will introduce you to our house-guests."

"A keen pleasure awaits me!" Justin put Lucy down at his feet, and she scurried over to Olivia and hid behind her. The dowager drew aside her skirts with a barely suppressed squeak.

Justin bowed low over each lady's hand, brushing kisses and breathing compliments. He *adored* Miss Lytton's gown (so did Quin), Miss Georgiana's ring, Lady Althea's ribbons . . .

Quin was rather interested to see that while Lady Althea fell into a perfect frenzy of dimpling, Olivia and her sister seemed more amused than admiring.

He took a deep breath and willed himself to calmness.

For a man who prided himself on not experiencing emotion, Quin had reacted to the news of Miss Olivia Lytton's betrothal to the Marquess of Montsurrey with a jolt of something so primitive that he had hardly recognized it.

He had to stop himself from sweeping her off her feet, carrying her to the library, and slamming the door behind them—after which, he would make damn sure that she broke off her betrothal.

But he never slammed doors. That was for . . . that was for other men. The emotional kind.

He wasn't emotional. It was a good thing he reminded himself of that, because he was in some danger of surprising himself.

Could he be experiencing some sort of temporary insanity? Perhaps there was a medical syndrome that encompassed kissing the vicar's wife, and given that no such matron was within ready grasp, kissing a stranger who appears on one's doorstep in the middle of the night in a rainstorm.

Of course, Olivia probably had every lecherous man in London panting after her, given her voluptuous figure. That gown she wore was made up of different panels that somehow swept around and under, and there was just a touch of lace over her breasts . . . perhaps they could call it the Olivia Syndrome.

The question was . . . what was the question? It was unusual for Quin to feel as if he were floundering between incoherent thoughts.

"As we have unequal numbers," his mother stated, "I regret that some ladies must necessarily remain unescorted. Tarquin, you may escort Miss Georgiana and Lady Althea to luncheon. Lord Justin, you may escort Miss Lytton. Lady Sibblethorp, we shall progress together." She paused for a moment.

"Miss Lytton, I would ask you to return that canine to the house before you join us. Animals are not tolerable in the vicinity of the dining table. In fact, I would prefer that the creature remain in the stables at all times."

"I do assure you, Your Grace, that if it were within my capacity to put Lucy in the stables, I would do so. But my fiancé, the Marquess of Montsurrey, begged me to keep her with me at all times before he left for the wars. I could not deny a request from a man engaged in the defense of our country."

"I am certain that he did not mean it literally," the dowager replied acidly.

"I'm afraid Rupert is always literal in his requests."

"Indeed." The dowager narrowed her eyes. "I had heard something of the sort."

Quin tensed at this, but Olivia merely said, "In fact, Lucy seems to have taken quite a liking to you, Your Grace."

As one, the entire company looked down to find that Olivia's dog was now sitting at the edge of the dowager's skirts, one tiny paw resting gently on the tip of her slipper.

She made a strangled sound. "Off!"

Lucy seemed unmoved by this command. She simply raised her long nose and gave a small *woof*, leaving her paw where it was.

"Tarquin!" the dowager said, staring down with the same horror with which one might greet the sudden appearance of a squid in one's bathwater.

Before Quin could come to the rescue, Olivia scooped up her dog. "I am so sorry," she exclaimed. "I had no idea that you were frightened by dogs, Your Grace."

The dowager regained her composure instantly. "Of course I am not frightened by canines. I merely find them to be unnervingly dirty. Given what I have heard of your fiancé, Miss Lytton, I think we can both agree that you may overrule his request. Put the dog in the stables. Begin, in short, as you mean to carry on."

It was Olivia's turn to stiffen. "I am quite sure you did not mean to speak of the Marquess of Montsurrey in such a manner, Your Grace." And then, as the dowager opened her mouth, Olivia added, "I myself would be reluctant to incur the censure of disloyalty, but I consider this of no account, since I am certain that you had no intention of making a suggestion that would be a wound to your credit, and give blemish to your courtesy."

Quin didn't even bother to untangle that; he could see that a gauntlet had just been tossed onto the flagstones at their feet. His mother held herself as rigidly as a soldier on parade, as did Olivia. They were of approximate heights and seemed to be displaying equal strength of will. And even more unnerving, each lady had a slight smile on her face.

"While Lucy will remain in my presence except at meals, as requested by my fiancé," Olivia continued, "I will do my best to keep her from your sight, Your Grace."

There was a terrible moment of silence, and then the dowager said, "That shall have to do."

Olivia sank into a curtsy, still holding Lucy under her arm. "I trust that you are not offended, Your Grace. I am heartened by memory of your own words: '*A true lady prefers gentle reproof to extravagant compliment.*'"

There was a soft gasp from the direction of Lady Sibblethorp, and Quin judged it time to separate the contestants before his mother forgot some of the precepts she held so dear; for her part, Olivia seemed to regard them as little more than weapons.

"Miss Georgiana and Lady Althea," he interjected. "May I have the honor of escorting you both to luncheon?"

"Miss Lytton," Justin chimed in. "May I give Lucy to a footman?"

But the dowager, chin high, ignored both of them. "I

gather that I have underestimated your attachment to the marquess, Miss Lytton."

"My fiancé does not carry his accomplishments on his sleeve, but I assure you that the sweetness of his disposition inspires loyalty."

The dowager nodded. Rather to Quin's surprise, there was a grudging respect in her eyes. "I would desire your forgiveness for the indignity of my suggestion."

Olivia's smile was very charming. "Your Grace," she said, "I heartily repent any untoward words of my own."

"For goodness' sake," Justin moaned, not quite under his breath, "I feel as if I am watching an elocution lesson."

Neither lady paid him the slightest heed.

"The Marquess of Montsurrey is very lucky," the dowager pronounced. "I shall write to his father immediately and inform him that his selection of a wife for his son does the family great credit."

Olivia bowed her head and dropped into yet another deep curtsy.

Quin, who had been momentarily distracted from the matter of Olivia's betrothal, just stopped himself from growling.

Lucky? If he understood correctly, Montsurrey's father had chosen Olivia, much in the same way that he himself was allowing his mother to pick a wife.

He suddenly realized that Georgiana was smiling expectantly at him. He bowed, as stiffly as a marionette. "Miss Georgiana."

She wrapped her hand under his arm. "Your Grace."

It wasn't leftovers.

It wasn't.

Ten

One Should Never Underestimate the Power of a Twist of Silk

*G*eorgiana appeared to be both admiring and rather awed. At the same time, she had composure and clear self-respect. This was how a lady should look at a duke. And she hadn't giggled once.

Lady Althea, on the other hand, giggled the moment he held out his arm.

"I hope that my mother's invitation did not draw either of you from London at an unwelcome time," Quin said, leading Georgiana and Althea across the terrace, one lady on either side. Cleese had set up a table at the far end, under the shade of the blooming clematis.

"Not at all," Georgiana answered. "I must confess that I was finding the season slightly tedious."

"You have been out a number of years, haven't you?" Lady Althea asked. Then she added with a charmingly flustered air, "I do hope that I haven't embarrassed you with that observation, Miss Georgiana. You look so young that one quite forgets how time passes."

Quin glanced down at the pretty bundle of femininity clinging to his left arm. Althea had apparently realized that she was falling behind in the ducal sweeps, and was making a stab at cutting her opposition out of the pack.

"I did indeed make my debut a number of years ago," Georgiana said, smiling at Althea as she sat down. Quin handed Althea into a chair beside her mother. Georgiana didn't seem to have turned a hair over Althea's jab.

"I have never thought that youth was a particularly good indicator of marriageability," Olivia remarked, as Justin ushered her into a seat to Quin's left. "There are so many more important factors."

Having been schooled by his mother in the fine points of etiquette, Quin noted that Miss Lytton should not have intervened in a conversation to which she was not a part. But obviously the rule was malleable: the dowager was likewise unable to resist.

"A lady's virtues," she pronounced, "are her dearest possession." She then added, "I consider age to be a negligible consideration."

"I quite agree," Olivia agreed, "though I would add that it depends on the virtues in question. All too often young ladies have all the virtues I most dislike, and none of the vices I rather admire."

"No one could dislike virtue!" Althea exclaimed.

"But I gather that you believe inexperience is a virtue, at least on the marriage market?"

"I suppose," Althea said, rather uncertainly. She had lost control of the exchange, and she knew it.

"And yet it can be so crushingly boring." With a brilliant smile, Olivia turned to Justin and asked him what the grouse season was like around Littlebourne Manor.

Althea opened her mouth and shut it again.

"Lady Althea," Georgiana said, "I remember hearing that you are a great lover of languages. I'm sure we would all like to know about your prowess in that area. I think that such skill is quite important if one is to entertain beyond one's local village, as I am sure you will."

It took a moment or two, but she soon had Althea babbling—in English—of her skills in Italian, German, and French.

Quin watched silently, thinking about Georgiana. Apparently she had not "taken," whatever that meant. Evangeline *had* taken, of course. He had had to fight off any number of suitors, although in reality the moment Evangeline's father got wind of a duke, the other suitors hadn't a prayer.

He'd always thought that her success on the market could be put down to the fact that Evangeline glowed when she was happy.

What a suitor could not know was that Evangeline did not glow when unhappy, which was a good deal of the time, as he remembered it.

Miss Georgiana was not the type to glow. She had very fair skin, almost as clear and pale as her sister's. Her nose was quite lovely too, though again, he would probably give the advantage to Olivia, by just a shade.

The only possibly unattractive note about her was that she was rather thin, more resembling a lean boy than a grown woman. Her gown had a décolleté neckline, but it could only do so much to accentuate the diminutive features that lay beneath.

Not that it mattered, he told himself quickly. A duchess is far more than her bosom. He was not a shallow man to be brought to his knees by a twist of violet silk and a pair of luscious breasts.

"I find it very interesting that you occupy yourself with the study of mathematics," Georgiana said, turning to him as the conversation about languages wound down. She was to his right, and Olivia on his left, since Althea had been placed beside her mother. Quin was trying not to look too often in Olivia's direction.

A gentleman does not ogle the fiancée of a man serving his country. Especially if that man is a nobleman, who could have taken the easy route, as Quin had done.

Not for the first time he felt a pang of acute guilt. It wasn't easy to stay a *moth of peace*, as Shakespeare had it. When he was a boy, he had dreamed of wearing scarlet and heading up a battalion.

"The study of mathematics," he said at length. "Yes, I am very interested in the mathematical arts."

"I have read about Leonhard Euler's work on mathematical functions," Miss Georgiana said, rather shyly. "I think it fascinating."

"You—*you* read about Euler?"

A slight frown creased her brow. "As far as I know, Your Grace, there is no law that says women may not read the *London Gazette*. Euler's work was rather extensively surveyed there a few months ago."

"Of course," Quin said hastily. "I apologize for sounding so skeptical."

Miss Georgiana had beautiful manners. She gave him a clear-eyed glance and a sweet smile. "Do you work on mathematical functions as well?"

"Yes, I do," he said, hesitating. But she smiled again, so he launched into a description of the Babylonian method of calculating square roots.

He emerged from his discourse some ten minutes later to discover that the table had gone absolutely silent, and they were all staring at him.

He looked to Georgiana to see whether she displayed the same thinly held level of disbelief. She did not: her eyes were alert and interested. "If I understand you correctly," she said, "you are trying to emphasize that this process will not work using a negative number."

"That is my understanding as well," his mother said.

Even a dimwit could have interpreted his mother's voice. Miss Georgiana had just passed the first test. Without being a bluestocking, she was clearly intelligent and interested in matters outside the household.

Olivia, on the other hand, was looking at him with distinct amusement rather than admiration, let alone awe. She was not enthralled by his mathematical lecture.

"Tedious, I know," he said, a bit sheepishly.

"Not at *all*!" Georgiana breathed.

"Yes, it certainly was," Olivia said at precisely the same moment. "Perhaps next time you could sell tickets beforehand."

"*Tickets*, Miss Lytton?" the dowager asked.

"Exactly," Olivia replied, giving her a serene smile. "I know it's a great fault, but I find I'm so much happier if I have paid for a lecture, even if I fall asleep during it. Education should be expensive, don't you think?"

"That is absurd," the dowager pronounced.

"As you yourself have written, Your Grace, '*A lady should always be aware of the weaknesses in her character.*'" Then she added, "It hardly needs saying that my mother is a great admirer of *The Mirror of Compliments*."

"I am aware of that," the dowager said, thawing a

trifle. "I have met your mother on several occasions, and she always struck me as remarkably sagacious for one of her rank."

Anger flashed through Olivia's eyes, and then her smile deepened. No dimple appeared. Quin mentally took a step back. Anyone who thought that smile indicated appreciation was completely deluded.

"You bring to mind another aphorism that might apply," she said sweetly. "'*Even the ghosts of one's dead ancestors would rather sleep than listen to someone twitter like a jug-bitten parrot.*'" She paused. "Although now I think on it, perhaps that cannot be attributed to *The Mirror of Compliments*."

"You have a lively sense of humor, Miss Lytton," the dowager remarked. It was not a compliment.

"I'm curious about the ghosts of my *living* ancestors, not the dead ones," Justin said, his eyes full of mischief. "What do they do when Quin launches into mathematical conniptions?"

Quin intervened. "Miss Lytton."

"Your Grace?"

"I promise not to inform you about square roots again without issuing tickets first."

"I, for one, would enjoy receiving one of those tickets," Georgiana said, giving him a warm smile. "And I apologize for my sister's irreverence. I'm afraid that we are used to funning between ourselves."

She was perfect for him in every way.

"I no longer have the moral fortitude to endure lectures in mathematics," Justin put in. "So, if you'll forgive me, Coz, I won't be buying a ticket to lectures on the complexities of square roots."

"Miss Georgiana," his mother said, "I should like to ask your opinion of stone window casements in the Gothic style."

"Your comment implies you once *had* the moral fortitude to endure mathematical lectures," Olivia said to Justin. Her eyes had a way of smiling when she was speaking—as if she were thinking naughty thoughts—that Quin found he quite appreciated.

"No, no, I've never had it," Justin replied, leaning slightly forward. "At least, not when it comes to mathematics. Now if you were talking about something truly interesting . . ."

"Fashion?" she guessed.

"I adore it!" Justin exclaimed, adding, "Life is nothing without the embellishment offered by the proper attire. But my true passion is writing poetry and ballads."

"Justin has written one hundred and thirty-eight sonnets, all for the same woman," Quin said, inserting himself into the conversation, though by all rights he should talk with Georgiana. Still, he had nothing to say about casements, a fact his mother had to appreciate.

"Really!" Olivia said, sounding quite impressed.

"It's called a sonnet cycle," Justin informed her.

"That is a great many sonnets, and even more rhymes. When you're writing such a cycle, are you allowed to repeat a few rhymes along the way? Say *love* and *dove*?"

"Not doves," Justin said with a wave of his hand. "Doves are for chimneys and the elderly. And *love* is harder to rhyme than you might think. How often can one write about *gloves*, for instance? After you've longed to be the glove on your lady's hand, what else is there to say?"

"Why would anyone want to be a glove on a lady's hand?" Quin inquired.

Justin rolled his eyes, something he was prone to do whenever Quin participated in a conversation. "Because that glove touches her cheek, of *course*."

"Other places, too," Olivia said thoughtfully.

Quin surprised himself by almost laughing.

"Such as her nose," she added.

"That is not very romantic," Justin said, shaking his head at her.

"I'm afraid that I don't have a romantic soul," Olivia said apologetically.

"I should hope not," the dowager said, intervening. "You are to be a duchess, Miss Lytton, and I assure you that a romantic soul is a marked detriment in a woman of our rank." She gave Quin a significant glance. "I'm sure we would all prefer to speak of something more elevating than Lord Justin's paltry attempts at verse. Lady Sibblethorp, how are your charitable endeavors with wayward youth progressing?"

As it happened, Lady Sibblethorp was more than happy to detail the blue shirts and sturdy shoes that her organization was handing out to blighted lads. Or youths from blighted backgrounds: the two categories seemed to overlap.

"How interesting," Georgiana said, managing to sound genuinely interested. "How did you decide on shirts and shoes, Lady Sibblethorp?" It seemed that she was both intelligent and charitable. Wonderful.

The lady in question swelled with pride and settled into a thrilling discussion of neckcloths, stockings, shirts, and coats.

Quin listened for just as long as he felt it absolutely necessary, and then turned back to Justin and Olivia. They had blithely ignored the dowager's instructions: Justin was reciting bits of his poetry and Olivia was making fun of them. They were obviously enjoying each other enormously.

"*I was born under a star,*" Justin was reciting, "*so the moon is within my grasp.*"

"What on earth do you mean by saying that you were born under a star? I was born at night, so surely I qualify. Does that mean the moon might drop into my hand?"

"It's a tribute," Justin explained. "I often compare my beloved to the Moon Goddess, Cynthia. She falls within my grasp because I am star-born." He paused. "Star-born. I like that. I have to remember to tell my tutor; he'll applaud, I'm sure."

"I thought Mr. Usher was supposed to be preparing you for the upcoming term at Oxford, rather than feeding your passion for poetry," Quin remarked.

"He has taught me no end of important things about mathematics," Justin said with a patent lack of veracity.

Quin frowned. "Just who is your beloved? You've read me a number of poems, but I believe I never asked for that salient bit of information. Perhaps a young lady you met while at Oxford?"

"Oh, I don't have one," Justin admitted cheerfully.

"One hundred and thirty-eight sonnets for a nonexistent lady," Olivia said, sounding quite impressed. "Do you ever describe her—this moon person, I mean?"

"Moon Goddess," Justin corrected. "Of course I do. She has silver hair."

"That's a surprise," Olivia said. Her voice was so droll that Quin found another laugh rising up his chest. "Let me guess. Sparkling eyes?"

"Generally speaking, they glow. They do sparkle in two poems, a sonnet and a ballad."

"She sounds a bit witchy. Aren't you worried she'll take on a jack-o'-lantern touch?"

"Absolutely not," Justin said with dignity. "My lady has no resemblance whatsoever to a carved turnip. She usurps the sun *and* stars with her beauty."

"What do you do about her clothing? Does she favor short-waisted gowns, or is she more old-fashioned, being a goddess and presumably long-lived?"

"I've heard enough of the poems to know that you should imagine Lady Godiva rather than a jack-o'-lantern," Quin put in.

"Your Grace," Olivia said, dimpling. "You surprise me!"

In fact, he surprised himself.

Justin rolled his eyes. "My poems are for *all time*. I'd merely date them if I described a gown. What if I described my moon goddess in a turban headdress? By next year she'd have turned to a frump, and I'd have wasted all that time on the poem."

"One certainly wouldn't want to write a poem that couldn't be reused," Olivia agreed. "I see that naked is best. Your Moon Goddess is making a brave strike against the tiresome rules of conduct against which I'm sure we all chafe."

"Do we?" Quin asked, leaning toward her. "Are you revealing a touch of the Lady Godiva in yourself, Miss Lytton?" He caught her gaze again, just until he saw a faint wash of pink in her cheeks.

He leaned back, vaguely aware that his heart was thumping in his chest in a thoroughly inelegant fashion. The mere mention of Lady Godiva caused him to picture Olivia, naked and lush, breasts playing peekaboo with a sweep of dark hair, that wicked mouth of hers laughing at him.

"My Moon Goddess is not naked!" Justin rolled his eyes yet again. "I simply don't mention her clothing. Besides, I'd rather write about how it feels to be in love. Here's one of my favorite couplets: *For you, I'd climb the highest tower; I'd dash across the sea.*"

"I hate to be pedantic, but those two lines are not in

iambic pentameter, nor do they rhyme," Olivia pointed out. "I'm certain that a couplet should rhyme."

"It seems more troublesome to me that the two activities are quite dissimilar," Quin put in. "Quite likely you could climb a bell tower if you had to, Justin, but you could not run, let alone walk, on water."

"Unless he's concealing signs of divinity," Olivia said, that dimple playing beside her mouth again. "He is star-born, after all."

They both glanced at young Justin, and then Quin's eyes met Olivia's again with a deeply pleasurable shock. "No visible signs," he commented. "No hovering halo."

Justin was a remarkably good-natured soul. "Philistines," he said, but without force. "Poetry need not rhyme. Only sticklers bother with that sort of thing."

"Couplets must rhyme," Quin said firmly. "But you're right about description. Why tie yourself down? I understand metaphors are *de rigueur* when it comes to verse."

"I suspect they are very hard to write," Olivia said. "The only poems I've managed to commit to memory use a great deal of metaphors, but I could never write one myself."

"For example?" Quin asked.

Her eyes laughed at him. "*There once was a maiden from Peedle, who was extremely good with her needle . . .*' I'll stop there, if you don't mind. But I assure you that when it comes to metaphors, there's nothing like a limerick."

"I've heard that one," Justin interrupted, looking at their guest with renewed respect. "I didn't think ladies enjoyed limericks."

"Generally speaking, they don't," Olivia told him.

"I'm an aberration. Most ladies would swoon to receive a pretty love poem from you. Just ask His Grace. Perhaps he wrote such verses in his youth."

Justin snorted. "Quin couldn't write a poem if Shakespeare himself prompted him."

"I could!" Quin protested. He was feeling rather reckless, drunk on the sparkle in Olivia's eyes. "My lady is a pink flower, and I'm . . . I'm a high tower. At least mine rhymes."

Olivia's little chuckle sent a rush of heat straight to Quin's groin. "You surprise me, Your Grace. I hadn't expected you to exhibit such metaphorical skill. Flowers and towers are surprisingly . . . evocative."

If he'd understood her correctly, she had just flipped his pitiful metaphor into something quite erotic. And, apparently, over his young relative's head.

"I could possibly work with *wild*flower, but not with *pink* flower," Justin said, frowning. "Too banal."

"You're right," Olivia agreed. "I think you should stay with the architectural metaphor, Your Grace. Perhaps you could do something with *castle*?"

Her smile dared him.

"*Castle* would be difficult," Justin said, with authority. "It doesn't rhyme with much of anything."

"The castle of your body is mine by right of conquest," Quin stated, picking up his wineglass. He took a sip and then looked at Olivia, knowing that his eyes were heavy with desire.

There was such a flare of heat between them that Quin was momentarily surprised that the tablecloth didn't spontaneously ignite.

"And the moat?" she asked, that wicked little smile playing around her lips again. "Surely . . . someone is going to—ahem—dive into the moat?"

Justin finally caught on and burst out laughing as well. "Ramparts," he said, almost choking. "You can't forget them, Quin!"

At this revelry, the dowager broke in. "I must ask if you have a humorous subject to share with the table."

Justin gave her a sweet smile. "We're discussing the architecture of medieval castles, Aunt. The subject naturally leads to merriment."

"Battlements," Olivia confirmed, nodding. "In the context of literature."

The dowager narrowed her eyes. Then she pointedly asked Georgiana and Althea about the use of figured velvet in bed-curtains. One had to assume that the question was relevant to matrimony. Quin promptly turned back to Justin and Olivia.

"I prefer dramatic ideas," Justin was saying. "For example, sixty-seven of my poems promise to do the impossible for love."

"I suppose that's where walking on water comes in," Olivia said. "What other kinds of things do you promise to do?"

"Walk through fire," Justin said. "Hold the world in my hand."

"Those two suffer from the same incompatibility," Quin said. "While I suppose you might walk through fire—though I think leap would be a more accurate description—you clearly have delusions of grandeur."

"Lord Justin, if you have a divine side, this would be a good moment to reveal it." Olivia looked hopeful.

"I think we can all agree that the two of you have sadly prosaic souls," Justin said. "Poetry is my *destiny*. Mockery won't stop me. Someday I'll meet a lady as beautiful as the moon, and I'll already have the poetry written."

"I have yet to meet such a lady," Olivia said. "Your Grace, have you been moonstruck at some point in your life?"

Quin looked at her and rejected the whole notion of the moon. "Too cool, pale, and insipid," he said. "I'd prefer a goddess who produces her own light rather than merely reflecting that of another."

"I can't imagine you in love, but one should *never* say never," Justin put in.

"Poetry might be His Grace's destiny as well," Olivia said, her eyes dancing. "Just look at his creative twist on a castle . . . and he didn't even get to the ramparts. Many people don't think of the design of fortifications in such suggestive terms."

"In what terms?" the dowager suddenly said, turning her head.

"As buildings," Olivia said innocently. "His Grace has an architectural turn of phrase."

Had Quin's mother possessed Justin's flair for the dramatic, she would have rolled her eyes. "We shall be hosting a small ball in a few days," she announced. "A quite small engagement, naturally. But I would be unsurprised if we commanded a hundred heads at the least."

She must be moving on to the next phase in the testing process, Quin realized. The thought sent an icy chill down his spine.

Yes, Olivia was charming. She was certainly amusing and undeniably sensual in her appeal. It didn't matter that she was betrothed to someone else. She was all wrong for him.

All wrong.

Quin snapped his head away and turned to Georgiana. Her eyes were clear, sweet, and a bit anxious. It couldn't be easy, being Olivia's twin.

Georgiana was an elegant piece of fine china, but in comparison Olivia beckoned like the promised land.

He wanted—no, he had to remember that he couldn't trust what he *wanted*. What he wanted was all wrong. He had to remember the wrenching awfulness of nights when Evangeline didn't come home, or the weary bitterness of listening to her scream at him, telling him of his manifest failures, his inability to satisfy her, to make her happy. . . .

He smiled down at Georgiana. "Now that I've bored all and sundry with my mathematical monologue, do tell me what pastimes you enjoy. That is," he added, "if you have free time. I know how busy young ladies can be."

She gave an odd little hiccup of laughter. "Tatting and sewing and the like."

"I suppose." Just beyond his left shoulder, her sister was laughing, and laughing made Olivia's breasts—

He pulled his attention back in line. "Which do you enjoy most? Tatting?"

"Do you have any idea what *tatting* even is?"

"Of course," Quin said, before he thought. "It's . . . something." He met her eyes, which were full of quiet amusement that brought a smile to his lips as well. "Sewing?" he offered.

"Tatting is a method of constructing a very sturdy kind of lace."

"Sturdy lace," Quin echoed. "That doesn't sound right."

"An oxymoron," she agreed.

"I gather you don't care for tatting." She smiled again, a kind of fleeting sweetness that was night and day to her sister's mischievous grin.

"Not as much as other things."

"What do you like, then?" Quin asked, truly curious for the first time.

She hesitated, and then: "I like to read."

"You're a bluestocking?"

"I don't think I deserve that label. I think of bluestockings as fiercely educated and extremely intelligent."

"I would have no trouble believing that you are quite intelligent, though I cannot speak to your education."

"I know your mother's book by heart," she offered.

He took her small, rather crooked smile and played it back to her. "*The Mirror of Compliments* is no substitute for Oxford University."

"Which does not allow women inside its august doors."

"That is true. So let me guess." He looked her over. She was a perfect bundle of English femininity: demure, yet with an undeniable backbone. Her options were limited, as she did not look particularly rebellious. "You play the harp. When you are not reading books about travels along the Nile."

Georgiana had a lovely calmness about her. He knew instinctively that she would never throw a scene, let alone china, even when she was irritated with him—as she was now. "I cannot play the harp. While I would quite enjoy reading about the Nile, I am happiest dabbling with what I believe you gentlemen call chemistry."

"Chemistry?" He never would have thought of it.

"That is perhaps too formal a word for what I do," she said, cocking her head to one side like a curious bird. "I like to mix potions. Olivia says that I am an apprentice witch."

"What sort of things do you make?"

"I try to improve products that already exist," she said. "Domestic products, for the most part. Duchesses have always—" She stopped, a lovely flush of rose sweeping up her cheeks.

"Duchesses?" he prompted.

She took a deep breath. "The ladies of great houses have always, of course, had more time and leisure than other women. So, many of them have given time to chemistry, for lack of a better word. Margaret Cavendish, Duchess of Newcastle, is now considered the first female scientist. Actually, she's the only woman scientist I know of, though she lived back in the seventeenth century."

"Except for yourself," Quin said.

"I'm nothing of the sort," Georgiana said, looking faintly horrified. "I merely dabble."

"Is your sister, Miss Lytton, also interested in science?" Quin inquired. "Is she also an apprentice witch?"

"Not at all," Georgiana said. "Olivia has quite different skills than mine."

"I suspect twins often define themselves in opposition to each other. Our local justice of the peace has two boys who are as dissimilar as they could possibly be."

"Olivia and I would confirm your hypothesis. In fact, I am fascinated by concrete objects, whereas Olivia is much more interested by language."

"*Language*? Do you mean the study of different languages?"

"We've studied several languages. But what Olivia truly enjoys is puns." She looked at Quin with a rather aggressive light in her eyes. "These days, we think of language play as mere twaddle, but I am of the belief that it will be a serious subject of study in the future."

"Puns," Quin repeated. "Words that mean more than one thing?"

"Exactly."

"Now that you say so, I noticed a distinct proclivity for puns during Miss Lytton's conversation with Lord Justin."

Georgiana colored again, to Quin's interest. Perhaps she guessed the sort of limerick that Olivia had aired—to wit, the lady from Peedle and her needle.

But at that moment Quin's mother cleared her throat. "I shall make final arrangements for the ball this afternoon, and I should be grateful if Miss Georgiana and Lady Althea would assist me in this matter." She gave both girls a smile. "I am most desirous to hear your ideas for the entertainment."

Test Number Two, Quin thought to himself.

While Lady Althea scrambled to assure the dowager that she was ready to help her in any way, Georgiana accepted in a far more dignified manner. In fact, Quin liked her.

Olivia, for her part, did not offer to help—not that her assistance had been requested nor, indeed, would be welcomed. She and Justin seemed to be making plans for some sort of excursion on horseback.

Notwithstanding the events of the night before, he had known Olivia Lytton for half an hour at the most, so it was obvious that he could not care for her. Not the way he had cared for Evangeline.

But Quin had never been any good at lying to himself. He did care.

For some inscrutable reason, he had taken one good look at Miss Lytton's pale green eyes and her luscious body and the way she held her shoulders upright, even when she was soaking wet, and he wanted her.

She was witty, lovesome, beautiful . . . wild.

Utterly wrong for a duchess.

He leaned forward. "I have a mare in my stables that will be perfect for you," he told her.

"Lord Justin has promised to teach me to fly a kite," she exclaimed. "I've always wanted to fly one, ever since

I saw them in Hyde Park the first time. Lady Althea, Georgiana, would you like to join us on a kite-flying expedition?"

"They would not," the dowager stated. "There can be no kite-flying today. After luncheon, we shall all walk to the village and deliver baskets to the poor. After that, the ladies will spend several hours planning the upcoming festivities."

"I would help you, but I know that you would be unhappy to share the morning room with little Lucy, given her marked preference for you," Olivia said, giving the dowager a beaming smile. "Perhaps familiarity will breed something warmer than contempt? No?"

"You may dabble with your kite-flying expedition tomorrow," the dowager continued, with crushing indifference, as if she were dictating the nursery schedule. "I cannot spare Lady Sibblethorp to act as a chaperone for the excursion, as we shall still be hard at work." She managed to make it sound as if the ladies planned to spend the afternoon digging in the mines. "It is possible that Lady Cecily will be kind enough to accompany you, Miss Lytton, if her ankle has mended appreciably. If not, I would feel comfortable were my son to accompany you on this excursion. I think we may eschew a chaperone on our own grounds."

Quin nodded.

His mother raised her finger as they rose from the table. "One's digestion is always the better for a brief stroll. Ladies, I would request that you join me in the Chinese drawing room as soon as you are dressed for walking, and we shall proceed to the village."

"I'm afraid that I have other plans," Justin said cheerfully. "Mr. Usher and I are going to be poring over

some very important lessons. Latin . . . mathematics
. . . it never ends."

Quin opened his mouth to offer a similar excuse
when he realized that Olivia was bending over the stone
balustrade, trying to pluck a spray of clematis that was
just out of her reach.

His entire body stiffened with a flare of lust so keen
that he drew in his breath. Those sweet and generous
curves were pure temptation. Without conscious voli-
tion, he found himself standing beside her, their bodies
touching as he reached for the flower she was straining
to reach.

The spray of blossoms snapped and he turned. For
once, Olivia was not laughing. She met his eyes for a
moment, then long eyelashes fluttered down and she
broke his gaze.

Who would have thought that pale green eyes could
look so smoky? He dropped back a step, swept into an
elaborate bow, the bow of a duke. As he straightened:
"Miss Lytton, may I offer you this flower?"

She curtsied. Quin cursed himself silently for noticing
that the movement gave him an even better glimpse of
creamy breasts. What in the bloody hell was happening
to him?

Then she straightened, and the look in her eyes made
the blood beat like thunder in his ears. Her gaze was
frank. *Carnal*. He wasn't alone.

But in a second, it all changed. "Darling!" Olivia
cried, turning slightly to the right and looking past his
shoulder. "Look what the duke was kind enough to
pluck from that vine. You must take it. You like flowers
so much more than I do."

Quin smiled politely as Georgiana took the spray of
blossoms.

And Georgiana smiled back: charming, pretty . . . a perfect lady. "How kind of you, Your Grace. The clematis smells so beautiful; we were remarking on it throughout the meal."

He hadn't even noticed its perfume. Sitting beside Olivia, he had caught a whiff of something different . . . better.

Lemon soap. Clean woman.

In comparison, clematis was overly sweet.

Eleven

The Art of the Insult

It was excellent that her sister had found the perfect husband. Of course it was. Not that repeating it over and over would make her feel any better. Envy was a rotten emotion, especially between sisters—and yet she was envious.

"It's beneath you," Olivia told her reflection in the glass.

"Did you say something, miss?" her maid asked from the other side of the room.

"I'm very happy with this walking costume," Olivia responded quickly.

Norah trotted over and twitched the hem of Olivia's gown straight. "That butter yellow suits you no end. And the spencer jacket is darling." She hesitated. "Is Her Grace accompanying you to the village?"

"Of course. She'll be watching poor Georgie to make sure that she doesn't put a step wrong."

"They all say downstairs that she's terribly strict," Norah confirmed. "I wouldn't want to be her daughter-in-law, myself."

"A terrible fate, no doubt, but I'm sure that Georgie can tame her."

Norah nodded, but managed to convey utter disbelief.

"Over time," Olivia clarified. "Do you think that perhaps you should weave a ribbon into my hair? Perhaps dull gold, to pick up the yellow?"

They both looked into the glass. Olivia's walking dress came with a pretty little jacket made of bombazine. It was short, stopping just below the bodice, and trimmed with a frill. Olivia fancied that it did an excellent job of emphasizing her curves.

"No," the maid said decisively. "I suggest a little hat, the one with the feather going sideways."

"Of course!"

"Her Grace is not going to appreciate your gown," Norah said, sorting through Olivia's hats and bonnets. "Not a bit."

Olivia groaned.

"The hem is too high, and she's likely to faint at the sight of your ankles. She has the butler measure all the maids' costumes weekly, to make sure they are precisely the right length from the floor. They aren't allowed to show even a twitch of ankle."

"My ankles are my favorite feature," Olivia said, looking at the mirror once again. Sure enough, they were on full display, accentuated by her utterly delicious new slippers. They looked positively bony. Truly: her best feature.

"They're going to be the gentlemen's favorite, too," Norah said with a giggle, "with those ribbons crossing up your legs. It's a good thing your mother isn't here to see."

"Oh, pooh," Olivia said lightly. "If a future duchess can't wear the newest design in kid slippers, who can? I'm sure the dowager would agree."

Or . . . she wouldn't.

By the time the party had assembled before the house and begun traipsing along the path to the village, Olivia had decided that the dowager's silent—yet ferocious—glances indicated that she was not in favor of the new short skirts, nor Olivia's delightful new slippers.

In fact, Olivia found it more peaceful to walk slightly behind the group on the way to the village. It was a charitable impulse, since the very sight of her ankles—and of Lucy obediently trotting beside those ankles—seemed to be driving the dowager toward apoplexy.

Yet as far as Olivia could tell, men were much more interested in bosoms and thighs than ankles. It was only women like herself, longing for bony body parts, who cared a twig about ankles.

It would be extraordinarily foolish to voice that idea to the dowager. One did not deliberately bait a lioness.

"Olivia!" Georgiana called, dropping back from the larger group.

Olivia twirled her parasol. It was a frivolous bit of lace and ruffle that looked like a giant buttercup. She loved it. "Yes?" she asked, knowing exactly what was coming.

But Georgie surprised her. "I didn't get a chance to tell you before we left the house. Those slippers are extremely fetching."

"I am showing off my best feature. And oddly enough, all the barely suppressed anger from the dowager is making me feel alarmingly at home. Perhaps I'll break out a limerick at the table tonight."

Georgiana carefully adjusted her parasol so that not

a touch of daylight reached her face. Needless to say, Georgie's parasol was altogether more substantial than Olivia's, with a high peaked top that shaded every inch of her from hair to toes. "Mother did not accompany us to this house party."

"In fact, no one has quoted *The Maggoty Mirror* in the last hour, and if I, for one, don't hear a few choice phrases from it soon, I might begin to forget its precepts. Although the living version does stalk before us."

"Mother is not here," her sister repeated, "and therefore you needn't behave as if she was on hand, trying to force you to do something you abhor—such as marry Rupert." She waved her gloved hand. "Look around you, Olivia. There's no one here but the two of us."

"If you manage to overlook the dowager, the duke, Lady Sibblethorp, and young Henwitty. Not to mention those poor footmen carrying the baskets and sweltering in their livery. I do wish Lord Justin had elected to join us on this excursion. I find walking unutterably boring, and at least Justin makes me laugh."

"What were you talking about in the drawing room before we left?" Georgiana asked. "You seemed to be having a wonderful time."

"Being shallow by nature, Justin and I have started a game to see which of us can come up with the worst insult."

"Why on earth would you try to make up insults?" Georgiana looked genuinely pained, likely thinking that Olivia was going to let fly at their hostess. "When can you possibly use them?"

"It's merely a game with no practical usage," Olivia explained. "Justin came up with this for a man: *You dog's-head, you rotten, roguey trendle-tail!*"

Georgiana glanced at the dowager's back. "For goodness' sake, Olivia, keep your voice down. I'm sure you're well aware that the two of you are engaged in an extraordinarily tasteless activity. What on earth is a trendle-tail?"

"I'm not sure," Olivia said now, wishing that she had never repeated it to Georgie. Of course her sister wouldn't approve of such a foolish way to spend one's time. "We both loved the way it sounded," she added in a weak defense.

"Trendle-tail," Georgiana repeated. "The word sounds vulgar. I'm sure it means something that you ought not be thinking about, let alone speaking aloud."

The duke dropped back and turned around. "A trendle-tail is a dog with a curled tail: in short, not purebred." He made no apology for eavesdropping.

Olivia's pulse instantly started tapping along at a faster rhythm. His Grace had the largest shoulders she'd ever seen on a peer. They were wasted on someone who apparently spent his time playing with scraps of paper covered with numbers.

"And what is *your* current entry in the game you are playing with my cousin, Miss Lytton?" he asked, looking at her with those intently dark eyes of his.

If she'd had her choice, she'd rather not have shared her contribution, but they were both waiting expectantly. "Mine is an insult for a woman. *You thin lean polecat, you of the grasshopper thighs and bony rump!*"

At that, the duke actually broke into a crack of laughter. It sounded a bit rusty, but it was laughter.

Georgiana, naturally, did not laugh. "I trust you weren't thinking of me," she hissed, under cover of the duke's laughter.

"Actually, no," Olivia said, nodding toward the lean, if lovely, Lady Althea.

"Your insult says more about you than her," Georgiana said, giving her a meaningful glance. Then she readjusted her parasol once again and slipped her hand under the duke's arm. "Do tell me more about infinitesimal calculus, Your Grace?"

Olivia had actually never heard Georgiana *coo* before. She bent over, pretending that one of her ankle ribbons had come loose, hoping the two of them would take the opportunity to walk ahead.

She could easily imagine them married. Lord and Lady Prim, the Duke and Duchess of Dandification, the—

The duke turned around. "Miss Lytton, we are loathe to leave you behind." He looked at her, unsmiling, and her unruly heart thumped again.

The group was clustered before a white gate in a fence that surrounded a small and rather dilapidated house. The dowager handed her cane to one of the footmen. "Give that gate a good beating, if you would," she commanded. "It will rouse the inhabitants."

"Excuse me," the duke said. He slipped his arm from Georgiana's. "Allow me." He unhooked the latch.

"You needn't, Tarquin," the dowager said. "I always signal my arrival thus. One wouldn't want the poor souls to run out half-clothed or some such. We would all be mortified."

Without a reply, the duke opened the gate and held it open for all of them to pass. Their bright bonnets and parasols seemed doubly so in contrast to the battered house and its neglected garden.

Then the front door popped open and children began to spill out, all bobbing up and down in a frenzy of curtsying.

"A very good afternoon to you, Mrs. Knockem," the

dowager said, nodding at a plain, tired-looking woman with red, knobby hands. All the children were lined up by now. "Avery, Andrew, Archer," the dowager said, nodding to each child. "I'm Alfred," the littlest boy said. "Archer is in the pub."

The dowager frowned. "In the pub, Mrs. Knockem? Surely Archer is extraordinarily young to be imbibing spirits."

"Our Archer is bringing home a penny a week washing mugs, Yer Grace. We're right proud of him."

"A penny is certainly not to be overlooked." The dowager looked at the line again. "Good afternoon, Audrey and Amy. Where is Anne?"

"She's inside, feeling a bit poorly," their mother replied, her hands twisting in her apron.

"Not in the family way, Mrs. Knockem?" the dowager inquired. "I understand she is walking out with the butcher's youngest."

"Oh no," Mrs. Knockem said, blinking madly. "Our Anne is a good girl. She's sat in a patch of something, and she's all covered with little bumps. We do call it the purple itch hereabouts."

The dowager gestured to the footman. "Bring the basket inside. Mrs. Knockem, if I might be so bold, one of my guests, Miss Georgiana Lytton, has quite remarkable skill at curing skin ailments."

Olivia leaned over and breathed in her sister's ear, "Lady Althea should just call for her carriage and return to London now."

But Lady Sibblethorp was apparently not ready to give up the fight. "My daughter, Lady Althea, has also made an extensive study of minor skin ailments," she said magisterially. "We shall examine the girl."

Mrs. Knockem didn't look particularly happy about

the imminent house invasion, but she seemed to realize that there was no stopping a flood once the riverbank was breached. She fell backward a step, blinking even faster.

Georgiana stepped forward. "Mrs. Knockem, you must be so worried. Could you tell me more about what happened?" She walked into the house, her arm tucked under Mrs. Knockem's, her head bent to hear her description.

The dowager waved Lady Althea and her mother into the house, and then turned. "You shall not be welcome, Duke," she said. "And Miss Lytton, I'm sure you understand that the canine must remain outdoors."

"I don't know anything about skin infections," Olivia put in, hoping madly that the dowager would touch something and catch a case of purple bumps.

"Quite," the dowager stated. The door shut behind her.

Olivia sighed.

Then she realized that she was standing in front of the line of small children, who didn't seem inclined to mill about the way children normally do. They were rather dirty and thin. And they looked anxious. "Let's see," she said to the eldest. "Your name is Apple because you have lovely red cheeks." She looked to the next. "You look very fast, so you must be Arrow. And this must be Apron because—"

"I'm not Apron," the small boy said indignantly. "That's for a girl!"

"Hmmm," Olivia said. "Then how about Ant? You are about the size of a peasecod."

"I'll get bigger," he said stoutly.

"Very true." She could see smiles popping up. The line had broken, and now they were clustering around her. "Let's try the girls. You must be Apricot, since your hair is a lovely shade of ginger that I heartily envy."

The girl giggled. "Me gram says it's the color of the devil's beard."

"It's not the most flattering of comparisons, but then we should all be so lucky as to have a fire that burns all the way through the winter, not to mention an apricot beard. And you," she said, turning to the last, very small girl, "you look like . . ." Her imagination failed.

"An acorn," came a deep voice just behind her. The duke leaned over and put a finger under the child's chin. "You are no more than a wee acorn."

She broke into a peal of laughter. "That's what me dad calls me, too!"

"All right, Miss Acorn," Olivia said, flashing the duke a surprised smile. "May I introduce Miss Lucy?"

Lucy had been sitting close to Olivia's ankle, but on hearing her name she stepped forward, her tail wagging madly.

The children clustered around her, squealing. Olivia held out Lucy's ribbon. "Would anyone like to take Lucy for a little walk?" A moment later Avery and Audrey headed to the village square, Lucy prancing before.

Olivia looked at the three remaining children. "So what is new and exciting in the village?"

" 'Zekiel Edgeworth bought a new mare!" Acorn exclaimed.

"Goodness me. And where does Mr. Edgeworth stable his horse?"

"Right there!" they squealed. Sure enough, there was a chestnut mare off in a corner of the yard.

"We're taking care of her," Ant said importantly.

Olivia held out her hand, looked down, and then stripped off her glove. "What *was* I thinking?" she said, causing another storm of giggles as she held out her hand again to Ant. "Now, Master Ant, will you introduce me to the fine steed living in your garden?"

"Isn't she beautiful?" Ant breathed, a moment later.

"She has some interesting aspects," Olivia acknowledged. "What's her name?"

"Well," Arrow said importantly, "Mr. Edgeworth likes to call her Starstruck. But we think that's a rackety name. So we call her Alice. See, she already knows her name. *Alice!*"

Sure enough, the mare looked up at that shriek, causing great gales of laughter. Olivia was trying her best to ignore the man at her shoulder. He was *Georgiana*'s future husband, for goodness' sake.

"Alice has a bad case of pigeon toes—or hooves, to be exact," the duke observed, coming even closer to her.

Olivia and children frowned at him. "We all agree that hooves like hers are very becoming in a horse," she announced.

There was a chorus of agreement.

"I certainly didn't mean to diminish her strong points," the duke said. He reached out and patted the mare's neck. He had removed his gloves as well. "For example, she has a large forehead and a long neck."

"A *very* long neck," Acorn agreed. "And a long back too, because we've all climbed on it once or twice. At the same time, I mean."

"That must account for the sway," Olivia murmured to the duke. He was looking at her in that intent way again, so she moved a step away under the guise of examining the mare's back.

"She has even better points than her neck," the duke said, his voice taking on a curiously innocent tone. "Any man would be lucky to have this mare."

Arrow seemed a little suspicious. "My pa doesn't say the same as you. He says as how Mr. Edgeworth threw away his coin when he bought Alice. He doesn't like Alice." He stroked the mare's nose consolingly.

"I was referring to her dark chestnut coat, of course," the duke said. "Soft eyes, a delicate mouth, and such long eyelashes." He too was stroking the mare—but he was looking straight at Olivia.

She had never heard a horse described in quite those words before. She stole another glance at his face. The duke did not seem the type of person who would engage in wordplay. Though at lunch . . . He'd certainly mentioned Lady Godiva in a suggestive manner.

"Her coat is extraordinarily velvety," he said to Ant. "Don't you all think so?" Six dirty hands patted the mare's belly, and a chorus of voices agreed with him. "One wants to keep touching her," he said. The laughter in his voice was positively wicked.

"And she has *very* smooth hooves," he continued, pointing down. "Nice and round in the front. Light on her heels, no doubt." The mare had succumbed to his blandishments and was bumping his shoulder, begging for more attention.

"Are you saying that she's light-heeled?" Olivia asked, still trying to figure out exactly how far his wordplay was meant to go. "Because she most certainly is *not*."

"That would mean our Alice was a hussy," Avery said disapprovingly. "You don't say that about a horse."

"You're absolutely right," the duke said. "I stand corrected. Alice is clearly a creature of virtue."

"You make very little sense," Olivia observed. "One would almost—almost!—think you implied that Alice is a high-flier."

"And she's not," Avery put in. "Mr. Edgeworth says she won't even jump the stile."

"We think it's because she's got such a round belly," Acorn put in.

"Indeed." The duke smiled again, and Olivia was furious to feel warmth creeping up in her cheeks. He couldn't be referring to her.

"Everything a man could desire," he said. "A lovely, plump buttock, too."

Yes, he *could* be referring to her. She stood taller, fiercely resisting the impulse to back her plump buttock out of sight. Maybe into the next county.

"It's because of all the grass we give her," Ant said importantly. "We tear it up on the Common and we bring her handfuls."

"What a lucky animal," the duke murmured. He was a devil . . . unless she was completely misunderstanding him.

How could he possibly mean what she—

"Well, Miss Lytton? Don't you agree with our assessment of this exquisite beast?"

The words jumped out of her mouth before she thought. "A plump *buttock*? Since when is that something a man desires in his mount?"

Stupidly, she caught the double entendre only after she herself made it. But the duke didn't miss the intimation. His eyes lit up with an unholy, smoldering light, a secret promise that made fire pool in her body.

"Why, Miss Lytton," he said, his voice a deep purr, "you surprise me."

It forcibly occurred to her that he had deliberately brought Lady Godiva into the conversation at luncheon. "Um," she fumbled. "I surprise myself." There was something hungry in his eyes that wasn't for her—couldn't be for her. She could never have what he was offering.

That hunger should be for Georgiana. From the time

she was ten years old she'd known that her future didn't include . . . *this*.

She couldn't think what to say.

The children had no such hesitation. "You're looking at Miss Lytton like the way our Annie looks at Bean," Apple told the duke.

"I expect you're walking out," Apricot chimed in. "Ma did say as how the duke was like to marry, remember?"

The duke didn't seem to be inclined to respond. One moment he had looked unemotionally *ducal*, for lack of a better word, and the next his face was transformed by a kind of rough sensuality.

"That's just how Bean looks back at Annie, too," Acorn put in, apparently taking silence as encouragement. "Like trouble, that's what Mum says." She turned to Olivia. "That's why Annie won't come out of the house. Because those purple bumps are all over her bottom, and how did they get there?"

Olivia frowned.

"Iffen she had had her clothes on," Acorn explained.

"See, Bean is the butcher's son, and they're walking out," Apricot added. "Though you shouldn't be saying things like that to fine folk," she told her brother with a poke to his middle. "This is a lady, and ladies don't know anything about their own clothes."

"We don't?" Olivia asked.

"You can't take 'em off yourself, can you? That's what Mum says. Though it could be she's wrong."

Alas, Olivia had to confirm. "You're right. My gowns are all buttoned up the back and I do need someone to help me undress."

"Well, the good news is that you won't get the purple itch, then, at least not on your bottom."

"*That* is very good to know," the duke said, gravely.

But he would never fool Olivia again. This particular duke may look as stiff as a poker, but there was something quite different inside.

A smile, a hidden smile.

Twelve

The Merits of Scrambled Custards and Gooseberries

*I*mmediately upon the little band's return to Littlebourne Manor—the unfortunate Annie's rash
having been inspected, diagnosed, and treated—the
dowager waved all the ladies off to their chambers to
change their clothing, then raised a finger at Quin.

"Accompany me, if you please, Duke," she said. "I
should be grateful for the support of your arm while I
take a brief turn around the gardens."

The moment they were out of earshot of their guests,
she stopped. "Tarquin, I am not enjoying Miss Lytton's
company."

"Yes," Quin agreed.

"Yet her sister Miss Georgiana appears to be a most
suitable candidate for your duchess. She was remarkable when talking to Mrs. Knockem and her wagtail of
a daughter—whose rash, by the way, is no more than

she deserves, given her loose behavior. At any rate, Miss Georgiana evinced compassion for the invalid, along with a kind, yet reserved attitude toward the family as a whole. She kept her distance, yet was never disdainful. I thoroughly approved."

Quin murmured something, thinking that Olivia didn't seem to care in the least about maintaining her distance from the Knockem family.

"In fact, the only drawback I can identify to the match," his mother continued, "is the elder sister. Yet since Miss Lytton will be married as soon as that young fool comes back from France, the pleasure of her company—or its opposite—hardly matters."

"Young fool?" Quin inquired.

"Montsurrey." His mother waved her hand impatiently. "Miss Lytton seems to have reconciled herself to the matter; I must credit her with that. And she was right about my slip of the tongue: I should not have maligned a peer of the realm, no matter what I may have heard about the future duke. Though," she added, "his own father described him as having brains more scrambled than an egg custard."

"An egg custard," Quin repeated.

"Irrelevant," the dowager said. "My point is that you must keep Miss Lytton and her dog out of my sight, Tarquin. As you know, I consider it very important that I carry out my tests in a judicious manner. I can hardly do so if I am engaged in fencing with a chit half my age."

"She held her own," Quin said, making quite certain that satisfaction did not leak into his voice.

"I am aware of that," his mother replied, rather grimly. "For my peace of mind, then, I would ask that you occupy the young virago and her mongrel while I continue to explore the characters of Lady Althea and Miss Georgiana."

"All right," Quin said.

His mother tightened her grip on his arm. "I do realize that Miss Lytton is a challenging and rather tiresome companion, and I apologize for burdening you with her company. At least I need have no worries that you will succumb to *her* charms. Her figure, for one, renders her most unattractive. What can she be thinking, wearing such a revealing costume when she carries all that extra flesh?"

Quin said nothing.

"Besides," his mother continued, talking to herself as she often did, "Miss Lytton seems admirably devoted to Montsurrey. Therefore, amongst ourselves, *en famille*, I believe we may dispense with a chaperone. Really, I have to credit Canterwick. I can see that she's just right for his boy."

"Boy?"

"Montsurrey must be five years younger than she is at the very least," her mother said, turning so they could stroll back to the house. "I find it amusing that both Canterwick and myself have looked to the Lytton family for a possible alliance with our children. It is true that the Lyttons are well connected on both sides, but they are hardly aristocracy. It is a tribute to . . ."

But Quin had stopped listening. Olivia was betrothed to a boy, a bird-witted boy, if he believed his mother.

Olivia—wry, witty Olivia?

Impossible.

"Don't you agree, Tarquin?" his mother asked sharply.

"I'm sorry. I'm afraid that I lost track of the conversation."

"I said that Miss Lytton was remarkably fortunate to have been chosen by the Duke of Canterwick to marry his son. Her birth is negligible, her figure forgettable, and her manner impertinent."

Quin stared down at his mother. "But she's beautiful."

"Beautiful? Beautiful? Certainly *not*. She's round as a gooseberry, which bespeaks a gluttonous turn of mind. And I don't care for her eyes."

"Actually, they are the color of gooseberries," Quin said. "A green such as I have never seen in a pair of eyes before."

"Unusual," his mother said. She didn't mean it as a compliment. "But her sister's eyes are entirely acceptable. And her figure is lovely. I find it odd that one sister should have such a squabby shape while the other is elegant in every respect. I expect it's a matter of self-control, always a lady's best weapon against the world's tribulations. Miss Georgiana obviously has excellent self-control."

"Yes," Quin agreed.

"She'll throw you no tantrums," his mother continued. A smile curled up the corner of her mouth. "I can see the two of you now, presiding over a cluster of small children. You would like that, wouldn't you, Tarquin?"

Black ice seized his heart; he didn't reply, but it didn't matter.

His mother went on, all the way back to the house, painting a picture of Quin and Georgiana, smiling affectionately at their brown-eyed children.

Thirteen

What It Means to Lead an Army

The next afternoon

Olivia's new riding habit had regimental flair: braid marched up the cunning little jacket and then down the skirt; there were tiny epaulets on the shoulders. Even the fetching little hat was not a bonnet, but a rakish version of a lieutenant's cap in dark crimson that flattered her hair and skin.

The costume made her feel as if her figure wasn't too plump, as if she wasn't too saucy (as her mother would put it). As if everything was right in the world, and she was the general of her own personal army.

A perfect illustration of the fundamental pettiness of her brain, she thought, walking slowly along the path to the stables. Georgiana felt happiest after she had cooked up some noxious brew that might—or might not—cure the second footman's baby of red blotches on its bum. Whereas Olivia felt happiest when she liked what she saw in the mirror and then headed out to engage in recklessly imprudent flirtation with a duke.

And not the duke she was marrying, either.

Worse yet, the duke her *sister* was marrying.

Obviously she couldn't flirt with the duke. The sooner she got it in her head that Sconce was Georgiana's future *husband*, the better. She actually gave a little shudder at the idea of flirting with her future brother-in-law. Only the most distasteful—not to mention disloyal—sister would do such a thing.

She was already feeling guilty enough. She had left Georgiana supine on a sofa, a wet cloth over her eyes. Olivia's exchanges with the dowager over the midday meal—which she herself had actually rather enjoyed—had given her sister a migraine headache.

Lucy gave a little yelp and ran forward, wagging her tail furiously. An elderly gardener was planting some seedlings in the shade of an old stone wall that separated Littlebourne Manor's gardens from the stables beyond. He was kneeling, back to her, the well-worn soles of his old boots cocked to each side.

"Thou art a hash little one, aren't thou?" the gardener said, scratching Lucy between her ears. His voice was warm and smoky, and made Olivia think about the qualities of voices: the way the dowager's voice was bright and cold, so different from her son's deep, intent voice. The duke sounded as if each word was chosen carefully, whereas her own tumbled out any which way, and often in an unladylike fashion—*you have a lively sense of humor*, the duchess had said the day before.

She shook off that thought and walked a little closer to the gardener. "Good day. Are you from Wales?"

The moment he heard her voice, he struggled to his feet, his joints creaking loudly, and backed against the wall, doffing his cap. "My lady," he said, eyes on the ground. "Not Wales." He sounded disgusted. "Shropshire." He was bowlegged and bent, like an apple tree on the ridge of a hill, fighting a blustery wind.

"I didn't mean to interrupt your work," Olivia said. "Please, go back to whatever you're doing. That's my dog sniffing your boots. Lucy, behave yourself!"

Lucy was dancing about, trying to lick the gardener's hand. Slowly, he reached down and gently pulled one of the little dog's ears. "She's a fair one, bain't she?"

"I don't think she's *fair*, if by that you mean beautiful." They both looked down at Lucy. "She's got very short fur, and there's that bite on her eyelid."

"O aye, she's lost a bit of her eyelid. But her eyes themselves are a fair treat," he offered. "Tail, too."

"It's a rat tail, though," Olivia pointed out.

He knelt back down on the brown soil, shoulder to her. Then he said, as if to his plants, "There's those as are decorative, like these flowers here will be. And then other flora that isn't a bit pretty, not until the petals drop."

Olivia came closer and peered past him. "Which flowers are unattractive until their petals drop?"

"Happen you walk in a cloud of petals jist dancing on the wind, then?"

She walked around so she was looking down at his weather-beaten cap, rather than his shoulder. "What a lovely description."

"This little mistress," he said, giving Lucy a nudge with his elbow that made the dog dizzy with delight, "is one of them as lift your heart when you're ornery, though likely there are them as would prefer something feather-tailed and furred."

Olivia found herself smiling down at Lucy. "You're right, of course. I didn't think much of her at first, but she's dear to me now." She bent over and peered at the ground. "What will those seedlings become?"

"Delphiniums."

"The tall, purple ones?"

"Aye."

Olivia frowned. "I thought those flowers need a great deal of sunshine. Will they get enough beneath this wall?"

"Her Grace likes them here, me lady." Rich soil ran like rain through his fingers as he patted the ground around each little sprig.

"I hate to plant things that won't live long. Perhaps the head gardener could teach Her Grace about delphiniums?"

He gave her a fleeting glance. "A lady likes her garden lush, neat, scented, sweet."

"That rhymes," Olivia said, thinking that Justin might learn from the gardener.

A warm hand suddenly touched her back. Olivia yelped and straightened.

"Miss Lytton," the duke said, his eyes dark and unreadable. "I apologize for startling you." He bowed. "I see you've met Riggle, our highly esteemed head gardener, who has been with us since I was all of six years old. Riggle, may I introduce Miss Lytton?"

Riggle looked over his shoulder and said something along the lines of "bain't it."

"I'm very pleased to meet you, Riggle," Olivia said. "Good morning, Your Grace." The duke had changed for riding as well. Breeches clung to muscular thighs; one quick glance made her heart speed to a red-and-gold beat.

Desire—for Olivia was not one to pretend to a more dignified emotion if the proper word presented itself—was proving to be an overwhelming sensation. She could imagine that fleeting touch of his hand down every limb.

Brother-in-law, she thought to herself. *Brother-in-law.*

"Don't tell me she's got you planting delphiniums again," the duke said. He bent over and looked closely at the plant. "Yes, those are palmate leaves. I told her not to, Riggle."

"Her Grace is a fierce believer," the gardener said, patting down another small plant.

"In what?" Olivia inquired.

"Her plans," the duke answered for Riggle. "My mother is apt to think that if everyone will simply adhere to a plan—preferably of her making—the world will be a sane and ordered place."

"To hope that a flower will bloom despite lack of sun shows an extraordinary confidence in one's plan," Olivia observed.

"I am surrounded by relatives with pretentions to divine powers." There was a spark deep in his eyes that spoke to her like a burst of laughter. It felt flammable, dangerous.

She couldn't *not* smile back at him, even though his face was—to outward appearance—serious enough. Still: *Brother-in-law*, she thought again.

"Riggle, we will take our leave of you," the duke said, taking Olivia's arm. "Miss Lytton, I've had two mounts prepared for us. Justin has already driven the pony cart around to the front to meet Lady Cecily, since her ankle is still unsteady."

Olivia said her good-bye to Riggle, and then walked in silence next to the duke. She had to say something . . . anything. It was almost the first time in her life that her brain was unable to summon a single word.

After lunch, her sister had been quite certain that the duke had taken a great dislike to Olivia, given her hoydenish behavior. But the duke didn't look as though he disliked her.

"Are you an enthusiastic horsewoman, Miss Lytton?" he asked, after a minute or two.

"Yes!" Olivia said, grateful to be given a topic of conversation. "I had a pony growing up, and nowadays my sister and I regularly ride in Hyde Park. Have you ridden there often yourself, Your Grace?"

"Not in some years," he said. "Does your fiancé like to ride?"

"Rupert? He has some trouble staying in the saddle," Olivia said, belatedly remembering that she shouldn't tell virtual strangers that Rupert couldn't stay on a horse until he was fifteen. "Though he's much improved in the last year. He has a weak . . . a weak knee," she added hastily.

"All the more reason to admire his decision to join the battle."

"His father was quite dismayed, but Rupert has a very strong will. When he puts his mind to something, no one can change it."

A fleeting frown crossed the duke's face. "I suppose—" He broke off.

"Yes?"

"Your fiancé sounds like an excellent man all around. Loyal to his country, brave even with the encumbrance of a physical disability, and resolute in his convictions in the face of his father's disapproval. I have met the Duke of Canterwick, and I would expect that he exerted considerable pressure on his son to remain in England. I look forward to meeting Montsurrey."

Olivia nodded. She couldn't say anything much without being disloyal to Rupert, and she had made up her mind that she simply wouldn't do it.

But the duke was not finished. "Canterwick apparently told my mother that his son's brains were as scrambled as an egg custard."

"Ah," Olivia said. Of course she agreed, but she had realized when the duchess was so dismissive of Rupert that she could either spend her entire life listening to sniggers behind her husband's back, or she could make it clear that no one should dare to insult Rupert to her face.

"The duke shows a dismaying inability to recognize his son's strong points," she said, suiting thought to word. "Rupert's thoughts are often remarkably clear." That was true enough. Rupert understood precisely what he thought of Lucy, for example. Olivia glanced down with a rush of affection. The little dog was trotting beside her, waving her tail so briskly that it kept hitting Olivia's leg.

"Parents are sometimes of that inclination," the duke said. His face was impossible to read.

"Of course, Canterwick would have preferred that Rupert remain in England, given that he has no other heirs," Olivia said. "But Rupert would not sacrifice his own and his country's honor merely for something as ephemeral as a title."

That drew a distinct frown from the duke. It may well have been the first time that anyone had envied Rupert; she felt quite sad that he wasn't here to enjoy it.

"Would you have liked to have joined His Majesty's Service, Your Grace?" she asked.

"Of course." He said it rather gruffly. "But I am already the duke, and a duke without an heir. I could not in good conscience leave my responsibilities in the hands of others."

"Rupert has no responsibilities as yet. He felt in his heart that he had to go." The duke really did look grim around the mouth, and Olivia started to feel a bit sorry for him. "He probably won't have any effect on the war effort," she offered. "He only has a company of one hundred men."

"As I understand it, the number of men is important, but not as important as one's strategic planning," the duke said.

Olivia didn't even try to imagine Rupert engaged in strategic planning.

"Are you worried about his safety?"

"Yes," Olivia said. And she was, oddly enough. For all her bleating over the marriage, something had shifted within her by the time she'd said good-bye. Rupert was not undamaged, but he was hers, for better or worse.

She hesitated a moment and then decided that she had better be absolutely straightforward. "You and I, Your Grace, have fallen into something of a flirtation."

He turned his head, rather slowly, and looked down at her. The flare in his eyes couldn't be described by a word as innocuous as flirtation. "I would not describe it as such," he said, echoing her thought.

Was he trying to shame her? If there was one thing Olivia hated, it was people who hid their emotions behind a mask of propriety. She'd had enough of that from her family. Though she loved them dearly, she'd long ago concluded that greed dictated her parents' relationship to her.

"I understand if you wish to pretend that the feeling isn't there, but I cannot agree with you," she said.

"In fact, I have described it to myself as being in the grip of compulsive lust," he said bluntly. "I assure you, Miss Lytton, that I have never kissed a strange woman in such an impetuous manner before you appeared at my front door."

Olivia felt a sudden flush break over her entire body. Her heart was pounding. She did not dare look at him. Part of her wanted to protest: didn't he realize that she was plump and unattractive? She peeked at him.

"You are betrothed," he said, his voice coming out in a growl.

"Since childhood," she said, nodding.

They were walking along a lilac hedge. The perfume of the blossoms floated in the air all around them. He stopped, dropping her arm, so she had to look up at him. A strong hand tipped up her chin. Their eyes met. "Olivia," he said. And that was all.

She was in his arms, and his lips came down on hers. For a moment they kissed the way they had in the silver room: a bit tentative, gentle, a sip and a taste. But then his arms tightened and she tilted her head just so, and the kiss changed. Her lips opened and he was there, tangling with her.

The fragrance of the lilacs faded. Instead, she smelled spice and soap, a mingling of gentleman and highwayman that was the duke.

He was right. This wasn't flirtation; this was craving, so deep and intense that Olivia's whole body vibrated with the need to be closer. She wrapped her arms around his neck, stood on tiptoe, allowed his hand to press her body against the hard planes of his body. The other cupped the back of her head, cradling it in a position that tilted her head so that he could kiss her hard, a hungry, smoldering kiss that told her without words that he didn't think she was plump and unattractive.

His hair fell from its ribbon and brushed her cheek. His eyes were closed, which made him look like a different man. Open-eyed, he was fierce, hawk-like, somewhat cold. With his eyes closed, he was someone else entirely.

A man in the grip of pleasure, her instinct told her.

His lips slid from hers, seeking the tender sweep of her neck. She gasped and shivered; his eyes opened.

"This is not flirtation." His voice rasped as his lips lit a trail of heat across her cheek.

"No," she whispered, trembling against him.

"It's a bloody forest fire," he said, dropping one last short, hard kiss on her lips and then putting her away from him.

Olivia swallowed.

"Yet you are betrothed." It was a statement, but those dark eyes were asking a question. Olivia felt as if the world peeled away from around them, as if there were only the two of them in the whole of the windy garden: this tall, hard man, his eyes searching her face, and Miss Olivia Mayfield Lytton, betrothed at birth to a marquess. Her heart thudded against her ribs, but . . .

There was Rupert to think of, and Georgiana.

She steeled herself and willed the words aloud. "A forest fire is no reason to betray the two people I . . . to betray my fiancé."

"Two people." He paused. "Georgiana?"

"That's irrelevant," she said quickly. "I didn't mean to—at any rate, it's completely irrelevant."

"No, it's not. She's here because my mother invited her."

Olivia nodded.

"It's not as if we were looking her over, like a horse at Tattersall's," he said somewhat defensively. "My first marriage went very poorly. My mother is anxious that I don't repeat the mistake."

Olivia touched his cheek, as lightly as a breath, but still her fingertips tingled. "Georgiana would never betray you."

"So you have heard the gossip?" His eyes were shuttered.

"My maid mentioned your former wife's reputation."

"Evangeline earned her reputation, I'm afraid." There was no shame, or condemnation in his voice. "I believe we had better continue to the stables, Miss Lytton. My aunt, not to mention young Justin, will grow restless if they are kept waiting in the pony cart."

Olivia again took his arm. Her knees felt weak.

"I take it, then, that Montsurrey has your loyalty."

She nodded, but realized he was looking straight ahead, and said, "Yes." It came out a croak. "He—he would be very hurt if I were to . . . It wouldn't do."

"A very English response," he said, glancing down at her. "It wouldn't *do*. But you're right. The very worst thing any man could do to another, especially one serving his country, would be to steal his future wife. Perhaps when he has returned safely, we might discuss this further?"

"You and I scarcely know each other," Olivia said, keeping her voice steady only with effort.

"I want to get to know you better. That's the point of the conversation." His voice was dark, husky.

Georgiana's hopeful face swam before Olivia's eyes.

She drew herself together. Rupert was one thing, but Georgiana was her twin, her other half. And she felt instinctively that her sister was right: this man was perfect for Georgie. Not for Olivia.

"One doesn't marry on the basis of madness," she said, dropping a cool edge into her voice.

He took another few steps without a word. Silence . . . silence just made Olivia even more conscious of the powerful body next to her. *Brother-in-law*, she said to herself.

"So are you familiar with this sort of madness?" His voice was colorless. "Does it come often to you?"

Like his wife. That's what he's thinking. She opened her mouth to deny it—and thought again. "Rupert and I have been betrothed since his birth. Of course I have not . . ." She tried again. "Neither of us had a choice of spouse. We both understood fidelity was not part of our fathers' pact, at least before marriage."

They were rounding the corner of the stables now. A stable boy peeked out the door, then popped back inside, followed by the clop of horse's shoes as a dappled mare emerged into the sunshine.

"I'll put you on your mount," the duke said.

He led her to the mare, then put his hands on her waist. For a moment they both froze. His hands tightened, and he lifted her carefully up to the saddle.

"Thank you, Your Grace," she murmured, slipping her leg around the pommel and tweaking her skirts.

"I prefer to be called Quin."

Startled, she looked down at him. "That would be quite improper."

"'Improper' would be if I pulled you off this horse in front of four servants and kissed you senseless."

"You can't!" she squeaked.

"I can." He said it calmly enough. "And I can only assume that it wouldn't disturb you, *Olivia*, given that you just characterized yourself as an accomplished flirt . . . to put your description in the best possible light."

What was she supposed to say to that? " '*Miss Lytton*' to *you*?" The duke had already turned away and leapt on his horse in one smooth movement. He was angry: she could see the contained fury in his body, in the way his cheekbones looked even more sharply masculine than usual.

But she didn't know how to respond. Everything in her—except her pride and loyalty—longed to reach out, touch his hand, catch his sleeve. Give him a feverish look, somehow, anyhow, lure him back so that he would kiss her again like that. As if she were desirable. Sensual.

Olivia glanced down and caught sight of her own leg curved around the pommel. The sight jolted her back to her senses. He wanted her now, for some reason.

But she was fat. Her leg was fat. He hadn't seen that yet, somehow. He'd overlooked it, but he wouldn't—*couldn't*—if they were ever in a state of undress together.

The thought made her stomach pitch, but she welcomed the faint queasiness. It was a call to reason. Quin would be happy with Georgiana. He would forget this nonsense, this "forest fire," as he called it.

She smiled at the stable boy holding her horse's reins. "Will you keep Lucy for me until I return? I do believe she thinks there might be rats in the stable."

"She'd be right," the boy said promptly. Lucy was nosing around at the wall, her tail stiff with delight.

"Find them," Olivia suggested.

He grinned and handed over the reins. She deftly

tightened them, nudged the mare, and set out after the duke. Quin.

They reached the house by a road that rounded a bend and placed them before the house. Littlebourne Manor had a magisterial façade, she realized, paying attention to it for the first time.

Rather than sprawling in many directions, like so many ancestral mansions that had been added to in bits and pieces, it stood upright, trim and perfectly symmetrical, surrounded by immaculately manicured lawns.

It was too neat for her. Each feature had its exact duplicate on the opposite side: windows, gables, chimneys.

"What do you think?" the duke asked, as she drew up her horse.

"It's too orderly for my taste," she said, with a wave of her hand at the windows marching along like tin soldiers. "I'm a quite haphazard person."

"What does haphazard mean in architectural terms?" he asked. But she could see Lady Cecily and Justin waiting for them, so she put her mare to a trot.

"I'm so sorry to have kept you waiting, Lady Cecily," she said, bending down once she reached the pony cart.

"You should be apologizing to *me*," Justin said with some indignation. "Aunt Cecily arrived only a moment ago, whereas I've had time to write an entire roundel. It's not bad either, if I say so myself." He waved a piece of foolscap at them.

"I will look forward to hearing it," Olivia said. "How is your ankle, Lady Cecily?"

"Excellent well! I put a poulder on it that I bought in Venice two years ago. The medicine is so powerful that it kept Helen herself young. And it's particularly for bones; I remember that the man selling it—'twas on the square before Saint Mark's—said that it would set your teeth and make them dance like the keys of a harpsichord. And so it did, though of course, it was my ankle, not my teeth."

"We'll go to Ladybird Ridge," the duke said to Justin. "Endeavor not to tip the cart over, if you can help it."

"It would be impossible to tip this thing over," Justin said, looking disgusted. "Now, if you'd let me drive your phaeton, I would at least having a sporting chance to roll it—"

The duke didn't bother to answer, instead turning to Olivia. "Shall we?"

"I wish your dear sister were with us," Lady Cecily called up to Olivia. "I gather that she has a headache, so I sent her a dose of this poulder as well. It's as precious as gold, I assure you, so I'm quite sure that she's already feeling herself again. Should we send indoors and ask if she'd like to join us?"

"No," the duke said, before Olivia could respond. "We're leaving now." And he wheeled his horse. It was a great black gelding that pranced forward and made a halfhearted attempt to shake him off.

Olivia turned her mare and followed.

Fourteen

The Flight of the Cherry Kite

Of course Olivia was no stranger to flirtation, let alone lust, Quin said to himself. It made complete sense. One didn't need to conduct a third experiment to prove this hypothesis: for whatever ignoble reason, he was particularly vulnerable to women who had a liberal relationship with the concept of chastity.

Even worse, he was more besotted now than he had been with Evangeline.

Evangeline had fascinated him: he had wanted to bring her home, cherish her, and make love to her. He had thought the curl of her hair and the tinkle of her laugh enchanting. But he could not remember feeling this sort of overwhelming sensuality, a wild madness that tangled up his reason and sent all the blood in his body to a place between his legs.

He didn't even have to look at Olivia to catalog her

features. Her eyelashes were a trifle longer at the corners, which gave her a wicked air, a touch of Cleopatra. Even thinking of her body made his tighten painfully. She was all curves and plump, creamy flesh.

And her eyes—they were honest. Unlike Evangeline, she told him the truth about herself, straight out. Both women were, one might say, less than chaste. But Olivia didn't pretend otherwise.

What's more, when he'd asked her in so many words if she would consider him rather than Montsurrey, she'd remained loyal to the marquess. He had the sense, as well, that she would always be so. No matter how coquettish she was as a young lady, once she married her returning warrior, she would be true to him.

There was another signal difference, too: Olivia was genuinely desirous. In his arms she was like a quick flame.

Evangeline . . . well, Evangeline had wanted words. That's what she'd longed for. When they made love she would squeal and push at his chest, hating the fact that he towered over her. For her, it was all about the time before, and the time after: the words. And he was so terrible at *words*.

He had slowed his mount to a walk, and Olivia caught up with him. She had a pretty flush in her cheeks from the exercise and wind.

"I like your hat," he said, suddenly finding a few words. It was like a cherry, perched atop a luscious mound of dark bronze-colored hair. Since it could have no useful function, it was obviously designed to make a man long to pluck it off.

She looked startled for a moment, and then beamed at him. "It wouldn't keep off the rain."

He turned onto a little dirt track, the pony clop-

clopping behind them. "We'll take the kites to the top of the ridge," he told her, nodding ahead of them. "They fly best on a hill, and this is a particularly windy spot. Sometimes we can spin out ells of string before they lose the current."

Olivia looked at him curiously. "You sound like a kite expert, which is rather like finding a grown man admitting to playing jack-stones."

His heart gave a thump. "I used to play—" he said, before he caught himself. There was no reason to tell her the details. He was coming to terms with the fact that she wouldn't be his. She belonged to another man, he of the patriotic bent and scrambled brain.

So he turned it into a weak retort. "Kites are not something one ever forgets how to fly."

"I suppose not," she said. But she looked curious, as if she saw through him.

He jumped from his horse, threw the reins over a bush, and came back to Olivia. It was ridiculous, really. He was damned sure that desire was etched on his face, which made him feel vulnerable and slightly mad. But he walked over and reached up to her waist anyway because, really, what are men? Merely animals, as subject to mating urges as any other biped. Or quadruped, for that matter.

"What are you thinking about?" she asked, shaking her skirts free as he put her down.

"Science," he answered, somewhat less than truthfully.

"Are you interested in more than mathematical functions, then?" She looped her mount's reins on the same bush.

"Yes. But I don't want you to fall asleep from boredom, so I won't elaborate; we'd have to bring you home in the pony cart." Justin was tying up the pony. He walked over to see if his aunt would like to descend from the cart, but she declared that she had a better view from her seat.

He took the kite box from the back of the cart. The lid opened as if he'd opened it yesterday, as if all those days in between hadn't existed. He had to take a deep breath before he pulled out the first kite: cherry red, a light and speedy one that tore through the air and generally plunged to the ground with equal velocity.

Underneath were two good, sturdy kites that had held up in wind after wind. And beneath that . . . he touched the small spines for a moment, his finger rubbing the delicate wood as if it could touch the child who used to hold it.

Then he swallowed hard and shut the box on that kite.

"I have three for us," he said, turning. His voice came out tense and dark, and he saw Olivia's eyes fly to his face. He forced himself to smile, grim though it probably was.

Justin hopped over. "I never liked that red one," he said cheerfully, as if the kites had no history. "Too frisky. I'll take one of the others."

"You have to tie the spool on," Quin said, handing it over.

Olivia snatched the cherry kite. "I love this one!"

"It matches your hat," he said, clearing his throat. "I'll tie on the spool for you." And then he bent his head to the task, avoiding her eyes. For whatever reason, he could read Olivia's eyes, and it seemed she might have the same power over him. He could have sworn that she saw his desolation, caught a glimpse of the black monstrous silence that lived within his chest.

"Now," he said briskly, after tying both their spools, "we'll walk to the top of the ridge."

It took time, and a great deal of laughter—not on Quin's part, but that was only because he rarely laughed—until all three kites were loose and free, bobbing in a current sweeping overhead.

"I love it!" Olivia shouted. She was running back and forth, her slippers twinkling under her hem.

As if it had been only five minutes, rather than five years, the cherry kite slid below the current, plunged down, jerked its way back up. Whereas Quin's kite reached its zenith and then stayed there, a solid scrap of white, bobbing far above his head.

Justin had flung himself on his back and was maneuvering his kite from there, indifferent to the possibility of soiling his magnificent mossy green riding costume.

But Olivia ran along the ridge, following her kite's erratic flight.

Justin looked drowsily comfortable, his eyes fixed on the distant speck of his kite. "You'd better go after Olivia," he said, throwing a lazy glance at Quin. "I can't see her anymore." With a sigh, Quin reeled in his kite.

Olivia had chased her kite somewhere . . . down or up or into the stand of trees at the end of the ridge. He glanced back and saw that Aunt Cecily was fast asleep, her jaw sagging comfortably.

He put down his kite and strode along the ridge. England was laid out before him, neat fields marked by hedgerows, a tiny carriage trundling along in the distance, the serpentine curl of the river over to the right. The wind smelled as if scythers were cutting grass, with a faint smoky undertone that suggested a bonfire.

For a moment joy bubbled up in his chest, and then

the familiar old feeling presented itself, as if for review. Guilt. Yet when he pushed it away this time, he felt different. Cleaner. More peaceful.

Perhaps it was time.

Suddenly he caught a flash of crimson that had to be Olivia's skirts. She had followed the ridge down the lee side, and was now standing under a tree, gazing up.

The cherry kite invariably found a tree to plunge into. He slowed and savored the walk toward her. His entire body was tight, fierce, as if he were barely in control. Which was absurd because he was *always* in control, and always had been.

Even five years ago, when he had turned away from the pier, knowing he was too late . . . he hadn't lost control. No. That wasn't entirely true; he shouldn't rewrite history. He had tried to throw himself in the water, bellowed for a boat, had to be restrained by the harbormaster.

But after . . . after, he walked away without a word. One foot before the other foot.

This was a different sort of emotion, like wildfire in his blood. Olivia had her hands on her hips, and as he watched she unpinned that silly little hat and put it to the side. He quickened his pace. She couldn't be thinking . . .

She was.

She unbuttoned her coat and placed it neatly on the ground.

As he watched, she reached up for the lowest branch and then scrambled up the trunk, placing her slippers against the bark with the agility and confidence of someone who has climbed a tree before. Indeed, many trees.

She was on the first set of branches, then the second, by the time he arrived at the trunk.

"Olivia Lytton!" he bellowed, standing below her. "What in the bloody hell do you think you're doing?"

She peered down at him through bouquets of green leaves. "Oh, hello," she called. "I'm rescuing my kite, of course." She was standing on a sturdy branch, looking as tidy as when she set out, like some sort of incongruous bird.

"Don't go any higher!" he ordered.

The sound of her laughter filtered down through the leaves, but Quin had already taken his coat off. He pulled himself in one smooth lunge onto the lowest branches. She was heading up again, so he maneuvered himself until he was below her and could catch her if she fell.

Which gave him a clear look up her skirts. She had one leg flung over a branch, and he saw a scarlet garter, and above it, a creamy thigh. His heart gave one ferocious thump and then settled into a faster rhythm.

For a moment he couldn't even breathe. Olivia's stockings were white silk and ended just below her knee. Above he could see a delicate line of lace . . . her smalls, he had to suppose.

Interesting. He hadn't known that ladies wore undergarments of that sort. Evangeline hadn't.

A wry thought flashed through his mind: Evangeline wouldn't have cared to waste the time. He dismissed the idea as beneath him.

"Miss Lytton, I can see your legs," he called, realizing as the words came from his mouth that the observation was also beneath him.

Olivia froze. But she had just thrown her weight onto that leg. So she pulled herself up on the next branch, almost slipping, but catching herself. Once on her feet again, securely holding on, she frowned down at him.

"Peering up a lady's skirts is not the act of a gentleman."

"I'm not sure but that climbing a tree disqualifies one for the title of gentleman—or, I might as well add, lady." He nimbly pulled himself onto the branch she had just deserted. "How much higher are you going? This tree won't take my weight above the height where you are now."

She pointed. The kite hung just out of her reach, caught by a loop of string. Quin tested the branch she stood on. "Move onto that branch next to your foot," he ordered. "I'm coming up."

Olivia hopped over to a nearby branch, as steady as if she were on ground. A second later Quin stood beside her. Up close, he could see that she was flushed with exertion, her bosom moving up and down. The bodice of her habit was made of fine linen, and her breasts strained against the cloth.

His hand clenched on the branch above their heads. Hopefully, she wouldn't glance at his breeches. "How can you climb a tree with a corset and all those petticoats?"

Her eyes shone with mischief. "It's a secret."

He leaned back against a handy limb, knees feeling a bit weak. "I am very good at keeping secrets."

"No corset," she said, half whispering, half laughing. "I learned long ago that it is simply impossible to climb a tree while wearing a corset. Not that I had tree climbing in mind when I dressed today. But I thought it was possible that flying a kite was a rather energetic sport as well. And it has certainly proved to be so."

"Just when did climbing trees become part of a lady's education?"

"The first time my mother put me on a reducing diet," she said, wrinkling her nose.

He frowned. "A *diet*?"

"I need to lose weight. I have ever since I was the tender age of thirteen, actually. Perhaps even a bit younger."

"No, you don't. I disagree."

"Well, I think I do. Your mother agrees, given the precept oft repeated in *The Mirror*: '*Virtue's livery is a comely shape.*' As does," she said consideringly, "most of the *ton*, given the number of slimming tips that have been whispered to me in ladies' retiring rooms."

The cruelty of Olivia being taught to loathe an aspect of herself that—to be frank—he thought was perfect made his heart feel as if something had broken loose inside. He straightened, leaned toward her. Her head angled instinctively, and their mouths met, hot and sweet, breath fast from the climb, or perhaps just proximity . . . She tasted like sunshine and grass. Like happiness.

Careful, he moved closer, not breaking the kiss, then leaned against the trunk of the tree and pulled her into his arms, being sure not to break her hold on the branch at shoulder level. "Olivia," he murmured against her mouth. "What's my name?"

She opened heavy-lidded eyes. "What did you say?"

"My name," he said, and then couldn't wait, snatching an openmouthed kiss, a silken mating of tongues.

"Quin," she said, drawing back. And then: "We're flirting again."

"We're out of flirtation and into the fire. But in any event, no one of our rank could possibly be kissing in a tree."

"So that means we aren't where we think we are?" Her eyes shone with amusement, and her lips were swollen from his kisses. "Or this isn't us in the tree? Or you're not a duke?"

"I must not be," he said thirstily, curling a hand around the back of her neck. "I'm not a duke. And you're not betrothed to a marquess, either."

They sank into the kiss as if they'd been kissing for years. His hands burned to take the kiss further, to run a finger, a hand, both hands, down the thin linen of her bodice. No corset.

He could hardly bear to look.

And then he did look, and actually groaned softly. "You have—" he said, and had to stop for a moment. "I think yours are the most beautiful breasts I've ever seen."

She glanced down and then at him. Oddly, for someone who seemed as experienced as she was, her cheeks turned pink and she looked self-conscious for a moment. Abashed.

But then she seemed to shake it off. "We need that kite," she said, pointing at it, which just strained her bodice even more. "Surely, Mr. I'm-not-a-duke, you can reach it?"

Quin wrestled with the part of his body that felt— strongly—that he wanted to reach not for a kite, but for the delectable female body that stood before him. She was still breathing quickly from the climb, or their kisses, or both, and the movement of her breasts bewitched him.

Leaves swayed all around them, creating a little bower, a room whose walls flickered with sunshine and green shadows.

If only there were a bed. He imagined her under him, struggling for breath, her cheeks a wild rose, hair around her head like a pillow.

"Don't look at me like that," she said sharply. "You mustn't."

"How about if I only look like this when we're high in a tree?" he suggested.

"This won't happen again."

"Precisely." So he looked again, head to toe. "You're exquisite, Olivia." He searched for more words, but couldn't find them, of course. He could never find the right words when he most needed them.

"You are very appealing as well," she said primly. "Not that it matters in either case, insofar as we are not birds and cannot live in this tree. I'm surprised your family hasn't come in search of us."

"Aunt Cecily was asleep in the cart, and I'm fairly sure that Justin is napping in the grass. His kite probably flew off by itself; he is far too lazy to retrieve it from a tree or elsewhere."

"Please, can you fetch my kite?" she asked, redirecting him to the original reason they had climbed so high.

Obediently, he stretched an arm and wiggled the kite free, managing to avoid tearing the fragile silk. He carefully let it spiral to the ground, controlling its fall through the branches and tossing the spool of string after.

"You are all dappled with leaves and sunlight," she observed.

"As are you," he said, running a finger down the curve of her cheek. "If Justin were here, he would make up a poem. I suppose we'd better descend from this tree. I'll go first, so I can catch you if you fall."

"Wait," she said, touching his arm lightly. Her touch sent a pulse of fire straight to his groin. "May I ask you something? What happened when you took the kites from the box, Quin?"

He hadn't expected that. Though he should have.

"Nothing."

She let her hand slide up his arm, over his shoulder, curl around his neck. "You don't want me to pull you off the branch, do you?" Her lips were smiling, but her eyes were serious.

"Time was when I would have begged you to," he said, the words coming from somewhere outside his control.

She waited.

But he couldn't bring himself to say more. "We should go back," he said, knowing the gruffness in his voice was its own confession.

"Did your wife like the kites? Was that one hers?" Olivia nodded toward the red kite on the grass below them.

"No. It was . . ." He had to wait a moment. Slap the layer of black ice back where it belonged until he was able to speak. "That was the nanny's. She was called Dilys. She was . . . she was . . . she liked bright colors and laughter. She was from Shropshire."

"Like Riggle?"

"I forgot you met him. Yes, she was his daughter. He's forgiven me, Lord knows how."

Her eyes met his, gentle and steady. "I am quite sure there was nothing to forgive. How old was your child?"

"Five." It came out a harsh whisper, and he cleared his throat, tried again. "Alfie would be ten now."

"Alfie?" Her whole face transformed when she smiled. "I love his name."

"He was named after my father: Alphington Goddard Brook-Chatfield. Though I called him Alfie, to my mother's enormous dismay. Dilys gave him the nickname; she'd been with him from birth. And—" He stopped, momentarily, then said steadily, "at the end as well. They drowned, you see. My wife, too."

Very delicately, Olivia slipped an arm around his neck. Then she let go altogether and stepped onto his branch. Quin felt a moment of panic, but the limb was stout. And she was close against him, clouding his mind. "I'm so sorry," she whispered.

"Right," he said, awkward as always. He should know what to say, he thought, frustrated.

Her mouth feathered over his. "Rupert sees his father every Thursday from two to three o'clock. I have the feeling that you saw Alfie more often than once a week."

"I couldn't stay away," Quin said, leaning back against the trunk again, one arm around her waist, the other holding tightly to a branch over their heads. "From the moment I saw him . . . I couldn't stay away."

She opened her mouth, but he silenced her with a swift kiss. "Don't tell me he's in a better place," he said, knowing his voice was stony. "Or that I was lucky to have known him as long as I did. Or that he's an angel. Or that I will meet him again when I cross the Pearly Gates."

"Is there ever a right thing to say?"

Quin thought about it. "Take me now?"

She laughed, and her laughter smoothed the jagged edges of his grief. "Nice and short. I won't say anything." She cupped her hands around his face and pressed a kiss on his lips that was like all the condolences he'd ever received in his life rolled into one.

He couldn't even speak after.

Her fingers swept up and into his hair, shaking free his ribbon. "Was your hair always white in front, or did it happen from grief?"

"Always there," he said. "I must have been one of the strangest-looking babies ever born in Kent."

Her fingers felt possessive of him, stroking through

his hair as if she'd owned him. Though that was impossible.

He cleared his throat. "I know that you're marrying the marquess." He felt as if his fingers were burning merely because they were touching her back.

She went still. She didn't move, but he felt as if she was about to step backward, so he tightened his grip. "Olivia! We're in a tree."

"We should climb down," she stated.

"One moment. If you weren't marrying that marquess," he whispered into her ear, "I'd change places with you."

"What?"

"I'd put you against the trunk. I'd—"

"Don't say it!" she squeaked. "I'm not some sort of acrobat who could . . ."

"Could what?"

"Well. You know."

"Is this the woman who almost told the entire table a limerick about a young lady who was particularly nimble with a *needle*?" He could feel laughter in his chest. It was unfamiliar, a bit intoxicating.

"Limericks are just extended jests. I memorize them because they make my mother so very enraged, and that allows me to maintain a small sense of self-possession. Now, could we *please* get down from this tree? I might as well add that my mother would explode if she could see me now."

"So would mine," Quin said comfortably, allowing his hand to drift down her back.

"Don't!" she ordered.

He stopped, his hand hovering just at the top of a magnificent curve. "Please?" His voice had a husky quality that would have embarrassed him on the ground, but who felt embarrassment up in a tree? He slipped his lips across her cheek, nipped her ear. "Olivia Lytton, I think you will always be my favorite tree-climbing companion."

"I expect I'm your only tree-climbing companion," she replied, giving him a mock scowl. "And now I am going to return to terra firma."

"Wait! I'm going down first." He swung down to the branch below. Then he looked up, feeling a wicked curl of anticipation in his stomach. When she didn't move, he bent backwards so he could see her face.

"You're planning to look at my legs, aren't you?"

"I love your legs," he said with perfect truth. "And if I didn't look at them I would be remiss in my duty, which in this case is to keep you from being injured."

She snorted, and then—much faster than he could have anticipated—pivoted, swung down, and alit beside him. The branch bounced and he instinctively reached out to steady her, but in so doing he lost his own balance and crashed through two layers of branches, landing hard on the ground.

The wind was knocked clean out of him, and the pain that resulted was spectacular. Black dots swam before his closed eyelids, and he couldn't seem to get air into his lungs at all.

"Oh, dear Lord!" he heard, before he could even see again. "Oh, Quin, oh, Quin, please don't be dead. Why did I do that?" Olivia was down from the tree. "Please be breathing . . . You're breathing!"

He *was* breathing. He was sure of it because every inhalation hurt like . . . a series of curse words crashed through his mind and only barely avoided escaping his mouth.

He felt Olivia patting him all over his chest. Although

pain likely impaired his mental acuity, Quin made an instant decision to keep his eyes closed. No man in his right mind would interrupt a woman on a mission. At least, this mission. He'd rather stop breathing than discourage her.

"I don't feel any broken ribs," she muttered to herself, patting even more firmly.

That could be because she had moved down to patting his abdomen, where he was fairly sure there were no ribs, but he wasn't complaining. Her hands hesitated for a moment, and then she very quickly, very lightly, gave him some pats below his abdomen.

A groan erupted from his lips before he could stop himself, and he grimaced. He wasn't used to being so undisciplined. He had always been in complete control of all his physical reactions, even with Evangeline, his own wife.

"Oh, Lord," Olivia cried again. "I'm going to fetch Justin. Please hold on! I'm afraid that you've broken something. I hope it isn't your back. I'll never forgive myself!"

The ragged sound of her voice made him open his eyes and snatch her arm just before she sprang to her feet. "I'm all right," he grunted. "Just give me a moment."

"I'm sorry!" Olivia said, her voice cracking. "It was so stupid of me, Quin. I never thought. That's how I always get down from the tree outside my bedroom. I just swing down fast and then find my feet."

"You climb out of your bedroom window?" He was forcing air into his lungs now and realizing that although his body ached, nothing felt as if it was broken.

"The tree is the only way one can leave my house without my mother knowing," she said. "Can you move your toes? I've heard that if a person can't move his toes, it's a terrible sign. I can see you moving other places, but . . ."

He raised his head, wincing. She was looking toward his feet, and therefore toward that part of him which was stirring. Damn well leaping out of his breeches. "My toes can move," he said, sitting up fast to block the view. His head spun.

Olivia didn't look as if she even recognized what she saw in the area of his breeches. It really wasn't clear to him whether she was merely skilled at flirtation, or more experienced.

Evangeline had not been a virgin when she came to his bed. He'd been surprised at the time, but when he got to know her better, he understood. Evangeline didn't have a voracious sexual desire, but she did have a voracious wish to be wanted, a longing so deep that no one man could have satisfied her.

His head was pounding, but even so, he could smell Olivia, some delicate, sweet scent that was hers, and hers alone. The scent was like bottled temptation. Like *need*.

Just having her kneeling beside him made him feel reckless. Even now, his body bruised and his head seemingly clamped in a vise, he wanted nothing more than to topple her backwards and then crawl on top of her.

And take her.

He groaned again at the thought.

"I'm going to fetch Justin," Olivia cried, jumping to her feet. "You're in pain. He can carry you to the pony cart."

"No!" Quin almost laughed at the idea of his slender cousin somehow managing to drag him along the ridge. "I can get up." And he did, bones protesting, muscles screaming. "It wasn't a long drop," he said aloud, as if telling himself would make it true. "And the branches surely slowed my fall."

"Nonsense," Olivia said crossly. "You could have been killed. You never should have climbed that tree after me. You're obviously too—" She stopped.

"Too old?" He gave her a scowl and started walking, slowly and painfully. He could tell already that he would be fine. But damn it, he really was too old to be climbing trees.

"Yes," she said baldly. "You are too old." Then she added, "How old are you?"

"Thirty-two," he said. "But at the moment I feel as if I were sixty-three."

"How many years ago did you lose Alfie?"

He didn't look at her, just walked. "It will be five years in October."

"You married quite young."

"Yes." But she seemed to be waiting, and words flowed from somewhere, so he said them. "I had just come back from France and Germany, and I went to London for my first season. It was Evangeline's first season as well. I didn't meet her the first two months, but as soon as I saw her . . ."

"Love at first sight?" she suggested.

"Something like that." He had never thought he was capable of love. But he had certainly been capable of fascination. Not to mention obsession.

Justin was loping toward them. "Lady Cecily wants to go home!" he shouted. "You'd better walk faster, Quin. She's as cross as a teakettle on the boil."

Olivia gave a little moan and started trotting toward the cart.

But Quin had lived through a thousand of his aunt's tempests, and he was in no condition to move faster. He just kept walking, thinking about what it meant to fall in love at first sight.

He knew that particular capacity was burned out of him, or perhaps it just wasn't part of his character. He really couldn't imagine anyone in his immediate family—other than Justin—experiencing such an emotion. Still, he couldn't help but wish that he'd met Olivia instead of Evangeline. Olivia was the kind of woman one could fall in love with, even at first sight.

Unless one had a heart like a withered turnip, which was about the condition of his.

Fifteen

"Turdy-fancy-nasty-paty-lousy-fartical rogue!"

So you flew a kite and then you climbed a *tree?*"
Georgiana's brow furrowed. "It sounds most peculiar to me." They had retreated to her bedchamber after
the evening meal.

"The kite was stuck in the tree," Olivia explained.

Georgiana put down her cup of tea. "When are you
going to grow up, Olivia?" Her tone was uncharacteristically sharp.

Olivia felt a pucker of hurt. "I consider myself to be
grown up."

"You climb trees," Georgiana said, counting off the
fingers on her left hand. "You think it's amusing to
insult a duchess. You bring Lucy into the house when
you know that you could simply put her in the stables;
Rupert would never be the wiser. You jest about with
Lord Justin as if you and he were the same age—and he
is a very young sixteen."

"I could not lie to Rupert about Lucy," Olivia said, seizing on the easiest of her sister's points to defend.

Georgiana shrugged. "Do you think that the whole table didn't hear you and Lord Justin laughing this evening? How do you think we felt, trying to have a serious conversation when all you care about is funning? The duchess said to Lady Sibblethorp that she felt as if she should take the nursery furniture out of Holland covers. I was humiliated."

"I'm sorry if I interrupted your conversation," Olivia said. Her voice was stiff, despite herself. "I truly am, Georgie. I didn't mean to. Justin was making up more silly insults and I couldn't help but laugh."

"You could," her sister said stonily. "We could all hear you, and even the duke couldn't help but listen. That long one you and Justin came up with . . . what was it?"

"Turdy-fancy-nasty-paty-lousy-fartical rogue."

"Exactly! *Turdy*? *Fartical*? How could you, Olivia? Don't you care for me in the slightest?"

"Of course I care for you! I didn't label you, nor the duke, *turdy*. Nor even the supercilious author of *The Mirror of Compliments*. We were just funning!"

"You're always funning," Georgiana snapped, picking up her teacup again with such a sharp, angry movement that tea slopped onto her saucer. "I can't manage this with you carrying on!"

"Can't manage what?" Olivia asked. Part of her wanted to snap back that she had avoided adult conversation in an effort to convince the duke that she was so uninterested in him that she'd rather converse with Justin.

But another part of her, the sisterly part, took a good look at Georgiana and saw the pinched, miserable look that her sister often had after a long night of sitting with the dowagers. She knelt next to her chair. "What's the matter, Georgie? I see I've been unbearably gauche. If I promise to make nothing but distinguished and righteously tedious comments for the rest of our visit, will you be happier?"

"It's not working," Georgiana replied, her voice catching.

"What isn't? You don't think you could care for Sconce?"

"I could," her sister whispered. "I really could. He's thoughtful and sober and everything I honor in a gentleman."

Olivia slid her hand over her sister's, which was clenched around the fragile bone china. "You're going to break the cup."

Georgiana looked down numbly and then put it away from her.

"Tell me what isn't working? I wasn't jesting with Justin the entire time, you know. I kept an eye on you and Sconce, and you seemed to be having an involved discussion about science. The nature of light, wasn't it?"

Georgiana looked up. "It was fascinating." But then she stopped.

"Well, that's a wonderful point of concurrence between you," Olivia prompted. "The sort of shared interest that will make a marriage long and vital. Just look at our parents."

"What about them?"

"They have always had one shared passion: the duchification of their two daughters. I wouldn't say they've been particularly successful at it in my case, but they certainly managed to turn you into a model of good breeding. After you marry Sconce, they'll have two duchesses for daughters. I expect any sacrifices they made will be thought worth it."

Georgiana nodded. "I think that, too. That is, I believe I would always be interested in what His Grace was investigating, whether scientific or mathematical. And he seemed interested in my ideas about chemistry as well. I don't think he was merely being polite."

"It's my distinct impression that Sconce is virtually incapable of prevarication," Olivia put in.

"Well, then, so he is interested in my potions. He even said that if I could give him the recipe for arthritis liniment, he'd like to have it made up for his head gardener. I gather the man is terribly bothered by years of being out in the damp."

"That's wonderful," Olivia said, wondering if her tone sounded hollow. "Splendid! And no one deserves it as much as you do, Georgie. So why aren't you simply ignoring your silly twit of a sister and chatting away with the handsome duke?"

"Do you think he's handsome?"

Olivia blinked. "There's no question. I think he's—" She snatched back the words. The last thing she wanted to do was tell her sister that she'd never seen, even imagined, a man as beautiful as Quin. "His aspect is more than tolerable."

"Don't you think his hair is rather odd?"

"No," Olivia said, thinking of the way it slid through her hands like silk, black and white together like the dual sides of life, darkness and light, good and evil, temptation and temperance. Mostly temptation.

"Well, I do. Do you suppose that if I mixed a dye myself he would allow it to be colored? Do you remember the zebra that came through in that travelling fair, Olivia? Sconce reminds me of that creature."

"Yes, I do, and the duke doesn't look in the slightest like a zebra. And no, he would never dye his hair. I don't think he's the sort of man who believes in deception. Or even knows how to engage in it." Olivia wasn't quite sure why she was so certain of this, but she was.

"I didn't think he would."

"What isn't working?" Olivia asked again, after a moment. "It sounds first-rate to me, Georgie. You have five times the *éclat* of poor Althea. Her maid was exactly right to describe her as a chicken in the rain. Sconce's mother couldn't possibly choose her over you."

"Dowagers always like me." Georgiana clearly did not view this as an advantage.

"And the duke likes you." Olivia consciously relaxed her jaw. She seemed to be developing a tendency to clench her teeth. "Yours would be a marriage made in heaven. Just think how happy Mother and Father will be."

"Do you really think so?" Georgie's face looked remarkably woebegone for a woman on the verge of betrothal to a duke. "It sounds possible now that we're talking about it, but when we were at the table, I found myself so angry at you."

"Why? That's what I don't understand, Georgie love. I've always been a bumptious fool compared to you, though I promise that I will be as hoity-toity as the best of them from now on. Why on earth were you even looking down the table at Justin and me?"

"Because *he* was."

Olivia cleared her throat. "*He* being the duke?"

"Yes." Georgiana's fingers were twisting in her lap. "When you laugh, he looks at you. Every time. I could not help but notice."

"I'm so sorry, Georgie. It's my stupid belly laugh, as Mother used to call it. It drove her mad as well. I'll be better tomorrow, I promise." Shame beat a rapid tattoo in her breast, but it was nothing she wasn't used to. "I didn't realize I had appalled the entire company."

"You don't understand," her sister said, staring at her entwined fingers. "You sit at the end of the table and we all can't help it, we look at you. It makes me feel like a paper doll."

Olivia frowned. "What do you mean?"

"Pale." Georgiana paused, and added, "Fragile and powerless."

"That is absurd! Just tell me what you want me to do, and I will. I don't need to make jokes. What else am I doing wrong?"

"You don't follow my point. When you laugh . . . everyone laughs."

"You must be daft. If you saw the dowager break a smile, let alone a laugh, I must have missed it. And as for your duke, Sconce has many virtues, but I wouldn't say that a gift for easy laughter is one of them."

Georgiana just shook her head. "The duke does know how to laugh. He's rather restrained about it. But I can see his eyes change when *you* laugh."

"Nonsense." Olivia said it stoutly, pretending she hadn't noticed the same thing.

But her sister reached out and tugged a lock of her hair. "You have a wonderful laugh, Olivia. I've always thought that was one of the saddest things about Mother and Father. They were so busy trying to make you into a duchess that they never laughed with you."

Olivia felt tears sting her eyes. "Oh, Georgie. I think that's the nicest thing you ever said to me."

"Your laugh has so much joy in it. If you ask me, Sconce is fascinated by you for that reason."

Anxious remorse crept up Olivia's backbone. She scrambled to her feet and turned around, busying herself with pouring another cup of tea. Her hands shook a little. "Of course that's not true, Georgie. You mustn't be absurd. I was laughing like a hyena, and the poor man probably couldn't hear himself speak over the noise." She put in three spoonfuls of sugar before realizing what she'd done.

She sat back down opposite her sister and stirred her tea. "Men aren't fascinated by ribald wit, Georgie."

"I suppose not. But anyone could see he's attracted to you."

"I'm a loud, fat woman who's betrothed to someone else," Olivia said flatly. "You misinterpret his attention because you love me."

"You are not fat! You're a peach, remember?"

"The truth is that I don't mind so much. You are a beautiful, willowy person, and I'm not. Rupert doesn't care at all."

Georgiana opened her mouth to argue, but Olivia held up her hand. "You're making far too much of the fact that the duke has glanced in my direction once or twice. From now on I'm going to act like the most top-lofty aristocrat of them all, so there will be nothing to perturb the ducal glow that surrounds our table."

Her sister smiled reluctantly. "I expect you're probably right. Given the loss of his wife and son, the poor man has forgotten how to have fun, if he ever knew. That's why he looks to you when you laugh."

Olivia only trusted herself to nod again. Some stubborn, stupid part of her wanted to howl, scream that Quin was *hers*. Which was ridiculous. She knew perfectly well that she couldn't leave Rupert. And Quin was her darling sister's best chance to become the aristocrat she was meant to be.

"What will you wear to the ball tomorrow?"

"I think the blue silk with Chantilly lace."

"Ah," Olivia teased. "The big weapons are coming out."

"I have the strangest feeling that Sconce's mother is throwing this ball as some sort of test," her sister said. "Isn't that odd? She seems to be interrogating both me and Althea, as if she were comparing our answers to an approved list."

Olivia shrugged. "You will triumph, in that case. What was our childhood, if not a series of tests?"

Her sister's brow pleated. "Do you really feel that way? And don't shrug again!"

"Yes."

"I suppose I see your point."

"Everything we were scolded for, or celebrated for, was directed at just one thing," Olivia said. "Becoming duchesses."

"I can see why you're bitter."

"You can?"

"Because you never passed a single test!" her twin said, hooting with laughter and running round the sofa as Olivia dashed after her, brandishing a napkin.

Sixteen

Various Anxieties Related to Children and Canines, but Not to Canapés

Whenever the Dowager Duchess of Sconce announced a ball—even a smallish affair—plans changed at all the great houses within a forty-mile radius. No one who claimed gentry status or higher would even consider missing such an occasion, unless it were for their mother's funeral.

And for some, even that would be a distinct wrench.

It wasn't that a Sconce ball was especially fashionable. Her Grace never bothered to import two hundred lemon trees heavy with fruit, or blanket the ballroom with orchids, or even send to Gunter's for specially made ices.

Rather, she followed the prescribed routine of the duchesses who had come before her: one ancestor had hosted King Henry VIII on two different occasions, greeting two different wives, and another had welcomed Queen Elizabeth three times.

To wit: The ballroom was scrubbed and polished to a fare-thee-well, a smallish orchestra was hired, a reasonable amount of food was ordered, and a great deal of excellent wine was brought up from the cellars.

And that was that.

The rest would take care of itself, to the dowager's mind, and it always did. There was nothing more pitiable than the sight of an anxious hostess.

As was her custom, in the early evening in question she presided over a small meal, to which were invited those guests who would stay at Littlebourne overnight, having traveled a goodly distance. Following the meal, the assembled guests were asked to proceed to the music room. Some time remained before the ball was to begin, and Her Grace had judged this interval an opportune time to address another item on her suitability inventory.

To this end, she issued a command, faintly disguised as an invitation. "I believe we should all be grateful if the young ladies among us would give us some light entertainment."

Lady Althea and Miss Georgiana immediately rose, as did the two Miss Barrys. (The Barrys lived on the other side of the county and were all very well in their way, but not eligible as daughters-in-law as a consequence of the unfortunate existence of an inebriate great-uncle. One never knew when that bad strain might pop up in the blood.) Her Grace positioned herself on a settee with a clear view to the instruments, instructing her friend Mary, Lady Voltore, to sit with her.

The Miss Barrys conducted themselves tunefully. Lady Althea sang very prettily. Miss Georgiana not only sang very well—a piece from an opera and then a light ballad—but she also accompanied herself on the harpsichord. It was eminently clear that Miss Georgiana Lytton would be an entirely commendable Duchess of Sconce. The dowager never permitted herself an excess of emotion, but she was inwardly aware that if she confessed to a weakness, it was her only son. The pain he had suffered after his first marriage was unacceptable.

"Your Grace?"

She looked up to find the Miss Barrys curtsying before her. "Yes?"

"Your Grace," one of them said, rather breathlessly, "would you be so kind as to allow Lord Justin to sing something for the assembled company?"

The other one dropped another curtsy. "Everyone would love it, we are sure."

The dowager allowed one eyebrow to arch. Yes, she had made the right decision when she dismissed the Barrys from her list of possible duchesses. "If Lord Justin would agree, I'm sure I have no objection," she said rather frostily.

Naturally, her nephew didn't take a hint from her tone, but leapt up in an unbecoming manner to sit at the pianoforte. It wasn't proper, to her mind. Ladies sang and played musical instruments. The only men who sang, let alone played, were of the professional sort, with whom one did not associate.

In fact, Justin was unsatisfactory in more than one way. This evening, for example, he was wearing purple. To her mind, wearing purple was like singing: gentlemen one knew simply didn't do it. But there was her own nephew (if by marriage), wearing the color of lilacs, with dove-gray lace at the cuffs, which made it worse. Vulgar was the word for it. The late duke would turn in his grave if he could see such a garment on a family member, half-French or not.

And why on earth were all those girls clustering around the pianoforte as if they were minnows nibbling on a crust of bread?

She shushed Lady Voltore, who was rambling on about a new type of rose, and turned her attention back to her nephew and his flock of admirers.

"What's that he's singing?" Mary bellowed. She was more than a little deaf. "It doesn't sound like 'Greensleeves.' I like it when they sing 'Greensleeves.' Tell him to play it, will you, Amaryllis?"

The dowager tolerated being on a first-name basis with Lady Voltore only because they had known each other since they were two years of age. "I cannot simply tell him to sing that," she said now. "I can request it, if you wish."

"Don't be absurd, Amaryllis. You paid for the fellow; you might as well get your money out of him." Mary had always been a touch crass, to put it charitably.

"I didn't pay for him," she said reluctantly. "He's a relative."

"Decorative? Yes, I'd say so. Does he work for the circus? I don't think I'd invite the circus into my house if I were you."

The dowager contented herself with giving Mary a look.

"I don't know where you hired that boy, but I have to say, I rather like him. Nice song. Nice face." Mary had a quite ribald chuckle. "Not so old but that I can appreciate a face. Why, he almost looks like a gentleman, barring that coat, of course. Makes him look like an organ-grinder's monkey."

Justin was surrounded by a positive flowerbed of young girls. One Barry hovered at each elbow, and Lady Althea was hanging over his shoulder.

The dowager duchess cocked her ear and listened for a moment. "*She was his sun,*" Justin crooned. "*She was his earth.*" Well, that sounded foolishly innocuous enough. But given that Lady Althea had been granted the incalculable honor of even being considered for the title of Duchess of Sconce, the least she could do was to behave in a dignified manner. The truth was that Althea was dizzy as a doorknocker, and she'd never make Tarquin happy.

Justin had started a new song, something about love. Love! Love was a destructive, disagreeable thing, to her mind. Just look what it had done to Tarquin: almost torn the poor boy to pieces.

She turned away, noting with approval that Miss Georgiana was sitting beside an elderly aunt on the late duke's side, engaging in a quiet conversation. She showed no signs of joining the throng around the piano, which said a great deal for her common sense.

And Tarquin?

It took a moment, but she managed to find her son. He was seated in a corner, and appeared to be watching Miss Lytton, who was sitting in another corner talking to the Bishop of Ramsgate. This evening Olivia Lytton looked the very picture of the future Duchess of Canterwick, the only possible objection being that her neckline was a bit daring.

The dowager squinted until she could see more clearly. The bishop, that old goat, seemed to be enjoying the view afforded by Miss Lytton's *embonpoint*.

But it was Tarquin whose face caught her eye. The expression on his face was somehow familiar. In fact, she had seen that look before, and she had hoped never to see it again. Before she even realized it, she was halfway out of her chair.

But she eased back.

It could not have gone very far. In fact, thinking carefully over the last few days, the dowager was quite certain that the relationship, if one could call it that, couldn't be said to exist. At least, not to Miss Lytton. That was important. Miss Lytton was already betrothed to a marquess. What's more, she seemed to be loyal to the poor fool.

Furthermore, Canterwick himself had insinuated to her that Miss Lytton might be carrying the heir to his dukedom.

Of course, that didn't mean that Olivia Lytton wouldn't throw over her fiancé in a moment if she got wind of the idea that she could exchange the marquess for a duke with a full twelve eggs to the dozen.

The dowager's fingers tightened on the arms of her chair. Miss Lytton was almost certainly another Evangeline.

Possibly carrying the duke's heir, even though the boy was only eighteen and as simple as they come, or so she'd heard. And now she was flirting with a bishop! Incredible.

"I must say, you have an ugly little dog, Amaryllis," Mary said, interrupting her thoughts.

"I don't own a canine!" Her irritation with Miss Lytton colored her voice.

"Whose is it, then?"

With a sense of misgiving, the dowager followed the direction of Mary's lorgnette. That odd dog belonging to Miss Lytton—one could hardly call it a canine, given its size and untidiness—was sitting at her skirts. Sitting with its horrid little paw on her slipper. Again!

For a moment she simply stared at the dog, aghast.

"Not bad in its own way," Mary said. "And it certainly adores you. Reminds me of the hunting dogs my husband used to have. They looked at him in just that way."

"I hate dogs. Take it off, if you please."

Mary gave that odd cackle of laughter that made her sound like a demented witch. "Nonsense, Amaryllis! At our age, we can't afford to coddle that sort of ridiculousness."

"I loathe animals with paws." It was a statement of fact, though she couldn't help noticing that this one seemed to have rather sweet eyes.

"You should give that up," Mary said. "Makes you look like a fool. You're too old to carry on like a green girl." And with that shot, she got to her feet, her knees creaking, and hobbled off.

The dog was an ugly little thing, with almost no fur and a distinct scar on its eyelid. Its nose was longer than any dog's nose needed to be. She glared at it and the dog lay down at her feet.

"There's nothing foolish about disliking paws," she said aloud. But she couldn't help frowning at the tiny black one that was inching close to her slipper again. Logically . . .

She pushed the thought away and looked back at Tarquin. Catching his eye, she gave a small but imperial wave. A moment later her son bowed before her. "Mother?" He had always obeyed her, even when he was a little boy. Too solemn, she'd thought at the time. He had inherited the title too young. But then he had eased into his duties so seamlessly that it felt as though Tarquin had always been the duke.

"I should like you to take Miss Georgiana for a turn

around the gardens," she stated. "She has been talking to Lady Augustina for a half hour now, which is sufficiently charitable for one night. You have time before the festivities will commence."

Tarquin bowed, silent as ever, and walked away. But his mother watched him and wondered.

Georgiana Lytton was the perfect wife for her son. She felt it to the depth of her bones. Georgiana was no namby-pamby miss, following rules just because they were there. She had a deep, ladylike decency about her. She would understand why *The Mirror of Compliments* had to be written: because civilization was the only thing that stood between mankind and raw pain.

The kind of pain that Evangeline had caused Tarquin. The dowager had written the book in the year after her son married his first wife, a tome born of desperation, sadness, and the conviction that if only ladies behaved like *ladies*, none of this grief would have to happen.

Yet the grief Evangeline had caused Tarquin when she leapt from his bed into those of strangers, neighbors, friends . . . that didn't even approach what he felt after she died. That foolish, foolish woman. Died and took little Alphington with her. She had honestly believed that Tarquin would never smile again.

There was no need for further tests. Georgiana was a perfect duchess. They could be betrothed within the day. For a moment she considered directing her son to issue a marriage proposal that very night, but then recalled that there were occasions when Tarquin— her mild, sober Tarquin—had dug in his heels. And given what she saw in his eyes while he watched Olivia Lytton, she needed to be very careful.

Tomorrow, she told herself, settling back into the settee. They could have this whole muddle solved tomorrow.

Seventeen

For Better, for Poorer, in Sickness and in Health

Georgiana was a very restful companion. They strolled to the bottom of the garden, where there was a little bench. Georgiana was as fascinated by the composition of light in terms of waves and particles as he was. It was a real pleasure to talk the question through.

Quin didn't even notice that it had grown a bit chilly until he inadvertently touched her arm and found it icy. "Miss Georgiana, you seem to be very cold. We should return to the house."

She ignored him. "I wonder whether it would influence the experiment if you slanted the paper that you are using to split the light into rainbows."

"What do you mean?"

"Well, if I understood you correctly, you are holding a card with a vertical slit up to the window."

He nodded.

"As the light strikes the slit, it divides into a rainbow, thereby demonstrating that light is made up of rays rather than particles. Though it is not clear to me why the rays evidence themselves merely because they went through a slit in paper."

"It may be because the rays bend as they go through. Though to be truthful, I'm not sure."

"What if the slit ran from corner to corner? Would the rays bend in the same fashion? What if the slit were parallel with the window frame rather than vertical? What happens then?"

He paused. "I don't know," he said finally. "But it's a very good point. I shall try that tomorrow." He put a hand under her chilly elbow and helped her to her feet. "I am growing cold as well."

Georgiana smiled up at him. "I didn't notice because our conversation had been so interesting." She took his arm and they began to walk back to the house. There was a contented silence between them. Quin was thinking furiously about the alignment of slits in relation to light, and Georgiana didn't seem to mind the quiet.

A patter of feet interrupted his thoughts, and he looked up just as Olivia burst around the curve in the path. He wasn't any good at describing such things, but her gown was made of a dull gold stuff covered in lace that went sideways. The lace was composed of little strings, thousands of little strings that dared a man to run his fingers around her.

The strings swayed when she ran. Just like that, his body went from chilled to hot. Heat sang to a pulse of blood raging through his body.

"Georgie!" Olivia said. "Your Grace." She dropped into a curtsy.

Georgiana's fingers tightened on his arm. "I'm sorry that you had to fetch me, Olivia. We were having a discussion about the scientific basis of light."

"Of course you were!" Olivia's smile was wide and utterly natural—until you looked at her eyes.

Or did he imagine that flash of possessiveness?

Quin deliberately put his other hand on top of Georgiana's fingers. "We were having such a fascinating conversation that regretfully I allowed your sister to grow quite chilled."

Georgiana glanced up at him, her eyes unreadable, and then back to her sister. "We are just returning to the house, Olivia. Thank you for coming to fetch me."

"I apologize for interrupting your conversation," Olivia said, her tone perfectly friendly. She fell back and walked at Georgiana's side.

"Did I hear you call your sister 'Georgie'?" Quin asked, looking across at her.

"Yes," Olivia said. "It's my pet name for her. Goodness, it is cold out here, isn't it? I can almost see my breath." She took a breath and huffed.

Georgiana laughed. "Don't be silly, Olivia! In order to condense the moisture in your breath sufficiently to be visible, it must be far colder outside than this."

Quin dimly registered Georgiana's response, but he couldn't find a way to bring words to his mouth. Whenever Olivia took a deep breath, her breasts strained against those delicate strings of lace. It seemed to him that a few of those strings were all that prevented her nipples from being exposed to every man in the ballroom.

A growl rose in his throat and he choked it back. "I like the name Georgie," he said. The words came with a husky intonation that sounded as if he meant something entirely different by them.

Georgiana—Georgie—looked up at him with a surprised smile. And Olivia blinked and looked away.

They both heard his voice, and they both misunderstood.

"Well," he said briskly, "I suggest that we go straight to the library and bake ourselves before the fireplace before we join everyone in the ballroom."

"Oh, I'm not cold at all," Olivia said lightly. "I'll warm up dancing." They were approaching the short set of stairs that led to the marble terrace. The very idea of Olivia in the arms of another man went through him like a sword.

It only took one smooth motion. He politely ushered Georgiana onto a step before him, slipped to the side, and stepped forward quite precisely so that his foot descended on the train of her gown, pinning her to the stair. Then he threw his weight forward, appearing to trip.

The scientist in him was quite satisfied by the prolonged ripping sound that resulted.

Swallowing a smile, he flowed into a smooth series of apologies—surprisingly fluent, for him. Georgiana remained calm, although many a lady would have been in hysterics. The seam at the waist of her gown had separated and now gaped open, revealing her chemise.

"I'll walk behind you," Olivia said to her sister. "We only have to make our way through the room and then straight up the stairs."

"Nonsense," Quin said. "I did the damage and I'll carry you to your chamber. Miss Georgiana, you have turned your ankle." He picked her up and discovered she weighed almost nothing. It was like picking up a bird, all hollow bones and feathers.

Georgiana didn't squeal, but she sucked in an anxious breath. "Olivia, you'll have to accompany us," Quin said, over his shoulder. "I can carry your sister upstairs, but I need you with me as chaperone."

Without waiting for an answer, he walked through the open doors. A rising spiral of conversation greeted them as people inquired what mishap had felled Georgiana.

"It's just a turned ankle," Olivia kept saying, walking just in front of them.

"I'm perfectly fine," Georgiana said, her voice as tranquil as ever. "In fact, I think I shall rest briefly and then return to the ballroom."

"I shall deliver you to your maid," Quin announced, making sure all in the near vicinity heard him. "You may, of course, make up your own mind about whether you feel it advisable to return. One wouldn't want to see you dance on an injured ankle, Miss Georgiana."

This flummery got them to the bottom of the stairs. Quin started climbing, thinking about the difference between the sisters. Georgiana felt like a bundle of feathers in his arms, whereas the idea of holding Olivia like this . . . carrying her upstairs to the bedroom . . .

He walked faster. When they reached the top of the stairs, he moved to the side to allow Olivia to go before them.

As soon as they were inside Georgiana's bedchamber, she politely but firmly freed herself and dropped a perfectly calibrated curtsy. "I thank you very much for rescuing me, Your Grace."

"I am happy to be of service; after all, it was I who was responsible for your predicament. And I think we should be on a first-name basis," he said, picking up her hand and kissing it. "My intimates call me Quin."

There was an odd look to her eyes, one he couldn't interpret, not the way he could read Olivia's.

"May I call you Georgie? The name suits you."

She nodded. "I would be honored." Then she turned to her sister. "Olivia, I'll join you downstairs in a half hour or so. Thank you again, Your Grace."

"My name is *Quin*," he insisted.

She really was a somber young woman; her smile came nowhere near her eyes. "Of course," she agreed. Then she closed the door in their faces.

Olivia stared, frowning, at the door, but Quin didn't give a damn about what Georgiana was feeling or thinking. He gave one swift look about and found to his deep satisfaction that there was no one within sight, and no one could see them from below. His hand closed on Olivia's like a vise and he pulled her down the corridor, flung open the door to his bedchamber, and hauled her inside like a recalcitrant child.

"Just what do you think you're doing?" she demanded in a harsh whisper.

Quin not only knew exactly what he was thinking, but he knew what she was thinking, too. She could protest all she wished, but he had learned to read her eyes.

Without a word he closed the door and backed her against it, and bent his head to her mouth, spurring the wild, searing passion that always flared between them.

"Quin," she gasped, but he was tilting her head to the side, unable to think, his entire body just a fierce ball of *want*. He throbbed to touch her, to have her, to be inside her.

"I need you," he said haltingly. He shaped his hands around her bottom and pulled her up, closer to him, molding her luscious body to his. "Olivia!" Her name came out low and deep, like a plea or a prayer. She was on tiptoes, kissing him back, and still it wasn't enough.

With a smooth swirl he plucked her from her place

against the door and placed her on his bed. He lowered himself on top of her slowly, making sure that every inch of him was against her softness, watching her to see that she understood what he was doing.

She made a sweet, inarticulate sound, more like a gasp, but she didn't say a word. Then she was kissing him too, and her body was soft under his muscled thighs, her fingers locked in his hair.

They stayed there, not moving much, for long minutes. It wasn't kissing the way Quin ever thought of kissing. He thought he knew exactly what a kiss was: a caress of the lips that might or might not involve an exploration of the recipient's mouth by the giver's tongue.

None of that made any sense compared to this. This was an inferno and a conversation, all at once. He felt every touch with double ferocity: the way her fingers caressed his hair and then clenched almost painfully if he nudged forward with his hips. Her breath, sweet and smelling of tea and lemons. The little sounds she made in the back of her throat, urging him on, telling him without words that—

He reared up, looking down at her, running a possessive hand down her neck, her shoulders, trailing onto her breast. He felt her shudder under his touch.

She opened her mouth, about to speak, so he put a finger across her lips. The tip of her tongue stole out and touched his finger. He pressed back, just a little, allowed his finger to slip through soft lips into liquid warmth. The groan was torn from his chest, reverberated through his entire body.

It crystallized his thoughts.

"I will not marry Georgiana." It was blunt because he wasn't good at words, even though he was a little more fluent around Olivia. Somehow, he could talk to her.

Her eyes flew open and her whole body went rigid. "Oh, God, I'm the worst sister in the world. Let me up!"

He shook his head, dragging his thumb along the curve of her jaw. "Your skin is beautiful."

"I feel sick to my stomach," she said, fierce and low. "And you—you're seducing me!"

"Yes."

"Stop it. And let me up!"

Reluctantly, he rolled to the side but kept his arm across her body. "I can't marry her, and it has nothing to do with you."

"Liar." She glared at him, and he took a moment to savor it. Olivia was like a flame.

"Actually, I never lie."

"You're lying now. If you had never met me, you would have married Georgie and been happy as two bedbugs in a mattress or, more to the point, two alchemists in a laboratory."

"I can't know for certain, of course, but I don't think so. It wasn't until my mother brought Lady Althea and Miss Georgiana here that I realized I could not simply marry whomever she chose for me."

"She chose rightly," Olivia said, stubborn as ever. "You're perfect for each other. This thing between us is nothing more than a forest fire, as you described it. Temporary. It will burn itself out. Let me rise, please."

"I don't believe that I know what love is, at least the sort that people talk about between men and women. But I would venture to say that some people characterize the feeling I had for Evangeline as love. I think *care about* is a more accurate description, especially if one understands the phrase to include an abiding desire."

She stilled. Raised a hand, touched his cheek. "I'm sorry."

"It wasn't a good marriage. She wasn't in love with me, and she had a deep urge to be with other men. It was problematic. But I cared about her, even when she made me a cuckold and finally left me. I couldn't stop. Stupid, I know."

Olivia leaned over and gave him a kiss that clung to his lips. "Actually, you should be proud of your loyalty. You are wonderful, Quin."

"No, I'm quite foolish. I should have stopped myself. Somehow."

"I don't think anyone has the ability to choose whether or not to fall in love."

"Exactly," he said with deep satisfaction. "I agree with you. When I told you that I don't lie, I meant it."

She shook her head. "I must return downstairs in case Georgie decides to rejoin the ball."

"I am telling you something." He tried to remember what it was, but it felt as if his entire body was focused on the plump, sweet curves of her lips.

"You never lie," she said, sitting up and breaking their eye contact. "I accept that."

"I'm not good at . . . interpreting complex statements."

She pulled up her knees, wound her arms around them, and then rested her chin on them, looking at him curiously. "And yet you're the most intelligent person I've ever met."

"Only because you haven't been to university."

She gave a deep chuckle. "Most people would prevaricate on hearing that compliment, and insist that I was exaggerating."

"As I said, I don't lie. The possibility is extremely good that I am the most intelligent person you've met. But that doesn't mean I'm the wisest. Witness the fact that I cared so deeply for Evangeline."

"A fact that proves you human."

"It's a miserable way to achieve humanity," he said wryly. "My point is that I couldn't say those vows without meaning them."

"Vows?" Her eyes changed. "Oh. The marriage vows."

"'To have and to hold,'" he quoted. "'To love and to cherish, till death us do part.'"

She swallowed. "Poor Evangeline."

"She's in the past now." And he meant that. "But I can't say those words to just anyone. They mean a great deal to me. They're powerful."

"Even though Evangeline was not respectful of those vows?"

"Yes. Do you know how she died?"

Olivia hugged her knees more closely. "No."

"She was leaving me. She had decided to run away to France with her current lover, a scrap of absurdity named Sir Bartholomew Fopling."

Olivia choked.

"I'm not joking," he said. "Fopling was a most gifted man: he could sing in any number of languages, dance everything worth dancing, and his cravats were always pressed. At any rate, she and Fopling took Alfie with them." He stopped and cleared his throat. "They left for France even though a storm was brewing. They were warned not to embark, but Evangeline bribed the captain. She was terrified that I was following her, that I would catch her."

"Are you sure you wish to tell me this?"

"Why not? It's no more than your maid would tell you if you asked."

"And were you following her?"

"I almost killed my horse riding him hard, but I was too late. The devil of it is that I still dream of that pier.

I'd missed them, and the only thing I could see was the sea, boiling with whitecaps. The boat went down only a mile or two from shore."

There was a moment of silence. "I suppose," Olivia said slowly, "that a future duchess should not engage in profanity, especially with regard to the dead. So I would say, Quin, while avoiding curses, that your wife was an ass."

He could feel a twisted little smile on his lips. "It was a long time ago. Five years. Practically a lifetime."

"Nonsense," she said. "One never gets over the loss of a loved one. Especially a child."

There was no point in answering that comment. It was cruelly true. "At any rate, I can't marry Georgiana." Then he added, just so she understood: "Ever."

"I think you could grow to love her—or *care* about her, if you prefer that term."

"Evangeline was not faithful to me, but I was to her. I was so feverishly in lust with her that there were times when I doubted my own ability to maintain my self-control. Though, of course, I did."

A shadow crossed her eyes. "Evangeline threw away something that every woman in this kingdom would love to have. She didn't deserve it."

"Deserve it or not, she had it. When I carried your sister up those stairs, I didn't feel even a shadow of desire."

She frowned at him. "Georgie has a perfect figure. In fact, she's perfect in every way."

"It felt as if I were carrying a child up the stairs, all long legs and hair."

"She's *elegant*," Olivia stated. "I would kill to have her figure."

"Really?"

"Of course. I have always wished to look precisely like her. Though obviously, not enough to avoid food," she added.

"That's madness. You have everything she doesn't."

Olivia opened her mouth, ready to argue.

"*Everything* she hasn't."

She frowned at him.

"Including me."

Eighteen

Madness, in All Its Forms

Quin's last two words—spoken with the reasoned calm that characterized him—shook Olivia to her core. "What?" she whispered. "What are you saying?"

"I'm saying that I care about you. Embarrassingly, I seem to care about you more than I did Evangeline. It may be that I am mad." He paused, considering. "I don't perceive any other signs of mental weakness, though, so I am inclined to simply acknowledge this as a human weakness. I am reluctant to label it a failing."

She shook her head, dazed.

"It could be that I am merely the sort of man who is ruled by lust."

Olivia took a deep breath. "I am honored by what you said. I assure you that no woman dislikes being told she is an object of desire. But you must listen to me, Quin. I will not betray Rupert by leaving him while he is overseas, in battle. More to the point, I will *never* betray my sister. You sat out there in the garden with her for almost an hour. You carried her up the stairs. You courted her."

"I was no more courteous to her than I would be to any other young woman under my roof."

"Sitting on a bench for almost an hour? I can't envision you doing that with any of your other guests."

"Your sister is remarkably intelligent; we talked about science. It is a pleasure to converse with her. However, a forty-five-minute conversation does not require that I marry her."

"Put together with everything else, it means that she has a reasonable expectation of marrying you. And I will not, ever, stand in the way of her wish. If the two of you do not marry, for whatever reason, so be it. I will never have it be said that I stole her chosen husband."

She stood up. "I must pin up my hair—"

He came at her in a low, silent rush, a surge of power and speed. "Don't marry me," he said, holding her tightly.

"I won't!" But he heard the catch in her voice.

"Just don't pretend that you don't want to. That there is nothing between us that is far beyond what I shared with Evangeline, you with Montsurrey, or even you with your sister."

Olivia's heart pounded in her chest so loudly that she thought he must be able to hear it as well. "I don't think it matters."

"It doesn't matter?" he bellowed it. "What matters more than that? What?"

"Hush!" she said sharply. "I'll be forced to marry you if we're caught here, and I shan't forgive you for it."

He jerked her a touch closer, so that her body was

flattened against his. "You don't know what I mean because you have never lost someone. There is *nothing* that matters more, not science nor mathematical propositions, not my title and my lands. . . . Nothing."

"There's honor," she said, feeling pain arrow into her heart. "My honor. I can't betray my sister or Rupert."

Something changed in his eyes. "Your love is not so boundless as the sea, or so deep."

"I never said that I loved you at all, let alone to the tune of those metaphors," she said, keeping her voice steady. "I hardly know you."

His fingers tightened on her hips, as if he were going to argue with her. Olivia felt a quiver deep inside. He knew what she felt for him.

But he let go. "My mother has always said that I'm a hopeless fool when it comes to emotion. I rarely feel it, and when I do it's like a kind of madness."

Olivia shook out her skirts, avoiding his eyes. She had the same madness, though she couldn't say that. If she did . . . he would take her. She could see it in his eyes. He would bellow "Mine!" and summon the whole party to the room.

And she would have to live with wounding—and betraying—her own sister.

No.

"I am retiring to my chamber for a few moments, and then I'll return downstairs," she stated. "If you would be so kind as to return to the ball now, there is a chance that no one will notice that we were both missing."

He bowed and she walked past him, closing the door quietly behind her.

Olivia's pulse didn't slow until Norah had pinned up her hair again, and she'd walked back to her sister's room. "Georgie?"

Georgiana was sitting by the fireplace, reading a book, the very picture of serenity. "Has it been long enough that I can go back downstairs now?"

"I believe that you have rested your ankle sufficiently," Olivia said, managing a smile.

"You don't think that I must pretend to limp, do you?"

"No, of course not. You bathed your foot in vinegar and cool water—though naturally you won't be so indelicate as to mention the particulars—and it felt well immediately. Perhaps you shouldn't dance, though."

"That will not be a sacrifice. I don't like to dance." Georgiana got up and smoothed her hair before the glass.

"You don't like to dance?" Olivia asked, surprised. "I had no idea."

"I am discovering that there are aspects to being a duchess that I do not enjoy," her sister replied, turning about. "Dancing, for example. And I don't enjoy chatting about embroidery either, as with Althea's mother this afternoon. For two hours."

"*You* chatted," Olivia said. "I lapsed into something akin to a stupor."

"If there had been a coffin available, I would have flung myself into it."

Olivia laughed. "Georgie! You're not yourself."

"I think I am becoming myself." Georgiana didn't laugh. "In the garden, I talked with the duke about the composition of light."

Olivia's laughter dried up instantly. "Of course. And that was far more interesting than embroidery. Of course it was."

"It's not fair that I can't go to university," her sister replied, her eyes fierce as a falcon's with a string on its leg. "I could do that, Olivia. I could do it as well as he. Maybe better."

"Really?"

Her sister nodded, curtly. "I don't know anything . . . nearly as much. But it would just be a matter of study. Like learning to be a duchess, but so much more interesting!" It was a cry wrung from her soul.

Olivia stopped short. "Are you saying that you learned how to be a duchess only because that was the available subject of study?"

Georgiana walked past her, into the corridor. "You're always too emotional. We were given a task. We could do it badly or well. I chose to do it well. You allowed emotion to get in the way of achievement."

Olivia followed and caught her hand. "Georgie!"

"Yes?" Her sister's eyes were cool.

"Are you angry at me?"

At that, they softened. "No, not in the least. I'm angry about the fact that I was trained to be the wife of a duke. Even if I had been trained to be the wife of a scientist, it wouldn't be good enough."

"You want to *be* the scientist."

A jerky nod. "I enjoyed talking to the duke. But at the same time, I felt such resentment that I could have choked on it."

Olivia leaned forward, kissed her cheek. "You could study anything you wish, Georgie."

Her sister shrugged, an unrefined gesture that revealed more than words that she was on the verge of cracking under the strain.

"I mean it!" Olivia continued, closing the bedchamber door behind them. "What on earth do you need a university for? Everything is printed in books, and we can get whatever books you want to read."

"You mean, you and Rupert?"

"Exactly. And we could ask a professor to come from

Oxford, or Cambridge. We'll pay him to teach you anything you can't get from the books. You'll learn like lightning, Georgie."

"I could." Her voice rose. "I really could."

"After you marry Sconce, you can buy whatever books you wish, not to mention discussing the ideas with him. It hardly need be said that neither Rupert nor I can provide you with any sort of serious intellectual conversation."

Georgiana started down the corridor but paused. "I know I told you he was perfect, Olivia, but he's not. There's no spark. None."

"Perhaps, over time?" Olivia said, forcing the words out.

"I thought . . . I truly thought that when I met the ideal man I would feel something. A wish to be with him. Passion, love, whatever you want to call it. At first, I believed that's what I was experiencing with Sconce. I do like talking to him. But I don't wish to call him by that ridiculous short name of his, Quin."

"You don't like his name?"

Georgiana began walking down the stairway. "It sounds like a piece of fruit to me, a quince by any other name."

Olivia stared at her back, pushing away the liquid, joyful feeling of relief that was flooding her entire body.

"And even if his appearance wasn't a cross between a zebra and a quince," Georgiana said over her shoulder, "he doesn't look at me the way he looks at you."

"He doesn't . . . ." Olivia said weakly.

Georgiana turned around at the bottom of the stairs. "I'm not *stupid*," she pointed out, unnecessarily. "I may have wanted to marry Sconce before I came to know him better. But even if I did still wish to marry him, which I do not, I am not a bone you can throw to him simply because you feel too guilty to act on your own feelings."

"I don't think of you as a bone!"

Her sister's eyes sharpened. "If you want him, Olivia Lytton, *take him*. He's a duke, for goodness' sake. You have a chance to make Mother and yourself happy. Rupert will come back one of these days, and his brain won't be any more powerful than when he left this country. What on earth are you waiting for?"

"Rupert," Olivia said weakly. "I can't betray Rupert."

"You would betray Rupert if you gave Lucy to a passing tinker. Personally, I think it's unlikely that he would grieve for more than five minutes over the prospect of not marrying you."

"I thought . . ." Olivia's throat swelled. "I thought it would betray *you*."

Georgiana's smile was brilliant. "If I wanted him, I would have dueled you for him. Rapiers at dawn. But I don't."

Olivia snatched her into a hug, careful not to muss her hair, and said, "We'll dower you, Georgie. You know that."

"Yes," Georgiana said. She looked happier than she had in years as they walked in the door of the ballroom. "You had better do that. Because in case you're wondering, I am not going to step into your shoes and marry Rupert. I still feel queasy thinking about that scene in the library. I'd rather stay an old maid. If I can find enough books to read, I shall do just that."

"You can do whatever you wish," Olivia said, feverish heat racing over her body. "One of us sacrificed on the ducal altar is enough."

Georgiana broke into a merry peal of laughter that

made two gentlemen turn and look. "If you're sacrificing yourself, then we should all be so lucky."

Olivia felt her cheeks heating up. "I know . . ."

Her sister put a fleeting finger on her cheek. "You deserve it after all the kindnesses you've shown Rupert. We can find him a wife, you know. Not Althea, but someone with understanding and kindness."

"And enough intelligence to run the estate," Olivia said. "Do you really think . . ."

Georgiana grinned and then glanced to the side. "Dear me, it looks as if the duke is dancing with Annabel Trevelyan. Now *she* would love to become his duchess."

Olivia spun; heard her sister's chuckle; saw Quin leaning against the wall staring moodily at the dancers.

"He remains where he can see you," Georgiana said into her ear. "And if you walked through the room and into the library . . . he would follow."

"I wouldn't dare," Olivia said, her heart in her throat.

"Is this the bravest woman I know?" Georgiana scoffed. "The woman who entered Father's study with Rupert, knowing that the next few hours would include the most unpleasant experience any woman could endure? You have courage, Olivia. Use it."

Olivia took a deep breath. At that moment, Quin turned his head. Georgiana was right: he was checking to see where she was.

He loved her. Or rather, to put it his way, he *cared* about her.

Rather blindly, she walked deeper into the room, trailed by the sound of Georgiana's laughter. At just the right moment she looked at Quin and let an invitation speak through her eyes.

He straightened instantly and his eyes flared in response. So she moved on, weaving through the room, pausing to respond to greetings, extracting herself as soon as she could, declining to dance. It was like a game, the most thrilling game she had ever played.

Quin was surely behind her, following her. She would have wagered her life that he couldn't resist the look she'd given him. Power was intoxicating . . . it sang in her blood, made her knees unsteady.

At the other end of the ballroom she went straight to the door that led into the library, opened it, and walked through.

The room was quiet, empty except for a footman. The duchess did not believe that her guests should be given the opportunity for dalliance, and to that end, posted servants in each room.

Olivia nodded to him. "Roberts. Are you having a quiet night?"

The footman relaxed his rigid pose, recognizing her. "Three couples so far," he said, a grin splitting his face.

"Let me guess . . . the betting-book is in play?"

"For each room," he said. "Tuppence a room. I wagered five couples would try for this one."

The door behind her opened quietly. She didn't have to turn; the air changed when he was near.

"Roberts," Quin said. His deep voice sent shivers down her spine. "Her Grace doubtless has some use of you in the back of the house."

Roberts was too well trained to show even a flicker of curiosity. He bowed and left as quietly as Quin had entered.

Only then did Olivia turn.

He was magnificent: wide shoulders, appearing even larger in a dark blue superfine coat that brought out the green of his eyes.

The look in those eyes had her retreating a step. "Quin!" she squeaked, breathless, silly, like a girl of thirteen.

"You summoned me," he said, direct as always. "And here I am, Olivia. I hope you meant it, because I think I shall never be able to resist you."

She couldn't think what to say. He was so beautiful . . . lean and powerful and muscled. Even his hair was extraordinary.

Whereas she was plump and ordinary.

He closed the space between them in one stride. Having him so close just made the contrast between them even more obvious. This was impossible. He took her hands in his and raised them to his lips, sending another shiver down Olivia's spine.

"I'm fat," she blurted out.

"You are not fat. You're the most beautiful, voluptuous woman I know." His eyes moved down her body, deliberately, slowly, then back to her face. What she saw in them sent fire squirming through her stomach and lower.

"I want every inch of you," he said, growling it. "I want to fall on my knees and worship at your hips." He reached out, shaped her curves from breast to hips with a burning sweep of his hand that a man was allowed to give only his wife.

But Olivia couldn't bear it if he found himself regretful later . . . if she ever saw the disenchantment in his eyes that she saw so constantly in her mother's. She hurried on.

"I won't make a very good duchess. I don't think the dowager likes me very much. She would prefer that you marry Georgiana. In fact, I'm fairly sure that she would be appalled by the very idea of your marrying me."

"That's precisely why my estate came equipped with

a dower house. I am not marrying my mother. I am marrying you." Quin's gray-green eyes were so . . . she'd never dreamed a man would look at her like that.

But she had a list, a mental list, of characteristics that disqualified her for the position of Duchess of Sconce. "I make coarse jokes. That is, my sense of humor is not very ducal."

His eyes laughed, even though his face was composed. "I know only one such poem, which my cousin Peregrine taught me when we were boys. *There once was a lady from Bude, Who went swimming one day in the lake.*"

He paused, waited . . . an invitation. Olivia could feel herself turning pink.

"*A man in a punt,*" she said softly, "*Stuck his pole in the water . . .*"

He picked up the verse. "And said: '*You can't swim here—it's private.*' The truth is that I never really understood it. Am I right in thinking that the lady is from *Bude* because she's swimming in the *nude* rather than a lake?"

"Yes."

"I do understand the *pole*. But once you have to explain it, the verse is not very funny. Are you certain that you want to be with someone who not only can divest every bawdy pun of its humor, but must, in order to see the point?"

"Are you certain you want to be with someone who doesn't share your love of science? I'm afraid . . ."

"What, dear heart?"

"You'll be bored with me." She said it in a rush. "I can't talk about the quality of light, and if you tell me about mathematical functions, I truly will fall asleep. I have a very trivial mind."

"You understand emotion; I don't. That doesn't mean that my mind is worthless. We like different sorts of things. Why should I bore you with talking about mathematics? You can teach me to laugh instead."

Something like a sob rose up in her throat.

"Will you teach our children bawdy verses as nursery rhymes?" he asked.

She considered. "Perhaps."

"Then you will have to teach me some first. I'm sorry to say that Alfie never learned a single verse of poetry."

His hands curved around her shoulders, slid up into her hair, teasing strands apart with his fingers. "Do you know that I find myself wanting to talk about Alfie for the first time since he died? I've said his name aloud to you and I don't feel as if I were falling into a black pit."

She swallowed hard.

"Perhaps," he said delicately, "we might bestow one of our children with the miserable doorknocker of a name, Alphington? Just so that he's . . . remembered?"

"Oh Quin," she whispered. Then, because his question didn't need answering, since he knew the answer as well as she: "Just how many children do you think we will have?"

"Many?" His eyes were steady on hers. "I always wanted the nursery to be full of children, so many that no one could be lonely."

Olivia's heart ached, for two lonely little dukes-to-be, Quin and Alfie. "Is that why you flew kites, so that Alfie wouldn't be lonely?"

"Evangeline refused to have any more children. She was horrified by the way that her body changed. Even more so because I loved how she looked."

"You did?"

"I thought she had never looked more beautiful;

she thought she had never looked more repulsive. She wouldn't let me touch her, or even see her unclothed, for two years."

Olivia blinked. "So she wasn't unfaithful the entire time you were married?"

"She was." He said it calmly, as if he were discussing the weather. "She felt differently about me than she did about her lovers."

Olivia thought, not for the first time, that there was no point in expressing aloud what she thought about Evangeline.

"I don't want to talk about my former wife," Quin said. "In fact, I'd just as soon never speak her name again."

"Are you sure? I'm so ordinary compared to you, Quin."

The look of complete perplexity in his eyes could not be feigned. "What the hell do you mean? You're beautiful, and funny, and everyone in this house loves you. With," he added punctiliously, "the possible exception of my mother, but she will learn to care about you."

A sob came, bringing a tear or two along with it.

"No," Quin said, pulling her into his arms. "No tears." He started kissing them away, brushing her face over and over with his lips in the softest of caresses.

Olivia nestled into his arms.

"Do you mind telling me what exactly brought you into this room?" Quin whispered between kisses. "When I saw you an hour ago, you were ready to sacrifice me for your honor."

Olivia laughed shakily. "I do feel terrible about Rupert. But Georgie says that we will find him the right wife: someone understanding, strong, and kind."

"Ah, so your sister saw the truth."

"She told me there is no spark between you."

"Just as *I* told you." There was deep satisfaction in his voice. "You know, your sister would make an extremely capable scientist."

"She *is* an extremely capable scientist, and she will be a brilliant one, once we buy her all the books she wants. Father never would, you know. He thought that books were unladylike, and Mother agreed."

Quin snorted.

She burrowed closer, reveling in the strong arms around her, the dark, spicy, masculine smell of his chest, the steel of his body . . . the hard nudge against her stomach that told her without words that he wanted her. That he thought every inch of her breasts and stomach and hips was worth kissing.

"I do feel some remorse about stealing you from Montsurrey. Stealing a man's fiancée while he is serving his country is not entirely honorable."

Olivia leaned against him, letting his heat warm her whole body. "Rupert lost air at birth," she offered. "He will never be all that he could be."

"He's more than enough," Quin said simply. "He's serving his country, risking his life to protect England."

A few more tears dropped onto Quin's coat. "You're right."

"We will always be friends to him." It was a vow of sorts. "He had you, and now I'm taking you away, and I will never forget what I forced him to give up."

Olivia sniffled ungracefully, took the handkerchief he gave her. "Rupert might be more resentful if you took Lucy."

Quin laughed.

"I mean it," she protested. "And Georgie agrees."

He nudged her head up, kissed her wet eyes again.

Then his mouth came down on hers. And his hands were everywhere: possessive, almost rough, claiming and branding her.

Olivia melted against him as if she had always belonged there. Quin's kiss was sweet, but under it was a hard demand, a man's onslaught. Her arms curled around his neck and she clung to him, opening her mouth, inviting him in. Her head reeled from the smoky male smell of him, the way he tasted like champagne and something else, something intrinsically Quin.

The kiss made her feel wild and deeply alive. He had his hand on her cheek, tilting her head back, kissing her fiercely.

This was *intimacy*, she realized suddenly.

Quin nipped her lower lip, and Olivia shivered against him as if she'd been struck by a cold wind. He gave a little growl in response and tilted her head even further back. Then his mouth slid from hers to the curve of her jaw, leaving her to move restlessly against him. His arms ran more slowly down her back, pulling her closer.

Olivia actually went up on her toes, so intent on the intoxicating warmth of his arms and his lips that—

She almost didn't hear the door opening.

Nineteen

Much Spontaneous Kissing.
And the Other Kind, Too

Olivia broke free with a gasp and turned, still in the circle of Quin's arms. The dowager didn't look particularly angry or judgmental. Instead, she was regarding them rather the way a small child might watch a caterpillar: with curiosity, but not revulsion.

"Tarquin," she stated.

"Mother," Quin replied, not moving his arms from around Olivia.

"What on earth are you doing?"

"Kissing Olivia," Quin said. "Spontaneously."

The duchess's brow might have furrowed—except one had to assume that she did not hold with extravagant facial expressions of that sort. "Miss Lytton, I might ask the same of you."

Olivia thought about saying, *Being kissed*, and decided that dissembling would be the more prudent course. "I expect that the exhaustion of the night has provoked a level of unwonted hilarity," she said, piling on words in the hope that the dowager would find herself confused.

What was she thinking? This woman wrote *The Mirror of Compliments*. She was perfectly at home in a maze of language.

"It does not look like an expression of hilarity to me," the dowager remarked. "Tarquin, I could remind you of the disastrous role that spontaneity played in your first marriage, but I shall not."

"Quite right," Quin said, his arms tightening around Olivia.

"I have no need to do so," his mother continued, "because this young woman is promised elsewhere, and kisses, whether spontaneous, hilarious, or otherwise, will have no consequence, given that fact. Miss Lytton, before you indulged in this fit of unwonted enjoyment, did you remind my son that you are soon to be a duchess?"

Olivia had the sudden feeling that the dowager was a vulture, circling far above. Which probably made her a wounded lion. Or something even more vulnerable: a rabbit thrown aside by the wheels of a carriage.

"Yes," she said. Then she looked at Quin. "As I informed you, Your Grace, I am indeed promised elsewhere."

"To the Marquess of Montsurrey," Quin said. "Once Montsurrey returns to England, you will be promised, and speedily married, to me." He turned to his mother. "Olivia shall be Duchess of Sconce."

"I do not agree."

There was a long moment of charged silence. "Perhaps I should leave you to discuss this by yourselves," Olivia said, gently freeing herself from Quin's embrace.

The dowager ignored her entirely, keeping her eyes fixed on her son. "Miss Lytton is more than suitable for a dim-witted simpleton like Montsurrey. Moreover, she has shown a laudable loyalty toward the poor fellow, and I wrote his father myself to say so. However, she is not suitable for you."

"I think she is," Quin stated.

Olivia slid to the side.

The duchess turned to her. "I trust you are not going to sidle from the room, like a guilty housemaid with a broken saucer?"

Olivia's back snapped straight. "I thought it would be more polite to allow you to continue this conversation with your son in private."

"I would agree, except that what I have to say pertains to you—and to your sister. *She* is suitable to become Duchess of Sconce, which is, by the way, a far older and more august title than that of Canterwick. You are not suitable for the position." Faced with the duchess's direct gaze, Olivia realized that she could either drop her eyes—and never regain a position of strength again—or fight back.

"My sister would indeed be a remarkable Duchess of Sconce," she said, hoping to avoid open warfare.

"That fact is irrelevant," Quin said. Olivia didn't have to turn to see that he was smiling; she could hear it in his voice. "I intend to marry Olivia, not Georgiana."

"For love, no doubt!" The duchess said it in a burst of fury. "And what has love gotten you, Tarquin, but a reputation for horns that hasn't left you even these many years later?" She turned to Olivia. "Do you know that he didn't speak for an entire year after his feckless wife drowned? Didn't *speak*?"

"I spoke," Quin protested.

"Oh, you may have asked for a slice of roast beef, but you didn't say anything worth hearing. Not for an entire year did you show interest in living."

"It was rather like sleepwalking," he agreed. Somewhat to Olivia's astonishment, he didn't sound in the least bit angry.

"Montsurrey is a noodle," the dowager stated.

Olivia stiffened.

"That is a fact," the dowager snapped before Olivia could say anything. "He is a fine match for you, but the same is not true for my son. You are, Miss Lytton—if you'll excuse my bluntness—overly fleshly, coarse, and rather ill-bred. The last is particularly surprising given that your twin sister has achieved the utmost level of refinement. More to the point, you are uninteresting. You demonstrate no ability to concern yourself in matters important to my son."

Olivia pulled her dumpy self very straight, and as tall as possible, and said with icy precision, "I will respond only to the claim that reflects on my parents, although I will note that your incivility warrants no response at all. My parents may not be members of the aristocracy themselves, Your Grace, but they are related to peers on both sides. In fact, my father's claim to the title *esquire* has been held for one generation longer than the Sconces can claim. And may I add that when it comes to matters of breeding, no one in my family has married into the *Bumtrinkets*?"

The dowager's bosom rose slightly into the air, resembling a balloon ascension Olivia had once seen in Hyde Park. "I was referring not to your birth," she said, biting the words with frigid disdain, "but to your manners."

"I like the way Olivia looks," Quin said, intervening.

For the first time, his voice had a distinct warning in it. "In fact, I adore the way she looks. And I think her manner is perfect for a duchess."

"I'm sure you do!" the dowager snapped. There were red flags high in her cheeks and her black eyes glinted with anger.

"What do you mean by that?" Olivia demanded.

"I mean that you are made of the same stuff as his first duchess, Evangeline. He *adored* her appearance as well, and found out too late that all that wanton sensuality tends to mask a woman who should be flattered to be called a trollop."

"Mother." Quin's voice was now as icy as his mother's. "You go too far. I beg you, for the sake of all of us, to modify your voice and behavior."

"I will not." The duchess was clearly beside herself. "The Duke of Canterwick wrote me before you arrived," she said, turning on Olivia with the look of a mother tiger facing a threat to her cub.

Olivia waited, head high.

"Have you informed my son that you may well be carrying the heir to the Canterwick title? You will note that I say nothing here about the fact that you are unmarried; that the duke is reportedly such an innocent that you almost certainly molested the poor man; nor that he is barely eighteen. Those are such deeply unpleasant facts that one can only hope that no one outside your immediate family ever learns them, Miss Lytton, because they do not speak highly of you."

"Are you *threatening* me?" Olivia gasped.

The dowager actually backed up a step, but then linked her hands at her waist and stood her ground. "Certainly not. Those of us in the peerage have no need to resort to methods such as you clearly envision."

Quin met Olivia's eyes with a silent question.

"No heir," she managed.

"Mother!" Quin's voice was lethal, and cold as ice. "You will show me the courtesy to instruct your servants that you will be leaving for the dower house on the morning. I refer not to the dower house on these grounds, but that attached to Kilmarkie, our Scottish estate."

To Olivia's surprise, it was she—and not the dowager—who blurted out "No!" in response to this command.

The dowager was utterly silent for a heartbeat. Then she bowed her head and descended into a curtsy.

Olivia grabbed Quin's arm and shook it. "You will *not* do this!" she said to him, not gently.

He frowned at her. "I don't—"

"Your mother and I have the perfect right to disagree about what is best for you without your interfering!"

"I wasn't interfering. I was responding to what my mother said about you. That, I cannot, and will not, tolerate from anyone." He looked at his mother and said it again, through clenched teeth. "*Anyone.* You should know that any man, whether in my family or not, who implies that Olivia and Evangeline have anything in common will give me satisfaction at the end of a sword."

"Oh, for goodness' sake," Olivia said, grabbing hold of his cravat, since shaking his arm had had no effect. "Could you descend the ducal mountain for one moment and pay attention? Your mother is worried sick about you, and you're threatening to send her off to Scotland? You weren't joking when you said that you don't always understand emotions, were you?"

The dowager made a small noise, but Olivia didn't look at her. She kept her eyes fastened on Quin.

He frowned at her.

"Of course your mother thinks that I resemble Evangeline—well, in everything except our figures. I came here betrothed to one duke, and when everyone expected that you would betroth yourself to my own sister, I stole you for myself. Your mother walked into a room and found the two of us unchaperoned, and lucky not to be sprawled together on the floor. I do look like the worst sort of hussy. If you are planning to duel every man who points that out, we shall have a very short marriage."

Quin's frown deepened.

"No time for all those children you envision," she continued, remorselessly. "No time to do anything but run around the country attacking people who are saying the obvious. Make no mistake, they won't just be saying it. Ten to one, they'll be making horns behind your back as well, at least for a few years."

Some sort of rationality was stealing into his eyes.

"Don't you see?" she said, letting go of his cravat. "None of that matters. Your mother loves you. She wants to spare you the horns, and the whispers, and the fat wife too—" She looked at the dowager. "That's the only part that I'm having trouble forgiving you for."

Quin reached out, spun her back to him, and pulled her into his arms, held her tight, so tight that she could hardly breathe. "I need you," he said, low and fierce, into her hair. "Oh, God, Olivia, how did I ever live without you?"

She reached up, pulled his face down to hers. "I'm yours, for good or ill."

There was a little click as the door to the ballroom closed, but Olivia paid it no mind.

"You're the missing piece of me," Quin said. "You make me *feel*."

"You have always felt. You're one of the most sensitive, loving men I know. Anyone can tell that."

He shook his head, so she just pulled his face to hers and gave him a kiss so searing that it said what neither of them were able to put in words . . . yet.

Without a word, Quin dropped into an armchair, taking Olivia with him. This time there was no stopping, and she knew it; he knew it. They kissed until little moans were coming again and again from her throat and she was trembling, touching him everywhere she could reach, fingers shaking.

Quin pulled gently on her bodice . . . and her breast tumbled into his hand. For a moment he froze. Then: "You're the most beautiful woman I've ever imagined, Olivia. May I?"

She wasn't entirely sure what he meant to do, but she nodded. She would always say yes to him, though it wouldn't be wise to let him know.

His mouth was hot and wet on the curve of her breast. She arched her back, offered herself until those searching lips reached her nipple.

Olivia wasn't quite sure what happened next. She would have thought the most she would do was gasp at the surprise, perhaps utter a ladylike squeak, even a tiny shriek . . . no. With an entire ballroom full of aristocrats on the other side of the door, she let out a full-throated cry, an expression of need and burning want.

Without pausing, Quin clamped a hand over her mouth and then suckled harder.

Olivia bit his finger, felt giddy spirals building in her body, sending her heartbeat into her throat.

He raised his head, dropped his hand from her mouth and rubbed a rough thumb across her nipple. Olivia arched back on his arm, mad with the need of it, dazed by the wild sensations coursing through her.

"We can't do this here," Quin said, his voice a growl against her throat.

"No?" She jolted, shocked by her own voice, by the pleading hunger. "Of course we can't." She sat up, preparing to stand.

Quin looked at her, a wicked invitation in his eyes, and rubbed a thumb over her nipple again. Her spine crumpled against him again, her legs falling open in an invitation he didn't take.

His hand stilled, finally. Olivia swallowed hard, fighting the impulse to beg for more.

"Are you quite certain that you are not carrying Montsurrey's child?" His voice held no condemnation, merely a request for information.

She turned her head against his chest. "Yes."

"But you and he . . ."

Olivia tried to think how to explain, while honoring her promise to Rupert. Georgiana was her twin, her other self; Rupert would understand that she had told Georgie the truth.

But Quin . . . Quin was the man who was going to take her away from Rupert. And even if Rupert didn't actually want her, he was nevertheless accustomed to her. For a man who loved familiarity, it would be a wrench to lose her. There was no question but that Rupert wouldn't want Quin to know about the limp celery.

"His father was concerned, because Rupert was going off to war," she said, choosing her words carefully.

Silence.

Then: "Canterwick forced you to sleep with his simpleton of a son out of wedlock because he was worried that he would have no heir?"

It sounded terrible, put like that.

"I wasn't forced."

"Did you volunteer?"

"No."

"That's rape," he said flatly.

"No! Rupert wasn't . . . Rupert would *never*."

"Then it was double rape of the both of you."

Olivia let out a huff of air. "You make it sound despicable. I'm very fond of Rupert, as is he of me. We got through it as best we could. And he did tell me a poem he'd written. It was very good."

"What was it?"

"It was about the death of a sparrow that had fallen from a tree. '*Quick, bright, a bird falls down to us, darkness piles up in the trees.*'"

Quin scowled. "I don't understand that any better than the limerick Peregrine taught me. What does he mean by saying that darkness piles up in the trees? As someone who is studying light, I can tell you that rays don't pile up anywhere."

Olivia tugged her bodice into place, and then leaned back against his arm so she could see his face. "Rupert's poem and the limerick aren't supposed to be dissected. They just cause a little rush of feeling, that's all."

"'Darkness piles up' is a feeling?" Quin sounded adorably confused.

"He's talking about grief: the grief he felt when the sparrow fell out of the tree. The bird was quick and bright, and then it was gone. Darkness piled up in the tree where the sparrow once sang."

His eyes changed.

"Yes, like Alfie," she said, and put her cheek against his chest. The emotion on his face was so raw that it was painful to witness.

They sat there for a while, Quin's arms tight around her. Strains of a contra dance crept into the silence, drifting from the ballroom under the door. The music was joyous and sweet, as if it came from miles away, from a world in which no little boys—or sparrows—fell from trees.

Finally Quin cleared his throat. "You do realize that Montsurrey—"

"Rupert," she corrected him. "Rupert hates to be called by his title. Were he able, he would be on intimate terms with the world."

"You realize that Rupert is more and more dislikable? He wrote the only piece of poetry I've ever understood, he's defending our country while I sleep comfortably at home, and I'm stealing his fiancée."

"Rupert would adore the idea that you were in the least bit jealous," Olivia said. "He may not think clearly, but he understands feelings, and it hurts him when people are dismissive."

"He certainly understands feelings."

"I think the damage in his brain freed him. He cries whenever he is moved, whenever he hears or sees something grievous."

Quin digested this in silence. At last he rose, setting her on her feet. "Are you certain that you wish to marry me? I didn't have a rush of feeling in response to that poem until you explained it. Why couldn't it be in full sentences?"

"Rupert very rarely speaks in full sentences."

"But he could have been more clear. Why didn't he say: *When the swift-flying sparrow died—likely of old age—and fell from the tree, I felt as if my heart grew very dark.*"

Olivia wrapped her arms around him. "You forgot *bright*, but I think you did well with *dark*."

"*Bright* doesn't make sense. Birds from the Passeridae family tend to be gray or brown. I realize that my version is much longer, but it's more precise. And grammatical."

"But your version talks about Rupert's feelings, whereas Rupert's spoke to you about your feelings for Alfie."

"Ah." He considered, and then: "I still find the conjoining of the specific words he chose to be quite illogical."

"Consider it the poetic equivalent of a mathematical function," Olivia suggested. "So, do you suppose we should walk into the ballroom and pretend nothing has happened? You'll need to tie your hair back."

"No."

"No to going into the ballroom, or no to pretending that nothing happened?"

"I have no objection to going into the ballroom, because that's the only way to reach the stairs to the bedchambers. I have changed my mind."

Olivia gave a little gasp. "Are you saying . . . ? *No!* That would create a terrible scandal. Absolutely not."

His hands tightened on her. "A sparrow falls every second, Olivia." He gave her a kiss that was an erotic demand.

It took a moment, but Olivia managed to pull herself away from his kiss and out of his arms. "Your mother would be horrified by such a scandal. You remain here for at least a half hour. I'll try to slip into the ballroom, and hopefully people will think that I was merely composing myself after having a conversation with your mother."

"There is a footman in front of the door."

"*What?*"

"My mother stationed him there after she left, to ensure our privacy. Look at the bottom of the door and you'll see the shadow of his boots. My mother's servants are trained to have their shoulders to the wall; if you open the door, you'll strike him in the back, which will attract attention."

Olivia bit her lip. "I had not planned to embark upon a life as an infamous woman with such speed."

He walked to the back of the room, wrenched open the window, and beckoned to her. "It's a good thing you're a nimble climber."

"Why? This is practically ground level."

Quin swung a leg over the sill and dropped the foot or so to the ground. Then he held out his arms, grinning up at her, his eyes frankly lustful. "I just realized that there is no way to reach the bedchambers without going through the kitchen."

Olivia pulled up her skirts as demurely as possible and managed to get a leg over the windowsill. It was harder than it looked, and she ended up toppling into Quin's arms in a flutter of petticoats.

"So," he said, holding her very tightly as he placed her feet on the ground, "we are not going back into the house. I think we'll go climbing instead."

"Climbing? Climbing where?" Olivia looked around. They were on the side of the house, around the corner from the ballroom. Except where yellow light spilled from the windows, the gardens were silver, cool with the light of a full moon. "Are you talking about a ladder reaching to your bedchamber? Because I absolutely refuse to climb a ladder. I am not a hapless fool, eloping in the moonlight."

"Didn't you tell me that I could only look at you *like that* if we were high in a tree?"

"I don't want to climb any more trees, Quin! What if you fall again? You're lucky not to have been killed."

Quin just grinned. "Even at my advanced age, I can climb this tree." He reached out a hand.

But Olivia hung back. "It's chilly out here. I don't know what you have in mind, but I'm sure it's not proper."

"It's not proper at all. And don't worry about the cold. I'll grab a horse blanket or two from the stables."

"You want to stay *outside*?"

Olivia was about to voice a whole string of objections, but Quin chose to counter her arguments by kissing her. The kiss was so successful that she found herself perched on the windowsill again, which put her breasts at a level that Quin obviously appreciated.

"It's a good thing that door is closed," Quin said sometime later, his voice rough with need.

Olivia gulped, and came to her senses. Her hairpins were long gone and her hair was around her shoulders. What's more, her bodice had fallen almost to her waist. Skin—far too much skin—gleamed in the moonlight.

"Oh, oh!" she cried, yanking at her gown. "Oh, no."

"Yes, yes," Quin said, his hands catching hers, holding them wide so that he could admire her breasts. "I will never have enough of you, Olivia. You're like a drug." He dropped her hands and bent his head again.

Olivia stilled, hand on the black hair that fell like silk onto her breast as he kissed her, open, wet-mouthed kisses that sent stinging needles, a sweet kind of torment, down her legs.

"I'm not cold any longer," she whispered, taking her courage in her hands. This was the right thing to do.

She was choosing her own duke.

"Where is your tree?"

She followed him. But in reality she followed the solemn laughter—and it was laughter—that bloomed in his eyes when she yanked her bodice up; the sweet heat of his mouth; the raw sound of his voice breathing her name.

She would follow him anywhere.

Twenty

The Lucky Lady from Peedle

The tree turned out to be behind the stables. And it wasn't just a tree. It was a house *in* a tree.

Olivia stood at the base, looking up with stupefaction. "What on earth is it?"

"A tree house. Alfie's tree house."

"Alfie had a tree house?" That was a stupid question; after all, there it was, a tiny house, perched in a tree. It even had windows and a door.

"Alfie liked to ask questions," Quin said, still holding her hand. "He had questions about everything: What was holding up the moon, why apples turn brown, and who made up the alphabet. One day he wanted to know why we live on the ground rather than in trees."

Olivia leaned over, brushed a kiss on his mouth. "He was your little sparrow."

"Yes." But his voice wasn't heavy with grief. In fact,

it was joyous. "I had the tree house built for Alfie because I thought it was a particularly good question and merited experimentation. We lived there for two days."

"And what did Alfie decide?"

"That the Dukes of Sconce live on the ground because it's very difficult for footmen to climb the steps up the trunk with a supper tray, and Cleese couldn't come at all. Alfie pointed out that Cleese is never happy unless he knows what everyone is doing, so it wasn't very kind to him if the two of us decided to live in a tree forever."

Olivia laughed aloud. "Reasoning that befits a future duke. Wait! Did I hear someone laughing beside myself?"

Quin pulled her against his hard body. "If you climb into that tree house with me, Olivia, there is no going back. I will never allow you to marry Rupert. And make no mistake—I allowed Evangeline to wander where she would, but I feel differently about you. If you even make eyes at a man, I'll probably kill him."

Olivia reached up on tiptoe, nipped at his chin. "That goes both ways. If I catch you ogling someone else's breasts the way you do mine, I won't kill her—I'll go straight for you. Consider yourself warned."

Quin laughed.

"That's twice in one minute," Olivia teased. "At this rate, you'll horrify my mother by turning into a belly-laugher."

"I was faithful to Evangeline," he said, ignoring her funning. "And I feel twice for you what I felt for her. I suspect I'm not capable of being unfaithful to you."

Olivia's smile wavered, and she felt a lump in her throat. She took a deep breath and turned toward the tree trunk. "How does one get up there?"

"There are steps nailed to the trunk. Wait one

moment." He ducked into the stables, reappearing with two blankets flung over his shoulder. Olivia was in the house a moment later.

The tree house had windows on all four sides open to the moonlight, which poured in like fairy dust turned liquid silver. It was just tall enough for Olivia to stand up in; Quin had to bend his head. The floor was covered with matting, onto which Quin threw the blankets.

Olivia hesitated. It was all very well for Quin to talk about how much he loved her breasts. But there was no way to block these windows. She had thought they would make love in a bedchamber, in the dark.

Quin sat down, held out his hand.

She gave him a weak smile.

"Second thoughts not allowed," he said cheerfully. He reached forward, grabbed her hand, and pulled her into his lap.

"It's just that there are no curtains."

"I know . . . and sound travels."

"You needn't sound so gleeful! I think I prefer the old Quin who never smiled."

"Too late." He nipped her ear, soothed the sting with a warm tongue. "I sent all the stablehands around to the kitchens except for two old men who are too deaf to hear you."

"Hear me?" The comment was not welcome. It made her seem as if she had no self-control.

In a swift roll, Quin toppled backward and positioned himself on top of her, settling between her legs. They fit together perfectly. Olivia felt as if her skin suddenly woke up. Perhaps she did have no self-control.

He propped himself on his elbows, staring down at her for a long moment. "'Til death us do part?"

The faintest shadow of heartbreaking anxiety was detectable in his eyes. Olivia swallowed a silent curse for his late wife . . . and nodded. "In sickness and in health."

When the Duke of Sconce put his mind to something mechanical, its intricacies were generally fathomed instantly, and Olivia's clothing was no exception. Faster than she would have believed possible, he divested her of slippers, gown, corset . . .

Kneeling at her side, his eyes fiery with desire, he reached for her chemise.

"No," Olivia cried, grabbing his hand. As it was, her chemise was traitorously delicate. Why had she chosen to wear something that was as transparent as a windowpane? She cast one look down at her body and found her chemise caught beneath her hips so that it strained against her belly. Why *had* she eaten all those meat pies? Couldn't she have pictured a moment like this one? She went rigid with mortification and regret.

If only she were Georgiana—someone with enough control that she wouldn't have eaten so much.

It would be so much better for both of them if she had Georgie's slender thighs. If she had her sister's legs she would flaunt them, roll on her hip and *know* that his eyes couldn't leave her.

She swallowed. "I will not do this unless I can keep my chemise on. I mean that." The words were as resolute as she could make them, bitten-off and stern.

Quin's brows drew together for a second, but he nodded. He looked like some sort of hawk, tamed to the hand but still wild. His skin glowed like honey in the moonlight. She sat up, pulling her chemise away from her skin so that it wasn't quite so revealing.

What did a lady do in this situation? Dimly, in a small

corner of her mind, Olivia realized that her mother's duchification program had neglected this entire subject. It hardly needed be added that *The Mirror of Compliments* was focused on preserving chastity, rather than abandoning it.

"I'm not sure what to do next," she admitted, hoping he wouldn't ask for any details about her supposed experiences with Rupert.

The look in his eyes was pure arrogant male delight. "Luckily, I do."

She waited.

"Take off my coat," he whispered, so softly she could barely hear him. A smile trembled on her lips and she reached out and pushed the coat off his shoulders. Then she unbuttoned his waistcoat, tossed it to the side, and tugged his shirt free from his breeches. She moved to pull up the shirt, but was diverted by the skin she found at his waist. She came up on her knees too, and ran her hands around his tight abdomen to the swelling muscles of his back.

"How is it you are so fit? Most men are rather soft, I have found."

He shrugged. "Physical exercise clearly has a positive effect on the human physiology. There seemed sufficient evidence to engage in it on a regular basis."

His skin was smooth and hot under her fingers. She let her hands wander under his shirt: up his broad back to his shoulders, back down again, up his front. Apart from some small shivers, he let her do as she wished.

When she brushed her fingers over his nipples, a hoarse grunt broke from his lips. She glanced and saw that his eyes were shut.

"Keep your eyes closed," she ordered, feeling a flash of courage. If his eyes remained closed the entire time, it would be as good as having curtains in a decently dark bedchamber.

He nodded obediently. She felt more confident when he wasn't looking at her; she needn't worry about how much that ridiculous chemise was revealing.

She managed to pull his shirt over his head, discovering that his torso was beautiful, with a narrow, taut waist. She caressed every bit of his chest and then—glancing again at his still-closed eyes—leaned in close and placed her mouth where her hands had been.

A low noise broke from his lips. "No opening your eyes," she warned. His lips tightened, but he nodded.

She bent to him again, kissing him, tasting him, dusting little kisses over his entire chest. And she kept coming back to his nipples because every time she rubbed her lips across them he responded. It was like champagne, that little sound he made. It was power, and she was drunk on it.

She forgot to keep an eye on his face, reassuring herself that he wasn't watching. Instead she came closer, squirming onto his lap so that she could rub more than her lips against him.

"Olivia." His voice was soft, liquid with passion.

Startled, she looked up, to find those gray-green eyes gazing at her. The moonlight frosted his thick lashes and he looked otherworldly: a fairy king, not a mere mortal. "You were to keep your eyes closed," she said, giving in to temptation and running a fingertip along his lashes. "You're so beautiful, Quin. Too beautiful for me."

He laughed at that. A third laugh, in the space of an hour.

She trailed her finger down, across his full bottom lip, leaned forward and carefully followed that line with her tongue.

"May I touch you now?" he murmured against her lips.

"Mmmm," she whispered back, loving the taste of him.

Big hands came to her back and pulled her against his naked chest. Olivia gasped as her breasts were pressed against him; they felt plump and wildly sensitive.

One hand held her against him while another slid down her back, slow and sensuous. "Aren't you going to remove the rest of my clothing?" He said it low and soft, like a dare he knew she couldn't resist.

She almost tumbled off his lap, turned to face him. "My breeches have a placket," he said, making no move to undo it himself.

Olivia leaned a little closer and found what he meant. She fumbled, her fingers trying to manipulate the buttons, aware that his breathing was fast and ragged. Once she saw how he trembled at her touch, she slowed down, caressing just inside the band of his breeches, loving his swift intake of breath as her fingers dipped lower.

Slowly, slowly, she eased the breeches over his lean hips, down powerful thighs. Once they were at his knees, he swiftly removed them and tossed them to the side. Now he wore nothing but smalls, which did very little to conceal what lay underneath.

No limp celery this—though Olivia instantly pushed away the thought as disloyal to Rupert. She may not be marrying him, but she would always be his true friend.

She was slow and careful working Quin free from his smalls, trying not to show awe at the size of him.

He threw the smalls after the breeches and came back to her, kneeling, hands quiet at his sides, but she could sense the leashed power in him, waiting to spring free. To spring on her.

A wave of anxiety flooded her again, sent her eyes skittering from him, from all that perfection, down to her thighs—only to find that blasted chemise had caught *again* and was emphasizing the fleshiness of her upper leg. Heat rushed into her cheeks as she plucked it free.

He said not a word. She looked up to see that he was regarding her with such a tender expression that she cringed. "Don't you *dare* pity me," she snapped.

Surprise flooded his eyes. "What do you mean?"

"Nothing," Olivia said. "I'm sorry. I misunderstood. Well . . ." To her dismay, she felt as if tears were threatening. Added quickly: "What do we do now?"

His face was serious again, the expression he had when he was thinking about light, or poetry.

"It's just that I'm not sure what to do," she said, her voice catching. Tears pushed at her eyes again.

"Dear heart," he said, "what's the matter?" He reached out and put his arms around her.

"Nothing," she muttered, feeling ten times a fool. "Kiss me?"

"Good idea." He kissed her slowly and sweetly, eyes closed—she checked before she relaxed into the feeling of being near Quin.

Then, when she was kissed into a hazy state, he moved so that she found herself on her back, her hair flowing around her. It was almost too much: trying to take in the sensation of his body heavy against her side, *naked*, his arousal urgent against her. And the moon was pitiless, casting its cool silver light everywhere.

It was pretty; she had to admit that. The inside of the

little house glimmered with light that looked magical. If only it weren't so *revealing*. A little less magic, that was all she asked.

"There's something wrong," Quin said, raising himself on all fours and looking down at her.

Her lip quivered and then, no longer able to choke them back, a tear spilled—even as she told herself, *Don't cry, don't cry, don't cry.*

Quin reached out with a thumb, gently rubbed it away. "Help me, sweetheart. Emotions are not my strong point. I need you to tell me what's the matter."

She shook her head. "Nothing! I'm simply being foolish."

His eyes searched hers and Olivia looked away, fast. He saw too much with those damnably intelligent eyes of his.

The next thing she knew her hands were caught and held above her head. "If you won't tell, I'll have to resort to logic. You're not afraid of being with me. And you told me that you're not a virgin, so you can't be afraid of pain."

Did she actually say that? He had inferred that she and Rupert had made love. And she couldn't tell him otherwise without breaking her promise.

"Unless"—he hesitated—"am I considerably larger than Rupert?"

Her gaze lingered on him with pleasure, and he seemed to throb and grow under that gaze. "Yes," she murmured, her voice throaty.

He laughed. "That is not fear that I hear in your voice."

"Does it bother you that I've—I've seen Rupert before you?"

He frowned. "Why should it? You didn't choose to

lose your virginity to Rupert, any more than he chose the reverse. I feel a measure of contempt for Rupert's father, but none for you."

It was very like Quin: both logical and fair. She managed a wobbly smile. "All the same," she began.

But he cut her off. "That's not it, Olivia. Please don't lie to me."

Her eyes fell.

"When I am in doubt, I make a list of questions," he said, leaning down and biting her earlobe so that she squealed.

"First question. Is darling Olivia afraid of my cock?"

He picked up her hand, curled it around his erection. Olivia gasped, delighted at its silky heat, smoothness, the way it jumped in her hand. She slid up . . . down. Took a quick glimpse and realized that Quin's eyes were shut, head thrown back. Just the way she liked him. She tightened her grip, wondered what he might taste like.

He moved her hand away, satisfied with her silent answer to his question. "Not afraid of it," he murmured, his voice a shade deeper, darker, than it had been.

"Second question. Is my Olivia afraid there might be pain?" He looked at her intently.

She shook her head.

"I didn't think so," he said with satisfaction. "Besides, I mean to make you so limp with pleasure that you'll be begging me for more of the same." This time his smile was pure unadulterated male.

Olivia's heart skipped a beat.

"Third question," he said, and he shifted onto his knees. "Could it be that foolish, foolish Olivia fears I won't like her body?" And then, quick as a cat, while she was still considering her reply—for even though he was right, she certainly didn't want to admit it—he reached out and ripped her chemise straight down the middle.

It was a good thing the staff had been sent away from the stables, because Olivia's scream of outrage could likely have been heard well into the gardens.

But Quin was already ripping away the last shred of cloth. Olivia squeezed her eyes, not wanting to see his face. That damn moonlight was everywhere, illuminating every curve and wobble.

He didn't touch her, and he didn't say anything. Olivia felt as though time stood still, leaving her stranded in the most humiliating moment of her life.

When at last he spoke, his voice was greedy and rough. "You don't really wish that you were a scrawny thing like your sister, do you?"

"Georgiana is not scrawny!" Olivia said, her eyes popping open.

"Like a stick of celery," Quin said. "Legs like a grasshopper's. A man wants this, Olivia." His hands came gently, shaping her breasts.

"I do know that," Olivia said, shivering as his touch sent flames licking over her body. "I like my breasts."

His hands slid lower, over the tummy that wasn't washboard tight, like his, or slender as a dancer's, like Georgiana's.

"A man wants *this*." His voice was still darker, rusty with passion as his fingers bit into her curves, sank into her warmth.

They slid lower, onto her hips. "You do remember that I never lie?" he asked, his eyes fixed on his hands.

Olivia looked down too, curious, seeing honey-dark hands gripping her hips. She looked like cream in the moonlight, as if her skin were glowing with some sort of inner luminescence.

"Yes, I remember," she managed.

"I think I love your hips and your arse most of all." The emotion in his voice was unmistakable. "But then I remember your breasts and how much I love them. I love every bitable, lush, delicious curve, Olivia, including those you haven't let me touch or kiss yet."

Until this moment, Olivia had been holding her body rigid, her thighs tight, her stomach pulled in. Now, slowly, she relaxed, watching him. Quin couldn't lie. She knew that; she had told Georgie that. She believed it.

The lust on his face, the way he was touching her, almost reverently, bending his head, now, kissing her greedily . . . That was the truth.

"Succulent," he murmured.

"You make me sound like a roast chicken."

"Ripe and plump and delicious. *Soft.*"

She shook her head. "Those are not the words a woman wants to hear from a man looking at her thighs." But she was feeling better, and they both knew it.

"Georgie does not have grasshopper legs," she said, poking him to make sure that he'd heard her. What he was doing now was going to make her collapse in a boneless heap, but she had to make sure he understood that one thing. "She has elegant, slender legs that any woman would love to have."

He looked down at her, eyes predatory, those big hands holding her. "Not *my* woman. Not you."

Olivia was about to defend her sister again, but he pulled her legs open and put his mouth on her, on that part of her.

She went rigid again for a second, long enough for a

rough lap and a sweet lick, a finger stroking where a tongue had just been, a . . .

And then she forgot about Georgie. Forgot her own name. Forgot everything except the man who drove her further into a firestorm with every lick. She couldn't stop twisting, or suppress the moans leaving her throat, one after another, undignified, guttural, *animal*.

Quin's hands were everywhere, touching her, adoring her, sliding under her and biting into her bottom, then soothing the little pain, sliding around her thighs, making it clear that every silky inch met with his satisfaction, finally inching up, parting her folds, one finger going . . . *there*.

Olivia stiffened again, a broken moan coming from her lips.

"You're so tight," Quin muttered. "That's it, Olivia. *Now*." One last rough lick, one twist of that clever finger . . .

The part of her that was Olivia—smart, wry, word-play-loving—was swallowed up by a wave of pleasure so acute that her body twisted, arched in a silent scream that matched the one coming from her lips.

Quin reared over her, caught her mouth in a wild kiss, pulled her into just the right position and thrust . . .

It was the tail end of that red-hot blindness, the utter rending of self, and for a moment Olivia didn't register the intrusion.

And the next moment she did. It was huge, scalding hot. *Excruciating*.

Still, it was Quin above her, head thrown back, eyes closed.

"You feel so . . ." His voice was ragged, rough with passion. He couldn't finish the sentence.

It was as instinctive as breathing. She rocked back, arched, took the last inches of him.

Changed her mind and wished she hadn't. Desire was one thing; agonizing pain was another.

His throat worked and he let out a low noise, a growl of male possession and pleasure.

If Olivia's mind had been fogged before, it was clear now. This hurt like . . . like . . . it helped to silently run over some curses that Georgiana would never utter aloud. He was not only huge, but he was burning her up. Who would have thought a body part could be so *hot*?

Suddenly his face changed and his eyes snapped open. "There's something about you . . ."

Olivia tried, unsuccessfully, to look as if she were enjoying herself.

"You were a virgin!"

She didn't bother responding. She was wondering whether women ever fainted during the act.

Quin dropped his body down a few inches, bringing his face closer to hers; Olivia suppressed a moan. Movement . . . not a good idea. A few silent curses that Georgiana had never even heard, let alone said aloud, drifted through her mind.

"Talk to me, sweetheart." Quin's voice cut through her body's violent protest. He shifted again.

"Stop that," she said grimly. "No moving."

He nodded.

"Do you remember that limerick about the lady who was good with her needle?"

Another nod.

"Why couldn't I fall in love with the man she learned her skills from? I don't want you to ever move again, not backwards or forwards. You're too *big*."

A gleam of laughter beat back the fierce hunger in his eyes. He dropped his head and gave her a lingering kiss. "I'll happily stay here forever," he whispered. "I think this is my favorite place in the world."

"They'll have to bury us in a large coffin," Olivia said, joking—because if she didn't, she might think too much about what a tragedy this was. They didn't fit together. He was simply too large.

"This will not work," she said, when Quin didn't respond to her sally about the coffin. He was kissing her cheek and her ear. All very nice, but as every nerve in her body was concentrating on the waves of pain sweeping from between her legs, she would be happy to dispense with the kisses.

"Actually, I take it back about not moving. I think it's probably time for you to move away," she said, trying to be nice about it.

He made a little murmur and started kissing her eyebrows. Annoying. Very annoying. "Out!" she said, giving him a little push.

"I can't. Someone told me not to move."

"This is not the time to develop a sense of humor."

He rubbed noses with her, such a startling, tender movement that she fell silent. "I wouldn't have thrust like that if I'd known you were a virgin. And I was under the impression that you informed me of your experience."

"You inferred such," Olivia told him. "It wasn't my—I couldn't clarify."

"But you left the duke thinking his son's heir might be on the way?" Laughter shone in his eyes.

"It served him right," she said, giving Quin a little bite on his chin, just because it was there, and he was beautiful. "Now, I hate to sound as though I have an appointment, but I'm sure there's somewhere important I should be."

"Hurts, does it?" He dropped a kiss on her lips.

"I cannot even describe how much."

"Because you're a lady?"

She nodded.

"If I had known you were a virgin, I would have pushed up your knees, and then entered you gently, and very slowly."

"It would have led to the same result." Olivia couldn't imagine that the mechanics could change, given the fixed sizes of their respective parts.

"But would you bend your knees? Just . . . to try?"

She bent her knees, grudgingly.

"Sometimes a woman wraps her legs around her lover's waist."

She could just see herself doing that. Like some sort of acrobat. Why hadn't she realized how unsuited she was for bedroom activities? She might not insist on the curtains being closed every single night, but lift her legs in such an undignified way? "Absolutely not. Never," she added, just to make sure he understood.

His eyes were laughing at her, but that was because he didn't understand just how much this all hurt.

"Olivia," he said, lowering his mouth on hers again, entirely relaxed, as if he meant to stay in the same position all night, "I love you." And then he kissed her, demanding that she open her mouth, so she did.

He plunged inside, his tongue playing a wet, hot game with hers, and Olivia understood for the first time. This kind of kissing was . . . *carnal.* It was outrageous.

"No wonder," she murmured.

He pulled back a fraction of an inch, arched an eyebrow.

"No wonder they don't allow debutantes to kiss," she explained. "It's just another way to make love, isn't it?"

In answer he took her mouth again, possessive, hot, sweet. All the sides of Quin at once.

"Dear heart," he said a while later, after his hand had drifted to her breast, "does it still hurt as much as it did?"

"Of course," Olivia said automatically. Even though she was enjoying his caresses—and how could she not?—she was always aware of the pain and the sense that something foreign and far too large was splitting her in half.

But then she wriggled a trifle and realized that it didn't hurt *quite* as much as it had before.

"It does feel a little better. I suppose you shrink when we don't do anything for a while."

He blinked. "Sweetheart, if you think a man who's found his way into the sweetest, tightest place in the world would shrink . . ."

She wriggled again, thought about that blissful feeling he gave her before all of *this* started. It wasn't fair to leave him without it. She wasn't afraid of pain. Or rather, she didn't believe in being afraid of pain.

"You should start again," she said. In truth, she was afraid, but that didn't mean she hadn't courage.

He looked unconvinced.

"Now," Olivia elaborated. "You can move back and forth now."

Slowly he withdrew. Oddly enough, once he was gone, she felt empty. Ridiculous, really. Then he was there again, slow this time, very slow. Part of her just wanted him to go fast, get it over with. Another part was entranced by the slow invasion. It did something . . .

She found her breath hitching, and her back arching a little.

"Better?" he asked, quietly, but she could hear the gruffness in his voice.

She nodded.

"Again?"

She acquiesced.

He pushed in, slow and steady. It wasn't comfortable. Not at all. But it was bearable. The rough sense of friction was even rather pleasant, for some strange reason.

And there was a trace of anxiety in Quin's eyes, pinching away some of his pleasure.

"I'm starting to love this," she said, giving him a big smile. "I could do this all night. I'll probably—"

"Liar," he growled, biting back the smile in his eyes. "I know this is hell for you, but Olivia, it is *heaven* for me. I never imagined anything could feel the way you do."

Braced on his forearms, he looked down at her, eyes heavy-lidded, slumberous with passion.

Olivia let the gladness of it fill her heart. She arched her back, moved toward him. It was an awkward movement, but he understood.

He threw his head back, eyes closed, and thrust forward fast and hard, once, twice, again . . . Just when Olivia started to think that perhaps it wasn't quite so horrible, Quin made a sound, a brutal, dangerous sound, and thrust into her a final time.

If he had fallen on top of Georgiana like that, like a felled tree, he might have killed her.

The good news was that because she had never taken to a lettuce diet, Quin felt exactly right falling on top of her. In fact, Olivia tightened her arms around his neck to keep him in place. The terrible burning between her legs seemed to have lessened, too. In fact, it felt rather tingly and almost comfortable down there.

It was so *intimate*. He was part of her. They were connected, two people, put together like a jigsaw puzzle that couldn't be put asunder. The thought made her a little teary.

"Quin," she said softly, turning her head, feathering kisses along his cheekbone. She wanted to share this ecstatic, perfect, most intimate moment.

He was asleep.

Olivia started laughing, and the giggles bubbling up her chest woke him. "Sorry, love," he said, voice dark with sleep, and shifted to the side. "No place to wash," he mumbled.

His eyes closed again. He was out.

Olivia tore a strip of her ruined chemise and cleaned herself up as well as she could. There wasn't very much blood, which was truly surprising. From the way she felt, blood should have gushed out of her.

But no.

She reached for the second blanket, pulled it over the naked body of her first lover—her only lover—curled up against his side, and settled herself to sleep.

Her body was throbbing and tingling in an unfamiliar way that made it hard to settle down. So she started thinking again about the blasted lady with her *needle*.

That was a ridiculous description for something that was more like a battering ram.

But . . .

There was something overwhelming, wonderful about the experience. It made her feel—

Absurd, she told herself, curling tighter.

No human can own another. Possessiveness? No.

She must have misunderstood the look in Quin's eyes. She wasn't even his wife yet.

Still, she fell asleep thinking about the way he looked at her as he thrust: ferocious, hungry, possessive.

Mmmm.

Twenty-one

The Definition of Marriage

Quin woke very early in the morning, as he often did. But he realized immediately that nothing else about this particular awakening felt familiar. Normally he woke on a soft, pristine bed, arms curled around no one at all.

But now he lay on a rough, hard surface, arms curled around a soft, sleeping woman. What's more, dawn light, unfiltered by draperies, bathed his face, and it sounded as if some tipsy birds were singing into his ear.

Suddenly the world—and recognition of just where he was and with whom—flooded back into his head. It was Olivia whom he had clutched all night, as if afraid she would escape. Olivia, whose laughing eyes and silly sense of humor and wry intelligence surprised him and delighted him . . . and made him mad with lust.

Olivia was *his*. Somehow he'd managed to find a woman who was the opposite of Evangeline.

Evangeline had played the virgin, but in truth, wasn't. Olivia had played an experienced woman, but in truth, wasn't. For a moment or two he puzzled over what precisely had happened between her and the saintly Rupert, but then he let it go. She would never tell; she must have promised Montsurrey.

If only he had known . . . He had thrust into her, believing that she was used to shaking the sheets with her fiancé, thinking she was a woman long pleasured. His former wife had trained him to it. To be blunt, making love to Evangeline had been like riding the public highway.

Making love to Olivia was all different, and not just because of physical differences. Every moan and shudder she gave seemed to ring changes in his own body.

And through it all came a wild sense of possession. Olivia was *his*, all his. No other man had ever touched her the way he had. The ferocity of his possessiveness was astonishing—and not logical.

He lay there for some time, listening to a thrush sing, and thinking about the kind of betrayal that makes a man desperate to find a woman who loves *only* him. Olivia's virginity was the most beautiful gift she could have given him.

His arms tightened even thinking of it. He had caused her physical pain, and he felt terrible for it. But knowing that he was the very first . . .

He shook the feeling away; it was illogical. It didn't matter how many men a woman had slept with. He had told himself that after Evangeline—on their wedding night—had detailed her many exploits (which had begun with a footman at the tender age of fifteen). He had been right.

None of those men had changed the essential Evangeline, or the way he'd felt about her.

But still, that glow—that ferocious, animalistic, possessive glow at the bottom of his heart—didn't fade away. He dismissed it as being akin to poetry: unaccountable, illogical.

Poor Olivia was undoubtedly sore after the events of the previous night. He eased her onto her back, then took his time caressing those creamy, soft, intoxicating curves. She slept on; he began embellishing his touch with a kiss now and then. She stirred a few times, but it wasn't until he had a hand exploring the delicate skin on her inner thigh, while his mouth inched closer to a sweet pink nipple . . .

She woke up.

She didn't murmur a greeting. Instead she sat straight upright and shrieked, "Ohmygoodness, where am I?"

Quin wasn't very good at answering questions at the best of times (unless, of course, they had to do with mathematics). Instead of answering, he reached up, pulled that luscious bundle of female flesh down onto his chest, and kissed her. Which made a feeling of possessiveness rage through his body again.

He let it happen.

It wasn't logical. Wasn't really *him*. It was powerful, though.

"Oh, Quin," Olivia whispered, considerably later. She was flat on her back, and he was inching his way down her body, kissing as he went.

"Hmmm."

"I love it when you growl in my ear."

Quin thought about that. "You make me sound like a rabid bulldog."

She threw her hands over her head in a happy stretch that signaled pure pleasure. "I don't mean you growl like a dog. You're—it's as though you're so happy to have *me* here."

"You're mine," he said, matter-of-factly. "Of course I'm happy you're here." He nudged her legs apart.

"Just what are you doing down there?" Olivia asked, peering down at him.

"Kissing your thighs."

She tried to pull her knees together. "Absolutely not. We must return to the house before your guests notice our absence. Thank goodness these birds made such a racket and woke us up."

He lapped a little design on her thigh that made her shiver despite all her busy conversation, slid his tongue a little closer to her hot middle, caressed her breast in a way that he now knew drove her half mad with pleasure.

"Why, why, Quin," she said, in that breathless voice he'd heard only a few times. "What . . ."

He ran a delicate finger over beautiful pink folds.

She sat up again. "No!" And she followed that up with a lot of babble. They had to go inside, they had to bathe and dress, they had to avoid his mother, they had to . . .

The one thing his beloved Olivia didn't realize about him yet was that when Quin made up his mind . . . he got what he wanted.

The only way to stop the flood of words and anxiety was to pull her into a kiss. Since his hand had found its way to the softest, wettest place in her whole body, he wasn't inclined to listen to protests.

Mind you, he wanted to do more than stroke her. But if he had momentarily lost self-control the night before, he had it again now. Olivia, sweet Olivia, needed to experience bone-numbing pleasure before he would venture near her again.

Finally he had her gasping and twisting against his finger and pleading, *please, please, please*. He ruthlessly rejected the urge to leap on top of her, and instead carefully pushed another finger next to the first . . . and that was it. She cried out, clutching at his shoulders, her whole body shaking.

It was so damned enticing that Quin actually had to stop for a moment and wrestle his own body back into submission.

She was everything he wanted . . . everything he could ever want.

He couldn't ruin it.

"Quin," she said, struggling for breath. "Oh, that. That."

He nodded, rolling over and giving his body another little lecture. No, he would not rub against her.

"Your turn," she said, looking like the brave little soldier facing a battalion of armed elephants.

That did it. His erection finally calmed enough that he could sit up. "Time to return to the house," he said, looking around for his smalls. It was the work of a moment to put on his breeches and shirt. "We should go back before too many servants are up and about."

"My knees are weak," Olivia said. Her voice was throaty and sounded as though she was inviting precisely that which she was not.

"Up," he said.

"You go," she suggested. "I'll take a little nap and follow later." She curled into a ball and tugged the blanket over herself again. Her eyes drifted shut.

"I can't leave you in a tree."

"Yes, you certainly can. You go inside and have breakfast with everyone. I'll come in later. That way no one will think that we spent the night doing wicked things in a tree, which I'm sure is what would come to mind if we appeared together. I know I often assume people are cavorting in trees."

"I cannot leave you here," he said patiently.

"I'll be fine. You're the one who fell out of that other tree, not me."

Quin squatted down. "Olivia, wake up. We're going inside, and I can't carry you down."

"Too tired. And too sore. I'm not climbing down until I've had a rest. Wake me in a few hours."

That was an order. Quin stood up, as best as he could, and looked down at his future duchess. She seemed to be sleeping peacefully, a hand under her cheek, her gorgeous, tousled hair curling all over the blanket. She didn't even have a pillow, and yet she looked blissfully comfortable.

He found he was grinning: he was rumpled and unwashed, and happier than he'd been in years.

She opened one eye.

"Bring some tea when you come back?"

"As I explained, footmen can't negotiate up the ladder while carrying trays. Wait a minute—are you, Miss Lytton, asking a *duke* to fetch you some tea?"

Her eye closed again, but he saw the little curl of a smile on her mouth. She was testing her power, his Olivia was.

"Yes," she said sweetly. "That's what marriage is all about."

"What is it all about?"

"Being nice because"—she smiled—"you want the other person to be *nice* to you."

He brought her tea.

And crumpets.

Twenty-two

Wreathed in Glory

Early evening

I simply cannot believe you did that!" It was a little insulting the way Georgiana was staring at Olivia, rather as if she were a two-headed calf at the fair. "No wonder you didn't come to breakfast. Or lunch."

"I slept right through both. But it wasn't as if we spent the night in the open air," Olivia tried to explain. "It's a tiny house; it just happens to be up in a tree."

Georgiana snapped her mouth shut. Her eyes were laughing, though. "I simply cannot believe it. No one could get me into a tree. I'm quite certain that you found the one man in the world who likes to climb trees."

"It's rather amazing, isn't it?" Olivia said. She could hardly put it into words. "He's everything I would have dreamed of, if I'd thought that I *could* dream."

Georgiana shook her head. "Even you couldn't have dreamed up a man who likes to sleep in trees."

"I know." Olivia was so happy that she felt as if she were about to burst. "How was luncheon?"

"We should join the party in the drawing room," Georgiana said, starting. "Her Grace is terribly irritable. She clearly suspects there's a reason you missed breakfast *and* luncheon. None of the houseguests have departed, and I gather some plan to stay for at least a week. She was quite short with Mr. Epicure Dapper—the gentleman with the remarkable addiction to puffed shoulders on his coats."

Olivia snorted. "How the mighty have fallen!"

"Lord Justin takes positive delight in tormenting her, you know. After luncheon, the young ladies all begged him to sing for them, and he sang *French* songs!"

"He is half French, is he not?" Olivia held open the bedchamber door so that Georgiana could precede her. "Why shouldn't he sing in his native language?"

"Oh, Olivia, you know perfectly well that French songs are nothing like English ones. They sound improper even when they aren't."

"Her irritability has nothing to do with Justin's propensity for singing in his mother's tongue."

Georgiana stopped short at the top of the stairway. "Don't tell me you crossed swords with her again last night."

"Aren't you glad you weren't with us? It would have given you a double migraine, if such a thing exists."

Olivia started down, but Georgiana caught her arm. "Tell me all, please."

"If you remember, *you* sent me into the library and said that Quin would follow."

"Which he did. I watched him track you through the crowd like a fox stalking a chicken."

"We had just worked out a few things to both of our satisfaction when the dowager entered the room. She interrupted us, if you follow what I'm saying."

"Just what *are* you saying?"

"Not that," Olivia said with a crow of laughter. "We were merely kissing."

"Oh dear."

"She was horribly cross about it. She said that I was too fat to marry her son," Olivia said, going straight to the only point that she clearly remembered. "Apparently, she believes I was a sensible choice for Rupert because my ample hips make up for his deficient brains."

"I cannot believe the dowager said such a thing!" Georgiana gasped. "She can be brusque, perhaps, but never uncivil. And such a comment—which is so untrue—goes far beyond garden-variety incivility."

"I assure you, she did say it, but she didn't truly mean it," Olivia said. "She's merely cross that now she will not have Wonderful You as her daughter-in-law—and really, who can blame her?"

"You are very kind, Olivia, but I am *disappointed*," Georgiana said, her small bosom swelling with such indignation that she bore a faint resemblance to the dowager herself. "For such a lady of consequence to fall below her own firmly held standards is shocking."

"It's probably my influence. I expect she is nothing but sunshine and daisies in the general course of events. I bring out the predator in her."

"That's no predator you're describing. It's rude, common behavior." Georgiana finally started down the stairs. "Well, the dowager may be unhappy, but Mother will be ecstatic."

"I doubt that very much."

"One duke is as good as another."

"Once she realizes that you refuse to take my place—well, I don't like to think. Remember, Father promised that one of his daughters would marry Rupert. Though really, Georgie, when I think on it, you *could* do worse. You are trained to the job."

"You don't want me to marry Rupert," Georgiana stated. "And I don't want to marry Rupert. And frankly, whereas you were always a good daughter except in the smallest things, I'm not."

"You're not?" Olivia asked.

"Mother and Father made the mistake of thinking that because I conquered every task they set me, I was therefore obedient. I'm not." She reached the bottom of the stairs and turned around to face Olivia.

"Georgie!" Olivia gasped. "You're—this is wonderful!"

"They also made the mistake of thinking that you *were* rebellious, simply because you recited limericks and generally carried on. But that was all flummery. You are the obedient daughter."

Olivia stepped down beside her. "I think I prefer being the rebel. I sound like a ninny."

"The Duke of Sconce would never be enticed by a ninny," Georgiana said with a grin. "He's mad for you. I expected him to break out and announce that he had chosen you to be his wife at the luncheon table, but he managed to restrain himself."

Just then one of the footmen standing along the walls of the entryway sprang forward and swung open the great doors.

Olivia turned, thinking it might be Quin. Then she froze in place, unable to speak. The person at the door was, most decidedly, not Quin.

Georgiana experienced no such hesitation. "Your

Grace," she said, as Cleese ushered in the Duke of Canterwick. "It is such a pleasure to see you."

"It's Rupert," Olivia blurted out. "Something's happened to Rupert."

"No!" The duke turned his head and saw her. "My dear, my dear, it's the best possible news!"

(As Olivia later told Georgiana, she would have thought that the *best possible news* would refer to her own pregnancy, and she had very good reason to know that wasn't the case.)

"Rupert has surpassed himself!" The duke shouted it. His entire face glowed with happiness.

"*What?*"

"Wreathed in glory," Canterwick said, still shouting. "Crowned in it! Earl of Wellington mentioned him in the dispatches . . . Prince Regent informed . . . special honors considered. Good evening, Miss Georgiana! And how are you getting along with Sconce, then?"

"Very well, thank you," Georgiana said, smiling. "I am so happy to hear your news, Your Grace."

"Not as happy as I am," the duke said, somewhat less *fortissimo*. "Happy is not . . . I can't even describe what I'm feeling. Couldn't believe it at first. His Majesty's messenger had to tell me four times. Then I sent a man to Dover to wait for my son and bring him here as soon as he touches shore. Should be any day, the messenger said. I came straight here to share the news. I have to tell *everyone*." He interrupted his crowing and moved to Olivia, putting his hands on her shoulders and giving her a paternal shake. "I can see that you're as dumbstruck as anyone, m'dear. Well, it's the truth. I see there's a bit of a party tonight, which is splendid. Splendid! I shall be able to tell everyone at once."

And with that, he drew Olivia into the drawing

room. The dowager moved forward with a smile; Quin turned around from a conversation. Before either of them could greet him, Canterwick waved the assembly to silence as if he owned the house.

He was something of an actor, Olivia thought, starting to get over the shock of his arrival and the astounding news he brought. First she had thought Rupert was dead, and now . . . Now?

"As you may know, my son, the Marquess of Montsurrey, is the major of the First Company of Canterwick Rifles," the duke was saying, once again at a near-shout. He rocked back and forth on his heels, the words tumbling out. "For one reason or another, the Rifles landed at Oporto in Portugal. Apparently, when my son discovered this error, he shaped up his men and took them across country to Badajoz, the fort of Badajoz."

The entire room was rapt, attention fixed on the duke. Except Quin; his eyes were fixed on Olivia's back. Olivia could feel her shoulder blades prickling.

"As I'm sure you know, Badajoz has been under siege, under the command of General Thomas Picton. There had been many an attempt to scale the ramparts—some of them detailed in the London papers—but to no avail. Not, that is, until my son arrived!"

Olivia doubted that the duke knew how triumphant his tone was whenever he said the words *my son.*

"He's glowing," Georgiana murmured to her. "Isn't it wonderful, Olivia? I mean, wonderful for Rupert. This will change everything for him."

Olivia nodded.

"The general labeled the Canterwick Rifles the 'Forlorn Hope,'" the duke went on. "That's the term they give to a company that has no hope of success. 'Forlorn Hope'! My son! Picton had to eat his words."

"I expect Picton didn't want to let them climb the ramparts," Olivia whispered back to Georgiana. "It's rather nice to see that even a general can't stop Rupert once he puts his mind to something."

"He and his men surmounted those ramparts, although every other English company had failed," the duke bellowed. "Scaled then *and* held them for several days, until the Fifth Division was able to return. They'd given up, you see. Given up and moved on, thinking the French were keeping the fort at Badajoz. They weren't, thanks to *my son*!"

Olivia couldn't stop herself; she glanced to her right. Quin was looking at her; their eyes met, and it felt as if a gulf had opened between them.

"Most of the French defenders retreated to San Cristobal, and surrendered from there," the duke said, his voice growing louder by the moment. "The marquess led his company up those ramparts, then held the fort, and captured many French soldiers. Held it. With one hundred men, he held the whole fort." The duke leveled a ferocious look around the room. "There have been those who said things behind my son's back. Made fun of him. Never again! They're talking of the Order of the Bath. An honor held by twenty-four men at the most. My *son*!"

There was a moment of silence and then, spontaneously, applause . . . spreading from hand to hand until the whole party was cheering, even tearful in some cases.

The duke suddenly turned to the side and caught Olivia's arm, pulled her to him. "Miss Lytton believed in him," he said, looking around the room, fierce. "I present to you my son's fiancée, the future Marchioness of Montsurrey."

Olivia almost tripped, caught herself, smiled. The applause briefly grew louder, then subsided as the Dowager Duchess of Sconce advanced majestically to stand before the duke. In the perfect silence of the room, she dropped into a low, and only slightly creaky, curtsy.

"Your Grace," she said, "it will be the honor of this nation to welcome your son back to the shores of England wreathed in rightly deserved glory."

Olivia did not look at Quin again.

She could not look.

Twenty-three

Why Heroes Are Not as Much Fun as Dukes

The dinner that followed the arrival of the Duke of Canterwick was never forgotten by any of the delighted and—after the joyous popping of champagne corks—inebriated guests. Though there was one participant who, even years later, would remember feeling utter despair in the midst of all that celebration.

Quin wandered among the guests feeling like a ghost: a human shell with a semblance of a face but no other distinctions than incredibly bad luck when it came to women.

He danced with Georgiana after dinner. He tracked Olivia from the corner of his eye, saw how she passed from man to man, how they ogled her and laughed with her and generally fell in love with her and into envy of the marquess.

Of course, no one would voice such a shabby emotion: not tonight, not after the French had surrendered that fort, which had been so hard-sought with lost English lives.

He walked from room to room, because if he kept moving, people didn't try to stop him and talk of the marquess. "Envy" was a pale word to describe the emotion he felt: it was more like rage, pure hatred, livid, bone-deep jealousy. His mother put a hand on his sleeve, stilled, let him go.

He didn't know what she saw in his eyes. It didn't matter.

The devil of it was that he would walk out of the room where Olivia was . . . and find himself walking back into it a moment later. He couldn't fool himself that he walked randomly. He tried to walk away. . . .

He found himself looking for her again. And again.

It seemed an eternity until the majority of guests retired to their rooms and the still excited and voluble duke was escorted to the Queen's Chamber, so called because Queen Elizabeth had slept in it on three occasions.

Quin went to his chambers and bathed. He put on his dressing gown, then dismissed Waller and dressed himself all over again. He slipped out of his room, down the corridor, opened the door to Olivia's bedchamber and entered.

She sat with her back to him, toes stretched out toward the fire, reading a book, just as in his dream. His body became a throbbing, aching torch.

He approached silently, swept her silky hair to the side, and bent down to kiss her neck.

His heart was pounding. He recognized the emotion flooding through his veins. He may not be the best at identifying emotion, but any fool could grasp this one. It was fear.

Rupert had done it. He was a war hero, now. A war hero.

Olivia had the choice of marrying a man who stayed at home, no better than a man-milliner, or marrying a man who scaled the ramparts, held the fort, and saved the day. Hell, Rupert might even have turned the tide of the war. He and his piddling hundred men.

His lips touched her neck as he breathed in that delicate combination of flowers and mystery that was his Olivia . . . as he waited with a sense of dread that stretched from the tips of his fingers all the way to his soul, wherever that mysterious organ might be situated.

He'd been in this state before: the first night Evangeline didn't come home. When she'd returned with the dawn light, she'd said that he was boring, with his talk of nothing but mathematics until she wanted to scream. She had spent the night with a local squire.

"I couldn't say no," Evangeline had said dreamily. "He had gone out on a hunt and startled a gang of smugglers, captured them all. He's a *hero*."

Even months later, when the "smugglers" came to trial and turned out to have been starving villagers, desperately trying to poach rabbits in woods the squire liked to think of as his own . . . even then she'd still thought of the man as a hero.

Now, here, Olivia's arms rose and caught him around the neck. Cherry lips, a gleam in her eye that was for him alone . . .

"I'm sorry," he managed to say, but not until minutes or even an hour later.

"What for?" He'd maneuvered her from the chair to the rug, firelight leaping here and there, flickering on her creamy skin. As it turned out, she was wearing nothing but a dressing gown, and though she had tried to keep it tied, he had managed to wrestle it open.

Blood raced through his body. But it had to be said. "You could have married a war hero if I hadn't taken your virginity. Every woman loves a hero."

"Isn't it wonderful for Rupert?" she said, smiling.

"Absolutely." His voice was hollow, but he kept it in check.

"We won't have any problem finding him a wife now," she continued. "Is something wrong, Quin? You aren't jealous of poor Rupert, are you?"

There was only one answer to that. "Yes."

She came up on one elbow, put a soft hand on his cheek. "Please don't tell me that you want to go to war."

"I can't. Too many responsibilities. But yes, I *would* like to. I've read Machiavelli, Julius Caesar, and de Saxe. I would like to do something that makes a difference in the world."

"I do see what you mean," she said, lying back and folding her arms behind her head. "You're saying that you have to stay home and take care of thousands of acres of land, and make sure hundreds of people in your care and working on your lands are fed and clothed and able to live another day . . . Wait! Is that making a difference?" She tapped her chin. "No, you're right. Unless you can go over to France and kill some people, your life is *wasted*."

Quin made himself say the words, forcing them out of his mouth. "Under the circumstances, do you still wish to marry me?"

She frowned at him. "Which circumstances? Rupert's triumphs or the battering ram episode of last night?"

"Battering ram!" Her indelicate simile caused him to momentarily lose track of the point, but he recovered. "Because of Rupert's triumphs. Because you could marry a duke who seems likely to be one of the greatest heroes the British Empire has ever known."

A little smile touched her lips. "Why, that *is* true, isn't it?"

"Yes."

"I could spend the rest of my life discussing what Lucy ate most recently with a great national hero . . . or I could lie on a rug with you."

His heart was pounding in his ears.

"Naked," she added. Her eyes said everything. "Vulnerable to attack by a ba—"

"Don't say that again." The clench in his heart eased. He stood up and pulled off his boots. She watched him with heavy-lidded eyes.

He threw the shirt away, pulled down his breeches. "Olivia."

"Mmmm."

"A *battering* ram?"

He threw off his smalls and her eyes went right to the spot. "That is an accurate description," she stated. "Just look at yourself."

Quin looked down. He was rampant, so to speak. And yes, formidable. "We really shouldn't make love again until Montsurrey is back in England and has been informed of the change of circumstances."

With a thrill of pure pleasure, he saw her eyes change and her lower lip droop. It seemed the battering ram wasn't all *that* terrifying.

He dropped to his knees and drew his fingers sensuously down the slope of her cheek, to her neck, slower . . .

"That doesn't mean we have to be strangers."

"No?" she whispered, winding her arms around his neck.

He lowered his head, a low groan escaping from his chest.

"No."

Twenty-four

Gallic Mustaches, a Friend in Need, and the Spirit of Adventure

*I*n later years, Olivia looked back on the evening she spent on the hearthrug, being ravished by a jealous, possessive, and altogether perfect duke, as a defining moment, the point that would forever separate her life "before" from that "after."

It was the night when she learned how breathtaking life could be.

And it was followed by the morning when she learned how truly fragile and dear it is.

She and Quin had crawled into her curtained bed, slept in snatches, woken each other up, laughed and whispered, and explored each other.

He departed as the sun was creeping over the horizon, having first told her exactly why the dawn rays stealing through the window were soft pink and not blinding white. She didn't even have to pretend to be fascinated; she genuinely was.

Although she fell back to sleep thinking of the light in Quin's eyes rather than that coming in the window.

The next thing she felt was a hand shaking her shoulder. "Olivia, wake up! *Wake up!*"

The barely contained panic in Georgiana's voice cut through dreamy half-sleep and snapped Olivia's eyes open. "What's the matter?"

Georgiana's sense of urgency was briefly derailed by her sense of decorum. "Why aren't you wearing a nightgown? No, I don't want to know." Georgiana hauled back the curtains with a jangle of curtain rings. "You must get dressed; Norah will be here in a moment, and she shouldn't see you in that state."

"What is it?" Olivia pushed the covers back, swung her legs over the side of the bed, and looked around for her robe. It was very peculiar to wake up naked, especially under the disapproving eye of her sister. "Has something happened to Mother or Father?"

"It's Rupert," Georgiana said, finding a discarded wrapper on the floor and throwing it at her. "Put this on, for goodness' sake."

"Rupert?" Olivia said, jumping up. "What has happened?"

Georgiana bit her lip. "He's badly injured, Livie. There's some question whether he will survive. I feel so—poor Rupert! Poor, poor Rupert." Her eyes were bright with tears. "And that's not all: the courier from Rupert's company no sooner told his father than the duke fell to the ground."

"*Dead?*"

"He's not dead. But he is insensible. He hasn't woken at all. The man arrived from Dover in the middle of the night, after we had all retired. Once Canterwick collapsed, the butler tried to find Sconce, but . . ."

"He was here with me."

"I guessed as much. So Cleese woke the duchess, and she summoned a physician. But Canterwick has not moved or spoken, and I gather the doctor is not hopeful. The duke looks as if he were dead, but he still breathes."

Olivia stood in the middle of the room, clutching the neck of her wrapper and thinking as hard as she could. "Is Rupert in London? I shall go to him immediately. He must be so frightened, and if his father cannot go to his side, then I must."

Georgiana shook her head. "He's in France. I think that's probably what his father found most shocking."

"In *France*?"

"I don't know all the details, but the courier said his men were taking him up the coast of France, trying to bring him to Calais, where they were planning to cross the Channel with the first boat they could commandeer, but—Olivia, it's just so sad—his injuries are too grievous. So one of his soldiers came without him, bringing the message for Canterwick, and was directed on from Dover to here."

Olivia sank back onto the bed, feeling temporarily overwhelmed. "He is too injured to cross the Channel?"

"I'm afraid so." Georgiana sat down as well and wound an arm around her.

"He must be terribly afraid. Unless . . . perhaps he's insensible?"

"I don't think so. Apparently he asked for his father."

"I expect he asked for Lucy, too."

"And you. He's very fond of you," Georgiana said.

"His father would have gone to him, if he had not

suffered this attack," Olivia said, her heart thumping miserably.

"One must suppose so. But it's a terribly dangerous endeavor, given the war. Rupert got only as far as Normandy. He might be captured at any moment."

Olivia stood up. "I must go to him. Now." She hauled on the bell. "I suppose I'll need a boat capable of crossing the Channel."

"You would do better to travel by coach until you're at a point directly opposite Rupert," Georgiana said, and then gasped, "but of course you're not going to France, Olivia! Don't be foolish."

Norah appeared in the doorway. "A bath," Olivia stated.

Her maid had a rather smug smile on her face. "I thought as much." She pushed the door open wider. Three footmen filed into the room, carrying buckets of water.

"And then a travelling gown, please," Olivia added.

"You cannot even consider such a rash gesture! Do you have any idea what the relationship between France and England is at the moment? What if you—*you*—are captured by the French, Olivia?"

Olivia considered that for a moment, then she shrugged. "We are at war. We have been at war for some time. We're still at war. I need to get to Rupert. I'm sure that any French soldiers I meet will understand."

Her sister groaned. "You haven't been reading the newspapers, have you?"

"Would it surprise you to hear that the answer is no?" The footmen had left, and the bath was ready. Olivia tore off her wrapper again. "If your sensibilities are going to be offended by my state of undress, Georgie, you had better leave now."

"You have nothing I don't have," her sister said, dropping onto a stool to the side of the bath.

"I just have more of it," Olivia murmured, poking a toe into the steaming water.

"You cannot take such a quixotic trip across the Channel," Georgiana insisted. "You haven't the faintest idea of the peril."

"I can live with the uncertainty," Olivia said. "Norah, will you please wash my hair as quickly as humanly possible?"

"Yes, miss," Nora said, tackling Olivia's hair as if it were a bundle of laundry.

"Since you do know all the danger *and* you read the newspapers, Georgie, you'd better tell me everything I absolutely have to know."

Her sister started to protest, but Olivia held up her hand. "You've known me longer than anyone else in the world. Do you really imagine that I would leave Rupert to die in some hut on the coast of France? Alone? I may not have wanted to marry him, but I am fond of him. In an odd way, I truly respect him."

There was a moment of silence, but for Norah's splashing.

"He is not your fiancé anymore," Georgiana said. But her voice betrayed the fact that she knew she couldn't win.

Olivia shook her head. "Stop."

"Then I am going with you."

"No, you certainly are not. Just how perilous is it to land on the French shore, anyway?" Olivia soaped an arm while she waited for an answer.

"According to the newspapers, French soldiers are constantly patrolling the beaches, looking for an invasion force and also for smugglers. You could be captured."

"Why on earth would they want to capture me?"

Her sister stared at her. "Do I really need to spell out what soldiers are capable of doing to women, Olivia?"

"Ravished by a Frenchman," Olivia said lightly. "There are those who pay for the privilege."

Georgiana gasped. "How can you respond with—with a vulgarity to such a terrible prospect?"

"I do not mean to belittle the terribleness of such an event, Georgie. But if I have learned anything during my betrothal to Rupert, it is that dwelling on the worst possibilities is not helpful. Therefore, I choose to picture any French soldier I might encounter as seductive and *gallant*." She spoke the last word using the French pronunciation, and considered. "Perhaps with a mustache that curls at the edges."

"I will never understand you! Just how *gallant* will those soldiers be if they believe you to be a spy?"

"A spy? Me? I look nothing like a spy."

"Who knows what a spy looks like? I have a definite understanding that there are women engaged in that business. I wonder if you're even allowed to ransom spies the way you can officers."

"Thank goodness you read the paper so assiduously," Olivia said. "Perhaps you can find out the answer to that question before my need becomes pressing." She stood up, letting the water sluice from her. "Norah, I'm sure you've gathered that I will need a small travelling bag."

"I will accompany you to France, miss," Norah said stoutly. "You will need someone to dress you, even in a French prison."

Olivia's smile included her maid and sister. "Neither of you is coming with me."

"You cannot go alone!" Georgiana protested. Then: "Oh."

"Exactly."

"You must send the duke a note now if you intend to leave immediately," Georgiana said. "Asking him to accompany you." She moved toward the little writing desk in the corner.

"I am quite certain that the duke is already preparing for the journey," Olivia said calmly. "Thank you, Norah, that is a perfect choice for travelling. Doubtless all the best spies wear dark plum."

"It will blend with the night," the little maid said, her voice squeaking with excitement.

Georgiana shook her head. "How do you know that His Grace is prepared? May I remind you, Olivia, that you met Sconce all of four days ago?"

Olivia grinned at her. "That man longs to serve the nation; if being a spy will allow him to, he'll be a spy. He positively writhed with jealousy at the idea of Rupert's going to war. He'll accompany me."

"And what will the dowager say to that?"

Norah shivered. "They do say below-stairs that the duke generally does whatever Her Grace demands."

"She will not be happy," Georgiana persisted.

"I would venture to say that *unhappy* doesn't approach her feelings on the subject," Olivia said, considering the matter. "But there's this to be said about it: If Quin stays in England because of his mother's objections, then he is not a man whom I wish to marry."

"A test?" Georgiana asked, her tone rather dubious.

Olivia nodded. "Do you remember that old story of the lady who was decreed to be a *real* princess because a pea had been hidden under her mattress? Well, this is my version. No prince is *real* if he obeys his mother."

"Rather than his fiancée?" Georgiana asked.

"Rather than the spirit of adventure!"

Twenty-five

The Matter of a Parental Blessing

Quin was in his gunroom, assessing the rather extraordinary number of weapons collected by his forebears. In the end, after careful consideration of what lay ahead, he chose a pair of small but deadly Italian pocket pistols.

"I trust these have been oiled recently?" he asked Cleese.

"Absolutely, Your Grace."

Quin handed Cleese the pistols and watched absentmindedly as the butler wrapped them tenderly in a fold of flannel and replaced them in a specially made case emblazoned with the Sconce coat of arms.

One duke upstairs, dead to the world.

The heir to that dukedom on a beach in France, dead—or very nearly so.

He felt as though he were living in a novel, the kind

with an improbable plot and histrionic characters. At any moment a piece of armor or something equally preposterous would fall from the sky.

"We'll take a boat from Dover," he told Cleese, watching him pack bags of powder and shot in the case. "Send a footman ahead to engage the best captain and vessel available. We'll anchor offshore and take a rowboat with muffled oars under cover of dark. With any luck, the marquess will be on English soil by tomorrow night."

"I trust that will be the case," Cleese said, looking as unconvinced as Quin felt.

The door popped open. "There you are!"

Quin looked up, and felt a surge of emotion so strong that he was dizzy. Olivia was dressed for travel. In the crisis, he had forgotten how beautiful she was: those green eyes, the color of sea glass, the mouth that was made for kissing. "Are you nearly ready?" she asked.

The very idea of allowing her on a boat, anywhere near the Channel, was unnerving. And yet he knew that he had no choice.

"We must leave immediately," she said. He saw anxiety in her eyes, but her smile was bright and brave.

"What on earth are you carrying?" he asked, as she carefully put a basket on the ground.

"Lucy, of course," she answered. "I'm afraid she's not very happy with the basket, but I don't want to risk her falling into the sea."

He stepped forward and took her hands, looking down into those lovely eyes. "Will you please remain here at Littlebourne in safety while I go to fetch Rupert? I will have the marquess at your side within twenty-four hours, if it's humanly possible. I'm sure his condition has improved while the courier was travelling to us."

Olivia's smile widened.

"I had to try," he muttered, as much to himself as to her.

"Your mother is waiting for you in the drawing room."

Quin took the pistol case from Cleese. With it, he was as prepared to protect his lady as he possibly could be. He was a crack shot, but he knew perfectly well that aim and a well-oiled pistol would go only so far. He would need luck.

Olivia stood at his left shoulder. "Quin, did you hear me? Your mother is waiting for you in—"

He turned and dropped a kiss on her lips. "I did hear you. I shall pay a quick farewell to Her Grace directly. Cleese, will you dispatch that footman to Dover, then collect my travelling bag from Waller, and make certain that Miss Lytton is comfortable in the carriage?"

Olivia had turned pink and rather flustered. "You mustn't kiss me in front of people," she whispered.

"Kiss you?" he asked, then: "Cleese, close your eyes." As always, the butler was prompt and obedient, and Quin kissed his lady again, hard and fast. "Is this better?" he whispered back, his voice roughened by a potent combination of desire and fear. "Our inestimable Cleese did not see that particular intimacy. But may I point out, dear heart, that our butler knows *everything* that happens in this household and was undoubtedly aware of my intention to marry you even before I was."

"Cleese, I must beg you to pay no heed to your master," Olivia said, rolling her eyes. "He's clearly succumbed to the stress of the situation." She moved toward the door, slipping away from his grasp. "Truly, Quin, we must hurry. I am worried that we will arrive too late." Her expression rather stricken, she added, "That is, I want to find Rupert as soon as possible."

Quin caught her hand, pulled her back to him, and gave her an openmouthed, hungry kiss. The kind he'd been thinking about ever since he left her at the break of dawn.

When he at last raised his head, she was sagging against him, her breathing unsteady. "I will kiss you," he stated, looking into her eyes, "before Cleese, or before the Regent himself."

Olivia blinked up at him, growing a little teary.

"Or the pope." He began punctuating his sentence with small kisses. "Or the emperor of Siam. Or the archbishop of Canterbury."

A voice came from the doorway.

"Tarquin."

He raised his head and nodded, acknowledging his mother. Then he looked back down at his future wife and dropped another kiss on her rosy lips. "Before any and every member of my family, including my saintly aunt, Lady Velopia Sibble, who would prefer that people communicated only with the deity of her choice, and then only in prayer."

Olivia shook her head at him. "I shall be in the landau." She paused before the dowager and dropped into a low curtsy, head bent. "Your Grace. You may characterize this a housemaid's scuttle if you wish."

"As you have doubtless surmised, I am leaving for France," Quin told his mother, as Olivia disappeared into the corridor. "I expect to return tomorrow, either with a wounded marquess, or the body of an English hero. It need hardly be said that I am hoping for the former."

"By all accounts, including her own, Miss Lytton did

not request your company on this foolhardy errand," the dowager pronounced. Her face wore an expression of grievous injury, and her hands were clasped like a marble saint's. The comparison ended there: the only female saint he could think of with a voice as commanding as his mother's was Joan of Arc.

"Miss Lytton did not have to ask for my escort," he confirmed. "However, I shall go to France, with or without her. May I accompany you to the drawing room, Mother? The tide waits for no man, and I intend to be in Dover in three hours."

"Given the present inclement political situation I would prefer that you did not travel to France."

"I am aware of that." He was running through lists in his head, trying simultaneously to soothe his mother and do the very thing that was terrifying her. "Cleese, please have some rope and a dark lantern put in the carriage. Oh, and a flint."

His mother ignored both his statement and the presence of the butler. "I must ask—nay, *demand*—that you reconsider this rash and dangerous venture. Montsurrey is undoubtedly at the point of death, if not already dead. I questioned Sergeant Grooper, the soldier who arrived in the middle of the night, and he described the marquess as barely able to raise his head from his pallet. That was a full twenty-four hours ago. He is surely dead by now."

"If the marquess has died, then I shall repatriate his body to England," Quin said firmly, guiding his mother down the corridor toward the drawing room. "He is a war hero. It is the least any English citizen could do for him."

"Why must it be you?" the dowager cried, the words bursting from her mouth in an uncharacteristically urgent—not to say emotional—manner. "We could appeal to the Navy! His Majesty would send a force. Or we could hire Bow Street Runners. From what I hear, they could take on a French battalion without any effort."

"His Majesty cannot risk the impression that a British force is attacking the shores of France, and the Royal Navy would face the same problem. But these are academic issues; there is no time to lose. I am beholden to Montsurrey. I shall do this myself."

"You most certainly are *not* beholden to Montsurrey! Did you not tell me that you'd never met him?"

They had reached the entry, and Quin stopped. "Mother, you know why I am beholden to the marquess. And you also know precisely why I would never allow Olivia—"

"Miss Lytton!"

He said steadily, "You understand why I would never allow Olivia to cross the Channel without me."

She was so pale that her rouge stood out in patches on each cheek. "This rash, imprudent effort is foolhardy in the extreme. The French will shoot at first sight. And you haven't even been on the water since your wife died!"

Quin's hand curled into a fist. "It is true that I have not been across the Channel, but only because I have had no need to travel to the Continent." Quin's even tone concealed the pit in his chest that had yawned open at the mere idea of crossing the same stretch of water that had swallowed his son. A duke should never be prey to such emotion, and he ruthlessly pushed it away. "Evangeline's death is irrelevant. Montsurrey needs me; Olivia needs me. And frankly, Mother, I could not face the Duke of Canterwick, should he recover his senses, knowing I had not made every effort to bring his son home."

His mother swallowed hard. "Canterwick would not do the same for you."

"As with Evangeline's death, that is irrelevant. We will put to sea at Dover, and the voyage should be a mere four hours with a good wind. I expect to be home tomorrow. Smugglers do this every day, you know."

"I am afraid of that water," the dowager said, her voice tight as a violin string. "I almost lost you to it before."

Quin nodded; they both knew there was more than one way to be lost.

He picked up his mother's hand and brought it to his lips. "You raised me to be a duke, Mother. I would disgrace my own title if I allowed a man of my rank to die on a foreign shore through my own cowardice."

"I wish I'd raised you to be a peasant," his mother said, her voice low.

"Your Grace," he said, bowing with a low sweep that signaled his deep respect for his mother.

She raised her chin, and then slowly descended into a curtsy of her own. "I would prefer not to be proud of a son who is walking into clear danger," she remarked. Her eyes were shining with tears.

"I will take your blessing with me," Quin said, ignoring her words and answering the look in her eyes. That was something he was learning from Olivia. If he concentrated, he *could* tell what people were feeling, just from looking carefully at their eyes.

His mother turned and swept up the stairs, her shoulders rigid, her head high.

Twenty-six

The Dangers of Poetry under the Moon

*I*t was almost three hours since they left the port at Dover in a vessel named the *Day Dream*, a schooner with a small cabin lying just above the surface of the water. Olivia stood at the porthole, watching black water fall restlessly behind their prow, as if it had somewhere to go.

"We'll take the rowboat up an inlet, if I understand you," Quin said from behind Olivia's shoulder. He was pouring over a detailed map of the French coast with Sergeant Grooper, the soldier who had come to fetch them. Though to be exact, Grooper had come to fetch Rupert's father.

Poor Canterwick. He still lay as if dead. Olivia had visited him before they set out, and had told him that she was going to France to find Rupert and bring him home. Perhaps he heard her.

"Aye," Grooper said. "The hut is just here." His stubby finger landed on a tiny inlet. "I memorized that town: Wizard." His finger moved again.

"Wissant," Quin corrected him. "I believe it means 'white sands.'"

Olivia hugged her cloak tighter around her. Quin had been interrogating Grooper for more than two hours, grilling him on the exact route up the French coast taken by Rupert's men. They'd been in a sloop, desperate to avoid capture. They had faced no problems until Rupert's condition became so precarious that they were afraid to keep travelling.

"Burning up," Grooper said from behind her. "Babbling of green fields and the like. And a lady he left behind."

Olivia turned and smiled faintly at the soldier. "May I inquire whether he was asking for someone named Lucy?"

"That's it! All the way down the coast, it seemed. Lucy, and more Lucy." He eyed her. "I'm thinking your Christian name might be Lucy, ma'am?"

"No, Mr. Grooper, this is Lucy." She gestured toward the little dog sleeping in a basket at her feet.

Grooper's bushy eyebrows flew up. "First time I've heard a man make such a fuss over a dog, I don't mind telling you that."

Olivia felt no need to explain Rupert, nor his devotion to Lucy, and merely nodded. Quin was bent over the map, evidently memorizing every tiny crevice on the coastline. His coat was pulled tight over his shoulders, emphasizing their breadth. His cheekbones stood out more prominently than usual. And that white shock of hair fell over his brow.

"What worries me most is that there's a garrison here,

damn close to the hut," Quin said, his finger sliding over from the inlet where Rupert could be found. "Have you seen soldiers conducting drills thereabouts?"

"I wasn't there but half an hour," Grooper said. "I'm not a man who's a dab hand at the sickbed. I set out for England the moment we had the major settled on a pallet. He hadn't much time." He shook his head. "I still see his father every time I close my eyes, just listing to the side like that, and then falling on the floor. I should have told his lordship more gentle-like. I just blurted it out."

"It wasn't you," Olivia said. "It was the distressing news, not you. No matter how you had phrased it, the duke stands to lose his only son, whom he loves very much."

"I saw that," Grooper said. "And I don't mind telling you that every man in the company feels the same about the major. 'The Forlorn Hope,' that's what they called us. Cause we weren't supposed to come to nothing and"—he stuck out his jaw—"we was the men that no one else wanted; did you know that?"

Olivia shook her head.

"The other recruiters for the army wouldn't take us, and we were just left behind, for one reason or another. They thought I was too old, though I know the battlefield as well if not better than any man. There was a few who had been lamed in the service, and they were told they should just go home."

Olivia made a sympathetic noise.

"Go home! Go home and do what? Take up knitting? You don't tell a soldier to go home just because he lost a few toes or has a gammy leg."

"But the marquess didn't agree?" she prompted.

"In the beginning, I was as nervous as any. He doesn't

think the same as the rest of us, that was plain. But then I saw what he was about. And once I saw that, I would have followed him anywhere."

Olivia beamed at him. "Up the ramparts, in fact?"

"That's right. See, the other companies as had tried before, they always went in the middle of the night, thinking to surprise the Frogs. But of course they didn't. Well, the major, he said we would just walk up there around noon or so and do it. He didn't seem to be worried about it at all, and so none of us were either."

"That's the attitude of a born leader," Quin said. He had straightened, pushed the map to the side, and now leaned on the table, listening.

Grooper nodded. "By then we'd marched across Portugal to Badajoz, and we knew he was a decent chap. Listened to us, he did. And told us what he thought, and didn't talk down." He paused. "Mind you, he was an odd thinker."

That was a kind way of putting it, to Olivia's mind. "So you took the fort."

"Easy as pie," Grooper said, his chest swelling with pride. "See, the Frogs was all eating. And when they eat . . . they *eat*. They go three courses, four, five. All of them, even down to the lowest soldier. The major, he worked it out. He'd had a French tutor, see, and he knew what they were like. And he told us in a way so we could all understand it, too."

Olivia smiled. She loved thinking of Rupert being greeted with respect rather than less-than-thinly-veiled contempt.

"We knocked out a few sentries right off, and then we just took the fort. And we didn't kill many of them French soldiers either; we let them run straight from the lunch table to San Cristobal. The major, he doesn't hold with killing, not unless you have to save your own life."

Olivia smiled. "That's Rupert."

"Did the marquess sustain his injury in the fight?" Quin asked.

Grooper shook his head. "It was the damnedest thing—if you'll pardon me, my lady. We was all done and we held the fort for three days, till the English forces could get back to us. They didn't think we had a chance, you see. Not after all the earlier attempts had failed." The disgust in his voice spoke for itself.

"We held that fort, and we did it nice, too. We had all the Frogs in the stockade, but we gave 'em blankets and plenty of food. Because the major said that a Frenchman deprived of his food will fight like a cornered rat. Sure enough, once they were all snug and well fed, they didn't seem to mind much. Never even tried to get out."

"Then what happened?" Olivia asked.

"The major, well, he liked to walk about on those battlements at night," Grooper said. "The guard up there . . ." He cleared his throat. "Well, he said as how the major was reciting poetry." The last word came out reluctantly, as if he were confessing that Rupert had begun smoking opium.

"Reciting poetry is not generally considered to be a hazardous activity," Quin observed.

"Not one for poetry myself," Grooper acknowledged, managing to imply that he considered poetry to belong in the same category as treason. "The major was up on those battlements, walking around and looking at the moon, and he took a header."

"He was looking at the moon?"

"We found a scrap of paper behind with a bit of verse on it, all about the moon. At any rate, the fall knocked his brains about. He didn't even wake up for a day and we thought he was gone for sure. But then he started talking of this Lucy—we thought she was his lady wife—so we decided as how we should get him back to England. Wellington's doctor, he said that we had to wait till the major died and just bring back the body."

"I'm glad you didn't wait," Olivia put in.

"The major wasn't like the rest of them commanders. He really *cared*." Grooper's voice was a bit rough. "We put him in a cart and brought him to the shore, then we took a sloop and brought him up the north coast of France easy as pie. And we would have come across to England, except we thought it was making him worse, with the pitching of the waves. It hurt his head."

Olivia put a hand on Grooper's sleeve. "You did just the right thing. His father may not have been able to say this before he collapsed, but he is tremendously grateful to you, as am I."

The sergeant looked at his hands and said, "Iffen we'd known Lucy was a dog, I don't know that we would have done it."

"In that case I'm glad you had no idea."

"We must be nearing the shore," Quin said, breaking in. "Olivia, you will wait here with Sergeant Grooper." He seemed to think that he had the ultimate say in that matter. "The captain will drop anchor and I will take the rowboat to the hut and fetch the marquess."

"No," Olivia said, keeping her tone even. "I intend to be in that rowboat."

"I beg to differ."

"I did not come all this way to sit safely offshore. If Rupert is alive, he may not be well enough to venture a ride in a rowboat as, indeed, Grooper and his fellow soldiers surmised."

"When we first discussed this possibility, we did not realize that there is a garrison of French soldiers a handsbreadth from the hut. I am extremely doubtful that Rupert and the two men who remained at his side are still at liberty."

Olivia pressed her lips together before they could tremble. "It is true that Rupert is not a very lucky person."

"I am certain that we can retrieve his body from the French if we pay enough," Quin said bluntly. "We will bring it back to England and he will be buried with honors, as befits his rank and his deeds. But you need not risk yourself in that particular endeavor, Olivia. I will bring Rupert home." There was a fierceness in his voice that turned the words into a vow.

Now tears *were* pressing against her eyes. Other than his father, Rupert had never had a champion. And now he had this magnificent, uncompromising duke. She felt sure that Quin would never allow the slightest insult against his erstwhile rival.

"Rupert would have been honored to know you," she said, her voice unsteady despite her best efforts. "And I shall be in that rowboat with you."

"No."

"If you do not permit me to accompany you, I will join you a few moments after I strike poor Grooper on the head and swim to shore."

"No need for that," Grooper said. He seemed to be enjoying the skirmish. "Never let it be said that I came between a married couple."

"We are not married," Quin said, eyes fixed on Olivia.

Grooper shook his head. "And here I thought nobility didn't have the loose ways o' the rest of us. You surely fight as if you'd taken the vows."

"I am an excellent swimmer," Olivia insisted, ignoring the sergeant's less-than-helpful comments. She was trying to make a point, but the moment the words left her mouth, and she saw the pain that flashed through Quin's eyes, she realized she had made a terrible misstep.

She was at his side in an instant, her arms tight around his waist. "I won't go in the water. I promise I won't go into the water." She brushed her lips across his. "If Rupert is still alive, I must be with him. He will recognize me; he has never met you."

"I'll bring Lucy with me."

Olivia knew in her heart of hearts that she had to have her way on this. "You cannot make this decision for me."

"You won't be safe." His voice was ragged . . . raw.

Though they scarcely noticed him, Grooper went up the steps to the deck, gently shutting the door behind him.

"You cannot keep me safe." She pulled him closer until she could feel his hard chest against her. "I cannot keep you safe either."

"Damn it, Olivia, these idiots stowed Rupert in a hut under the very noses of a whole garrison of French soldiers. If the Frenchmen were to capture you . . . *no*."

"They will not capture me," she said. She felt the knifelike agony in his eyes sink into her own heart. "I didn't come all the way to France simply to wait in the *Day Dream*." Then she had an inspiration. "They won't capture me because I will be with you."

"With me," Quin muttered. His jaw clenched.

"I want to remain with you. Not only will I be safer, but I couldn't bear the tension of not knowing how you were faring." She felt a pang of guilt. She was manipulating him. "What if those soldiers catch glimpse of the *Day Dream*?"

"They will not," he said flatly. "We will anchor offshore and shutter the lantern." But his eyes searched her face. He was listening to her.

"I cannot leave him to die alone." She put every bit of willpower she had in her voice.

"Dear heart." He rubbed his thumb gently along the line of her lower lip. "Rupert is dead. I'm trying to work out how to carry his body down the inlet without alerting soldiers. And if by some remote chance he is alive, I will have Lucy with me. Surely she will be introduction enough."

"No." She'd never thought, never imagined, that someone like Quin could love her. Still, she understood instinctively that he had to—he absolutely had to—respect her. He had to trust her even when his instinct was to deny her. "His father is gone. I am the only person in the world who cares for him, Quin. The only one. *I must go to him.*" She held his eyes. "My personal safety is immaterial. This is a question of ethics."

There was a moment of tense silence.

"You have a point," Quin finally said, his voice reluctant.

She held her breath.

His arms tightened about her. "You are Olivia, after all."

"What do you mean?" she whispered.

"You love your sister enough to give me up. You love Rupert, the poor scrambled egg. You love Lucy with her bitten eyelid. You even love your misguided parents."

She cleared her throat. "You omitted one person in that list."

"You are the most loyal person I know. You will

never give up Rupert's secrets; you will never steal a man whom your sister wants. Therefore, obviously you could not live with yourself if you did not make every effort to be with Rupert."

Olivia opened her mouth to say something about love, something about how much she loved the complicated, harsh, and altogether fascinating man who stood before her, but there was a splash, followed by the sound of an anchor being lowered as quietly as possible.

"Very well," Quin said tightly. "I don't like it. But I understand."

Olivia reached up on tiptoes and brushed a kiss across his lips again. "I love you."

His hands tightened on her arms and he kissed her. He said nothing. But it didn't matter. Olivia understood love as well as any other woman, and when a man looked at a woman with desire and possession and caring all mixed up . . . he loves her, whether he articulates it or no.

She smiled. "The rowboat is waiting for us. It's time to go."

Twenty-seven

"And Miles to Go Before I Sleep"

Up on the deck, the first thing Quin realized was that the rowboat was far too small, hardly bigger than his bathtub. It would barely take his weight, let alone his and Olivia's. And it certainly couldn't take a third person, dead or alive.

The captain of the *Day Dream* leaned close, his voice low. "It's the only one I have with muffled oars. It slips through the water with no more sound than a man pissing in a pond. For those with a need to reach the shore quiet-like, this is the one."

The man showed every sign of being a smuggler. Quin paused, then nodded, consciously releasing the tension in his jaw. If they survived the next few hours, he didn't want to keel over like Rupert's father; he had noted that tension had an extremely deleterious effect on the human body.

Two dead dukes, both betrothed to Olivia and neither with a surviving heir, would be absurd.

He cautiously lowered himself from the schooner into the little boat and reached up for Olivia, whom the captain helped down. They had to sit with their legs sharply bent, knees pressed against knees, Lucy clutched in Olivia's arms. The pang of desire he always felt at her touch, ordinarily so thrilling, was now an irritant, a spur to his underlying sense of panic.

But he slipped the muffled oars into the water, and indeed, the boat made no more sound than a reed in the wind. Rocks reared on the port side, and in the near distance a blur of sand shone in the moonlight.

He mentally calculated the exact place where the inlet let into the sea, and was gratified to catch a patch of darkness just where he'd predicted it would be. Somewhere a curlew called a night anthem, notes tumbling with the gentle sound of the waves. Olivia's eyes were shining. "I love the smell of the sea," she whispered, her voice just a thread of sound in the night.

In truth, the water didn't smell like the terrible, engulfing entity that had stolen his son. It smelled like brine and seaweed, and reminded him of his childhood, when every physical quality of the world was a mystery waiting to be solved.

Ahead of them was a bright spark in the darkness, slightly to the right of the inlet. He tapped Olivia on the knee, pointed.

"Rupert?"

"The garrison." He pulled to the port side, heading straight for the dark shadow that signaled the mouth of the inlet.

Perhaps they truly would be lucky . . . in and out like a fox.

Then the little boat was slipping up the inlet, which was overhung with branches, just as Grooper had described. All the while, Quin was calculating how to bring the three of them back down the inlet, given the size of the rowboat. It was not possible.

He would have to take Olivia back to the *Day Dream*, get her safely aboard, then return for Rupert's body.

The boat slid like a ghost through the water, and the stream bent slightly to the right again. A second later, they nosed onto the beach. Quin clambered to shore, made the boat fast, and turned to help Olivia and Lucy.

He held her for a moment. "I don't want you here," he whispered.

"Let's go," she said, her voice brushing his ear.

He took her hand. It was hell to care about someone. How could he have forgotten that? He used to worry about Alfie every time he was ill. Anxiety was tiresome.

They climbed up the bank and veered to the left. In his mind's eye, he followed Grooper's finger on the map, translating map distances into steps. If there were ever a situation in which his mathematical skill was useful, this was it.

They moved silently forward, feeling their way as much as seeing it; after a time the dark exterior wall of a hut loomed precisely where it should be. Quin put a hand on Olivia's shoulder and tightened it in a silent message. She nodded, her eyes huge in the moonlight.

He followed the wall of the hut, turned the corner, and pushed gently on the door. Inside there was a faint brush of movement; instantly he whispered, "God save the King."

The door swung inwards. Quin walked into total darkness, and waited until the door shut behind him. Then a dark lantern slid open. Its wavering flame illuminated the faces of two drawn and exhausted English soldiers.

"Thank God you've come," one of them breathed.

"He lives?"

A jerky nod of the head. "Barely."

"Your names?"

"Togs." Another jerk of his head. "That's Paisley."

Quin nodded at the lantern. They shut it again and he slipped out, returning with Olivia, her hand warm in his.

When the lantern was opened once more, its light shone on the clear planes of her face, the glowing strands of hair escaping from under her hood, the generous line of her lower lip.

"*Lucy*!" Togs gasped. There was a wealth of meaning in his voice. They thought she was worth risking their lives for. Quin could see it in both men's eyes. A silent growl rose in his throat, startling him.

Olivia shook her head, unloosed her cape, and put Rupert's little dog on the floor. She smiled at the bewildered faces and pointed. "This is Lucy."

"The marquess?" Quin asked. He had stopped thinking about corpses and was now desperately calculating how to get both Olivia and a grievously injured Rupert back in that tiny rowboat. His remaining behind was out of the question; Olivia couldn't row far enough to reach the *Day Dream*. He would have to take one, then return for the other—which meant that he would have to leave one temporarily behind.

Togs shook his head and drew back a rough curtain in the corner, revealing a slight figure lying on a thin mattress on the floor.

Olivia rushed over and fell to her knees. Lucy was already there, nosing her master's cheek, her thin tail wagging madly.

She picked up Rupert's hand. It was odd to realize only now that his fingers were long and delicate. They weren't like Quin's powerful grip, but they were beautiful in their own way.

She leaned close and said, "Rupert!" He didn't stir.

Lucy pressed close to Olivia, trembling, and then she suddenly took a little hop and landed on Rupert's chest. Olivia reached out to remove her, but the dog was licking his cheek, his nose, his eyelids. Instead Olivia said, low and urgent, "Rupert, I've brought Lucy to you. It's *Lucy*."

His eyelids trembled.

She rubbed his hand faster and glanced over her shoulder at Quin. "He's waking!" she mouthed.

Lucy was still licking Rupert, her warm tongue bathing his cheek, his ear. He opened his mouth and rasped one word. "Lucy."

Olivia bent even closer. "Rupert, it's Olivia. Lucy and I have come to take you back home."

For a second he said nothing. Then his eyes slowly focused on Lucy's brown pointed nose and shining eyes. A smile trembled on his bloodless lips.

His eyes moved to Olivia. "Knew you'd come."

The words were slurred. Olivia saw with a lurch of her stomach a trickle of dried blood leading from his ear.

She felt a sob rising in her throat. He didn't . . . he didn't look as if he had long to live.

Quin's hand came on her shoulder and squeezed. He squatted down beside the pallet. "Lord Monts—"

She shook her head.

Quin started over, his voice calm and deep. "Rupert, we've come to take you home."

Rupert's eyes wandered from Lucy. "Who?"

"My name is Quin."

"Ah." His eyes were closing. "Miles to go."

"Yes," Quin agreed.

He saw the truth of it in Rupert's face, before the man even spoke. "Too many miles . . ."

Olivia's hand closed around Quin's wrist. "We must take him now to the boat. *Now*. Otherwise . . . he will die here, in this hovel."

Rupert didn't look like someone with the indomitable will that had driven a company of one hundred men over the walls of a fortress. There was a kind of acceptance about his face that spoke for itself. Quin thought he would almost certainly die very soon.

"We cannot remain here for more than a few hours at the most," he said.

"The Frenchies almost caught us this morning," Togs put in. "We heard them coming . . . they was set to enter the hut, but one of the dogs startled a duck and they went after their supper instead. We didn't have a boat because we sent Grooper over in it."

Quin frowned, looking at the silent Paisley.

"He don't speak," Togs said. "Not even a word. He's the best sailor of us. He got the boat all the way here, but he couldn't come across to fetch you because he don't speak. The major said as how it didn't matter to him as long as Paisley could hold a gun the right way up."

The silent man nodded.

"You both stayed with him," Olivia said, her smile, warm despite her fear, lingering on each of their exhausted faces.

"He's our commander," Togs said. And Paisley nodded tersely.

They were good men. Quin had to get them out as well, before the French stumbled by the hut again in the morning and decided to explore.

Tension mounted in Quin's chest. Rupert was near

death, and the two soldiers were exhausted to the point of collapse. He would bet that they'd had little—if anything—to eat in the last few days.

He crouched down, close enough to catch the warm, flowery scent that was Olivia, and said quietly, "I must leave you here for a short time, dear heart."

She turned her face and her lips brushed his, sweet and heady. "That's exactly what I was thinking."

"I'll be back for you. An hour at the most."

Quin realized that Rupert's eyes had drifted open again, and that he was watching them.

"Happy . . . you." The words floated on the air.

Quin had to clear his throat. "I'm going to carry you to the boat." He slipped one hand under Rupert's torso and discovered that he weighed almost nothing.

"Take Lucy," he whispered to Olivia.

Olivia retrieved the little dog from Rupert's chest, but stopped Quin before he could pick up the injured man. Rupert looked very ill and impossibly young. He didn't seem sixteen, let alone eighteen.

"You did it, Rupert," Olivia whispered, leaning close. "Your father is so happy, and so proud of you. You have crowned the Canterwick name with glory."

Even in the low light, she could see a faint smile in his eyes, a tired smile.

"And you're also a wonderful poet," she said, cupping his cheek with her hand. "You must heal, so that you can write more poetry."

He shook his head, just slightly.

The truth of it was in his face. Olivia's eyes filled with tears. "Then fly, Rupert. Be free. Leave all this darkness to us."

The smile was there again. He turned his head, just slightly, lips against her hand, and closed his eyes.

Olivia stayed still for a moment, a tear splashing onto the rough blanket. Then Quin ran a hand over her hair, and she rose.

She waited until Quin was standing with Rupert in his arms. "If he fails," she told him, "you cannot leave him. He *must not* die on that boat with no one but Grooper by his bed. Do you hear me?"

Her voice was barely above the sound of a nesting bird, and yet he heard every word. "Olivia, no!" It was a plea and a protest at once.

"The French patrol in the morning," she said. "Not until morning." Her eyes moved back to Rupert's face.

She was right. Rupert probably didn't have until the morning, but if they waited in the hut . . . men had taken more than the few hours that remained until dawn to die. And if that were the case, they would all be caught.

Olivia handed Quin Lucy's cord, and he wound it around his wrist. Outside the night air still hung heavy with no hint of dawn. He had time to row down the little inlet, out to the *Day Dream*, time to make Rupert comfortable. . . . He had time.

When they were settled in the rowboat, an operation that required considerable finesse, given the boat's diminutive proportions, Rupert stopped breathing.

Lucy gave a little whimper and licked his cheek; Rupert's chest moved again.

Quin bent to the oars, but he had to be silent, silent . . . He couldn't row too vigorously or the oars would catch the water and splash.

When at last he reached the *Day Dream*, Grooper was waiting at the gunwale. With the soldier hauling from above, getting Rupert on board was quick work, but at the sight of his beloved major unconscious,

Grooper's eyes grew large. He was a man of action, the one who had crossed the Channel to alert Rupert's family, but he was not a man who could stand to see a man suffering.

They managed to get Rupert into the bed, and Quin drew the blanket to Rupert's chin and placed Lucy at his side. The journey from the hut, although short as the crow flies, had been punishingly arduous, and he could see that for Rupert it had been excruciating. His face was even more drawn, and his breathing, the shallow respiration of a man at the limit of his tolerance. His thin fingers clenched Lucy's fur.

"Brandy," Quin barked over his shoulder, only to realize that Grooper, his capabilities exhausted, had fled to the deck. He wrenched open a cabinet and snatched a bottle, which turned out to be the finest French cognac, the kind even dukes drank only sparingly. Oh, for the life of a smuggler.

Turning back, he dribbled a little brandy into Rupert's mouth. The marquess gasped; his eyes flickered open.

A familiar feeling of helplessness clutched Quin's heart. He knew he should say something, but he had no idea what. It was rather as if he were facing Evangeline again, when she would accuse him of being no more emotional than a piece of wood, and he hadn't the faintest idea what she wanted from him.

Probably Rupert would like to hear poetry—but Quin didn't know any poetry. His tutors had never bothered with that sort of thing. His mind spun with furious frustration. If only Rupert wanted information about wave patterns . . .

"Who?" Rupert's eyes searched his face, confused.

"I'm Olivia's friend," Quin reminded him. "We

brought Lucy to see you, and we've come to take you home to your father, to England."

Rupert's fingers curled around Lucy's ear and he gave it a little tug. Lucy nudged his hand.

"Too many miles," he said.

Quin silently agreed with Rupert. What was one supposed to say to a dying person? A psalm, he thought, except he couldn't remember any.

"Sleep," Rupert said, his eyes drifting shut again.

Suddenly, somehow, Rupert's poem came back to Quin, as clearly as if Olivia had recited it to him a moment ago. Before it could vanish, he said it aloud: "Quick, bright, the bird falls down to us, darkness piles up in the trees." It made no sense in this context, but he said it again, more slowly.

Rupert's face brightened and he said something, so quietly Quin almost didn't catch it. "And they fly . . ." A long silence. His breath stopped, started again.

Quin looked desperately at the porthole. There was no sign of dawn yet. He knew what Olivia would say. He knew what she wanted. He knew . . .

Rupert's chest stopped moving again. Then he took another breath, like a little gasp.

So Quin sat, holding tight to the hand of the man who was giving him Olivia, who had written a poem that spoke to Alfie's death, who was flying with sparrows fallen from trees.

And all the time the dearest person in his life was back there on a foreign shore without him, guarded only by two exhausted and trembling soldiers.

Damn, but he must love her to—

The thought cracked like thunder in his head. He froze, noting that Rupert had stopped breathing again, but he'd done that before . . . *Love*?

His mother had told him when he was only a child that love . . . what had she said about love?

That it was dangerous and not for people of their rank. That it was impulsive and the sign of someone foolish and ill-bred.

But . . . when did she say that he wasn't able to love?

He loved Olivia, more than life, more than light, more than . . . anything.

The analytical part of his brain, which had been counting silently, spoke up, suggested that the bird was winging its way through some other sky, a silent sky.

Quin looked down and saw that it was true.

Rupert was gone. Gently, Quin disengaged his hand and tucked Rupert's sheet more securely about him.

Lucy was curled next to her master's body. She lifted her long nose and looked at Quin, whimpering a little. He couldn't fix Rupert, the way she was asking him to. And it didn't seem right to leave her next to her dead master. So he plucked her up, stashed her inside his coat, and ran up the stairs.

Once in the water, he set himself to the oars faster than he should have, catching the water, sending it arcing . . . He had time. He still had time. His heart beat the same sentence over and over. The eastern sky wasn't yet turning pink. It wasn't dawn. He had time.

He tried to slow down, make the oars quieter . . . couldn't stop himself, rowed as fast as he possibly could.

He was still too late.

Twenty-eight

One Putain, Two Putain . . .

*A*fter Quin left, Olivia waited outside the hut, her cloak wrapped close and the hood up, head tipped back against the rough planks. A light wind drifted by, carrying the scent of rotting fish and the peppery, sweet smell of crushed strawberries.

The stars seemed too bright for spring. They should have been so distinct, so clear, only on the coldest of winter nights. Minutes passed . . . until finally she knew for certain that Quin had not come straight back, that he was waiting at Rupert's deathbed.

The stars wavered above her, but tears never fell. That was a point of pride. No crying. Instead, to distract herself, she watched for a falling star, though she knew it was a foolish superstition to think it proclaimed the creation of an angel.

And all the time she listened for the tramp of soldiers' feet, for a burst of French jests. The men who had guarded Rupert had fallen asleep on the floor, telling her to rouse them if she heard anything.

"The battalion marches at the same time every morning," Togs had told her, his voice raspy with the relief of giving over Rupert's care. "Still hours from now."

No stars fell, but she was still watching for them when a hand clapped over her mouth and pulled her into the woods. She was too shocked even to scream.

It wasn't dawn! There wasn't even the faintest hint of light, and there had been no cheerful French badinage, no tramp of boots to warn her.

By the time she gathered her wits and began to struggle, it was too late. With one swift movement she was pushed down and flipped onto her stomach. All those years of French tutoring stood her in good stead, though: "*Aidez-moi!*" she shrieked when the hand left her mouth. "*Lâchez-moi immédiatement! Coquins! Vermines!*" The only response was a foul-smelling scarf, tied so tightly around her mouth that it jerked her head back.

Still shouting, though her words were muffled, Olivia twisted, trying to kick the man pinning her to the ground. But her captor swiftly wound a rope around her wrists, hauled her upright, and gave her a rough shove.

"*Allez!*" The word sounded with the ping of a fat hailstone striking a window. Then a poke between the shoulders forced her forward. "*Avance!*"

She walked, telling herself that Quin would be there any moment, that the English soldiers would wake to discover her missing. She caught a glimpse of the sleeve of the man shoving her. It was ragged and blue, the kind of thick fisherman's shirt she remembered seeing on a childhood trip to Brittany. *Not* a soldier's uniform. Her heart was pounding so hard that she could feel the pulse in her ears.

By the time they broke out of the wood, the eastern sky was lightening. They continued to walk, through thick scrub, the smell of the sea keen in the wind. Olivia tried biting at the scarf in order to get it away from her mouth, but to no avail. She intentionally stumbled in an attempt to slow them down, but the man simply hauled her upright and thumped her in the back with something hard.

These brutish attacks had made her back bruised and painful, and for the first time, she felt truly frightened. A battalion of French soldiers was one thing. Surely they wouldn't injure a woman, even an English one. But what if this thug belonged to a gang of smugglers? Or pirates? Or just common criminals?

The possibilities were all unpleasant.

They had been following the line of the shore, winding along, when the man suddenly directed her up a small trail that led inland, over some bluffs. Olivia's skirts caught on a sturdy bramble, and she stopped, thinking the man behind her would untangle her. Instead the hard object jabbed her in the back again and she stumbled forward, her skirt letting go of the bramble with a long ripping sound. Now her back felt as if it were on fire.

Her eyes were pricked with tears, but if she hadn't wept over Rupert's death—or not much—the last thing she would cry over was this farcical situation. Not dangerous, she told herself; rather it was *farcical*. Quin would save her. The moment he knew she was missing.

The important thing was that Quin was with Rupert.

Furthermore, Rupert wasn't in that smelly hut, but in a proper bed, on the *Day Dream*, with Quin. If there was one person she would want to sit next to her death-bed, it would be Quin, with his honest eyes and the reassuring low bell-sound of his voice.

After what felt like hours, they stumbled out of the scrub and into a gravel yard, on the far side of which lay a two-story brick building surrounded by a wall. A sentry stood at the gate in the wall.

"Who goes there?" he said, without much interest.

All of a sudden Olivia felt utterly calm. At least now she would know what was happening. They had arrived somewhere.

"A *putain* using Père Blanchard's hut." Her captor's voice was toneless, and accompanied by a hard prod in the direction of the gate.

Olivia almost fell at the feet of the sentry. He was slim and weary, with a mustache so luxuriant that it looked as if his face had sprouted wings.

"I am not a *putain*," she cried, her voice strangled by the scarf. She was fairly sure that a *putain* was the French word for a strumpet, a night-walker. Whatever it was, she was certain that it wasn't nice.

The sentry narrowed his eyes at her and then glanced at the man behind her. "What's the use of bringing her here?" he wanted to know. "Send her back to the village."

"She isn't from hereabouts, so that won't work. I don't recognize her." Olivia lifted her chin and gave the sentry a fierce stare, willing him to order the scarf removed so that she could speak.

"Pretty," he said, not noticing her glower—likely because he was too busy staring at her chest. "Take that cloak off, Bessette."

With a jerk the cloak disappeared from around Olivia's shoulders.

"Plump as a partridge," the sentry said, with a toothy smile. "Are you vending your wares, *Madame*?"

Furious, she shook her head.

"Just another wayward wife." He pulled on his mustache until his face looked lopsided. "What's the world coming to? *Le Capitaine* or Madame Fantomas?"

"Madame. No need to bother *Le Capitaine* with this one. Think we can get twenty francs off her husband for retrieving her? See this cloak? Nice made, and it's lined."

"Might be *petit bourgeoisie*. Madame will decide. Take that scarf off her mouth, Bessette. I have to make sure she's not a spy. *Le Capitaine* would want to know."

There was a disgusted snort from Bessette. "*Le Capitaine* is too pickled in brandy to know what to do with a spy even if we did find one. This is no spy. She was leaning outside Père Blanchard's hut, easy as can be, waiting for someone. You know there's only one reason a woman goes there."

"We should burn that hut down," the sentry said, pulling at his mustache again.

Bessette started fumbling with the knotted scarf and Olivia prepared a stream of vitriolic French, but the guard waved his hand. "Just take her in to Madame Fantomas. We got some excellent hams when we found the butcher's wife bent over the apothecary's counter, remember. Tell Madame we want our normal cut."

Olivia felt as if she would burst with rage.

"This little *Madame* is a fierce one," the sentry added, finally meeting her eyes. He actually fell back a step. "Take her away, Bessette. I can't be seen dallying with a trollop. My wife will hear of it."

"Your missus is not one to cross," Bessette said with

a rough chuckle. "Especially if she heard what this one is like. Hips and breasts, just as a man likes them."

"True enough," the sentry said, his eyes lingering on Olivia's breasts. "Best not hit her like that, Bessette. She'll have her husband on you if she gets a bruise."

Bessette snorted. "Not after he learns where I found her."

Once past the gate, rather than walk up to the building's entrance steps, they veered off to the right. Olivia was forced to duck her head as they descended a deep, damp flight of stone steps that opened straight into a large kitchen.

To label the kitchen antiquated would be to pay it a compliment. It was primitive. The chamber appeared to have been carved from stone, with little attempt to smooth the walls. Two pits had been hollowed from the rock and were in use as fireplaces, with holes apparently venting to the outdoors.

But it smelled like a kitchen: chickens were going on spits, and an aroma of yeast and flour was in the air. Four or five very young men, wearing uniforms in various states of disrepair, were turning spits, sharpening knives, or washing potatoes. In the very center of the room was a long table, at which a woman was kneading a lump of dough with ferocious energy.

For the first time since she'd been abducted, Olivia stopped twisting her wrists in a vain attempt to loosen the twine holding them together, and just took in the sight. Madame Fantomas—for it must be she—was like a circus embodied in one person: a big, bold pirate of a woman. Her black hair was tied up so that it rose above her head in a towering fountain, above arched eyebrows and a mouth painted crimson. She wore a low-cut gown, and over that a gore-splattered apron, the entirety lightly dusted with flour. And dangling over the gown and apron, almost to her waist, were ropes of beads: great chunks of turquoise, gold chains, even a cross. They weren't necklaces of a sort Olivia had seen before.

Madame was kneading a huge glop of dough, powerful muscles flexing as she shoved forward, wrapped, and turned. After a moment she pushed it away and reached for a glass of red wine beside her, clinking her thumb rings against it. Rings adorned all her fingers, enough rings to hang a full set of bed curtains. She had the eyes of a goose Olivia had once seen run wild and peck a baker. Mad eyes.

"I brought you a *putain*," Monsieur Bessette offered, from behind Olivia's shoulder. "Found her in Père Blanchard's hut, waiting for her man."

"*Putain*, my ass," Madame said with a snort. "Take that thing off her mouth, you fool. You've got yourself a high-flier there . . . nationality to be determined. Could be for sale, but chances are she's a *très-coquette*, having a bit on the side."

Without taking her eyes off Olivia, she pinched off some raw dough and ate it.

Bessette didn't bother trying to untie the scarf; he just pulled it straight off Olivia's head.

There was a second of silence, then two things happened at once: Olivia burst into a violent stream of French—a commentary on Bessette, together with the illegality of kidnapping in general—while Madame Fantomas swiveled and bawled, "This tastes about as good as pig's slop." With that, she picked up the huge, squashy pile of kneaded dough and threw it squarely across the kitchen.

Olivia broke off her tirade.

The dough hit the wall and slid down, landing on the unevenly bricked floor.

"Feed the *putain*!" Madame barked. They all stared. "*Now*!"

"I am not a *putain*," Olivia shouted, deciding that she had to make as much noise as Madame if she wanted to be noticed. "I was merely waiting for the return of my fiancé. And I don't want anything to eat."

"You may not be a *putain*, but you're a fool with an English accent," Madame said with another swig. "What the devil is an Englishwoman doing at Père Blanchard's hut? Are you a spy, then?"

"Absolutely not!"

"Good. Because there's nothing here to spy on but a groggified captain and a bunch of French boys whose balls are too small to hold up their breeches." She waved her hand at the young men turning the spits.

"I am no spy," Olivia stated. "I demand to be released. My fiancé will be wondering where I am."

"The *putain*!" Madame bellowed, turning her head and glaring at a boy at the side of the kitchen. Then she looked back at Olivia. "Spy or not, what are you doing here? Because we don't get many female smugglers over here, not that you look the type anyway."

The boy got to his feet, trotted over to the side of the kitchen, and plucked the top off a large earthenware container. It was oozing, bubbling . . . the source of the vinegary sharp smell of growing yeast. He poured it into a shallow bowl on the far end of the table. Presumably that was the *putain*.

"I am in this country on an errand of mercy," Olivia said, keeping her head high. "I am betrothed to a duke, and I demand to know on what authority this miscreant captured me and brought me here. And I want my hands freed!"

"Sakes alive, a virgin," Madame said with a twist in her smile. "Isn't this my lucky day?"

Olivia spun to face Bessette. He turned out to be a burly man with a large head and ears that stuck out like pink flower petals. "You!" she said furiously. "Monsieur Bessette, you must undo these ropes from my hands *at once*!" Then she turned her back to him and waggled her fingers in his direction.

To her satisfaction and relief, she felt him fumbling at the twine.

"The mushroom," Madame commanded. The boy poured a thin stream of foul-smelling, cloudy black liquid onto the bubbling yeast and began mixing it.

"Treat her gently!" Madame barked, apparently referring to the yeast, not to Olivia.

When Olivia's hands were free, she shook them for a moment, trying to restore their circulation, then folded her arms over her chest and turned back to Madame. "Am I to suppose that you make a habit of kidnapping women at your whim?"

"Not unless they are worth some money."

"How much money do you want?" Olivia demanded.

"For what?"

"I assume I am to pay for my freedom."

"Your French is too good for a mere English maiden," Madame stated, narrowing her eyes and ignoring Olivia's comment. "You're a spy."

"You said it yourself: there's nothing here to spy on."

"True. Then . . . you're spying on *me*."

Olivia rolled her eyes. "Believe me, Madame, no one I know would have the faintest interest in you and your kitchen, though it would serve nicely in an exhibit of primitive cooking amongst savages."

"Not so!" Madame said, slapping her hand down on the floury board so that a cloud rose in the air. "All the great bakers of Paris and London want my recipe for bread. And you—you have come here, straight to the place where I am, because you know of my great talent."

"I know nothing about bread," Olivia stated.

"Then *you* are the savage! The great Napoleon himself said my bread was blessed by the gods. And I share the secrets of my *putain* with no one. No one!" Her voice rose to a shriek.

Olivia stood her ground. Although it might seem rather paradoxical, she was feeling quite calm now. Marauding gangs of lustful soldiers were terrifying, but battles with a lunatic cook were a routine part of running a large household. "If you think anyone would try to steal the recipe for that disgusting concoction, you are quite mistaken."

"She is a spy," Madame announced. "A cookery spy. And a terrible liar, which is true of all the English."

"I am not," Olivia snapped.

Madame ticked off the presumed lies. "A virgin? I don't think so."

Olivia opened her mouth and shut it.

"Betrothed to a duke? Also unlikely. You're well enough, but you're no beauty. Betrothed to a draper rather than a duke, I'd guess." She turned and hauled on a bell cord hanging at the wall. "She'll have to go into the catacombs until *Le Capitaine* wakes up. How much did he drink last night?"

One of the boys turning a spit looked up. "Two bottles, Madame."

She snorted. "He'll not wake before evening, then." She pulled out a ring of keys. "Put her in the far end, Petit."

Olivia gave the boy a look.

"She's a lady," he protested. "Ladies don't belong in the cells."

"She's damned lucky they've put the Guillotine to rest," Madame replied, finishing her wine. "They used to do it properly in Paris. People made a living, just whacking the heads of aristos like I might a bean row. Bessette, go along with them."

"I *demand* to speak to whoever is in charge of this establishment!" Olivia said furiously.

"I am," Madame stated.

"You! You're a servant, not the commander of a garrison."

"Wine!" Madame bellowed. One of the boys trotted over and poured her more red wine. "It's me whenever *Le Capitaine* is drunk or asleep, which gives him about one hour to my twenty-three."

Olivia eyed her red wine.

"Strengthens my blood," Madame said, grinning. She reached into a sack of flour and sprinkled some on the table. "Give me a bit of that *putain*. I'm starting over."

Bessette grabbed Olivia's arm, holding it hard. "It's in the back with you. Do I have to tie you up again?"

Olivia shook her head, glaring into his pale blue eyes. "My fiancé will likely kill you when he finds how you have treated me."

Bessette grinned, showing blackened teeth. "Won't be the first who tried. I hope you don't mind if I keep your cloak. I can sell this for ten sous."

"There's no need to wrench her arm," the young soldier said, stepping forward.

Madame didn't look up from the flour she was delicately sifting over a small pile of frothing yeast. "English *putain*, don't think you can seduce the poor lad into giving you the key to your chamber. The only way out is through my kitchen, and I don't leave my bread. Ever."

Twenty-nine

Lost Treasure

Quin had woken Togs and Paisley from a sound slumber, knowing already that they had no idea what had happened to Olivia. There was no point in tearing into the exhausted Englishmen; how could they be blamed for sleeping through her disappearance, after all they'd been through? Now they milled about like sleepwalkers.

Quin's heart was beating in his throat so violently that he could hardly form words. He dispatched them back to the schooner, with instructions to send Grooper back with the rowboat to wait at the top of the inlet.

He paused to get his bearings and to work out the exact location of the French garrison in relation to the hut. He started off at a steady jog, Lucy trotting at his side. Either the French soldiers had captured Olivia, or he would force them to assist in locating her.

As he ran steadily up the bank and then through a scrub forest, he turned over the various possibilities in his mind. Yes, England was at war with France, but that meant different things to different people—and he wasn't entirely convinced that a provincial garrison would feel much desire to capture an English lady.

Though the odds of one English duke's subduing an entire garrison of French soldiers, bristling with everything from pistols to bayonets, were not good. It wouldn't be helpful to Olivia if he ended up skewered on a bayonet in a valiant but failed rescue attempt.

Just then a hare bounded across his way, and he heard a surprisingly deep bark in response. He looked down to find Lucy still running along beside him, as fast as her stubby little legs would carry her.

Quin paused just long enough to scoop up the dog and took off again. By his reckoning, he should be very close. Indeed, a moment later the scrub gave out at the edge of a raked-gravel yard, on the other side of which, behind walls, stood a brick structure.

The garrison did not give the impression that it was prepared for military action. The gravel had been raked with no regard to a few wildflowers sprouting up here and there, waving gently in the area that appeared to have been designated for formation drills. A sentry sat at the front gate, fast asleep. Quin walked straight past him through the courtyard and ran up the steps to the main entrance, Lucy under his arm.

Inside, he put Lucy down and poked his head into a dusty receiving room, an unused office, and a long mess hall. Toward the back he found a room that showed signs of heavy use. Open crates holding rifles lined the room, suggesting it was an armory, but he'd guess that the worn billiards table in the center received the most attention.

He headed up the staircase without meeting a soul, the click of Lucy's toenails only making the silence feel more profound. The first bedchamber he looked into, however, was occupied. For a moment Quin stood in the doorway, assessing the situation. A large and rather malodorous man was snoring loudly, facedown on a bed whose sheets had seen better days. A table at the far wall of the room glittered with a row of brandy bottles, the same sort he'd given Rupert in the schooner. Thrown on the chair was a stained captain's coat.

A small pistol lay on a side table; he removed its bullet and tossed the bag of powder out the open window. Then he put it back where he'd found it, caught up the back of the captain's shirt, and shook him.

The man snorted and rolled on his back. Quin recoiled as a breathful of rancid brandy reached him.

Half a minute later the captain was awake and the bed was sopping wet; Quin had been forced to empty a water pitcher over his head, and it was only the threat of the chamber pot that actually got the man on his feet.

"Who the devil are you?" he said, his face pale gray in the sunlight, his eyes red-rimmed and dull. He reached out, steadied himself against the wall.

Quin pointed one of his pistols at the man's head. "I have come for my fiancée. She's English and was abducted on the shore near here a few hours ago."

Ignoring the pistol altogether, the captain sat down, shuddering like an ear of corn in the wind. "No Englishwoman would be here. We're at war with you, if you didn't notice."

"Did your men capture her?"

"I doubt it. Most of them are too young to find their own winkles without a map. I need sleep. Get yourself the devil out of here, will you?" He sank back down onto the soggy bed and closed his eyes.

Quin looked around and saw a half-drunk bottle of brandy. He upended this too over the captain's head, who lurched upright, his face contorted. "What the devil?" he croaked. "You're a madman."

"Find my fiancée," Quin said, keeping his voice even. He raised the pistol and shot the first of the brandy bottles lined up on the far table, causing Lucy to flinch and then bark. Glass shards and brandy rained down onto the floor, and its heady aroma filled the room.

"Stop!" the captain screamed. "You're insane. All you English are mad as spring hares."

Quin switched pistols and shot the second bottle. "I'm the madman who will have you arrested as a smuggler if you do not send your regiment out to find my fiancée. I don't care how young your men are. You will find her or I'll destroy every bottle in the place, and I'll make sure your cozy smuggling operation dries up as well."

"And how would you do that, being a benighted Englishman?" But the captain was just blustering. He was a weak and feckless type, who would always choose the path of least resistance. Sure enough, he hauled on a bell cord.

A minute or so later a very young soldier poked his head in the room, wrinkling his nose at the odor. "*Oui, mon capitaine?*"

"Is the regiment out on patrol?"

"No, sir. Everyone is still resting."

Quin finished reloading and shot a third bottle.

"Get them up and send them down to the shore!" the captain screamed, to the sound of glass tinkling to the floor. "Find this man's woman. *Une anglaise. Mon dieu*, my head is killing me." He fell back onto his bed.

The young soldier saluted his moribund captain and then looked to Quin. "We're about to patrol the shore in search of smugglers, as we do every morning and afternoon," he said, without betraying by the blink of an eyelash the fact that they were standing in a smugglers' haven. "We will look for your wife, sir."

"Good," Quin said, biting the word off. He was aware that he was in a state of barely modulated panic. If these soldiers hadn't captured Olivia—and obviously they hadn't—then where in the bloody hell was she?

He started down the stairs. He would check every house in Wissant, and then return here to see if the patrol discovered anything.

The damnable thing was that he knew this particular sensation. It fell on his shoulders like a familiar but loathed garment. He had felt it when he realized that Evangeline had taken Alfie and headed for the Channel. He had tasted it, bitter on his tongue, as he galloped toward Dover, hoping to intercept them on the pier.

It had driven him half-mad once he was there, watching the water. And he felt it now. It wasn't *safe* to love someone.

His mother was right about that.

But it was too late to avoid the condition.

Thirty

The Princess and the . . .

*B*essette, followed by Petit, marched Olivia through a door and down a damp and chilly vaulted brick passage. It went on, wound to the left, its walls broken occasionally by solid doors with barred openings at shoulder level.

"What is this place?" Olivia asked.

"The catacombs," the young soldier answered. "They built the armory on top of them, and decided to use the catacombs for the kitchen and cells. You're at the far end. She's given you the best cell—it's got a hole in the corner."

Bessette shoved open a door to reveal a bare stone room with one rickety wooden chair, lying on its side. Sure enough, there was a stinking hole in the far corner. A high, tiny window, also barred, revealed sky and a bit of grass; she was, for all intents and purposes, underground.

"You cannot leave me here," Olivia said, grabbing his arm. "My fiancé is a duke. And I am a lady."

"I hate *le ducs*," Bessette said, grinning at her again. "I'm not fond of Napoleon either, but I really hate you aristos." He shoved her in and slammed the door. He pulled the key free and handed it to Petit, who had trailed them all the way down the passage. "Don't let this one seduce you into giving up the key," he advised. "Madame Fantomas is not a pretty sight when she's angry. Think about her rolling pin."

"It won't matter what Madame thinks by the time my fiancé gets through with you," Olivia shouted.

The only response was the sound of footsteps receding down the passage.

Olivia took a deep breath, which was a mistake; she nearly gagged at the stench coming from the hole. Presumably she would grow accustomed to the smell in a few minutes. Or perhaps fresh air would blow through the window. Perhaps pigs would fly.

One had to think that by now Rupert had either rallied or . . . not. Which meant that Quin would have returned to shore and must now be looking for her. He would be frantic.

Her situation wasn't as terrible as the dire possibilities Quin had envisioned. After all, she hadn't fallen into the hands of a garrison of soldiers thirsting for English blood. A mad breadmaker and a boozy captain didn't strike fear in her heart; if she died of anything here, it was likely to be the stench.

She turned the chair over and dusted off the seat with the hem of her ruined gown, placing it in such a way that, once seated, she could see out the window. The grass bent at one point and she stood on the chair to see if someone was passing, but it was only a black cat, nosing along in pursuit of a mouse.

By the time the key rasped in the lock again, the light had grown stronger and taken on a yellow hue. The same young soldier, Petit, poked his face around the door. "*Mademoiselle*," he whispered, "we've prepared something better for you. At least until *mon capitaine* wakes. I'm sure he'll let you go once he realizes you're here. But no one can go against Madame Fantomas, except for him."

"I would appreciate anywhere that doesn't include a hole," Olivia told him.

Petit was probably about sixteen, though he seemed even younger. His eyes were the color of robins' eggs. "We decided that French honor would not allow us to leave a lady in a room such as this, even if you are a spy."

She laughed. "I promise you that I'm not."

"As you have seen, Madame is rabid," he said, holding open the door. "We don't cross her because there's no point to it, and besides, she weighs twice as much as any of us. A man named Oboe pinched her once and she struck him on the side of his head with a rolling pin. He never recovered his hearing in that ear."

He escorted her a short way to another cell, which had no hole, and therefore no stench. But the more salient distinction from the first cell was that against the wall under the window there was a stack of mattresses—each covered in a different rough linen ticking. The covers were striped and flowered, which made them look absurdly incongruous in the dank cell, and the stack actually reached as high as her head. A little stepladder leaned against it.

"We each brought our mattress down here for you," Petit said, waving at the stack. "There's twenty of us, and we hauled down fourteen. We thought that was enough to keep the damp off."

"That was astonishingly nice of you!" Olivia exclaimed. "In truth, I was beginning to be very fatigued."

"Ladies don't belong on the ground. *Maman* would have killed me. May I help you?" He moved next to the stepladder.

"*Merci beaucoup*," she said. She took his hand and climbed the ladder, toppling onto the highest mattress when she reached it. She came onto her knees and looked over the side. Petit's nose was level with her perch, and all of a sudden it felt rather precarious.

"You'd better lie down," he said, frowning. "You could crack your head like an egg if you fell off."

She nodded in agreement. "Do you happen to know whether my fiancé, the Duke of Sconce, has come looking for me?"

"We're not allowed outdoors at this hour. I can find out at four in the afternoon when we go out for patrol."

"*Merci*," she said, but there was a noise down the passage and he backed out, slamming the barred door firmly behind him.

For a moment she just sat, her head close to the stone ceiling. She was so weary that she felt dizzy. The mattresses were lumpy and uneven. But they put her on a level with the small window, which in turn was level with a patch of bright grass outside.

Finally she lay down, facing the window, and watched the grass sway. Despite the fact that there were so many mattresses, they were remarkably uncomfortable. It felt as if there was a lump at her back, as if somehow a rock had gotten mixed into the stuffing.

She turned this way and that, trying to find a comfortable position that avoided the lump and would allow her to fall asleep. In the end, she curled around it, willing herself to lie very still. In her sleep, she relaxed and so woke, hours later, with something hard poking painfully into the middle of her back.

She shifted off the hard thing—it was not merely a knot of straw. It was too hard for straw. And she saw that the sun had moved all the way across the room and was now striking the opposite wall.

Just then Petit pushed open the door. "Hello," she called down softly.

"Good afternoon, *Mademoiselle*." He held a tray. "I have brought you something to eat. Madame takes a sleep in the afternoon, though unfortunately she does not leave her kitchen."

He climbed up a step and handed over the tray. "That's her bread," he said, nodding at it. "Even though Madame is completely mad, there are bakers in Paris who would love to know what she puts in her *putain*."

"Goodness," Olivia said, adding anxiously, "Do you know if the duke has asked for me?"

Petit nodded. His eyes were twinkling. "*Mon capitaine* was forced out of bed by him, and he never rises before evening. Your duke fairly tore the place apart. Unfortunately, *Le Capitaine* had no idea you were here."

Olivia groaned. "Did the duke leave?"

"Yes, but he will return in an hour or so. *Le Capitaine* promised to send out the patrol to try to find you before he went back to bed. Bessette plans to demand fifty guineas of your duke, but Madame says you might be worth a hundred."

"In that case, I'll be out by nightfall."

"How is your mattress?" Petit asked, a quizzical look on his face.

"While I wouldn't wish to seem ungrateful, I'm a bit afraid of falling off. May I ask why you put quite so many on top of each other?"

He turned red, and suddenly looked even younger. "We thought that it looked too much like a bed with just one or two mattresses."

"It *is* a bed."

"Yes, but if it looked like a bed, there was the chance that Bessette might decide to . . ." He waved his hand, embarrassed. "You'd be there, you see, on a bed. But this way it is difficult to reach you."

"You are brilliant," Olivia said, sincerely. "If there are any coins to be given out, I shall make sure that they come in your direction."

He grinned. "It was my idea, but we did it, all of us. So, is it comfortable up there, my lady? The mattress is . . . smooth?"

"Of course," Olivia said, rather less than truthfully. She hesitated and then asked, "Aren't you rather young to be a soldier?"

"I'm almost sixteen," he said stoutly. But then he added, with a little droop to his lips, "Nothing ever happens in this garrison, because *Le Capitaine* is interested only in brandy. My mother forced me to be here rather than join a proper regiment." He looked disgusted.

Olivia smiled at him. "I think your mother is very wise."

"Petit! Time for review!" The words echoed down the long stone corridor.

"What is needed is a distraction that might cause Madame to leave her kitchen," he said, his brown eyes now sparkling. "Something that will disrupt the garrison before your duke hands Bessette those guineas he is demanding." He grinned. "I shall think on it."

He disappeared, slamming the door behind him. Olivia heard the lock slide into place.

A distraction? What good would that do, unless she could escape from this cell? She ran her hand over the uneven mattress, thinking about the light in Petit's eyes. One could almost think that he had tried to drop a hint about her mattresses.

Carefully, she slid her legs over the side and stood on the stepladder. She slipped her hand between the first two mattresses, but she could still feel the lump beneath her fingers. She tried the next two, and the two before that . . .

It was a key.

A key tucked between the mattresses, a big iron key that looked exactly like the one the young soldier had used to enter her cell. A smile spread across her face. She would wait for Petit to create the distraction he had promised, and then walk straight out of the building and into Quin's arms. And if Madame Fantomas tried to stop her on the way through the kitchen, she'd thump *her* on the head with a rolling pin.

A bellow sounded down the corridor. "Spy, what do you think of my bread?"

Olivia grinned. "I've had better," she shouted back. "*Putain!*"

Thirty-one

The Bark of Cerberus

Quin was murderous, exhausted, and on the verge of sheer panic by the time he reached the village of Wissant. Lucy was as tired as he was, so he was carrying her tucked inside his jacket, which wasn't comfortable for either of them. And then it transpired that no one had heard anything of *une anglaise*, though they knew that some English soldiers, one of them gravely wounded, had been living in Père Blanchard's hut.

"The soldiers were not hurting anyone," the smith told Quin, arms folded over his formidable chest. "Yes, they were English." He shrugged. "So are you. I would guess that Bessette scooped up your woman."

Quin's eyes narrowed. "Bessette?"

"A warthog of a schemer. He'll have handed her over to Madame Fantomas, and he'll want a reward."

"Where will I find this Madame Fantomas?"

He snorted. "Where else? The garrison, right under the nose of that drunken sot."

"Don't you speak against *Le Capitaine*," the smith's wife said, suddenly appearing in the door behind him. "He's keeping our boys safe." She eyed the shock of white hair falling over Quin's brow. "Touched by an angel, were you?"

"By the devil, more like," he answered.

He headed back to the garrison, a few furlongs up the road from the village. He didn't think he'd ever been so fatigued, or so filthy, in his life. His hair ribbon was long lost. Every inch of his clothing was caked with dust or worse.

But when questioning the villagers, all that dirt had worked to his advantage: he'd had the distinct impression that while they might not have been eager to help a member of the aristocracy—no matter the nationality—the look and dress of a madman had fit right in.

When he reached the garrison, the sentry had woken up.

"I want my fiancée," Quin said, dispensing with the preliminaries.

"I can tell you who has her, but I should have something for my pains." He pulled nervously at his mustache.

Quin leaned toward the man and spoke in a voice that was calm, but lethal. "I've had a long day. Your pains? I would be happy to rip your head from your shoulders, and then you will forget your pains."

"Bessette is waiting for you around the building," the sentry blurted out, jerking back.

Transaction concluded, Quin walked around the side of the garrison, one pistol at the ready and the other stuck in his waistband.

"Here!" A low voice called to him from the trees.

Lucy was sniffing at one of the windows, set close to the ground. "Come!" he called to her, walking toward the woods.

She ignored him, barking at some invisible quarry. A rat, no doubt. He started toward her, but a burly man stepped from the shade of the wood. The smith was right: *warthog* suited him.

"You have my fiancée," Quin growled, leaving Lucy to her rat and striding over to him.

Something about the look in Quin's eye must have unnerved him, because he stopped grinning and rubbed his hands together. "You'll need to pay me fifty guineas for my protection," he said briskly. "She was waiting around Père Blanchard's hut. We always receive a share when we pick a woman up wandering about where she doesn't belong. Between men. That's not even to mention the fact that no English are allowed on these shores, as I hope you know."

Quin let his hand draft back to the butt of his pistol. "I don't have it."

Bessette shifted his stance, just enough to show that he too was armed. His little warthog eyes glinted. "I'll ask you to fetch the sum before I hand over your woman."

"If I return to England to raise that sum, there's no guarantee that I'll be able to come back immediately," Quin pointed out. "Nations at war tend not to have regular ferry service."

Bessette spat out his soggy cigar at Quin's feet, narrowly missing. "Boats go back and forth every day, so you'll be back by morning. If you give something toward her keep, we won't introduce her to the pleasures that only French—"

Quin's left hand shot out and he twisted Bessette's scarf around his throat, so quickly that the man didn't have a chance to gasp. He watched dispassionately as Bessette's bulbous face reddened to a beet color; there was some sort of hubbub going on behind him, but he didn't want to risk turning his head. Instead he watched Bessette's face for a slackness that would indicate he was near expiration for lack of air.

When it came, he eased his grip. "My fiancée. Now."

Bessette gargled. Quin couldn't make out what he was saying. For one thing, strangled French was none too easy to understand, and for another Lucy was barking furiously somewhere behind him. Likely the soldiers had returned from their useless patrol.

With his free hand, he pulled the pistol from Bessette's breeches and threw it to the ground, shoving his own into the soft folds of the man's stomach. "You're a petty blackmailer, if not worse, and I'm convinced the village would be better off without you." He tightened the scarf again. He waited for a bit and then relaxed his grip just enough so that Bessette could make pleading noises. "Where is she?"

"Madame Fantomas," Bessette said, his voice a whisper. But his eyes shifted. Quin noted the twitch, calculated the probabilities, and moved to the side just as Bessette attempted to knee him in the groin.

"Where will I find Madame?" Behind him, Lucy was barking again.

"Catacombs," Bessette gasped. Then he crumpled. Quin let go of the scarf, allowing him to fall to his knees, but he kept his weapon trained on the man's head.

"Madame Fantomas put her in the catacombs." Bessette's shoulder moved, just a twitch. The fool was planning another attack. One swift and well-aimed kick with Quin's boot and the man rolled on the ground instead, hands between his legs, sobbing with a high-pitched squeal.

"Where are the catacombs?" Quin demanded. He scooped up Bessette's pistol to empty the chamber. Then he froze, realizing he smelled smoke.

He spun around to find that thick smoke was billowing out of the small windows flush with the ground. No wonder Lucy had been barking—something was on fire.

Damn it, he didn't have time for this; he had to find the catacombs. But Bessette had scurried into the woods the moment he'd turned his back. Quin briefly considered giving chase, but he was likely needed to help with the fire. The drunken captain certainly didn't seem capable, if indeed he had made it out of bed.

He ran around the side of the building, ducking to avoid the cloud of black smoke pouring from the windows. It had an acrid, deeply unpleasant odor, as if putrid water had caught on fire.

Lucy raced ahead of him, and the sight of her brought an idea to mind so terrible that he almost stumbled. It couldn't be that Lucy had been barking at Olivia—which would mean that the catacombs were below the garrison?

He burst into the courtyard to find it full of soldiers darting here and there chaotically. No one seemed to be making a concerted effort to put out the fire. The captain was standing at the top of the steps, bellowing and waving his arms. His men were trotting out the front door carrying out crates that clinked gently. It seemed the brandy took first priority.

A hand caught Quin's arm. "Sir, sir!"

He turned. A young and very frightened soldier stood before him, face blackened with soot.

"She's in there," the boy panted. "Past the kitchens. She was supposed to come out when I got Madame to leave her kitchen—she had the key!—but she hasn't come, and I couldn't get through the smoke."

The boy was pointing, hand shaking, to a doorway from which smoke billowed like a sheet in the wind. "The catacombs," he gasped. "She's in the catacombs and there's no other exit!"

Quin looked in time to see Lucy race under the smoke and disappear through the door.

A curse ripped from his lips as he pulled off his coat and jerked sharply on his linen shirtsleeve, tearing it off. "Ignore that bloody captain and his brandy," he shouted at the boy. "You must put out the fire! Organize the men."

Without waiting for a response, he tied the sleeve around his nose and mouth and lunged down the steps, bent double to avoid the thickest smoke. Olivia. Olivia, Olivia, Olivia. It felt as if the very beat of his heart was sending her name coursing through his body.

At the bottom of the stairs he squinted, able to see just enough to realize that he was in a kitchen. *Past* the kitchen, the boy had said. He saw smoke pouring from a chimney on fire, likely feeding on years of grease. He couldn't see a door, but he heard Lucy bark somewhere to his right. He moved in that direction, half-blind and choking, toward the bark.

If anything, the smoke was worse in the passage he found. He shouted Olivia's name, took in a lungful of smoke, reeled, and nearly fell. He flattened himself on the pavement, turning his head so his cheek was against the cool stone, and was rewarded with a gulp of relatively clean air. Holding his breath, he thrust up and forward, flattened himself again, took another breath. By now, he'd inhaled enough smoke that it felt as if the fire was in his lungs, not the chimney.

But Olivia was here, somewhere. Five years before, he had not entered the Channel's frigid, treacherous waters to save Alfie. He *could not* have saved Alfie. But he could make it down this bloody passage. He would not allow another person he loved to die gasping for air.

Another gulp of air and he heaved himself forward again, trying, against his body's protests, to think. He had to find Olivia and get her to one of those windows. They were tiny, too small to push her through, but if he could hoist her up to the window on his shoulders, she would be able to breathe. Air on the ground was damnably short, even with his nose pressed against the stones. In fact, the relentlessly calculating part of his brain informed him that he would die in minutes if he did not breathe some fresh air.

Another breath. The bleak truth of it came with tingling in his extremities. He would not survive this. He would not find Olivia, nor save her. His lungs burned, telling their own story.

Still, at least this time he knew that he had given it his all: he hadn't stood, powerless, on the dock. He had thrown himself into the water.

He forced himself to crawl forward again, and then he heard a strangled woof. He reached out, thinking he'd touch fur, and felt a bare arm instead. A limp arm.

A *window*. He had to get her to a window. Indeed, he had to get them both to a window. He felt up her arm, panting her name, but had to stop in order to dip his head to the stone floor once again. He sucked up what air he could, choked, tried again. Olivia was lying face-down, which might have saved her.

He refused to think about the other possibility.

She lay halfway across a threshold. He tried to peer into the room, but oily black smoke obscured everything. But Lucy had barked at a window . . . without further thought Quin took another breath, then he staggered up and hauled Olivia's slack form into the room. His body overruled him in a desperate attempt to find air. Dropping Olivia, he sucked in a gulp of smoke and doubled over, coughing so hard that he felt as if his ribs would break.

Black dots floated before his eyes, and he stumbled forward, hitting some sort of soft pallet. He leaned against it for a second, trying to gather strength. He knew the window was up there; if he could hoist Olivia onto this thing, he could put her face close to it.

They would have to abandon the little air there was at ground level. But the logical part of his brain registered that his loss of vision wasn't only due to the smoke. His sight was closing down along with his lungs. They would not survive unless they got to that window.

He crouched down, took in a breath, managed to roll Olivia's limp body over his shoulder, and staggered to his feet. It was a sign of his diminished mental power that he felt no surprise when a ladder appeared just where he needed it. He put a foot on the lowest rung.

Lucy. He propped Olivia against the ladder, reached down and felt fur, picked up the dog by the scruff of her neck.

The black dots were swirling now, like a storm coming in at sea. How much time did he have before unconsciousness? A minute? Less? He snatched Olivia's skirt, dropped Lucy into it, and stuffed the fold of cloth into his mouth, holding the dog between them.

He forced his second foot onto the ladder. His thighs felt like steel bars, inflexible and impossibly heavy. But he pushed himself up and up again, until at last he toppled Olivia on top of the pallet. There was the window. *Bless you, Lucy*, he thought.

Lucy rolled free, scrabbled to her feet, and tottered toward the fresh air. Quin sucked in one lungful and then pulled Olivia across the pallet, putting her mouth next to the bars. She had not moved. She was utterly limp.

Dead, he thought. She was dead.

"Come on, Olivia," he said, his voice coming in a rasp. "Breathe, damn it, breathe!"

But her face lolled against the bars. He could see no signs of life.

A tearing pain seized him. His heart was cracking, breaking right there in the smoky room. "Don't leave me!" he shouted hoarsely. He grabbed her shoulders and shook her, hard. "Don't leave me."

As his vision cleared, he could see that Olivia's face was faintly blue. He suddenly remembered to feel for a heartbeat, but when he pressed his hand to her chest he couldn't feel anything. Then he realized he was trying to find a heartbeat on the wrong side of her body.

"My brain's garbled," he mumbled. Then, fiercely: "You must breathe." He shook her again, willing her to open her eyes, but her head fell back like a blossom on a broken stem. Her face swam in front of his eyes and he realized that he was crying, his hands moving over her chest, trying to find a heartbeat that wasn't there.

Lucy was there too, barking hoarsely at her mistress's ear.

But Olivia did not move. She would never move again.

He lowered his face to her neck, trying to smell that wonderful, elusive perfume that was Olivia, but all he could smell was smoke.

Something twisted hard inside his chest, and all the grief he had never expressed came boiling up, sobs rising so hard that his body jerked as if he were having a seizure. There was no stopping these cries; the world turned into a black swirling hole of grief. Alfie, Olivia, even Evangeline and Rupert . . . they were all dead.

Howls tore through him, bringing with them words that he had never spoken aloud, because a duke is always controlled, a duke never pleads.

This duke pleaded.

Please, God, help. Help.

Finally he realized that he could see Lucy licking Olivia's cheek; the room was clearing of smoke. The chimney fire must have been extinguished. Lucy uttered a bark that sounded like a low bell, like that of a Great Dane.

The bark of Cerberus, the dog who guards the gates of Hades, perhaps.

His last sob brought with it a strange clarity, a deep calm. "I cannot bear it," Quin said, talking to the thin air. "I cannot bear this again." He couldn't go back to his sterile house, to the pages of mathematical equations, to his mother's strictures. Without Olivia and Alfie, there was no point in living.

Lucy was still licking Olivia's cheek. He reached to push her away—and he thought he saw Olivia shudder. He grabbed her shoulders and lifted her toward him. "Please, Olivia! Breathe. Please!"

Nothing.

He pulled her body against his and rocked back and forth, those damned tears falling again.

She coughed.

Tarquin Brook-Chatfield, Duke of Sconce, made a fool of himself that night in France. He always remembered it, and looked back with a tinge of embarrassment.

The man who never cried, not even at his own son's funeral, wept.

And when Olivia Mayfair Lytton came to, coughing and hurting, but otherwise fine, she—who never cried either—wept as well.

Thirty-two

A Warrior and an Amazon

*I*t was the mattresses," Olivia told Petit two hours later. She was sitting on a chair in the middle of the courtyard, taking deep breaths of fresh, sea-scoured air. Her chest ached, but it was already feeling much better. A steaming hot bath had helped. "Your mattresses saved our lives."

But his eyes were agonized. "It was I, I, who almost cost you your life! I blocked the chimneys to force Madame to leave the kitchen, and then one of them caught on fire. By the time I realized you had not used your key, I couldn't get through the smoke. I *failed*!"

"It was an accident," Olivia told him. "But you must promise never to do something so dangerous again."

"I will not," Petit gasped. "Never, never, never."

"You can make up for it," Quin said, appearing at his shoulder. "Carry Lucy to the rowboat next to Père

Blanchard's hut, if you please." He handed over the little dog. "She's too tired to walk with us. Give her to a sailor named Grooper, who should be waiting."

"I will run all the way," Petit said, suiting action to word and tearing out the front gate.

"My goodness." Olivia watched him go. One of Lucy's ears was just visible, blowing backward in the wind. "Lucy must feel as if she's in a race."

"Petit is taking the road," Quin said. "We'll cut through the woods, and we should meet him not long after he arrives, even given his gallop." He bent and picked her up in one smooth movement. "Time to go home."

"You mustn't!" Olivia protested. "You *can't*! I weigh too much." But he merely pressed a kiss on her forehead and walked out of the courtyard, leaving the sordid garrison behind.

His body ached, but he never gave way to fatigue. It was half a league to the inlet where the rowboat waited for them, but the duke's muscles seemed to be made of steel.

Olivia was quiet, her arms around his neck, her cheek against his chest, so grateful to be with him, and alive, that she couldn't speak. But when he walked through the woods and she heard the sound of running water, she insisted on being put down.

"We're almost at the *Day Dream*," Quin protested. "I want to get out of this bloody country."

She ran a hand along his cheek. "Please?"

He groaned, but he put her on her feet.

It was early evening, and the air was warm and smelled of flowers. Bluebells stretched down to the edge of a lazy stream lined by young oaks. "They're so beautiful," Olivia breathed, kneeling in a patch of blossoms.

Quin just growled. "Enjoy them now, because you won't see these flowers again. We are never returning to France."

She laughed. "Of course we will return, after the war is over. I want to meet Petit's bride someday, and learn if the drunken *capitaine* sobers up. Besides, I heard you making plans for cognac to be sent to Littlebourne Manor on a regular basis."

"The best I've had in years." Quin looked unrepentant.

"I hate to say it, but Madame's bread was astonishingly good. Worth a trip to France." Her voice trailed off as she looked up at him.

Quin had bathed as well, and washed away the streaks of black soot that made him look like a thief in the night. Even so, there was something different about him. The cheekbones that seemed aristocratic in England now seemed harsh and undomesticated. He wore no coat, and one shirtsleeve had been ripped away, baring his muscular arm. He was the embodiment of an avenger.

"What?" he asked, scowling down at her.

"You look like a warrior," she said, her whole body thrilling in a distinctly uncivilized way to the barely suppressed violence pulsing in his every sinew.

He crouched beside her, and his thigh muscles bulged in a way that made her long to run her fingers over them. A lady would never notice that. Her mother would be scandalized, and she could not have cared less.

"I thought I had lost you," he said, his voice stark and uncompromising. "It turned me into a madman, so I should probably warn you that I may never be the same again, Olivia."

She came up on her knees so that their eyes were level.

"My last thought before I fainted was of you. I knew you would come. I love you, Quin."

"I never understood much about love," he said, not touching her. "But I do know that I love the way you hold your own against my mother, and your bad jokes, and your silly limericks, and your violet dress, and the way you can climb a tree and fly a kite."

She smiled. That was good enough.

"My mother told me long ago," he continued, "that it was a good thing that we were an unemotional family, because love was dangerous. I proved her hypothesis by falling in love with Evangeline."

Olivia bit her lip, ready to argue.

"But I love you so much more." His voice grated and nearly broke, but he steadied it. "I love you more than anything in this world, more than my own life. If love is dangerous, then I don't want to live in safety." His voice was rough and savage, and doubly honest for its hunger.

Olivia shifted backward, still on her knees. "Just looking at you makes me ache . . . *here*." She put a hand on her stomach, let it drift lower. "And *here*."

His face changed from deadly to sensual. "Olivia." He breathed the word. Then: "*No*." He tried to make the word into a command, but she was pretty sure that warriors married Amazons, which meant it was time she became as bold as any Amazon. Not that history was her strong point.

"I'm not afraid when you are with me." She undid the top button of a villager's dress, kindly given to replace her ruined travelling costume. "I'm not afraid of Bessette, because I saw what you did to him back at the fortress."

Quin's jaw clenched. "Unfortunately, I think the bastard will survive. If I had known that he had given you those bruises, I would have beaten him to within an inch of his life the first time I encountered him."

She smiled, and slipped free two more buttons. "And I'm not afraid of French soldiers, because all the ones around here are your cousin Justin's age, though they might not be quite as poetic."

"I wouldn't be surprised if Petit returns to his room to scribble verses to an English moon goddess." He was watching her hands.

Olivia undid the last button and eased the gown over her shoulders. "Most of all," she said, coming to her feet, "I'm no longer afraid of myself, of my own body." The gown pooled at her feet, leaving only a chemise.

"No corset," he growled, not moving. "I'm going to destroy all your corsets when we reach England."

"What's wrong with a corset?" she asked, teasing him by slowly, slowly inching up the hem of her chemise.

"Holds you in," he said, his eyes flaring. "I can't stand to see your curves confined."

She knew her smile was radiant; she felt not even a tinge of embarrassment as she pulled her chemise over her head and tossed it aside. Quin froze, a muscled, wild man crouched at her feet. She simply waited in that patch of French bluebells, a ray of dusky sunshine playing on her breasts and stomach, and let him look as long as he wished.

To be strictly honest, she did position her legs in the best possible fashion—knees together, bent slightly to the side. She had never felt more sensual or more desirable. Being naked in the outdoors, even though—or, perhaps, especially because—Quin was still clothed, was intoxicating. Her whole body softened with desire, sang with it.

Still, he didn't move, that new, ferocious demeanor clinging to him. "Olivia," he growled finally.

"Yes?"

He may be ferocious, but she was a *woman*. His woman. She saw the fire blazing in his eyes, and the way his hands were trembling. For her.

"Move your legs apart."

She shifted into the immodest pose he wanted, and even that didn't embarrass her.

"You're perfect," he said hoarsely. "And you're mine." All of a sudden strong arms circled her hips and a swipe of his tongue between her legs made her shriek.

"Like honey," he said, taking another lick that made her gasp. A sweet, insistent ache spread quickly down her legs, and Olivia wound her fingers into the clean silk of his hair and hung on.

Quin took his time, holding her upright after her legs lost strength, his hands digging into the voluptuous curves of her arse, his tongue as demanding as the rest of him. He didn't stop until she was sobbing with pleasure, shaking all over, trying to speak but unable to find words.

He rose to his feet and ripped his shirt over his head. A moment later she found herself on her back in a heap of discarded clothing and bluebells, a naked, hard body looming over her. But his jaw was clenched, eyes worried. "I can't stop myself, Olivia. And it might still hurt."

But she was already arching toward him, her hands clenching on his forearms. "I feel empty," she whispered. "I want you inside me."

He reached down with one hand and closed his eyes for a moment. "You're so ready." His voice rasped.

"Oh," she cried, pushing against his finger, against

the rough stroke of his thumb. "I . . . can you . . . yes!" The golden sunshine hurled into her again, streaking along her veins.

Quin waited through the spasms that shook her, then reared back and put his huge hands under her bottom. His face was desperate but still wary.

"I want your—" she said, but had to stop for a shaky breath.

A gleam of laughter lightened his eyes. "Don't you dare say anything about a battering ram, Olivia Lytton."

She pouted at him, loving the way his eyes caught on her plump lips. "But I *want* it." And she meant it.

If possible, he felt even larger than the first time. But it was all different; she shrieked when he thrust home, and not from pain. Her legs instinctively rose and clenched around his hips, holding him fast.

A low cry tore from his lips. "Not—not so fast," he gasped. He came down on his elbows and kissed her. "I love you." The words came out low and fierce, a warrior's vow. He drew back, thrust again. Stopped. "There's no reason to live without you, Olivia. None."

Her lips trembled and her eyes swam with tears. But he bent his head, caught her mouth again. "No tears," he said. "You lived. I lived. *We lived.*"

"I love you," she said, her hands trembling as she tried to pull him even closer. "I love you so much, Quin."

Their eyes met. "Please," she gasped, not really certain what she was begging for. But Quin knew. He came home to her, and she took what he gave her, took it and gave it back.

Thirty-three

The Merits of Simple Words

Quin did not find the right words until they had washed in the stream and put their clothes back on. But for once it didn't bother him that the words he wanted didn't come immediately: what he and Olivia felt was more than language. It was like light, he realized. Something plain and simple that split into a rainbow when examined closely.

"You have changed my heart," he said at last. "I'll never be comfortable without knowing where you are."

The shimmer in Olivia's eyes threatened to spill over again. But she was safe and in his arms. He began to walk, bending his head to kiss away a tear or two.

There was still a long tramp through the forest to the inlet overhung by trees, and he hadn't slept in two days. But Olivia's whispers gave him strength, and everything she told him, even the silliest of limericks, really meant only one thing. She loved *him*, that cold and unemotional man whom Evangeline had declared unlovable.

When they reached the rowboat, Grooper was asleep on the riverbank, Lucy curled up under his arm. And the world—Quin's world—was in place, and would be for the rest of his life.

When their carriage drew up at Littlebourne, followed by another, which was hung with black and carried Rupert's body, the household poured out to greet them.

The Duke of Canterwick—still unsteady from his bout of unconsciousness—clung to their hands, thanked them over and over for bringing his boy home, and then left, a broken man.

The Dowager Duchess of Sconce broke her most cherished commandment as regards a lady's composure and burst into tears in plain sight of the entire household.

Miss Georgiana Lytton screamed, grabbed her sister, and shook her. It hardly need be said that an outburst of sobbing, happy hysteria indicates that a person has (if only momentarily) cast aside precepts such as "*Your demeanor should ever augment your honor.*" It was a good thing that Georgie and Olivia's parents were not there to see the general laws of the universe dispensed with (at least, to Mrs. Lytton's mind).

Poor Mrs. Lytton would have been even more shocked if she had overheard the conversation between her daughters later in the day.

"But you cannot bear Lady Cecily for more than a half hour! You'll be driven mad by within a week. Don't you remember the trip here, when you and I—"

"It doesn't matter," Georgiana said firmly. "Lady Cecily's nephew is an Oxford don, Olivia. A *don*!"

Olivia put down her teacup and eyed her sister. "Being a don must be a good thing."

Georgiana ignored that; she was bubbling with excitement in a very un-Georgie-like fashion. "Mr. Holmes begins a series of lectures on Laplace's *Mecanique Céleste* and Newton's *Principia* next week. Women are not allowed to attend such lectures, but he obviously cannot deny his own aunt!"

"And her companion. But Georgie, are you quite certain you can endure it? Remember, lecturing seems to be a family trait: you're facing *hours* of Lady Cecily's opinions regarding digestive processes."

"Lady Cecily is very kind, Olivia. Just think; she's going to sit through those lectures for my sake."

"She's going to do exactly what I would do in that situation, and sleep through."

"If I had to be a companion to a *murderer* in order to go to those lectures, I would," Georgiana said with conviction.

"You raise an interesting question," Olivia said mischievously. "Could it be that the sainted Mr. Bumtrinket, late husband of Lady Cecily herself, died a questionable death, perhaps from a potion bought from a Venetian quack?"

"*Olivia*!" Georgiana said, shocked as always.

"Worse! What if you are driven to homicide?"

"Stop that! You are being quite improper."

"There was a talkative old woman named Bumtrinket, Who nattered day and night like a cricket," Olivia laughed, dancing out of the way as her sister made a grab at her sleeve. "Her tongue never ceasing, Was vastly displeasing, Until her companion smacked her bum with a picket!"

"You reprobate!" The perfect princess actually

chased the imperfect princess clear around the library settee before she remembered that *dignity, virtue, affability, and bearing* precluded bodily assault.

Olivia's world, like Quin's, was firmly in place. Georgie might be going off to Oxford and eschewing the life of a duchess, but the tattered shreds of the duchification program clung to her. And Olivia was about to fulfill her mother's dearest hope . . . although it could be said that her success was directly tied to the failures of the very same program.

Quin and Olivia walked behind the Duke of Canterwick when Rupert was buried with honors: not in the family tomb, but in Westminster Abbey, as befitted an English hero who trailed clouds of glory. His place was marked by a very simple marble tablet engraved with his name and a fragment of an odd poem.

A few years later, a young poet named Keats stood puzzling over the inscription one long afternoon. Sometime after that, a middle-aged poet named Auden found himself fascinated by it for a whole week. Fifty years later, an erudite dissertation discussed the complexities of fragmentation . . . but that was all in the future, a puzzle that lay ahead for those interested in twists of language.

For Tarquin Brook-Chatfield, Duke of Sconce, complicated words never had the same incantatory force as they had before his second marriage. He never worried if he couldn't find just the right ones.

There were only three that truly mattered, and they bore repeating: "I love you; I love you; I love you."

"I love you."

Epilogue

Thirteen years later

*T*he young girl had ebony hair with a shock of white over her brow. Lady Penelope Brook-Chatfield didn't know it yet—although at age twelve, she was beginning to guess—but she was the most beautiful lady of her age between Kent and London and even beyond. Cherry lips, high cheekbones, and the scream of an Amazon.

"It all adds up," Quin mumbled. "She's going to be a terror. They'll line up begging to marry her, and then we'll have to give her poor husband hardship pay."

"Pish," Olivia said lazily, enjoying the way the summer heat hung in the air even in the shade of their favorite elm tree, the one at the end of Ladybird Ridge. Small white butterflies danced below its lowest branches.

Penelope ran by, chasing one of her cousins with a shriek that reminded one of the new steam engines. "My papa is too!" she screamed. "My papa is *fierce*!"

"You don't look fierce," Olivia said, twining her hands into Quin's hair. He lay on the quilt next to her, whispering things into the tummy that rose in the air between them.

"I'm being nice to the new baby," he said, dropping a

kiss in the appropriate place. "I'm saving all my ferocity for Penelope's first suitors."

A scrambling noise could be heard in the tree above them. "Be careful," Quin called. "Mama is here and you must be particularly careful these days, you know."

"I know." There had been lots of rain this summer, and the tree was thick with dark leaves. Thin legs emerged from the canopy and waved for a moment, until Quin got to his feet, took hold of their owner, and placed his son safely on the ground.

"Papa!" Penelope screeched, running back toward them, her hair streaming in the wind. She must have lost another ribbon. "Aunt Georgie says that you haven't killed any pirates, so come and tell her that you do it *all the time*!"

"You really must give her a better understanding of what a local militia can and cannot do," Olivia murmured.

Quin put his hands on his hips and shouted, "Tell Georgiana that it's Uncle Justin who is good at rounding up pirates."

Penelope arrived in a flurry of long legs and silky hair. She grabbed his hand. "That's absurd, Papa. You know that Uncle Justin is too busy singing. If you wished to kill a pirate, you could do it before breakfast. Come tell Aunt Georgie *that*." And she dragged him away.

Master Leo Rupert, who held the title of Earl of Calderon (though he didn't know it yet), fell onto his knees beside his mother and showed her a little collection of twigs, all broken off at precisely the same length. Leo was imaginative, dreamy, and much quieter than Penelope. He was always thinking as hard as he could, harder than most five-year-olds.

"Will you build something with the twigs?" Olivia

asked, pushing herself into a sitting position. "Perhaps a house?"

"I'm too young to build a house," Leo said, with just a shadow of annoyance. "People my age don't build houses, Mama. You should know that." He stowed the twigs carefully in his pocket and got up from his rather grubby knees.

"What will you do with them?"

"Alfie and I will build a road. I'll ask Uncle Justin if he will help us." Then he gave her a smile that was all the more beautiful for being quite grave and rarely used. "Where's Lucy?"

"She's sitting in the pony cart," Olivia told him. "You know Lucy doesn't like leaving Grandmother's knee these days."

"I shall show these sticks to Grandmother," he said, and wandered off.

Olivia watched him go, wondering. Her husband returned, and sat down just behind her, spreading his hands over her belly and pulling her against his warm chest. "This baby is bigger than either of the other two," he observed.

"Quin, do you think it's truly all right that Leo plays with a friend named Alfie all the time—and no one can see Alfie but him?"

Quin pulled her even more snugly against him and kissed her ear. "Do you think he does it simply because it makes his Papa so happy?"

Olivia tipped her head back against his shoulder. "No. Leo would say that Alfie is his *own* friend, just as he has said, many a time over the last year. As for the size of my belly, I begin to think I might be carrying twins."

"You're carrying *twins*?" Quin exclaimed. "Could

you rethink that idea? I'm not sure we can handle two more."

Olivia laughed. "Is this the same man who said he wanted the nursery full of children?"

"That was before I knew how loud they can be. With Georgiana's two, and Justin's boy arriving tomorrow—and you know that child is a perfect terror, Olivia—the house shakes at its foundations."

"Kiss me," Olivia asked, looking up at her beautiful warrior prince of a husband.

His first kiss was adoring, but it gradually deepened and turned into something else: a possessive, marauding kiss. His hands edged from her tummy up toward her chest, a softer and more voluptuous curve.

"You mustn't!" Olivia said with a little gasp, sometime later. They were both breathing quickly.

"Let's go home," Quin said into her ear. "I want you. I want my wife on a Sunday afternoon in a sultry, sunny English summer. I want her naked and lying on our bed so that I can—"

Penelope skittered to a halt beside them. "Are you kissing *again*? Grandmother says it's time to go home, and Nanny says that there are lemon tarts for tea. Come *on*!" She ran ahead, her half boots twinkling under her skirts.

Quin helped his beloved to her feet, took her hand, and entertained her all the way back to the pony cart with so many whispered suggestions that she was quite rosy when they at last reached the end of Ladybird Ridge.

"Humph," the dowager said, seeing Olivia's face. "Too hot out here, I shouldn't wonder. Lucy is overheated as well."

Quin bent down and gave Lucy's ear a tug. "Then we

must go home," he said, nodding to the groom driving a second cart now full of his children and their cousins. He took the reins of the pony cart. "We mustn't discomfort Lucy. And I think my wife would also be the better for—"

Olivia elbowed him.

"A nap," he said, kissing her nose.

The dowager duchess looked at both of them and then away at the neat fields that spread out from the seat of the Sconces. It was not every day that she thanked God that she had chosen Georgiana to undergo that absurd series of tests she had devised, and that Georgiana had brought along Olivia.

But almost every day.

Historical Note

This novel has so many literary antecedents that I can scarcely list them: Renaissance plays, *The Scarlet Pimpernel*, a short story by David Foster Wallace. My primary debt, of course, is to Hans Christian Andersen's *The Princess and the Pea*. His fairy story was panned by literary critics of his day as too chatty and informal, and they greatly disliked the double entendres surrounding that intrusively hard pea found in a maiden's bed.

Andersen's shocking pun gave me the idea of creating a heroine with a particular propensity for improper wordplay. We think of limericks as a form popularized by Edward Lear in *The Book of Nonsense* (1846), but in fact the form is much older than that. (For example, a fascinating example appears in the September 1717 diary entry of one John Thomlinson, a reverend who liked to record the scandals occurring in his parish.) Help with Olivia's bawdy humor came from the Renaissance playwright Ben Jonson (*"Turdy-facy-nasty-paty-lousy-fartical rogue!"*), as well as the writers of the British television classic *Black Adder* (*beardy-weirdy bottle-headed chub!*)—whom Jonson would proudly claim as offspring.

I am also indebted to Jonson for the name Cecily Bumtrinket, a servant mentioned in one of his plays, whom I turned into a duke's daughter. Another inspired name is Lord Justin Fiebvre . . . a character written for my twelve-year-old daughter's delight; she is among the most fervent of the Beliebers. The novel's conclusion was inspired by *The Scarlet Pimpernel*. As a teenager, I adored the scene in which Sir Percy lifts his wife as easily as if she were a feather and carries her half a league to the shore so they can escape from war-torn France in his luxurious schooner, the *Day Dream*.

On a historical front, jack-o'-lanterns were carved from turnips, but they did exist. And the Siege of Badajoz really happened, though I altered its details to serve my purpose—to turn Rupert into a hero. In closing, I'd like to note that Rupert's middle names are Forrest G.

G for Gump.

Questions for Readers, for Book Clubs, for Roving Page-Turners

Dear Reader,

What follows are a few notes about less obvious aspects of *The Duke Is Mine* that might be fun to chat about—as well as some suggestions for what you might read next.

1. In the fairy tale *The Princess and the Pea*, the girl who arrives at the gate in the middle of a rainstorm turns out to be a "perfect" princess. Olivia, my heroine from *The Duke Is Mine*, by contrast, is no perfect heroine; she's impudent, bawdy, and plump. Do you like your heroines to be less than perfect? How did you feel about the fact that she's curvy? If you like Olivia, you might like Josie, the heroine of *Pleasure for Pleasure*: she's another woman whose figure doesn't suit

the current style, but who learns to love herself precisely as she is.

2. In a deep sense, *The Duke Is Mine* is about perfection, and what that means. Think about Tarquin, who has an Aspergers-like inability to express emotion and relies on logic, and Rupert, who is all emotion and little logic. Olivia teaches Quin a great deal about expressing his feelings, but so does Rupert's poem, which gives him a way to grieve for his son. What do you think makes up a perfect hero? For me, he's a man who can run into a burning building to save his beloved—but isn't so constrained by his masculinity that he's unable to express emotion. Quin and Rupert are both heroes, but in very different ways. Another hero along those lines? Simeon, the hero of *When the Duke Returns*, rescues his wife from a boat occupied by violent, escaped prisoners.

3. Many readers have asked me why I'm rewriting fairy tales. The answer has to do with my father, Robert Bly, and his interest in reworking fairy tales (most famously, *Iron John*). But I also like them because they present a challenge: can I surprise my readers when they already know the outlines of the plot? If you enjoyed tracing how the design of *The Princess and the Pea* appeared and disappeared in *The Duke Is Mine*, you might also enjoy *A Kiss at Midnight*, my adaptation of *Cinderella*, as well as my version of one of everyone's favorite fairy tales, *When Beauty Tamed the Beast*. I'm often asked whether I'll write more fairy tales; as I write this letter, I'm working on

The Ugly Duchess (Duckling), and I can envision at least one more fairy tale after that.

I hope you enjoyed *The Duke Is Mine*—and any other books of mine that you might read. If you'd like more information about my novels, just check out my website, www.eloisajames.com. And I'm often on Facebook, at www.facebook.com/eloisajamesfans. I'd love to chat with you there.

With very best wishes,

Eloisa

*Turn the page for a sneak peek
at the newest romance
from Eloisa James,*

The Ugly Duchess,

available September 2012
from Avon Books

A Rather Long Preface

March 1805
45 Berkeley Square
The London residence of the Duke of Ashbrook

*Y*ou'll have to marry her. I don't care if you think of her like a sister: from now on, she's the golden fleece to you."

James Ryburn, Earl of Islay, and future Duke of Ashbrook, opened his mouth to say something, but a mixture of rage and disbelief choked his throat.

His father turned and walked toward the far wall of his library, acting as if he'd said nothing particularly out of the ordinary. "We need her fortune to repair the Staffordshire estate and pay a few debts, or we're going to lose it all, this townhouse included."

"What have you done?" James spat the words. A pounding, terrible feeling of dread was spreading up his limbs.

Ashbrook pivoted. "Don't you *dare* speak to me in that tone!"

James was aware of rage burning up his spine and took a deep breath before answering. One of his resolutions was to master his temper before turning twenty—and his birthday was a mere three weeks away. "Excuse me, Father," he managed through stiff lips. "Exactly how did the estate come to be in such danger, if you don't mind my asking?"

"I do mind your asking." The duke stared back at his only son, his long, aquiline nose quivering with rage. James came by his temper naturally; he inherited it straight from his irascible, reckless father.

"In that case, I will bid you good day," James said, keeping his tone even.

"Not unless you're going downstairs to make eyes at that girl. I turned down an offer for her hand this week from Briscott, so I didn't feel I had to tell her mother. But you know damn well her father left the decision over who marries his daughter to her mother—"

"I have no knowledge of the contents of Mr. Saxby's will," James stated. "And I fail to see why that particular provision should cause you such annoyance."

"Because we need her damned fortune," Ashbrook raged, walking to the fireplace and giving the unlit logs a kick. "You need to convince Dora that you're in love with her, or her mother will never agree to the match. Just last week, Mrs. Saxby inquired about a few of my investments in a manner that I did not appreciate. Doesn't know a woman's place."

"I will do nothing of the sort."

"You'll do exactly as I instruct you."

"You're instructing me to woo a young lady whom I've been raised to think of as a *sister*."

"Irrelevant! You may have rubbed noses a few times as children, but that wouldn't stop you from sleeping with her."

"I can't."

For the first time, the duke looked a trifle sympathetic. "Dora is no beauty. But all women are the same in the—"

"Do *not* say that," James snapped. "I am already appalled; I don't wish to be disgusted."

His father's eyes narrowed and rusty color rose in his cheeks, a sure sign of danger. Sure enough, Ashbrook's voice emerged as a bellow. "I don't care if the gal is as ugly as sin, you're taking her. And you're going to make her fall in love with you. Otherwise, you will have no country house to inherit. None!"

"What have you done?" James repeated through clenched teeth.

"Lost it," his father shouted back, his eyes bulging a little. "Lost it, and that's all you need to know!"

"I won't do it." He stood up.

A china ornament flew past his shoulder and crashed against the wall. He barely flinched. His father was given to fits of temper, and James had grown up ducking to avoid everything from books to marble statues.

"You will, or I'll bloody well disinherit you and name your cousin Pinkler my heir."

James's hand dropped from the door handle, and he turned around. He was well aware that he was on the verge of losing his temper. While he'd never had the impulse to throw objects at the wall—or his family—his ability to fire cutting remarks was equally destructive. He took another deep breath, trying to curb the fire in his belly. "While I would hesitate to instruct you on the legal system, *Father*, I can assure you that it is impossible to disinherit a legitimate son."

"I'll tell the House of Lords that you're no child of mine," the duke bellowed. Veins were bulging on his forehead and his cheeks had ripened from red to purple. "I'll tell 'em that your mother was a lightheeled wench, and that I've discovered you're nothing but a bastard."

At the insult to his mother, James felt his fragile control snap altogether. "You may be a craven, dim-witted gambler, but you will *not* tar my mother with sorry excuses meant to cover up your own idiocy!"

"How dare you!" screamed the duke. His whole face had turned the color of a cock's comb.

"I dare say only what every person in this kingdom knows," James said, the words exploding from his mouth. "You're an idiot. I have a good idea what happened to the estate; I just wanted to see whether you had the balls to admit it. And you haven't. No surprise there. You gambled our lands on the Exchange. You invested in one ridiculous scheme after another. The canal you built that was only seven feet from another canal? What in God's name were you thinking?"

"I didn't know that until it was too late! My associates deceived me. A duke doesn't go out and inspect the place where a canal is supposed to be built. He has to trust others, and I've always had the devil's own luck."

"I would have at least visited the proposed canal before I sank thousands of pounds into a waterway with no hope of traffic."

"You're nothing more than an impudent ass!" The duke's hand tightened around a silver candlestick standing on the mantelpiece.

"Throw that, and I'll leave you in this room to wallow in your own fear. You want me to marry a girl who thinks I'm her brother in order to get her fortune . . . so that you—*you*—can lose it? Do you know what they call you behind your back, Father? Surely you've heard it. The dam'fool duke!"

They were both breathing hard, but his father was puffing like a bull, the purple stain on his cheeks vivid against his white neckcloth.

The duke's fingers flexed around the silver piece.

"Touch that candlestick and I'll throw you across the room," James said, adding deliberately, "Your Grace."

The duke's hand fell to his side and he turned his shoulder away, staring at the far wall. "And what if I lost it?" he muttered, belligerence underscoring his confession. "The fact is that I did lose it. I lost it all. The canal was one thing, but I thought the vineyards were a sure thing. How could I possibly know that England is a breeding ground for black rot?"

"You idiot!" James spat, and turned on his heel to go.

"But you must save the estate," Ashbrook hissed. "The Staffordshire estate's been in our family for four generations. You *must*. Your mother would be devastated to see Ryburn House sold. And what of her grave . . . the cemetery adjoins the chapel, you know."

James's heart was beating savagely in his throat. It took him a moment to come up with a response that didn't include curling his hands around his father's throat. "That is low, even from you," he said finally.

The duke paid no heed to that weak rejoinder. "*Are* you going to let your mother's corpse be sold?"

"I'll think about marrying some other heiress," James said. "But I will not marry Daisy." Theodora Saxby—known to the family as Dora and to James alone as Daisy—was his dearest friend, his childhood companion. "She deserves better than me, than anyone from this family."

There was silence behind him. A terrible, warped silence that . . . James turned. "You didn't. Even you . . . couldn't."

"I thought I would be able to replace it in a matter of weeks," his father snapped, the color leaving his cheeks so that he looked positively haggard.

James's limbs suddenly felt so weak that he found

himself leaning back against the door. "How much of her fortune is gone?"

"Enough." Ashbrook dropped his eyes, finally showing some sign of shame. "If she marries anyone else, I'll . . . I'll face trial. I don't know if they can put dukes in the dock. Probably be the House of Lords. But it won't be pretty."

"Oh, they can put dukes on trial all right," James said heavily. "You embezzled the dowry of a girl entrusted to our care since the time she was a mere infant. Her mother was married to your dearest friend. Saxby asked you *on his deathbed* to care for his daughter."

"And I did," her father replied, but without his usual bluster. "Brought her up as my own."

"You brought her up as my sister," James said flatly. He forced himself to cross the room and sit in a chair opposite his wretched father. "And all the time you were stealing from her."

"Not all the time," his father protested. "Just the last year. Or so. The majority of her fortune is in funds and I couldn't touch that. I just . . . I just borrowed from . . . well, I just borrowed some. I'm deuced unlucky, and that's a fact. I was absolutely sure it wouldn't come to this."

"Unlucky," James repeated, his voice liquid with distaste.

"And now the girl is getting a proposal or two, I don't have the time to make it up. You've got to take her. It's not just that the estate and the townhouse will have to go; the name won't be worth anything either, after the scandal. Even if I pay off what I borrowed from her, it won't cover my debts."

James didn't reply. The only words going through his head were flatly blasphemous.

"It was easier when your mother was alive," the duke said after a minute or two. "She helped me, you know. She had a solid head on her shoulders."

James couldn't bring himself to answer that either. His mother had died five years earlier, and in a mere half-decade, his father had managed to ruin an estate stretching from Scotland to Staffordshire to London. And he had embezzled Daisy's fortune. And . . . *"Bloody hell."*

"You'll make her love you," his father said encouragingly. "She already adores you; she always has. We've been lucky so far that Dora is so homely. The only men who've asked for her hand have been such obvious fortune hunters that her mother wouldn't even consider them. But that'll change as the season wears on. She's a taking little piece, once you get to know her."

James ground his teeth. "She will never love me in that way. She thinks of me as her brother, as her *friend*."

"Don't be a fool. You've got my profile." A glimmer of pride underlaid his words. "Your mother always said that I was the most handsome man of my generation."

James bit back a comment that wouldn't help the situation. He was beginning to feel an overwhelming sense of nausea. "We could simply tell Daisy about what happened. What you did. She'll understand."

His father snorted. "You think her mother will understand? My old friend Saxby didn't know what he was getting into when he married that woman. She's a dragon, a positive dragon."

In the seventeen years since Mrs. Saxby and her infant daughter had joined the duke's household, they had managed to maintain fairly cordial relations—primarily because Ashbrook never threw anything in the widow's direction. But James knew instantly that his father was right. If Daisy's mother got even a hint that her daughter's guardian had embezzled her inheritance, she would be battering on the door of a high judge before evening fell. Nausea drove James's stomach into his throat at the thought.

His father, on the other hand, was cheering up. He had the sort of mind that flitted from one subject to another; his rages were fierce but short-lived. "A few posies, maybe a poem, and Dora will fall into your hand as sweetly as a ripe plum. After all, it's not as if the girl gets much flattery. Tell her she's beautiful, and she'll be at your feet."

"I cannot do that," James stated, not even bothering to imagine himself saying such a thing. It wasn't a matter simply of not wishing to say such inanities to Daisy herself; he loathed situations where he found himself fumbling with language he found tedious in the extreme. The season was three weeks old, but he hadn't attended a single ball.

His father misunderstood his refusal. "Of course, you'll have to lie about it, but that's the kind of lie a gentleman can't avoid. She may not be the prettiest girl on the market—and certainly not as delectable as that opera singer I caught sight of with you the other night—but it wouldn't get you anywhere to point out the truth." He actually gave a little chuckle at the thought.

James heard him dimly, concentrating on not throwing up as he tried to think through the dilemma before him.

The duke kept talking, amusing himself by laying out the distinction between mistresses and wives. "In compensation, you can keep a mistress twice as beautiful as your wife. It'll provide an interesting contrast."

There was no human being in the world he loathed as much as his father. "If I marry Daisy, I will not take a mistress," he said, still thinking frantically, trying to come up with a way out. "I couldn't do that to her."

"Well, I expect you'll change your mind on that after a few years of marriage, but each to his own." The duke's voice was as strong and buoyant as ever. "Well? Not much to think about, is there? It's bad luck and all that rot, but I can't see that either of us have much choice about it. The good thing is that a man can always perform in the bedroom, even if he doesn't want to."

The only thing James wanted was to get out of the room, away from his disgusting excuse for a parent. "I will do this on one condition." His voice sounded unfamiliar to his own ears, as if a stranger said the words.

"Anything, my boy, anything! I know I'm asking for a sacrifice. As I said, we can admit amongst ourselves that little Dora is not the beauty of the bunch."

"The day I marry her, you sign the entire estate over to me—Ryburn House and its lands, this townhouse, the island in Scotland."

The duke's mouth fell open. "*What*?"

"The entire estate," James repeated. "I will pay you an allowance, and no one need know except for the solicitors. But I will *not* be responsible for you and your foolish schemes. I will never again take responsibility for any debts you might incur—nor for any theft. The next time around, you're going to prison."

"That's absurd," his father spluttered. "I couldn't— you couldn't possibly—no!"

"Then make your good-byes to Staffordshire," James said, rising to his feet for the last time. "You might want to pay a special visit to my mother's grave, if you're so certain she would have been distressed at the sale of the house, let alone the cemetery itself."

His father opened his mouth, but James raised a hand.

"If I let you keep the estate, you'll fling Daisy's inheritance after that which you've already lost. There'll be no estate within two years, and I will have betrayed my closest friend for no reason."

"Your closest friend, eh?" His father was instantly diverted into another train of thought. "I've never had a woman as a friend, but Dora looks like a man, of course—"

"Father!"

The duke harrumphed. "Can't say I like the way you've taken to interrupting me. I suppose if I agree to this ridiculous scheme of yours, I'll have nothing to expect but humiliation."

It was an implicit concession.

"You see," his father said, a smile spreading across his face now that the conversation was over. "It all came well. Your mother always said that, you know. All's well that ends well."

James couldn't stop himself from asking one more thing, though God knows, he already knew the answer. "Don't you care in the least about what you're doing to me—and to Daisy?"

A hint of red crept up his father's cheeks again. "The girl couldn't do better than to marry you!"

"Daisy is going to marry me believing that I'm in love with her, and I'm not. She deserves to be wooed and genuinely adored by her husband."

"Love and marriage shouldn't be mentioned in the same breath," his father said dismissively. But his eyes slid away from James's.

"And you've done the same to me. To your son. Love

and marriage may not come together all that often, but I have no chance at all. What's more, I am beginning my marriage with a lie that will destroy it if Daisy ever finds out. Do you realize that? If Daisy learned that I had betrayed her in such a callused way . . . not only the marriage, but our friendship, will be over."

"If you really think she'll fly into a temper, you'd better get an heir on her in the first few months," his father said with the air of someone offering practical advice. "A woman scorned, and all that. If she's disgruntled enough, I suppose she might run off with another man. But if you already had an heir—and a spare, if you can—you could let her go."

"My wife will *never* run off with another man." The words growled out of his chest from a place he didn't even know existed.

His father heaved himself out of his chair. "You as much as called me a fool; well, I'll do the same for you. No man in his right mind thinks that marriage is a matter of billing and cooing. Your mother and I were married for the right reasons, to do with family obligations and financial negotiations. We did what was necessary to have you, and left it there. Your mother couldn't face the effort needed for a spare, but we didn't waste any tears over it. You were always a healthy boy." Then he added, "Barring that time you almost went blind, of course. We would have tried for another, if worse came to worst."

James pushed himself to his feet.

"Neither of us raised you to have such rubbishing romantic views," the duke tossed over his shoulder and left the room.

Having reached nineteen years of age, James had thought he understood his place in life. He'd learned the most important lessons: how to ride a horse, hold his liquor, and defend himself in a duel.

No one had ever taught him—and he had never imagined—how to betray the one person whom you truly cared for in life. The only person who has truly cared for you, other than his mother, and she'd been dead for years. How to break that person's heart, whether it happened tomorrow, or in five years, or ten years in the future . . .

Because Daisy would learn the truth someday. He felt it with a bone-deep certainty. Somehow, she would learn that he had deliberately set out to make her marry him, that he had pretended to fall in love . . . and she would never forgive him.

More romance from
USA Today bestselling author

Eloisa James

978-0-06-202127-4
Stern and gruff, powerful and breathtaking,
the Earl of Marchant is well worth taming . . .

978-0-06-162684-5
Kate has no interest in marriage or princes
or fairy tales . . . but she never dreamed
there would be magic in one kiss.

978-0-06-162683-8
Should a noble rogue choose an acceptable bride . . .
or pursue true love to possible ruin?

Visit www.AuthorTracker.com for exclusive
information on your favorite HarperCollins authors.

Available wherever books are sold or please call 1-800-331-3761 to order.

EJ1 0911

At Avon Books, we know your passion for romance—once you finish one of our novels, you find yourself wanting more.

May we tempt you with . . .

- **Excerpts** from our upcoming releases.

- Entertaining **extras**, including authors' personal photo albums and book lists.

- Behind-the-scenes **scoop** on your favorite characters and series.

- **Sweepstakes** for the chance to win free books, romantic getaways, and other fun prizes.

- Writing **tips** from our authors and editors.

- **Blog** with our authors and find out why they love to write romance.

- **Exclusive content** that's not contained within the pages of our novels.

Join us at
www.avonbooks.com

AVON

An Imprint of HarperCollins*Publishers*
www.avonromance.com

Available wherever books are sold or please call 1-800-331-3761 to order.

FTH 0708

More romance from
<u>USA Today</u> bestselling author
ELOISA JAMES

978-0-06-162682-1

The Duke of Beaumont needs an heir, so he summons his seductive wife, Jemma, home from nine years abroad.

978-0-06-124560-2

Married by proxy as a child, Lady Isidore has spent years fending off lecherous men in every European court while waiting to meet her husband.

978-0-06-124557-2

Enough with proper tea parties and elegant balls; what Harriet really wants is to attend an outrageous soiree where she can unleash her wildest whims and desires. But to attend such an event she must disguise herself . . .

978-0-06-124554-1

Unwilling to lose the woman he still lusts after, the Duke of Fletcher is determined to win back his beguiling bride's affections.

Visit www.AuthorTracker.com for exclusive information on your favorite HarperCollins authors.

Available wherever books are sold or please call 1-800-331-3761 to order.

EJ2 0911

*G*ive in to your Impulses!

**These unforgettable stories only take a second
to buy and give you hours of reading pleasure!**

Go to *www.AvonImpulse.com* and see what we
have to offer.

Available wherever e-books are sold.

AVONIMPULSE

IMP 0811